YO...
CO...
TH... ...AN
SAID.

★   ★   ★

Ann thought she'd misunderstood him. "What?"

"We want you to come with us."

"Why? I haven't done anything."

"So you say, but your husband is dead and we need you to identify the body."

"What did you say . . . about my husband?"

"He's dead. Murdered. You wanna talk to us about it or not?"

★   ★   ★

"Realistic courtroom page turner."
—Michael Louis Minns,
     author of *The Underground Lawyer*.

ACT OF PASSION

HARRISON ARNSTON

HarperPaperbacks
A Division of HarperCollins*Publishers*

This is a work of fiction. The characters, incidents, and dialogues are products of the author's imagination and are not to be construed as real. Any resemblance to actual events or persons, living or dead, is entirely coincidental.

HarperPaperbacks *A Division of* HarperCollins*Publishers*
10 East 53rd Street, New York, N.Y. 10022.

Cover photograph by Herman Estevez

First printing: March 1991

Printed in the United States of America

HarperPaperbacks and colophon are trademarks of HarperCollins*Publishers*

10   9   8   7   6   5   4   3   2   1

For: My wife, Theresa, whose boundless support, understanding, and love make my existence a joyful experience.

Special thanks to: Attorneys Arthur Deckelman, Linda Hughes, and Joseph Sicignano, for their invaluable counsel on matters legal.

Thanks also to the many people working within the confines of the Pinellas County (Florida) Criminal Courthouse, who requested anonymity and shall receive it.

My sincere appreciation is expressed to my agent, Susan Lipson, and my editor, Carolyn Marino. Their ideas and hard work helped turn the manuscript for this novel into something I can point to with pride.

PART ONE

We are apt to shut our eyes
against a painful truth . . .

Patrick Henry

PROLOGUE

CHICAGO, 1946.

JUST HOURS AGO, THE YOUNG ATTORNEY HAD COM-
pleted his very first criminal trial, the successful defense
of a young street punk named Vincent Sabbatino. Now,
as he answered a knock at the door of his modest home
on Chicago's North Side, he was astounded by what
he saw.

Three men stood on his doorstep. He recognized the
small man standing in the center of the trio as Vito Gallia,
current capo of Chicago's criminal empire; the giants
flanking him were obviously Gallia's bodyguards.

"May I come in?" Gallia asked.

"Of course," said the stunned attorney.

As he led his uninvited visitors into the front room,
the lawyer gave his wife a look that sent her scurrying

upstairs. He walked over to a small table and raised a decanter. "Some wine?" he asked in Italian.

Gallia said no. The other two remained silent.

The lawyer returned the decanter to the tray. "What can I do for you?"

Gallia took a seat on the worn sofa, removed an envelope from the inside pocket of his exquisitely tailored blue serge suit, and laid the envelope on the small coffee table in front of him. "You did well today, counselor," he said, in a voice as cold as his soulless eyes. "Vincent Sabbatino is very grateful, and so am I. I'm sure this will cover your expenses."

The lawyer glanced at the envelope, then stared at his infamous visitor. "I've already been paid by the court," he said haltingly. "I was appointed to this case by the judge."

Gallia snorted. "I know all about it," he said. "They figured you'd screw it up, but you fooled them. You busted your ass for two weeks preparing for this case, and it paid off. Jesus! That judge is sure pissed at you." He laughed, a deep, throaty laugh that almost brought tears to his eyes. "Vincent was supposed to take a fall today and you saved his ass—for a lousy thirty-five bucks! Jesus! You've got balls, counselor. What'd you stick your neck out for?"

The lawyer blushed. "I—I was just trying not to make a fool of myself, that's all. Look, I'm no criminal lawyer. I'm a business lawyer. I've never handled a criminal case before. I wanted to give it my best. I had no idea. . . ."

The visitor appraised the attorney for a moment. Then he said, "Well, now you do." He leaned forward and, in a voice that was almost a whisper, said, "Vincent is not an isolated case. I have some other ... associates ... who need a lawyer at certain times. People I can't be connected with, you understand? I want you to handle them for me."

The lawyer shook his head. "I'm sorry," he said, aware of the beads of perspiration beginning to form on his forehead. "I don't wish to be disrespectful, but I handled Vincent's case only because I was appointed by the court. We lawyers can't refuse a judge's appointment."

"I know that," Gallia snapped. "You think I don't know about lawyers? I happen to believe you're a good one."

"But I'm not a criminal lawyer," the young man protested. "I don't feel comfortable with criminal work. I'll never feel comfortable with it. I prefer to work with paper—trust deeds, contracts, leases. Those are things I understand."

"And how much money does that earn you?" Gallia asked, waving a thin hand in the air, already knowing the answer to his question. The dark, cold eyes took in the sparseness of the room, warm and homey but furnished with an odd collection of marred, chipped, obviously secondhand pieces. Then Gallia motioned toward the lawyer. "Look at you! Where'd you get that cheap suit? Montgomery Ward?"

In fact, the suit had been purchased at Sears, Roebuck—on sale. A jacket and two pairs of pants for twenty-three dollars. Up until this moment, the attorney had thought it looked pretty sharp. "My business is small right now, but it's growing," he said, feeling awkward and defensive in the presence of this notorious gangster to whom money meant nothing.

"Don't be a fool," Gallia growled. "You're wasting your time on that shit. You're a natural as a criminal lawyer. You had that jury in the palm of your hand today. You shouldn't be so selfish. Think of your family. I can make you very rich, counselor."

The mention of his family sent a chill down the lawyer's spine. Was he being threatened? He didn't know, but he was a man who believed principles to be the very foundation of his being. Without them, he was nothing. "I'm sure you can," he said, as he rose to his feet, picking up the envelope from the table with a hand that was beginning to shake. "Please," he said, "I've shown you respect. I can't take this, and I can't work for you."

Gallia rose slowly to his feet and glared at his host for a moment, then expelled a sigh. "Not many people refuse me, my young friend. Are you aware of that?"

The beads of sweat had become little rivers of moisture streaming down the lawyer's ashen face. He started to wipe the sweat from his eyes but stopped himself. "I'm aware of who you are and what you are," he said. "Again, I mean no disrespect, but I'm the wrong one for you. There are many others who are available—and willing."

For a moment Gallia said nothing. Then, in a flash of anger, he snatched the envelope from the lawyer's hand and hurled it at him. The envelope bounced off the lawyer's chest and fell to the floor. "If you want to show respect," Gallia snarled, "you'll take my money, counselor. That you *will* do." Then, pausing, he allowed a false smile to reach his lips and said, "As for the rest"—he extended his hand—"have it your way."

The two men shook hands, then Gallia whirled and

stalked quickly out of the room, his bodyguards scrambling to keep up with him.

After the lawyer had secured and bolted the door, he went upstairs and told his wife what had happened.

Her eyes widened in fear. "My God!" she said, bringing a hand to her mouth. "What are you going to do?"

The attorney turned the still unopened envelope over in his hands. "This will go to the church," he said. "As for the rest ... I think we'll be all right."

"Are you sure?"

"No," he said softly.

1

ANN HEARD THE DOORBELL RING.

It had to be Cathy, she thought. The two had been together for much of the warm Florida evening, and when Cathy had finally agreed to return to her own home, it had been with considerable reluctance. After what they had witnessed, that was understandable. Now, Ann assumed, Cathy had had second thoughts and had returned to look after her.

As Ann got up to answer the door, she reeled uncertainly and leaned against the refrigerator for a moment to steady herself. Then she swayed gently forward, trying to concentrate on what she would say to Cathy when she greeted her. Cathy had never seen her drunk. It was embarrassing. Oh, well. She was such a sweetheart, she'd understand. Thank God for people like Cathy,

Ann thought, opening the door.

Her eyes widened in shock as she saw two policemen. The taller, older one removed his Smokey the Bear hat and said, "Mrs. Cohen?"

"Yes?" The world spun before her eyes, and her brain, marinated in vodka, struggled to comprehend why these men were ringing her doorbell at—what, four in the morning? She was guessing. She had no idea of the time.

"I'm Sergeant Weber of the Pinellas County Sheriff's Department," the policeman said, in a deep voice that seemed to come from somewhere beyond his head. "This is Deputy Quill. May we come in?"

"What for?" Ann asked, uncomprehending.

"We'd like to talk to you for a moment. Would that be all right?"

"Did I do something wrong?" she asked.

The policeman had a strange expression on his face. "I don't know. Did you? I noticed your car's still warm. You look a little intoxicated. Maybe you were driving under the influence. Maybe you were doing something else. Were you?"

"No!" Ann ran her hands through her hair, trying to get it away from her face. "I would never drive when I've been drinking. I didn't start drinking until I got back. What do you want?"

Weber glanced at the one named Quill and then turned back to Ann. "Mrs. Cohen," he said harshly, "we need to talk to you. It's real important. Is it all right if we come in for a moment?"

"I still don't understand," she said. "What do you want?"

Weber didn't answer. "It won't take long," he said.

Ann took a step backward and waved them inside. The two policemen followed her to the kitchen and sat down at the table with her. Weber had a piece of paper in his hand. "Mrs. Cohen," he said, "I'd appreciate it if you'd sign this form. It's a waiver. We call it a Consent to Interview form. It means you gave us permission to come inside and talk to you without your lawyer being here. Would you sign it, please?" He handed her a pen.

"What would I want a lawyer for?"

"I dunno. It's just the way we gotta do things. Would you sign it, please?"

She hesitated for a moment, then signed the form, slid it and the pen back across the table, and watched as both policemen also signed it. Then the other cop, the young one, his face a blur, asked, "Do you own a gun, Mrs. Cohen?"

"Shure," she said, trying, but failing, not to slur her words. "Marty 'n' me."

Quickly, the older one asked, "Could I have a look at it?"

"Why?"

Again, the policeman didn't answer. "I'd like to look at your gun and then we'll talk some more. Would that be all right with you?"

As drunk as she was, Ann knew something was very, very wrong. They were treating her as though she were a retarded child. She could sense that, and yet she was a cooperative person by nature. Drunk, confused, traumatized by what she'd seen earlier in the evening, she nodded her head. Immediately, Weber pulled out another piece of paper and placed it on the table.

"What's thish?" Ann asked.

"It's called a Consent to Search form, Mrs. Cohen."

"A what?"

Weber took a deep breath, glanced at his partner, and then returned his gaze to her. "A Consent to Search form. You've just given us permission, as part of a routine investigation, to look at the gun you own. In order to keep the books straight, we need your permission in writing. That way, you can be sure that we aren't doing anything that might infringe upon your rights. Just sign on the last line." He pointed to the line, handed her the pen, and waited.

Keep the books straight, he'd said. She could understand that much. She was an accountant. She knew it was important to keep the books straight.

She scrawled her name.

"Where is the gun?" Weber snapped.

The room was beginning to spin. "Ish in the bedside table," she said. Weber took the paper, shoved it in his pocket, and disappeared in the direction of the bedroom, while the other one stayed in the kitchen, keeping an eye on Ann, who watched the table move in a clockwise arc. She was trying to understand what they were doing here. She was certain it was some awful mistake.

A few moments later, Weber returned, holding a plastic bag in front of him, using only the thumb and forefinger of his right hand. He held the bag as one might hold a soiled diaper, away from his body. Inside the bag was the gun. The policeman whispered something in his partner's ear, then they both looked at Ann. The one with the gun left the house and returned shortly with yet another piece of paper. This one he called a property receipt. He signed it and asked Ann to do the same. Again, she scrawled her name across the bottom of the page.

Then the one called Weber turned to her. "Mrs. Cohen, can you tell me where you were earlier tonight?"

Quill tapped Weber on the shoulder and whispered, "You didn't Mirandize her yet."

Weber grunted. "She signed the waiver. That's enough."

Ann shook her head. "I don't wanna talk about it. I wasn't driving drunk, if thash what you're worried about. I would never do that."

"Did you have a fight with your husband?"

She looked at him with half-open eyes. Then, ever so slowly, a strange smile came over her face. A fight. How silly. A fight? Tonight? Of course they'd fought. Tonight and every night. It was their life. But she couldn't tell him that. That was private. "I don't wanna talk about it," she said.

Weber looked disappointed. "Mrs. Cohen," he said, "this is really a waste of time. You know you want to talk about it, and you should. After all, it's four in the morning, you're still dressed, you've been driving your car, and you're drunk as a skunk. Why don't you tell us what happened? Believe me, you'll feel a lot better about it if you do."

She tried to look into his eyes, but her own refused to focus properly. "What are you talking abou . . . about? I told you I didn't start drinkin' until I got back home. Please. I didn't drink 'n' drive. I know I'm a little drunk, but I have a good reason. Nothing you'd understan'."

"Try me," Weber said.

She wanted to cry. There were policemen in her kitchen and they wouldn't leave her alone and she didn't know what they wanted. "Jus' leave me alone. Please! I've got enough troubles tonight. Can't you see that?"

Weber leaned forward, placing his face inches away from her own. "I'll tell you what I see," he said, his voice sounding like thunder. "I see a woman who's all messed up because she did something she's real ashamed of. Maybe you had good reason, did y'ever think of that? Maybe the judge will take that into account. You don't look like a criminal to me, Mrs. Cohen, so why don't you cut all this crap and just tell us what happened? We're on your side, if y'wanna know the truth."

It was so confusing. She was trying to understand, but she couldn't. She had no idea what this man wanted her to say. She started to cry.

"I'm afraid you'll have to come with us," Weber said.

She thought she'd misunderstood him. "What?"

"We want you to come with us."

"Why? I haven't *done* anything."

"So you say," he said. "But your husband is dead and we need you to identify the body."

He said it as though he were talking about nothing more serious than a thunderstorm: unceremoniously, unfeelingly, unsympathetically. So much so that Ann thought she had misunderstood him. "What did you shay . . . about my husband?"

"He's dead," Weber said flatly. "Murdered. You wanna tell us about it or not?"

Ann stared at him as though he were insane. She'd

just seen her husband, not more than five or six hours ago, engaged in some sick sexual ceremony with his mistress. There was no way he could be dead.

"You're crazy," she blurted.

The policeman hesitated for a moment and then said, "You're a cool one, lady. I'll give you that. But he's stone dead and we need you to ID the body, so let's get with it."

Involuntarily, Ann's hand went to her mouth.

"Mrs. Cohen?"

It was the other cop, the young one. As before, Ann tried, but failed, to look at him. She finally let her head drop without answering. She heard him say, "Would you stand up and put your hands on the wall, please, feet apart?"

The trip to the morgue was a blur, and when they got there—incredibly—the body they showed her *was* Marty. He was lying face up on a stainless steel table, his body covered with a plain blue sheet. Another smaller sheet with a hole cut in it had been placed over his head in such a way that only the actual face was visible. She didn't know it at the time, but the medical attendant, unaware of the suspicions of the policemen, was trying to be gentle with her. The back of Marty's head and part of his brain were in another part of the room, inside a large glass jar, awaiting analysis. But what Ann saw was horror enough.

There were two innocent-looking holes. One just above the left eye and another to the right of his nose. As Ann stared at the body, she saw no blood. The face, while recognizable, seemed distorted somehow. She'd never seen a gunshot victim before. She'd never expected to. Certainly not her own husband.

The vision before her eyes was more than she could stand, as the truth finally smashed through the barrier of drunkenness. Her husband was lying dead before her eyes. The source of her pain was dead. If there was a scintilla of lingering hope, hidden deep in the recesses of her mind, that somehow she might still save her marriage, it was gone forever.

Whatever had gone on before was history. Marty'd gotten himself killed. He'd never given her a chance. He'd never given *them* a chance. He was dead. It was over.

Overwhelmed by shock and despair, she started banging her fists against the sheet-covered body. "You bastard!" she screamed. "You lying, rotten bastard! How could you *do* this?"

One of the policemen grabbed her; then they led her away and put her in a chair in the hall just outside the room where Marty lay.

She felt faint. She bent over and put her head between her legs, trying to will herself not to pass out or be sick. A wave of doubt washed over her. It still didn't seem possible. Perhaps she was imagining this entire scene. Perhaps it was nothing more than a horrible hallucination brought on by her emotionally distraught condition, exacerbated by too much booze.

"Is that your husband, Mrs. Cohen?"

In the distance, she heard the sound of the policeman's voice. She couldn't speak but was able to nod her head.

"For the record, we need to hear you say it."

With great effort, she said, "Yes."

"You wanna tell us about it now?"

She covered her face with her hands. For a while, no one spoke. Then, in the distance, she could hear other sounds. New voices. She couldn't make out what they were saying, because they spoke softly, but after a time, the now-familiar tone of the sergeant could be heard as he directed his attention to her.

"Mrs. Cohen, we have some questions we want to ask you. Under the law, you're entitled to have a lawyer present while we do that. But, as I'm sure you'll agree, you're not in very good shape right now. So we're gonna find a bed for you in the hospital where you can sleep it off, and then you can call your lawyer in the morning. That sound all right to you?"

She was numb. Completely confused. Utterly destroyed.

"What?" she asked weakly.

"Do you understand what I've just said?"

She wanted to scream at them but couldn't. "I'm gonna be sick," she said, her lips quavering.

She heard someone in the distance say, "Shit! Get a policewoman out here!"

She felt strong arms lifting her to her feet. And then, she was sick right there in the hallway. She heard curses, more curses and then—finally—she achieved the goal she'd set for herself earlier in the evening.

She passed out.

CHAPTER

2

ANN COHEN AWOKE AT 7 A.M., HER MIND STILL MUD-
dled by alcohol. For a moment she stared at the flat gray
ceiling. The ceiling in her own bedroom was textured
and white, and there was a spot directly above the bed
that she had repaired herself after a swag lamp had
been moved. It was always the first thing she saw in
the morning, that little bump in the ceiling. The bump
wasn't there.

Where was she?

Her head hurt terribly. Images formed in her consciousness: strange, disjointed, terrifying images, mate-
rializing quickly, then disappearing, as though she were
watching a movie being shown at triple speed.

Where was she?

Where was Marty?

Marty? There was something about Marty.

The bastard!

Police. Visions of policemen danced before her eyes.

Marty wasn't there. But that didn't mean anything. He could be out in the kitchen, thinking up excuses for his behavior last night.

More lies.

She was aware of extreme physical discomfort. Every muscle in her body ached, her head was pounding unmercifully, and her stomach was heaving.

She tried to sit up but couldn't. Her stomach hurt too much. She smelled of disinfectant.

She looked around the room. God! Where was she? It looked like a hospital room, but there were bars on the window. A jail?

The heaving in her stomach intensified. Desperately, she pushed herself from the bed and staggered toward the bathroom, leaned over the toilet, and retched uncontrollably. Feeling dizzy, she found her way back to the bed and fell on it, her body covered in a cold sweat.

She closed her eyes. For a moment, all she could hear was the pounding of her heart, and then, as she drifted back into unconsciousness, she heard voices. Familiar voices.

One was her own. The other belonged to someone she'd known briefly many years ago.

A young man.

A handsome young man.

So long ago. . . .

It was twenty years ago. She was twenty-five years old and still a virgin, but the virginity had become an intolerable burden. Someday she'd meet Mr. Right. But when that joyous day finally arrived, she wanted to be a woman of the world, not an inexperienced accountant from Chicago who still lived with her mother and father and attended mass every Sunday.

So she made a major conscious decision.

She thought of it as preparation for the future, a rite of passage to be conducted far away from home, where no one would ever know. How else would she learn the techniques so vital to a solid marriage? How else would she learn to judge a man in bed?

They were all rationalizations, of course. In truth, she was simply dying of curiosity. For over ten years, and for a host of reasons—fear, religious beliefs, parental influence—she'd suppressed a keen awareness of her ripening sexuality and had believed she would remain a virgin until marriage. But lately, the curiosity had overwhelmed her and she'd become fascinated with the idea of making love to a man. And being loved. This was, after all, the beginning of a new decade. The old rules were being quickly struck down. There was the pill now and, with it, the new freedom.

Her curiosity had to be satisfied, and soon, she thought, or she would never be able to put it out of her mind.

She hadn't wanted her first sexual experience to be with anyone from the office, or any of a number of men she'd dated over the years. She wanted to lose her virginity to a stranger. Not just anyone, but a carefully chosen stranger she'd never see again.

So she'd gone to Italy, alone, for a two-week vacation. It was a dual-purpose trip. She'd always wanted to visit the country of her grandparents and see the ancient cities with their ageless splendor: Rome, Venice, Naples, the Vatican. She'd kill two birds with one stone. She'd see Italy and, while there, lose her sacred virginity to a wonderfully romantic Italian with flashing eyes and old-world charm. Once that had been taken care of, she'd have a number of other discreet encounters until she was satisfied that she could truly please a man. The right man. A man she would spend the rest of her life with. Faithfully.

During her sojourn in Rome, she'd met a number of Italian men, but they were all so uncouth. Their eyes flashed with lust, but they had no charm. In the middle of a crowded street, or on a bus, with no concern for her embarrassment, their hands would reach out and squeeze her breasts or her buttocks. They were little more than animals, touching her as though she were nothing but a piece of meat. It repelled and frightened her.

Then she'd met the American. A graduate student from Toledo, he was visiting the home country of his grandparents just as she was. He'd been funny and handsome and attentive, as they rode together on the tour bus. For three days, he'd pursued her relentlessly in a way she could understand and accept, until she'd finally given in, almost desperate to have this thing over with.

In Ann Martino's fantasies, the sex act had always seemed sweet and pure. Soft candlelight, violins in the background, the aroma of freshly cut flowers mixing with the pleasant scent of a man's cologne. Her lover's soft hands caressing her skin tenderly, his lips traversing her body with little kisses, his voice murmuring adoring passages taken from romantic poems.

But this . . . it hadn't been romantic at all. The small bed in the cheap hotel had squeaked. There was no music. There were no flowers. He smelled of beer, not cologne. And he was in a terrible hurry. His hands were rough, his kisses rougher. And when he finally spent himself, his face was contorted in an expression that seemed to be anything but an exultation of joy.

She had discovered that being a woman of the world had its negative aspects. All in all, from the first deep kiss to the moment when he was, once again, fully dressed, about six minutes had gone by. He hadn't cared about anything except his own pleasure. At that point in her life, it was the biggest disappointment Ann Martino had ever experienced.

Four years later, at the age of twenty-nine, Ann Martino was in full flower, an almost awesome beauty. Her Italian heritage had given her smooth, flawless skin a nearly permanent tan. Her large, dark brown, slightly hooded eyes sparkled with amusement. Her slightly angular face featured pronounced cheekbones, full lips, and a sharply chiseled chin. Her face was framed by soft, fine, dark brown hair that fell to her shoulders. Her five-foot-six body was supple from years of ballet lessons. She had slightly sloping shoulders, full high breasts, a small waist, and long muscular legs that moved with a vivacious quickness.

And to a degree, she had become a woman of the world. In the intervening years, the early disappointment had been tempered by more fulfilling encounters. Not many, but enough to allow her some measure of confidence in herself—and her sensuality. Her initial curiosity, and subsequent disappointment, had been replaced by the realization that she enjoyed sex, the inherent guilt of a "good" Catholic woman notwithstanding. But an enduring relationship had eluded her, in part because of her high standards, and in part because her beauty and intelligence intimidated a lot of otherwise well-qualified candidates.

She wanted a man who was bright, kind, attentive, and sexy. Someone with a sense of humor and an ego under control, a man who would see her as an equal partner, a helpmate, a soul mate, and a friend. She hadn't found him, and she was beginning to think she never would.

When Marty Cohen, one of the senior accountants, asked her out for dinner one Friday night, she almost said no. Marty was two years older and just a couple of inches taller. Not particularly good-looking, he was intelligent, funny, and friendly. He was also divorced, with children. Not exactly prime material. But she didn't say no. Her shopping list of standards was becoming condensed.

He took her to Doro's, one of Chicago's better Italian restaurants, where the maître d' greeted Marty effusively, as he'd been primed to do earlier in the day, an urging enhanced by a ten-dollar bill. "Mr. Cohen," he gushed, "how nice to see you again. Your table is ready."

They were seated and presented with menus and a wine list. The waiter was there instantly. "May I get you something from the bar?"

Marty smiled at her. "Would you like a drink, or would you rather have wine?"

"I'd rather have wine," she said.

Marty picked up the wine list and handed it to her. Then he grinned at the waiter. "My lady is a connoisseur. She'll choose the wine and then the entrée as well."

Ann was impressed. It wasn't often she encountered men who accepted women as equals. For the first time in her life, a man was actually suggesting she be the one to order the meal. A refreshing experience.

She ordered the wine, then leaned back in her chair and appraised Marty carefully. In this setting, he seemed better looking than in the office. The rimless glasses he wore seemed to add a couple of years, but they also gave him a professorial air. Behind the glasses, his eyes seemed to twinkle. She saw kindness there.

"Well," she said, "you seem to be well-known around here. Do you come often?"

"Not as often as I'd like," he said. "At these prices, once a week is extravagant. By the way, the Pontet-Canet was an excellent choice, although the 'sixty-nine would have been a little better. The 'sixty-eight was not well-rated."

The game had begun.

"I'm thinking of your wallet," she said. "The 'sixty-nine is twice the price. The difference in the wine isn't worth it."

He smiled. "True. And most considerate of you. Are you always this considerate?"

She didn't answer. "Why did you tell the waiter I was a connoisseur?"

"Because you are."

"How do you know that?"

His smile widened. "Because for some time I've been asking about you. I wanted to know all about you. I won't pretend otherwise."

She was both flattered and uneasy. "Really? And what have you found out?"

He leaned back in his chair, removed his glasses, and rubbed his nose. "I know that you're second-generation Italian, you've never been married, you live at home, and your father is an attorney. Your only brother, also a lawyer, lives in Seattle; you're an expert on wines and food, an excellent cook, and a hell of a tennis player. You're highly intelligent, extremely competent, and you work too hard. Why do you work so hard?"

He'd almost taken her breath away. "Because I want to advance," she said. "In this world, a woman has to work much harder than a man just to stay even. It isn't right, but that's the way things are. I accept that. I intend to overcome it."

"I think you will," he said. "You have the drive and the talent. That's a winning combination."

"Thank you," she said. "What else do you know about me?"

"I know you work out three times a week, so you must care about your health. There's no regular man in your life." He leaned forward and stared at her, the expression on his face something close to awe. "And," he continued, "you're unaffected by the fact that you are one of the most beautiful women in Chicago. You're a very unusual person, Ann."

She couldn't help it. She blushed. There was a certain frankness about him that she found appealing, and a certain zeal she found unsettling. They'd worked together for three years, in the large accounting firm of Collins and Wilson. Well, together was the wrong word. He worked on the twenty-third floor and she on the twenty-second, so they hadn't actually seen that much of each other.

"You have two children, don't you?" she asked, trying to change the subject.

"I have two girls and a boy," he said. "I see them on weekends. Since the divorce, I see them more than I did when I lived at home. I guess because I make more of an effort now. Before, I took them for granted. Now, I don't."

"That's honest."

"I'm always honest," he said.

The waiter arrived with the wine, went through the obligatory ceremony of removing the cork, testing its moisture content, pouring Marty a taste, and then half filling their glasses. After he left, Ann said, "It must be awful, getting divorced. The thought of loving someone, sharing your life, having children, then seeing it all come apart. It scares me to death."

"Is that why you've never married?"

"No," she said. "I just haven't met the right man yet."

"And what will the right man be like?"

She blushed again. Clearly, he was a man who liked to control the conversation. He seemed to be teasing her, but she couldn't be sure. His questions were posed in a friendly way, but—

"I don't think I've established criteria," she said. "Maybe it's chemistry. When I meet him, I'll know."

"You're a romantic," he said, smiling. "I guess that comes from being Italian. Well, I'm also a romantic. It can create problems."

"What do you mean?"

"Had I not been a romantic," he said, "I wouldn't have married when I did."

"Why not?"

"Because I wasn't in love."

"So why did you marry?"

"Because I thought I was. We were both so damn young we didn't know the difference between love and infatuation. I married her right out of high school. We were so different in every way. I figured I could overcome it all, and for a while it seemed as though I was able to, but I couldn't. While I worked my way through college, she started having babies. Once I graduated and got a job, I really tried. I helped around the house and babysat while she went out with her old girlfriends, just to give her a break. I even cooked some of the meals, the whole thing. But it just didn't work.

"The differences killed it. I'm a neatnik, she's a bit of a slob. I like opera, she likes country music. I like people, she doesn't. I could go on. Had I not been a romantic, I would've foreseen what lay ahead. As it turned out, we brought three kids into the world. It was wrong for both of us. I won't pretend otherwise."

He sighed.

"When I made the decision to marry her, I meant it to be forever. It was a total commitment. Hell, nobody thinks about divorce when they get married. You think it can't happen to you and when it does—well, it's a shock. Maybe not the divorce. By the time you get to that part, you've been through hell already. The tough part is accepting the failure."

"How long has it been?" Ann asked.

"A year and a half. I live in a crummy apartment, cook my own meals, do my own laundry, but it's worth it. The kids are much better off. They're sad, of course, but the turmoil is gone. No more screaming fights. I think they're grateful for the peace and quiet. Children are amazingly resilient."

"Your wife hasn't tried to turn them against you?"

He shook his head. "Ex-wife. No, thank God. I think in some ways she's as relieved to be out of the marriage as I am. Now that I'm gone, she seems to have taken a new interest in the house and in herself. The place is cleaner than it's ever been, and she looks great. She's dating, having some fun, and I think, before too long, she'll be married again. To the right guy, this time. I wish her the best." He waved his hand in the air, signaling his desire to change the subject. "Enough of this. Tell me, why is it you never became a model? You're certainly better looking than most models I've seen."

She laughed. "You're a real smoothie, Marty. You like to flatter women, don't you?"

"I mean it. Don't you think of yourself as beautiful?"

She shrugged. "I suppose. But the idea of being a model never occurred to me. I find that sort of thing—well, not demeaning, but certainly not fulfilling. I don't mean to denigrate women who pursue that kind of career, but it seems so phony. So keyed to appearance alone. I guess I want to be thought of more as an intelligent woman than a beautiful one. Outward appearances are worthless, when you get right down to it."

"Is that why you became an accountant?"

"I suppose. That, and the fact that I'm a bit on the shy side. I've always liked working in an atmosphere that's quiet. The aloneness of this work is not a detriment. I see it as an asset. I like the solitude."

His eyebrows rose. "That surprises me."

"Why?"

"Because you seem so people-oriented. I would have thought you'd thrive in a job that kept you in constant contact with others. Sales, something like that."

She sipped her wine. Usually, when men flattered her, she could see the lust in their eyes. But not Marty. What she saw in his eyes was understanding, and intelligence, and maturity.

Maturity. That was what impressed her so much. He was different from anyone she'd ever met. Sure of himself and yet not afraid to admit mistakes. There was none of the machismo that most men exhibited when they were around her, thinking it would impress her.

Marty was different.

They talked all through dinner. She was amazed at how much they had in common. Food, wine, tennis, the arts: the list was seemingly endless. Coupled with what she already knew about him, it made quite a package. He expressed his feelings honestly and openly, exposing a sensitivity she found captivating. By the end of the evening, she was really enjoying his company.

But she knew she had to be careful. He was, after all, a co-worker. That was bad enough, but he was also a divorced man with many responsibilities.

Three kids. What if she fell in love with him? She wanted her own children, not someone else's. They lived with their mother, but you never knew.

After thinking it over carefully for two days, she decided it wasn't worth taking the chance. She would not go out with Marty Cohen again. But the next day, when he asked her for another dinner date, she heard herself saying, "Sure! I'd be delighted."

They dated for eight weeks. Every Friday night. Nothing more than dinner and conversation. And every time they saw each other, her interest in him grew. Their dates followed a rather pristine pattern. Each time, he would drive her back to the office after dinner, to her car, and they would go their separate ways. There was never a sexual overture. Just a chaste good-night kiss. She sensed that he was deliberately taking his time, waiting for the message to be transmitted by her. A message she never consciously gave.

Finally, after eight weeks, he made his move.

And when they finally made love, it was romantic.

It was more than that. It was sensational.

They'd just left the restaurant—Doro's again—when he suggested a walk. It was a short one, ending at the Tremont Hotel, just around the corner from the restaurant.

"I've rented a room," he said matter-of-factly.

She wasn't really surprised. All evening, he'd seemed charged with anticipation. Shoving his hands in his pockets, he stared at the ground, scraping the toe of his right shoe along the concrete. At that moment, he seemed like a little boy, something else she found endearing.

"I want to make love to you, Ann," he said. "Not in some seedy little apartment like mine, but here, in the Tremont. It's one of the smaller hotels but very, very nice. And very quiet."

"You've already rented the room?"

"Yes. I know how presumptuous that is, but if you come up and you feel the slightest bit uncomfortable,

I'll understand. I promise. I do want to make love to you. I won't pretend otherwise."

It was a phrase he used constantly. For some reason, the words of one of her college psychology professors popped into her head. "Speech patterns are a clue to the true character of the human being. For example, if someone constantly says, 'To be honest,' you'd be wise to consider the possibility that the opposite is true."

She giggled aloud as she thought it through. He wanted to make love to her, he'd said. He wouldn't pretend otherwise. Did that mean that he *was* pretending otherwise? And what would that be like?

"What's so funny?" he asked.

She turned and looked into his almost pleading eyes. "Nothing's funny, Marty," she said. "I'm just a little nervous."

She chastised herself for being so critical. If she continued to analyze every word a guy uttered, she'd never find Mr. Right. Besides, she wanted this man. Still, she felt unsure, cautious.

"Let's go," he said, taking her arm, his face breaking into a wide grin as he opened the lobby door.

Upstairs, he fumbled with the room key but finally got the door unlocked and pushed it open. She stepped inside. It was more than just a room. It was a large, tastefully furnished suite. Both the main living area and the bedroom were bedecked with vases of freshly cut flowers. Soft music came from a radio on one of the bedside tables. A number of thick red candles sat on the dresser, waiting to be lit. Beside the bed, a silver ice bucket rested in its three-legged stand, the half-melted ice cradling a bottle of Dom Perignon. The '69 vintage.

Interesting. Marty had said he lived in a dump. He'd also talked about the alimony and support payments he was required to make. Ann knew what almost everyone in the office earned. Clearly, what little Marty had left over from his salary was being lavished on her. She felt flattered.

He'd thought of almost everything. It was as though he'd been able to penetrate her mind and visualize her fantasies of years ago. She found it comforting and frightening at the same time. Obviously, Marty had skipped out of the office early, rented the room, arranged for the flowers and the other things, and then returned to work.

"You seem quite sure of yourself, Marty."

He looked just the opposite. "Not really," he said. "I just thought I'd show you the room. If you're uncomfortable, we'll leave. I was just hoping that you had some of the feelings for me that I have for you."

She pondered his words for a moment. "May I use the bathroom?"

"Of course."

She went into the bathroom, more to consider her options than anything else. When she closed the door, she noticed the peignoir hanging on the back of the door. It was blue: silk, not nylon. The manufacturer's label was still attached, although the price tag had been removed. A gift. Another enticement.

He *had* thought of everything.

For a moment, she sat on the edge of the tub, wondering what to do. Then, slowly, she began to remove her clothes.

When she came out of the bathroom, the candles

were lit, casting a soft glow over the room. Marty was already in bed, the covers drawn up to his waist, his naked chest exposed. He held two glasses. "You look incredible," he said softly.

"Thank you. Can you tell me something?"

"What?"

"Why am I so damn nervous?"

He put the wineglasses down on the bedside table and reached for her hands. "Sit down," he said gently.

She sat on the edge of the bed. She could feel her heart pounding unmercifully. Her knees seemed to be shaking. She knew her hands were icy cold.

"Ann," Marty said, "you can't be any more nervous than I am."

"You're nervous?"

"Of course I'm nervous. If I wasn't nervous, I should be put in a home. Here I am in a hotel room with the most beautiful woman I've ever seen in my life, a woman I want to please so much I can hardly stand it, and—" He stopped talking and kissed her gently on the lips. His tongue darted inside her mouth and explored, then receded. "I want to please you, Ann. Let me show you how much pleasure I can give you."

"May I have some champagne, please?"

"Of course." He handed her a glass, then brought his own up and touched it to hers. "Here's to the future," he said.

Her nervousness started to subside. He had a way about him, a soothing, calming way. And later, when they began to make love, he was so careful, so patient, so affectionate, so considerate. His hands were soft, his touch gentle, and when they held each other close, she could feel the thundering of his heart pounding against her breasts.

His sexual technique was masterful. He'd said he wanted to give her pleasure, and he was doing just that, in a way no other man had ever done. She was aroused beyond anything in her experience. Overcome with passion, she abandoned all inhibitions, matching each move with one of her own, moaning with desire as she did so.

It was magic. Pure magic. A seemingly endless series of delightful sensations took her from one peak to an even higher summit of pleasure. And when it was over, she lay in his arms, listening to his breathing, secure in the knowledge that, at long last, she'd met Mr. Right.

She was certain of it.

CHAPTER

3

SIX MONTHS LATER, ON ANN'S THIRTIETH BIRTHDAY, Marty Cohen proposed. The ring was a full carat, an almost flawless stone, and when he placed it on her finger she felt a small twinge of anxiety. Just a small one.

She was certain he was the man for her, but there was a side to Marty that was unfathomable. A mysterious darkness would flash across his face for a moment and then be gone. And occasionally, he seemed a little selfish.

But she loved him. Madly, joyfully. That much she knew. No one was perfect, including herself. Marty was definitely Mr. Right. Almost everything she'd ever dreamed about. In fact, she was surprised at the depth of her feelings. She loved him so much.

She'd met his children, and they did seem reasonably well-adjusted, as well-adjusted as any children caught in the middle of a divorce. They treated Marty with reserved affection. There were hugs and kisses, but they seemed forced, somehow. There was nothing to indicate that any of them held animosity toward him. She assumed the slight reserve toward their father stemmed from their natural confusion and torn feelings.

After spending many hours with the children, she made a judgment. Whatever was bugging them was obviously due to the influence of their mother. Marty insisted that Ruth was doing nothing to turn them against him, but Ann was sure the opposite was true. Marty just couldn't see it. She was sure Marty would be a fine father to *their* children.

She felt comfortable around him. Felt more alive when she was with him. So she accepted his proposal, with only one caveat. "I don't want to wear the ring until we've told my parents," she said. "You're coming to dinner tomorrow. We'll tell them then, and I'll put on the ring. Do you mind?"

"Are you saying I need their permission?" he asked, a slight edge to his voice.

"No, of course not. I *want* to marry you. I *will* marry you. I just want to tell them before I wear your ring, okay?"

"Okay," he said.

Marty and Ann arrived together, but in separate cars, having come directly from work. Ann's parents greeted Marty warmly, and they all went into the front room to have some wine. The smells emanating from the kitchen were, as usual, mouth-watering.

Ann could tell that Marty was on edge. She squeezed his hand tightly as she announced, "Marty and I have something to tell you." Her voice sounded unusually reedy. "We're getting married," she said.

Her father looked positively stricken as he sat stiffly in his big leather chair, not saying a word. Her mother burst into tears but embraced Marty tightly and planted a big kiss on his cheek.

A few moments later, her father pulled himself together and toasted them both. Dinner progressed rather well, Ann thought. But later, after Marty had left, her father lost no time in venting his feelings.

"I don't understand it," he said, shaking his large head in genuine confusion. "You've waited all this time to get married. You're thirty years old! You're well-educated, you have a good job, you have friends, you have everything. And you're gorgeous. You know that? Gorgeous! And you want to throw it all away on a guy with three kids?" Again, he shook his head. "Princess, I just don't understand."

Ann took one of his hands in both of hers and held it tightly as she explained. "Daddy, I'm not throwing anything away. Marty is a wonderful man. He's bright, and giving, and very loving. His kids adore him. It wasn't his fault he got divorced. The woman is just . . . a bitch! What else can I say?"

"You've met her?"

"No."

"Then how do you know? You believe everything the man says? Maybe she's wonderful."

Ann groaned, released her father's hand, and stood up

to pace the kitchen floor in the old house on Chicago's North Side.

"I think I'm a pretty good judge of character," she began. "Marty and I have a lot in common. You know that. We both like the same things: tennis, good music, art, people. Our attitudes on almost everything are in balance. But, as important as all those things are, I'm in love with him. That's what really counts. He makes me feel so alive! God! When I'm around him, I want to sing! And he feels the same. I've never known anyone like Marty. He really loves me, Daddy, and that's what counts, more than anything."

She stopped pacing and moved toward her father, wrapping her arms around his neck.

"You know I've had some relationships with men," she said, her voice almost a whisper. "I'm not a little girl anymore, Daddy. But I always knew they weren't right for me, you know? Look at you and Mamma. You have less in common than Marty and I do and just look at you. You've been married for thirty-five years and you still act like kids. Why? Because you're still in love with each other, that's why. And it's a beautiful thing to see.

"That's the kind of relationship I want, Daddy. And Marty can give it to me. He's funny, he's honest, he likes to laugh, he's—oh, Daddy! I know you'll love him if you'll just give him a chance. I just know it."

As much as he wanted to believe her, her father found it difficult. He'd spent little real time with Martin Cohen, but from the first he hadn't really liked the man. There was something about him. He was too self-assured, too glib, too *accomodante*. There was a lack of passion, a certain coldness that seemed hidden beneath the pleasant surface. But his daughter's mind was obviously made up. He wanted his daughter to be happy. If this man could do it—well, so be it.

Ann's mother had a different approach. She expressed her feelings to her daughter as they sat together on the bed in Ann's bedroom.

"What about children?" she asked.

Ann avoided her mother's gentle gaze. "Marty's already got three children," Ann said. "He has to pay child support and alimony and—well, we don't think we'll have any for a while."

Her mother's eyebrows moved upward. "No children?"

"Not right now."

Her mother placed an arm around Ann's shoulder. "Ann, sweetheart. I'm sure Marty is a wonderful man. I trust your judgment. Your father and I have only known him for a short time, but I can see why you love him."

"You can? Oh, Mamma, he's terrific!"

"I know. Your father knows that too. If he seems upset, it's just because he loves you. No man in the world would be up to the standards your father has set for you. I sometimes think his attitude has been a major reason for your taking this long to get married."

Ann shook her head. "No. It really isn't, Mamma. I just never met a man, until Marty, who had that certain spark, you know?"

"I know," Ann's mother said, with a gleam in her eye.

"It has nothing to do with Daddy."

"All right. But I want to tell you something. The greatest joy in my life has been watching you and your brother from the day you were born. I'm not very good at verbalizing my feelings, so I can't really explain what's in my heart. But as much as I love your father, there is no joy like that of having your own children."

She sighed.

"You're thirty years old, Ann. As you get older, you'll find the time goes by much faster. If you and Marty have decided not to have children for some time, it may mean you'll never have any. And that is a tremendous sacrifice, my dear. Just tremendous."

Ann gripped her mother's hand. "I realize that, Mamma," she said, "but it's only until Marty's ex-wife gets married again. Once that happens, his payments are reduced. Then we can afford to have children. It's not that he doesn't want any."

"But what if she never gets married? You told me she's a real *strega*."

"She is. But you know how it is. Those women seem to have no problem attracting men. I'm sure she'll get married soon. Marty says she's got a boyfriend."

"You're sure?"

"I'm sure."

"And you're sure he wants children?"

"Yes. I'm very sure about that. We've talked a lot about it."

"And did he agree that the children will be brought up in the Catholic faith?"

Ann nodded. "He's already agreed to that. His first wife was a Unitarian. Marty's kids go to church, not synagogue. He's really not a religious person, but he said he'd come to church with me, just to keep me company. It was quite a concession for him, because he didn't want to when we first talked about it, but it shows how caring he really is."

"And you're only delaying the children because of money?"

"Yes."

"Then let us help. We have more than we need. It all ends up with you and Paolo eventually. Let us help you now, so you don't have to wait to have the children."

Ann threw her arms around her mother and hugged her tightly. "Oh, Mamma," she said, "I'd love to do that. But Marty's so proud, it would really bother him. He takes his responsibilities seriously. That's why he got married the first time, remember?"

She could feel her mother's body sag.

"Mamma, please don't worry. We *will* have children, and soon. I know it. Please trust me."

"It's not a question of trust," her mother said. "It's a question of practicality. You aren't getting any younger."

"Don't you think I know that?"

Her mother placed a hand on her cheek and smiled. "I guess you do at that. All I want is for you to be happy. As happy as I've been. That's what I want for you, Ann, happiness." Her mother stared at her with those soft, dark eyes of hers. Eyes that missed nothing. It made Ann strangely uncomfortable.

Six months later, Ann Martino married Martin Cohen. Her father gave her away, weeping as he did so. He said later they were tears of joy, but Ann wasn't so sure. Although he'd never uttered another negative word about Marty Cohen, there was an uneasy stiffness in the relationship between her father and her husband that hung in the air like stale cigarette smoke.

After a thoroughly romantic, magnificent Hawaiian honeymoon, Ann and Marty moved into a downtown apartment, within walking distance of the office. It was small, but that was all right. It made their modest collection of furniture look more imposing. It was cozy, convenient and theirs.

They made love every night, and sometimes in the morning as well, and later they would smile knowingly at each other as they walked hand in hand to the office.

Weekends were heaven. Sometimes, they'd never get dressed at all. Other times, they would have Marty's three kids over and the five of them would explore Chicago.

Things seemed to be running smoothly. Marty had asked her to wash and iron his shirts instead of sending them out because—he said—they never seemed to get them right. She hated ironing, but she did it willingly, because he'd asked her to. He wasn't much at helping around the house, but that was all right. As a senior accountant, his responsibilities were greater than hers, which meant he had to bring work home from the office. So she would do the housework while he worked at the kitchen table.

They settled into a routine. Friday night was restaurant night. Then, the first Sunday night of every month, they ate with her parents. The second Sunday of every month, they ate with Marty's mother, a dour widow with a negative attitude about everything. Ann, with her vivacious, warm personality, tried mightily to win the affection of the woman, but it wasn't working.

Aside from the grandchildren, whom she saw infrequently, Marty was all Mrs. Cohen had left. Clearly, she resented the fact that he'd married again; perhaps she hoped that by remaining unattached, he would focus all his attention on her. She fawned over him and ignored Ann, almost to the point of rudeness. Marty had warned her about his mother's attitude—it explained why he'd kept Ann away from her during their courtship—but the overt hostility still came as something of a surprise.

Another surprise was Marty's obsession with television sports. During their courtship, he'd taken Ann to a few Cubs games at Wrigley Field, and they'd been fun; but now he showed a fanatical addiction to games on TV: baseball, football, both college and professional, basketball, even hockey. No matter how much work he brought home, he always seemed to have time for sports, sitting in front of the television set and soaking up the games like a sponge. There were times when he seemed more interested in watching television than in making love. Ann took to reading the television listings before deciding what to wear on any given night. There was no point in wearing some sexy see-through confection before a Black Hawks game, for he would hardly notice. But on nights when there were no games on, he was attentive and romantic.

She never outwardly expressed her annoyance. Marty had told her what a complaining bitch his first wife had been, and Ann was afraid that her complaints would only force a comparison, something she wanted to avoid. She wanted him to be happy because she loved him, and because she knew the happier he was, the happier she was. So she cheerfully acquiesced to his wants and needs, thinking it was the right thing to do.

But the first small, acid drops of disillusionment had begun to eat away at the foundation of their marriage.

A year after their wedding, Ann and Marty moved from the rented apartment in Chicago to a new house in Minneapolis, where Marty had been transferred. It was a decision they'd made together. The move meant a promotion and raise for Marty, and the company had a place for Ann as well, with a raise for her, too.

It was their first house, with all of the attendant excitement, but it brought added responsibilities. There were lawns to mow in summer, sidewalks and a driveway to shovel in the winter, as well as many other humdrum things that needed to be done.

It fell upon Ann to do most of them. Marty was working most of the time, either at the office or at home. When he'd work at the office, Ann would stay as well, because she hated being alone in that big house. So they turned one of the bedrooms into an office, so Marty could work at home while Ann did the housework.

He would have the children one weekend a month. The first three times, Ann met them at the train station, entertained them throughout the weekend, and drove them back to the train station, while Marty spent most of his time in his home office. She thought it strange that she should be the one to accept the responsibility, and on this issue she complained bitterly.

"They're *your* children, Marty," she said, after returning from the station, alone, for the third month in a row. "The least you could do is drive them to the train."

He slammed his pencil down on the desk and glared

at her. "For Christ's sake! You know how far behind I am. These reports have to be ready for tomorrow's meeting."

"Reports! You always have time to catch a game on television. Why can't you take some time for your own children? Why do I have to be the one? You're not being fair. They come to see you, not me! If you really don't have the time to spend with your kids, tell them. They'll understand if you're busy. But you just ignore them. I don't see why I have to be the one to take them to the zoo, or the park, or the arcade. I have things to do too, you know."

It was their first real screaming, yelling, let-it-all-hang-out fight. And it frightened Ann terribly. Marty seemed on the edge of physical violence. There was a lot of waving of arms and slamming of hands against the wall. But in the end, Marty apologized, agreed with her point of view, and promised to take the responsibility upon himself.

And he did—for the next two months. Then he started telling Ruth he was too busy to take the kids. It was three months before they visited again, and three months after that. It wasn't nearly enough. So they talked about it and came to an agreement. The kids would come every month. Ann would take the major responsibility, but Marty would carve out a full four hours a day on Saturday and Sunday for alone time with them.

He seldom kept his promise, and that was disturbing. But what was even more disturbing was the looks the kids would give her. They seemed to understand exactly what was happening. They liked her. Truly liked her. Loved her, in fact. And the looks they gave her seemed to be looks of pity. It was as though they were telling her they'd been through this once before. It was all new to her, but old hat to them.

They were just kids, she reminded herself. Kids! What did they know? What *could* they know?

The big change came after four years of marriage.

They were eating dinner, half listening to soft music in the background while they ate and talked about the day's events. Just a normal Tuesday evening. Then Marty said, "Ann, honey, there's something we need to discuss." The tone of his voice made her look up from her plate in surprise. He seemed suddenly very tense.

"Discuss? Discuss what?"

He averted her stare, and said, "I talked to Andy Duggan today."

"Andy? Your old tennis pal? I thought he moved to Florida."

"He did."

"He called you?"

"Yes."

"What about?"

Marty leaned forward, placing his knife and fork on his plate. "Ann, he's making a fortune down there. In one year, he's made over a hundred grand." He repeated it, louder this time. "A hundred grand!"

She had a funny feeling in her stomach. "Good for him. So what's that got to do with us?"

"He wants me to join the firm he's with."

She was stunned. "He's involved with rest homes!"

"They're called adult-care living facilities."

She stared at him. He had the strangest look on his

face. The darkness was there again—in the eyes—only this time it was deeper, stronger. "Are you serious about this?"

"Yes, I am," he said flatly.

"I thought you wanted to discuss it. You sound like you've made up your mind."

"We are discussing it."

There was a harshness in his voice that was new to her. It was troubling. "Marty," she said, "you're an accountant. You've been an accountant all your life. I thought you liked being an accountant."

"I do."

"So? Why would you all of a sudden want to be involved in developing adult-care—whatever you call them?"

"The money's better."

She was flabbergasted. "You make very good money now," she said. "Between the two of us, we're doing great. Andy's business is so . . . iffy. It may be good right now, but what about two years from now? You know what goes on in Florida. Boom and bust. Half those people are crooks. You don't really want to be a part of that, do you?"

"You're talking about something else," he said. "Adult-care living facilities never go bust. People can't help getting old and feeble. It's a cinch, and Andy's the proof."

She couldn't believe what she was hearing. "Marty," she said, keeping her voice as calm as possible, "you're doing very well right here. We both are. We have a nice home, and good friends, and . . . you can't seriously be thinking of throwing this all away because of a single phone call from Andy Duggan! He's such a blowhard.

He's always been a laughingstock at the club. He's so stereotypical, with his flashy clothes and stupid jokes. How do you know he's really making that kind of money? I wouldn't believe a word he says."

"You done?" he snapped.

She was speechless. He was looking at her as a stranger might. "Now, listen to me," he said. "Andy says he's gonna make close to two hundred thousand dollars this year, and I believe him. Andy's a lot of things, but he's no liar. And you can bet I'll check it out before I make the final decision."

"Before *you* make the final decision?"

"Sorry. Before *we* make the final decision, all right?"

"Marty—"

"Listen. Just listen. Two hundred thousand! You know damn well I've got more on the ball than Andy Duggan ever had and I won't pretend otherwise."

She ran a hand over her forehead. "Marty, I know you're bright, but—"

"Jesus! Give me a little credit, will you? Andy and I talked about this over a year ago. He wanted me to go with him then, and I thought about it for a while, but I figured I'd wait to see how he made out. Well, now I know. He's making out great."

She was astonished. "You never mentioned it to me," she said.

"I know I didn't, and for good reason. I figured there was no point in discussing something that might never happen. I didn't want you to get upset. Then, when I didn't hear from Andy, I sort of forgot about it. But when he called today and told me how great he's doing, I realized it was time to talk about it. It's a hell of an opportunity. It's right, Ann."

"Right? How can you make such a decision on the basis of one phone call?"

"Ann, I've thought about this for a long time. Look! I'm an accountant because I was trained for it and it seemed like a nice secure job. But these days, you have to make your own security. I make less than forty grand a year. You make less than thirty. That's not bad, but hell, we'll never be able to afford kids at this rate. It doesn't look like Ruth will ever get married again. With the alimony and the child support, half of my damn income goes to her. You contribute more net income to this household than I do. That's not fair.

"If I can make the kind of money Andy's talking about, we could start having a family right away. I know that's what you want, and I want it too. But we're limited here. Don't you see?"

She didn't answer. She was afraid her words would betray her anger. She hated to fight.

"And another thing," he said, moving right along, "the weather here in Minneapolis is lousy. How many times have we had to get up at five in the goddam morning to clear the driveway of snow?"

"We?" she said. "What is this 'we' stuff? I'm the one who shovels the snow!"

"I know that," he said, "and I'm trying to change it. Don't you see? You're stuck with the snow because I spend all my time working. Florida is a paradise. Warm all year—hell, we could play tennis twelve months straight. Wouldn't you like to get out of the damn snow and cold?"

The darkness was gone from his eyes now, replaced

by that twinkle she loved so much. Ann felt confused. "Marty, I'm used to the cold. So are you. Sure, it's nice to get out of here on vacation, but . . . to live in Florida! That's where old people go to die! God, Marty. It's so backward. Alligators and cockroaches and old people. There's no culture, no galleries, no theater, no nothing! In the summer, it's unbearable. Miami is a joke. They don't even have major league baseball there. You know what a baseball nut you are. Can you really live without the Twins?"

"There are more important things than baseball," he said. "And Andy isn't in Miami. He's in Clearwater."

There were more important things than baseball, he said. That was interesting. Very interesting. She let it pass.

"Whatever," she said, "it's still Florida. Is Andy prepared to offer you a salary?"

"Salary plus commission," he said, gloating.

"How much salary?"

"Twenty-five to start," he said. "Listen to me. I know I can do it. Like I told you. I've been thinking about this for a long time. The market down there is booming. Exploding! Suppose it all falls flat. So what? I can always find work as an accountant. But opportunity knocks, love. Anyone who fails to grab this kind of opportunity is crazy. The chance to make that kind of money? You want kids or don't you?"

"You know how much I want children. How can you say a thing like that? This isn't about kids. This is about moving to Florida."

He threw up his hands. "Okay! I don't want to argue with you. Tell you what. We give it a try for two years.

That's all. Two lousy years. If you hate it after two years, we'll come home. That's a promise. Whaddaya say to that?"

"Two years? What do we do with this house?"

"We sell it. Houses are cheaper in Florida. We can get a castle for what we paid here."

"Marty. Are you really serious about this?"

The darkness flashed over his face again. "I've never been more serious in my life," he said.

They talked about it long into the night. Talked instead of argued. As was often the case, Ann expressed her concerns but not her hurt. And when they finally kissed each other good night, the decision had been made.

Actually, two decisions had been made. They would move to Florida, and they would start trying to have a family of their own.

Two months later they were in Florida, driving on a busy highway north of Clearwater, looking for a house. They both saw the billboard at the same time.

FLORIDA'S FINEST! THE CLUSTERS! TREES! PONDS! SPACE! THREE- AND FOUR-BEDROOM VILLAS FROM THE LOW 80'S. ONLY SIX LEFT! TURN LEFT NEXT LIGHT.

Marty wheeled the car over to the left side of the crowded six-lane highway and prepared to make a left at the light, as the sign directed.

They'd been prowling around Florida's Pinellas County for three days now, looking for a suitable place. Andy Duggan had researched several resales, but for some reason none of them appealed to either of them. What they'd really wanted—what they'd agreed upon before leaving Minneapolis—was a nice new three-bedroom detached house. But so far nothing had really caught their fancy. There were plenty of homesites for sale that would allow for a custom-built house, but that called for a four-month wait. And Marty wanted to move now. Right now.

Marty made the turn and drove up a long, winding road that broke out into a new housing development much different from anything they'd seen to this point. There were sixty "villas" in all, five villas per "cluster." Despite the fact that the villas were joined on at least one side, they looked very attractive from the outside, with their natural cedar siding blending into the heavily wooded site.

Villas. How Europeans must laugh at that, Ann thought. In Europe, a villa was a *villa*. These were townhouses.

"Well?" Marty said. "Wanna take a look?"

"Why not?" Ann said. "I'd like to see what they look like on the inside."

Marty parked the car and they went inside the model home. They were greeted by a smiling, bovine real estate agent who fawned over them as if they were her long-lost relatives. "Where are you from? Minneapolis? How nice! What brings you to Florida? Really? How wonderful! Which firm? Oh, yes, I know Andy. He's in commercial and I'm residential, but I know him. You'll love it here. We have a lot of folks from your neck of the woods. Everyone is so nice! Palm Harbor is marvelous! Great shopping, schools. Do you have children? Oh. . . . Well, when you do, the schools here are just wonderful, and close. Aren't the grounds lovely?"

She took them on a tour of the model.

"There are five designs, each one unique. Notice the lovely appliances. I'm sure you'll appreciate the size of the refrigerator, Mrs. Cohen. We've spared no expense. Every appliance is top-of-the-line. There's a synagogue just four miles from here. . . . Oh, really? Well, then, St. Luke's is less than a mile away. This model has over twenty-one hundred square feet of living space. We have others that are larger and some that are smaller. Whatever your needs might be."

Ann listened to the patter with half an ear as she wandered through the rooms of the model home. She was impressed with the spaciousness, the appointments, and how well the villa was laid out. Every inch of space was utilized. There were lots of closets, a well-lighted eat-in kitchen with a wall of windows that looked out over a large stand of tall pine trees, and the master bathroom was a delight, with an oversized bathtub and marblelike counters.

The development was spread over fourteen acres of lush grass, flower beds, and thick stands of oak and pine trees, less than three miles from the Gulf of Mexico and adjacent to one of Florida's premier golf and tennis resorts. The grounds were immaculate, and the trees abounded with industrious squirrels and blue jays, all chattering away as they went about their tasks. It did seem like a paradise. Florida didn't seem so terrible after all.

Twenty-four of the houses were owned and occupied by full-time residents, the real estate agent explained. Thirty more were owned by people from Ohio, Michigan, New York, New Jersey, and three other states, "snowbirds" who spent anywhere from one to four months a year in Florida. That was a plus, the agent pointed out. The Clusters was a development destined to remain quiet, restful, beautifully maintained, and one that truly emphasized a quality of life found nowhere else. Six were still for sale, but they were going fast.

Ann and Marty Cohen brought that down to five less than six hours later. They chose a unit about a hundred yards from the model that was identical in design. When they closed their deal four weeks later and moved their belongings from Minneapolis, it seemed like a good move. Even with unpacked boxes cluttering every room in the house, Ann could still stand on the rear deck of their villa, look out at the expanse of pine trees, and revel in the naturalness of the place.

Maybe it would all work out, she thought.

CHAPTER

4

MARTY COHEN ATTACKED THE BUSINESS LIKE A MAN possessed. Within three years he was averaging better than seventy thousand a year and reveling in his success. But there was a downside to his accomplishment. The long hours cut into evenings and weekends, and when he was home he was often too tired to talk, much less do anything else.

Ann, working as an accountant, earned just under thirty, so together the couple was doing well financially. They managed to travel abroad for an annual vacation, trade their cars every other year, and enjoy other material fruits of their labor, but it wasn't nearly the marriage Ann had envisioned.

They rarely ate dinner together, either at home or at a restaurant. Some nights, Marty would arrive home very late, sit up in bed, and regale Ann with tales of triumph, but it wasn't a conversation. It was a dissertation by Marty, with Ann the sole audience, listening intently, asking questions that were rarely answered, until he'd finished what he wanted to say and rolled over to fall into a deep sleep. The lack of contact, both verbal and physical, troubled her. But more importantly—to Ann—she had failed to conceive.

Their sex life had become a sometime thing. While Ann's desire remained undiminished, Marty's had waned dramatically. He would claim tiredness, or stress, or any number of things, but she feared she was losing her allure. And on those special nights when she was most likely to conceive, she often had to beg Marty to make love to her. She wasn't always successful.

Her failure to become pregnant finally drove her to a specialist, who examined her carefully, then arranged a follow-up appointment for the next week, at which time he would discuss the results of a number of tests.

"You say you've been off the pill for three years?" the doctor said, as he looked at her test results.

"Yes," Ann replied. "Ever since we moved to Florida."

"I see. Well, the tests show no abnormalities. There's no reason I can see why you haven't conceived, although I would suggest that you increase your frequency of sexual intercourse during ovulation. Have you talked to your husband about a sperm count?"

Ann squirmed in her chair. "Yes, I did."

"And?"

"He says he'd rather not. He feels that since he's already fathered three children, there's no need for a sperm count. He feels the problem lies with me."

"But he fathered the children some years ago, didn't he?"

"Yes."

"Things can change, Mrs. Cohen. Your husband might have any number of problems that could remain undetected unless he's checked." The doctor pursed his lips for a moment. "You might tell him that. Other than what we've talked about, there's not much else I can suggest."

"Thank you, Dr. Stein."

The doctor stood up and extended his hand. "Good luck."

"Thank you."

On one of those rare evenings when Marty was home for dinner, Ann decided to confront the issue head on. "Marty," she began, her voice filled with trepidation, "I want to talk to you about our children."

He looked as though he'd been stabbed in the heart. "Not that again."

"Yes, that again."

"What now?"

"Marty," she said, marshaling her courage, "I talked to the doctor today. He says the results of my tests show there's no reason in the world why we can't have children . . . unless something's happened to you."

He slammed a hand on the table. "Dammit! I told you I'm not about to go through that crap. You know what they make you do? They make you go into a room and jack off into a jar, for Christ's sake. Jack off into a goddam jar! The hell with that. There's nothing wrong with me, dammit. I won't do it."

"But Marty," she insisted, "you said you wanted children. *Our* children. How are we ever going to have children if you refuse to look at the possibility it could be something you're not aware of? There's nothing to be ashamed of. Just for your own peace of mind, you should do it. At least, then you'd know."

He leaned back in the chair and tossed his napkin on the table. "I already know."

"Marty," she insisted, "you know what the doctor said. We have to do it every day during my ovulation, and that's right now. We haven't made love in over a week. At least you could make *that* effort."

He sighed deeply. "Ann, I've been thinking. I think we need to reexamine our priorities."

"What do you mean by that?"

"I've been meaning to talk to you about this for some time."

"About what?"

"I think we're both too old for children."

It was so strange. She wasn't surprised by his words. What astonished her was the fact that she'd anticipated them. They were exactly the words she'd heard him say in her mind, many times, as she lay awake, staring at nothingness, listening to the breathing of her husband as he slept beside her. Sometimes, she would lie on her side, staring at him in the dim glow cast by the night-light on the wall. She'd lean over without touching him and look at his face and whisper to him. "Who are you, Marty? Who are you really? Where did the man I fell in love with go? Can you bring him back?"

She brought her mind back to the present. "Too old?" she said. "I don't think we're too old."

Marty shook his head. "You're being a romantic again. You're not looking at the facts. Look, right now we have a terrific life-style. We have the freedom to come and go as we please, we've got money in the bank, a great social life . . . the American dream. I'm really thinking of you. With a kid, you'd be stuck. Diapers, baby food, all that stuff. I've lived it, so I know what I'm talking about."

Ann fought to control the anger in her voice. "I've told you many times that I'm prepared to take full responsibility for those duties. I don't expect you to change diapers."

He slammed a hand on the table. "All you can think of is having some little cuddly baby in your arms," he said. "Well, babies grow up. They become people. That's when the problems start. You're not giving that any consideration."

"You must think I'm an idiot!" she yelled. "Of course I've given it some thought."

"Oh, really?" he countered. "I don't think so. Soon we'll both be over forty. Think of the way things will be down the road, when the kids are teenagers. I say teenagers—plural—because you certainly won't want to stop at one. I can't see you wanting to bring up an only child. So there'll be two, or maybe three. What about when the oldest turns fifteen, for example? Hell, we'll be in our fifties. That's when the real problems come up. Look at the problems our friends have with their teenagers now. Drugs, sex, the whole bit. If our kids survive that, you've got college to consider. Do you know what it costs *per year* to send one child to a decent college these days? How about twelve thousand dollars!"

"I'm aware of that," she said flatly.

"Okay, take three kids for four years. That's a hundred and forty-four thousand minimum! What if they want to go to graduate school?"

"You never used to talk this way," she said, feeling the anger building quickly.

"I know," he said, "but we were both younger then. When we first got married, I expected Ruth to remarry right away, but she never did. If she had, I would have wanted kids right then, but you know how strapped we were. It's only in the last few years, thanks to my decision to get into this business, that we've really been able to put some money away. If we have a kid, that'll go by the board. You just haven't thought it out."

"Yes, I have," she snapped. "Damn it, Marty, you talked me into moving to Florida because you said you could do better financially. You said that was the only thing holding you back. Well, you *have* done better. Much better. And it's only been three years. If you wanted children three years ago, you should want them now. Unless you lied to me back then."

That cloud of darkness flashed across his face. "I never lied to you," he said. "It's just . . . you don't look down the road like I do. You're the eternal optimist. You see the birds, but not the crap they leave all over your car. Supposing this business falls on its ass. Suppose I have to go back to being an accountant. We can't afford it!"

She was exasperated by his newfound negativism. Always, he'd talked about having children as a high priority—until now. "Marty," she said, "there are lots of people who have children in college who don't make what we make today. We can start a fund right now for them. That way, the money will be there when we need it. You're giving me fluff here. The truth is, you just don't want children, do you?"

"That's not true!" he insisted. "I want them as much as you do. But I realize how much they'll change our way of living."

"You mean *your* way of living!" she yelled. "You! Oh, you had it great! You fathered three kids, and as soon as the first one neared puberty, you took a hike. You simply don't want to go through it again, do you?"

"No, I don't," he said. "I won't pretend otherwise. It's too late for us, Ann, and the sooner you accept that, the better off we'll be."

For a moment, they simply stared at each other; then Marty broke the eye contact by dropping his gaze. "Yes," he said, "I fathered three children, but I was a lot younger then. Damn it, Ann, I'm thirty-nine years old. I'm too damn old to be a father again. I don't have time to be a good father. And if I can't be a *good* father, I don't want to be a father at all. You're just being selfish."

There was more, but Ann tuned him out. The argument was lost, and she knew it. For Ann, there could be no independent action. To be sure, she could refuse to go back on the pill and take her chances, but what would that accomplish? Even if Marty did manage to make love to her more than three times a month, and even if she did get pregnant, she'd have a child its father didn't want. Would that be fair to the child? No. Did she want to leave Marty Cohen and find another man? A man who would want children as much as she did? That was ridiculous. She'd married Marty because she loved him. Certainly, he wasn't everything she'd thought he'd be, but he was still her husband.

Two days after the argument, they were barely speaking to each other. The third night, he came home with a large bouquet of flowers in his arms and told her he was sorry. "I haven't changed my mind," he said, "but I love you. I want you to be happy. Forget about the pill. If you get pregnant, I'll accept that as God's will."

She pulled him toward her and hugged him tightly. "Thank you, Marty."

"But I won't go to the doctor," he said. "I don't like the idea of jacking off in some jar. It's too disgusting."

Again, she held him close, but she knew he was insincere. His words were hollow. And she began to realize, for the very first time, that Marty Cohen was a consummate liar.

CHAPTER

5

A FEW MONTHS LATER, WHEN SUSAN, MARTY'S OLDEST child, now a stunning eighteen-year-old college student, arrived for a short visit, Ann found out how right she was.

Over the years, Ann had developed a closeness with Marty's children, especially Susan, a bright, vivacious young woman who wanted more than anything to be a television news anchorwoman. Susan was studying hard in college, majoring in broadcasting. With her brains, her looks, and her motivation, she was a cinch.

They were walking through the bird sanctuary near the Clusters, waxing philosophical and discussing a variety of things, when Susan said, "It's a shame you never had children of your own, Ann. You'd make a wonderful mother."

"Why, thank you," Ann said, pleased with the comment.

"In fact," Susan went on, "I often think of you as my mother. That sounds crazy, I know, but I've always been able to say things to you I never could to my real mom."

Ann squeezed Susan's arm and said, "You're very sweet."

They sat on one of the wooden benches that fronted a large pond. Three egrets walked by slowly, oblivious of the humans in their midst, their spindly legs moving in slow motion.

"In a way," Susan said, "it's kind of sad that Dad had the vasectomy right after Billy was born. If he'd known he and Mom would end up getting divorced, he probably would never have done it, but you can't really see ahead much, can you?"

Ann stared at the center of the pond and tried to will her heart to stop pounding. "How...did you know about that?" she asked. "You were just a child."

"Mom and I were talking about six months ago," Susan said. "Every once in a while she gets a little bitter. I guess the fact that Dad got married again and she never did—well, I think she resents that. I'm sorry, I shouldn't be talking about her. It's not fair."

Ann grabbed Susan's arm. "No. It's all right. What did she say?"

Susan thought about it for a moment. "She was upset about something, and a little drunk, I guess. Anyway, she was crying and laughing and carrying on about you. She's still jealous, you know. Even after all this time.

Anyway, she said, 'At least she'll never be able to bear him children.' I asked her why and she told me."

A look of horror came over Susan's face.

"You knew, of course?" she blurted out.

Ann smiled bravely and nodded. "Of course I knew. Your father has always been very honest with me."

"Thank God," Susan said, clutching her chest. "For a moment there, from the look on your face, I thought—"

"It's all right, Susan," Ann said. "I get these strange looks from time to time. I think it has something to do with the tides or the moon. Feel like a hot dog?"

"Yeah."

"Okay, just up the road here."

They walked up the road in silence. A forced silence. Ann wanted, more than anything else in the world, to scream at the top of her lungs. The effort required to suppress the impulse almost took her breath away.

Susan's visit continued for two more days. Her presence forced Ann to go through the motions of daily life disguising her anguish behind a facade of tranquility. Outwardly, Ann seemed cheerful and happy, but inside the turmoil was like nothing she'd ever experienced before.

Could Susan be mistaken in what she thought she'd heard? No. Susan was an intelligent woman and would not have misunderstood, so the words had to have been spoken. But had the words been true? Perhaps Ruth had uttered them maliciously, knowing they would eventually reach Ann's ears. Susan was Ruth's daughter, after all, and Ruth was no doubt aware of the closeness that had developed between Ann and Susan. And Ruth was a jealous, vindictive woman, wasn't she? Or was she . . . really?

Jealous, yes. Perhaps even bitter. But vindictive? No. Ruth had never displayed vindictiveness in the past. In truth, the actions of Marty's former wife seemed well-meaning. Much to her credit, Ruth had never tried to turn the children against their father or Ann. Why would she suddenly change now? Could her loneliness have finally taken its toll? Could it be that vindictiveness repressed for eight years was now manifested in this terrible lie? Ruth was drinking, Susan had said. Maybe that was it. People said lots of things they didn't mean when they were drinking. Could Ruth's comment about a vasectomy have been something as simple as a thoughtless, drunken lie? That was a possibility. Or, was it something as simple as the truth?

There was only one way to find out. As much as Ann abhorred confrontations with Marty, there was no escaping the need for one now. She decided she would wait until after Susan left, early Monday morning.

After dropping Susan at the airport, Ann drove directly to work. Sitting at her desk at the accounting firm, the bright mask fell away, revealing the pain etched in her face.

Cathy Pollard, Ann's best friend, noticed it immediately. "What's wrong?" Cathy asked, as she lingered over a file folder on Ann's desk.

Ann looked up. "Wrong? What makes you think there's something wrong?"

"What makes me think something's wrong? Would the fact that you forgot to put on makeup this morning be a clue?"

Ann's hands flew to her handbag. Quickly she withdrew a small case and opened it, peering into the small round mirror. "Oh, my God!" she exclaimed. "You're right. I completely forgot."

"No offense," Cathy said, laughing, "but you look like shit. Anything you want to talk about?"

"No," she said. "Nothing's wrong, Cathy. Really. I just was in a rush this morning, that's all."

Cathy, whose lankiness was emphasized by her passion for long-distance running, was a sweetheart of a friend, even if her manner of speaking was sometimes too direct. With her short blond hair, flashing blue eyes, and sardonic sense of humor, she never failed to brighten Ann's day. But now her face expressed her concern. "Ann," she said, "don't bullshit me. You're a terrible liar. The agony is written all over your face. Come on! What are friends for?"

Ann looked at Cathy with eyes suddenly misting. "I really can't talk about it now. Okay?" She put down the compact and took one of Cathy's hands in both of hers. "I'd like nothing better than to tell you, but I'm just so confused, so upset. Will you bear with me?"

Cathy squeezed Ann's shoulder. "I'm sorry, Ann. I don't mean to pry. Of course I'll bear with you. Just remember. If you want to talk, I'm right in the next office."

"I know that," Ann said.

With mixed emotions, Ann watched Cathy walk away. She wanted very much to talk, but it wasn't time yet. Not until she knew the truth. Not until after the dreaded confrontation with Marty.

For most of the morning, Ann kept mulling this over

while she went about her work, until the work took over, as it usually did. Accounting, with its majestic precision, was an endeavor requiring the utmost concentration. Thoughts of Marty receded.

Then, just before lunch, Ann had an idea. She picked up the phone and called Dr. Norma Wells, her ob-gyn. Norma would know what to look for.

After getting home late, Marty showered quickly, put on his terry-cloth robe, and plopped himself in front of the television set, his usual routine for a workday. In a few minutes he'd be asleep. Normally, about an hour later, Ann would wake him, and he'd stagger off to the bedroom with hardly a word. That was what their life had become, except for occasional weekends and vacations, when some semblance of togetherness still existed.

Tonight was going to be different, Ann thought, as she headed for the bedroom. She undressed and soaked her body in an oil-rich tub of hot water for twenty minutes, allowing the heat and oil to relax every muscle. Feeling equal to the task ahead, she toweled off and carefully applied makeup. Next, she spent ten minutes teasing her hair until it had that wanton look Marty liked so much.

Satisfied, she rummaged through the closet looking for various and sundry items that Marty had bought her over the years, the sexy lingerie he loved her to wear when they made love. Once, she'd loved wearing it for him, finding excitement in the desire it aroused in him.

Like many men, Marty wanted his wife to be a whore in bed, and Ann had no problem with that. She enjoyed it too, being naughty and uninhibited, sure that the intense intimacy was bringing them closer together. But, as the years went by, Ann felt the spontaneity go out of their lovemaking, and that did present a problem.

The clothes served to arouse Marty sexually, but once aroused, he became interested only in his own pleasure. Hers became secondary. Without the accouterments, Marty was rarely interested.

She sighed as she put them on now, all of them black: the garter belt, the net stockings, the strapless half bra that left her nipples exposed. She slipped on the six-inch heels and the lacy, diaphanous peignoir. Then she studied herself in the full-length mirror on the back of the bedroom door.

She looked like a thousand-dollar-a-night hooker. That's what Marty had said years ago, offering it as a compliment. How long ago? When was the last time she'd worn this outfit?

A niggling doubt crept into her thoughts. Maybe that was the problem. Marty had certain ... needs ... that she'd failed to cater to of late. Maybe she was the one at fault, as Marty had often claimed.

She pushed the thought away. No, it wasn't just her fault. Marty had become selfish in their lovemaking even before she'd stopped wearing the sexy clothes. She'd tried to discuss it with him, but he'd sloughed off her complaints as just another example of her childish romanticism. Funny, he hadn't thought it so childish when he was courting her.

Stung, she'd responded by giving him what he wanted, because it made him happy. But only for a while. As the years had passed, nothing seemed to satisfy him, and for Ann, sex became a chore instead of a pleasure. Eventually, she had felt little incentive to spend an hour preparing for a lovemaking session that would last five minutes. That's why she'd stopped wearing the clothes.

She forced herself to concentrate on the present. Tonight, she was filled with purpose. Fixing a smile on her face, she walked slowly into the living room, the floor-length peignoir trailing behind her. As expected, Marty was asleep on the chair, his arms draped over its arms, his legs apart, his robe tied loosely.

She turned off the television set and switched on the stereo. Soft music washed over the room. Then she went to the dining room, removed two candles from the table, lit them, and placed them on the living room coffee table. She started to turn off the lamps until she realized she'd need the light. For the task at hand, candlelight wouldn't be enough.

She knelt down in front of Marty and pulled gently at the robe. It fell away. Carefully, she took his limp penis in her hands, then bent over and took it in her mouth. Marty stirred, opened his eyes, and mumbled, "Ann, it's late. I'm tired. You're sweet, but I'm just not in the mood tonight. Okay?"

She stopped what she was doing and looked up. "I understand, sweetheart," she said huskily. "You just relax. You don't have to do a thing. Not a thing."

Her eyes were half closed, her lips moist and parted. Again, she took his limp penis into her mouth. As her tongue played with the tip of it, she could feel its response. She kissed it tenderly, then brushed her lips against his testicles. Gently, she cupped them in her hands, kissing and licking them, all the while looking for the telltale scar.

"Ann, you're really sweet," Marty protested, "but I'm just bushed. Why didn't you tell me you were horny?"

And then she saw it, exactly where Norma had said it should be, a very thin, almost imperceptible scar about an inch long. Her heart almost stopped beating.

It was so strange. She'd made love to Marty a thousand times, doing exactly what she was doing now, except for the fact that, in the throes of passion, she'd usually had her eyes closed. She'd never seen the scar before only because she wasn't looking for it. And now that she had seen it, she wanted to retch.

Quickly, she stood up and drew the peignoir tightly around her. "Where'd you get the little scar?" she asked, the huskiness in her voice replaced by a shrillness she'd hoped to avoid. Too late. The anger was fueling her now, threatening to overwhelm her. She didn't care. Not anymore.

"What scar?"

"Here," she said, leaning over and jabbing a finger into his scrotum. He recoiled so quickly he almost knocked the chair over on its back. "It's just a little thing," she said coldly. "Were you in an accident or something?"

He was on his feet almost instantly, bending over in pain and staring at her in shock. "What the hell's the matter with you? Are you crazy?"

The smile was gone from her lips. Her eyes were thin, angry slits. "I asked you about the scar, Marty," she said.

"Forget about the damn scar!" he snarled. "It happened when I was a kid. I don't remember how. What's the difference?"

"What's the difference?" she screamed. "I'll be happy to tell you." Her voice was so loud it was drowning out the music, but she didn't care. "Before we were married, we talked a lot about wanting our own family, remember? And since then we've had a hundred conversations about the same thing. But you kept giving me these well-thought-out, logical reasons why we shouldn't have children.

"You were so rational, so wise. You weren't making enough money, you said. You were paying too much alimony, you said. You wanted to get established in business, you said. Always something. Then, the other day, you hit me with 'We're too old to have children.' But it was all a sham, wasn't it, Marty?"

Stunned, he mumbled, "I don't know what the hell you're talking about."

"Oh, yes, you do," she said, her voice a snarl. The anger was unbridled now, naked, free to drive her in whatever direction it chose. Never in her life had she completely lost control of her temper or surrendered herself to any emotion other than lust, but this rage was almost a living thing. Instead of being frightened by her loss of control, she felt relieved to have set it free.

"You had a vasectomy right after Billy was born," she screamed. "We could *never* have had children, and you knew it all the time, you lying, filthy *bastard*!"

His eyes widened and his jaw dropped. "That's not true!" he protested, just as she thought he would. But it was no use. She knew.

"It *is* true," she yelled. "Don't insult my intelligence

any further. I can see the scar, Marty. It's there, right where it should be. God help me, I never noticed it before, but it's there. You're the one who lies, just as you've been lying to me all along. How could you? How could you do such a thing?"

The air of defiance left him quickly, like a balloon stuck with a pin. His hand reached out for her, but she slapped it away. "Ann," he said, his voice almost pleading, "I love you. I wanted to tell you, but I thought— well, if I told you, you might not marry me. I know it was a terrible thing to do...."

He stood there, with a puppy-dog look on his face that infuriated her. She'd always thought of Marty as a strong man, but now she saw him for what he really was: a weak, spineless nothing. She wanted to hit him. No, at that precise moment she wanted to kill him.

Suddenly she became aware of the extent of her rage, and the realization frightened her. She whirled and ran into the guest bedroom, slamming the door shut and turning the tiny knob that locked it.

Then she threw herself on the bed, crying into the pillow, staining it with her makeup, wanting more than anything to die right there, right this minute, so she'd never have to see another human being again.

For fifteen minutes, Marty stood at the door, begging her to come out, telling her how much he loved her, how sorry he was, and a hundred other things that meant nothing. She never answered him until, frustrated, he threatened to break down the door. That brought her to her feet.

"Marty," she screamed, "if you touch that door, I'll call the police! I mean it. You leave me alone!"

After some more unanswered pleading, he finally did. And through the night, she sat in a chair by the window, looking out into the darkness, wondering what had happened to her world.

In the morning, Marty was at the door again. "Ann," he said softly, "are you all right?"

She hadn't slept at all. "I don't want to see you," she said. "Go to work and leave me alone."

"I'm not going anywhere until we talk about this. Ann, we have to talk, really."

"Tonight," she responded. "We'll talk about it tonight."

"Are you going to be all right?"

"I'll be fine," she said bitterly. "You just get the hell out of here."

"But we'll talk tonight?"

"Yes."

She watched him through the window as he climbed into the car and drove off. Only then did the muscles in her body relax, if only a little. She finally left the small prison she'd created for herself, showered, and dressed. Then, nursing a cup of strong coffee, she phoned the office, claiming a migraine headache, and then, on impulse, phoned the church and made an appointment with Father Cassidy.

For Ann, like many Roman Catholics, the teachings of the church had ceased to make much sense. But she chose to believe that the fault lay with those men charged with the responsibility of making policy, not the church itself. Having been religiously inculcated at a young age, she felt compelled to attend mass on a regular basis—alone—because without it she felt less than whole, for reasons she couldn't fully comprehend.

She liked Father Cassidy, a small, wizened man of sixty-six, even though he was an Irish priest from the old school. A kind, gentle man, he loved to tell stories, especially funny stories, and despite his clinging to the old values, he was well-liked and well-respected by those who attended the church.

When he would rant and rave about birth control or abortion, or a score of other things that seemed diametrically at odds with the ways of the twentieth century, most would simply tune him out, convinced that God would forgive them even if Father Cassidy wouldn't.

The diminutive priest greeted her warmly, ushered her into a small private office, and offered her some coffee. They talked about nothing for a few moments, and then Father Cassidy asked, "So, Ann, what troubles you?"

She took a deep breath, and then proceeded to tell him everything. While she explained, he sat quietly in his chair, the tips of his wrinkled fingers placed upon his pursed lips, his head moving up and down from time to time. He didn't say a word until she'd finished.

At that point, he let out a deep sigh of his own, clucked his tongue for a moment, and then, with his hands clasped together, leaned forward. "You're sure about the vasectomy?"

"I'm sure," Ann answered. "He admitted it."

"Did he indeed?"

"Yes."

"I see. I'm so sorry."

"I am too, Father."

"Well, there's nothing to be considered, Ann. The road ahead is clear."

She looked at him with eyes filled with confusion. "Clear? I don't understand."

Father Cassidy sighed again. "Ann, in the eyes of the church, your marriage is a fraud. Martin—I cannot call him your husband, I'm afraid—has committed a number of sins, the fact that he married you under false pretenses paramount among them. That particular sin"—his eyes hardened as he said the word—"makes your marriage a nullity. In the eyes of God, you have never been married. And you must take immediate steps to rectify that situation."

"You mean . . . ?"

"Yes. An annulment. It must be done immediately. And you must make arrangements for either Martin or yourself to live somewhere else. To continue to live together would mean you would be living in sin and damned to a life in hell. There is no other possible course of action."

Ann shook her head. "Father, I can't . . . just like that."

"But you must," he insisted, his hands flat on the desk. "If you want to reach some future accommodation with your husband, that is both understandable and Christian. But it must be done outside the physical bonds of matrimony. You must realize that at this moment you are aware of Martin's sin. You have no marriage. What took place was a fraud. It must be addressed.

"I realize that we live in a society of laws aside from those of the church. Naturally, you'll have to attend to those as well. But my concern is for your eternal soul. I can only advise you that under the laws of the church you are required to address this issue in the only way acceptable. An annulment *must* be sought. I'm sure it will be approved. What you do from a legal standpoint is of no concern to me. It's only church law that matters in any case."

His words only served to intensify the agony that seemed about to crush her. "Father," she said, "surely— I came here seeking some sort of solace. Right now, notwithstanding the position of the church, I—"

He was on his feet. "Ann, you will find your solace only in prayer, by the giving of your heart and soul to Jesus Christ, our Savior. Ask of Him and it will be given. But you cannot live in sin. Please."

He walked over to a small file cabinet, sorted through some files, and withdrew a number of papers. Returning to his desk, he handed the papers to Ann.

"You will find everything here. Follow the instructions on the first page. Once the papers are completed, get them to me and I will forward them to the diocese. I'm sure there'll be no delay." He was staring at her. "Do you understand?"

"Yes," she said, as she took the papers, folded them, and placed them in her handbag. But she didn't. She'd gone to Father Cassidy for comfort, and instead, she'd been given a lecture on church law. Why couldn't he have just offered some plain, simple compassion?

The lie she'd told earlier was becoming reality. A headache gnawed at her temples, threatening to develop into a debilitating migraine. She rushed home, took two painkillers left over from a year-old prescription given her when she'd sprained her ankle, and lay on the bed with a cold towel over her face. As she waited for the pills to take effect, she thought about what Father Cassidy had said.

He was right, of course, as far as it pertained to the church. But was that what she wanted? Did she really want to leave Marty? That was the question.

No, not now. She couldn't think of that now. Divorce? Out of the question! She loved him.

She rubbed the towel over her face.

Love? How could it be love? Marty was selfish, egotistical, and took her completely for granted. How was it possible to love such a man? What was the strange chemistry that attracted her to him? How could she ever look into his eyes again, knowing what she knew? How could she feel about him the way she'd once felt?

Exhausted and confused, she lay on the bed, in deep despair, until she felt the welcome anger rising within her, filling her with resolve. Yes. Father Cassidy was right. She had to leave Marty.

She searched her mind for the name of a lawyer she could talk to. There were lawyers she knew from her accounting work, but she really didn't want to get her personal life tangled up with work. There was the lawyer who'd been involved with the house sale, but he seemed like an idiot.

Then she remembered a man named Bill Connally who lived in the Clusters. He'd given a talk at one of the homeowners association meetings. He'd seemed knowledgeable and, perhaps more important, quite friendly.

When the headache had receded to a dull thud, she got up and looked through the Yellow Pages until she found his small display ad. She pressed the numbers on the phone.

. . .

Bill Connally shook Ann Cohen's hand and showed her to one of the two chairs that fronted his desk. He took a seat beside her. "Would you like some coffee?" he asked.

She shook her head. "No, thanks," she said. "Thanks for seeing me so soon. I really appreciate it."

"No problem at all," he said in a resonant voice. "After all, we're neighbors. How can I help you?"

Up close, she was incredibly beautiful, even more beautiful than the night he'd seen her sitting in the crowd when he'd addressed the homeowners group on some problem they were having with a service contractor.

He'd never forgotten that night. He was a criminal attorney, but since most people thought of lawyers as jacks-of-all-trades, he'd agreed to give them some advice rather than send them looking for someone else. In the first place, he was a homeowner himself, and as interested as anyone else in the welfare of the Clusters. In the second place, homeowners meetings were a good way to get to know people in the neighborhood. Especially the women.

He'd been introduced at the meeting before his talk, and when he'd met Ann she'd reminded him of Vivian. Not that Ann and Vivian looked that much alike, except for the same big, expressive eyes. It was more the body language and the voice. Above all, the voice. If he closed his eyes, Ann Cohen *was* Vivian. Throughout his presentation to the homeowners, he'd had to fight to keep from looking at her, and her alone. And later, during the discussion period, when she'd asked a number of questions, he'd found the sound of her voice unnerving.

She'd come to the meeting with friends, and Bill hadn't seen a husband hovering around. But later he'd learned that she was married, and happily so, he'd tried to put her out of his mind.

When she'd called this morning, he hadn't hesitated to rearrange his schedule to accommodate her. And now she was sitting in his office, looking distressed. Her eyes were a little puffier than he'd remembered, but that was probably because she'd been crying. A divorce, he assumed. He felt his pulse quicken. Divorce wasn't his bag, but for her he'd do it.

Connally was forty-three but looked much younger. He had closely cropped brown hair, shaggy eyebrows, and deep-set brown eyes. His face was rugged and square, with lots of laugh lines around the eyes. His six-foot frame was well muscled, but his most arresting feature was his voice. It was a radio announcer's voice, mellifluous, almost mesmerizing in its fluid grace. Each word was uttered in clear tones, in such a way that those who heard were compelled to listen carefully. As a prosecutor, he'd had an enviable string of victories, and there were those who credited his voice with his success. It wasn't true, of course. His success was due to his intelligence, his innate ability to understand the workings of the human mind, and an actual desire to work long hard hours.

Now he was on the other side of the fence, defending rather than prosecuting. He enjoyed being on his own, freed of the awful bureaucracy found within the office of the State Attorney.

The agonizingly painful death of his beloved Vivian

had scarred him deeply. Once a devoted husband and expectant father, he was now a shameless womanizer who believed in playing as hard as he worked. At this moment, he'd have liked nothing better than to be playing with Ann Cohen rather than discussing a possible divorce. Perhaps, after the divorce, there would be time for play.

"I don't know where to begin," Ann said, in a voice filled with despair.

"Take your time," he said softly. "There's no hurry."

"Well," she said, "I guess—I thought I should talk to someone . . . about a possible . . . annulment."

Bingo! he thought to himself, as he reached for a yellow pad and started making notes. "I'm very sorry to hear that, Ann," he said, not at all dismayed by his lie. "I'll be happy to help you in any way I can. Why don't you tell me what's on your mind?"

It took her a while, but she finally started talking. As she described her marriage problems, he asked questions, made more notes, and gently urged her on. They spoke for half an hour, and when they were done she seemed drained. Clearly, she was a woman who'd been betrayed and used. She was bewildered, confused, and deeply hurt.

"How about that coffee now?" he said, as she leaned back in the chair, looking drawn and tired.

"Yes," she said. "I think I'd like a cup."

"How do you take it?"

"Black," she said.

The attorney went out into the foyer of his small office and motioned to his secretary. "Sharon, would you bring two black coffees inside?"

"Yes, sir. Do you still want—"

"Yes. Hold the calls."

"Phil Medgars called. He's been arrested."

"What this time?"

"DUI."

"How long ago?"

"I guess it happened this morning. He called twenty minutes ago."

"Okay. You can start the paperwork. I shouldn't be more than another half hour."

Bill went back to his inner office, waited for the coffee to be served, and then took a position behind his desk.

It was a small office in a building shared with a real estate outfit. Keep the overhead down, that was the deal. He worked alone, with just a secretary. A very small operation, but it was slowly starting to come together. Another six months, and he'd be making as much as he'd made when he was a state prosecutor. Without the crap.

What the hell. He was alone now, in the prime of life. No wife, no kids, no responsibilities. He'd always dreamed of being a big-shot criminal lawyer, and now he had the chance to go for it. That's why he'd never seriously considered marriage again, not until he'd made it. In the meantime, there were plenty of women. Women who liked him a lot.

"Ann," he said, his announcer's voice sounding confident and sure, "it sounds to me like you have a clear case of fraud. There's no question that the marriage can be legally annulled. However, I think divorce would be the better course of action."

"Divorce? I don't understand, Mr. Connally. If Marty lied to me—"

The lawyer held a hand in the air. "Ann, if you don't start calling me Bill, I'm going to be very upset. We're neighbors, after all."

She smiled weakly. "All right . . . Bill. I thought—"

"Here's the difference," he said, interrupting her. "In the eyes of the law, an annulment means that the marriage never took place. Do you understand?"

"Yes."

"Okay. Now, if the marriage never took place, the court has a devil of a time determining who owns what. That's number one. Number two? There's no alimony granted. So to seek an annulment would not be in your best interests financially. A divorce would be much more advantageous to you in all respects. Now, I realize that your church doesn't recognize divorce, but they'll probably annul your marriage in their own way, the legal aspects being irrelevant to them. How much does Marty earn?"

She was taken aback by the question.

"Marty? He . . . I guess last year it was about sixty thousand. Some years it's worse, and some years it's better."

"And you? What do you earn?"

"I make just under thirty."

The lawyer smiled. "Well, right there, you see? It would be much better for you to get a divorce. Much better."

"But Marty already pays alimony to his first wife," Ann said.

"I know. You told me that. It has little bearing on your

situation, other than his ability to pay. As they say, you can't get blood out of a stone, but it sounds to me like Marty is able to provide for your needs. With that, plus what you earn, you should be fine."

They were talking about money. Money and divorce. She found the fact that she was seriously considering such a thing frightening. "I'm not sure I know what I want," she said, her resolve suddenly retreating.

Connally noticed it immediately. "Well," he said, "there are a number of considerations here. Keep in mind I'm a lawyer, not a psychiatrist, but I think the damage that has been done to you by Marty is something you'll never be able to put aside as long as you're still emotionally and physically tied to him. And it looks to me as though the damage is considerable.

"Your husband acted in an unconscionable manner. I don't think you'll ever be able to live with that. Do you?"

"I don't know," Ann said. "I really don't."

She was vacillating. He could see that. For some reason, it annoyed him. He'd met Marty Cohen and disliked him instantly. The man was an arrogant asshole. A big stickman as well, he'd heard around town. Well, so was Bill, if the truth be known, but Bill was single, not married to a woman like Ann Cohen. Anyone who screwed around on a woman this beautiful needed his head examined.

"Well," he said softly. "I don't want to talk you into something you don't really want. All I can do is give you legal advice, and as far as that goes you don't have much of a problem. No problem at all, in fact. As for your feelings, I think it would be best if you came to grips with them without undue influence from me."

"I appreciate your consideration," she said sincerely. "You seem so ... understanding. I can't tell you how much I appreciate that right now."

He got up from behind the desk, walked over to where she was sitting, and took a seat beside her. He reached over and patted her hand. "I do understand, Ann. It must be terrible to love someone and then find that—well, my heart goes out to you. It really does."

She was fighting back the tears again, but it wasn't working. Dabbing her eyes with a linen handkerchief, she looked at Bill. "What do you think I should do?"

"You want an honest answer?"

"Yes. I really do."

He didn't hesitate a second. "I think you should divorce the son of a bitch," he said.

CHAPTER

6

FOR THREE NIGHTS, UNABLE TO BEAR BEING IN THE same room with Marty, Ann used the guest bedroom as an emotional and physical retreat while she considered her options. Instead of fixing breakfast for the two of them, her normal practice, she would stay in her room until Marty had left. She arrived at work late, staying an extra hour to make up the time. Lou Holt, her boss, seemed perplexed but didn't complain. Cathy, dying of curiosity, nevertheless held her questions. After work, Ann would eat at one of a variety of fast-food joints on her way home, then lock herself in her prison, trying to ensure as little contact with her husband as possible.

Unable to sleep, she would sit by the window and stare blankly at the darkness. The harsh, life-wrenching reality of divorce was almost impossible for her to consider seriously for many reasons. She'd been raised in a home filled with love and understanding. Her parents had been her role models, with their easygoing affection for each other, their unabashed desire—even now—and their total trust. With her naïve romanticism, Ann had taken it for granted that her marriage would mirror theirs.

Then there was her basic philosophy of life itself. She'd always lived by a credo that to fear the worst was to ensure the worst, or at the very least invite it. So the thought of divorce was something that had never entered her mind until now. She'd waited until the age of thirty to pick her man, and the specter of having been terribly wrong, and the horrible nightmare of starting all over again, was more than she wanted to accept.

Her father had said that Marty was used goods. Divorce meant *she* would be used goods, and that terrified her. She'd observed countless numbers of divorced women in her social activities, watched them going through their acts, looking for someone to ease the pain. She'd seen them at parties, pathetic creatures, fawning and smiling and listening to the dirty jokes, enduring the suggestive touches, bearing the burden that went with being alone.

She was thirty-eight. She'd read the surveys and knew the odds. The chances of a thirty-eight-year-old woman finding a man—any man—were slim. With the benefit of hindsight, she realized she'd compromised her standards once and now she was paying for it. She knew she'd never be able to compromise her standards again. That, in itself, ruled out any chance of finding another man—

which meant living out her life alone.

Unless . . . unless she stayed and accepted Marty for what he was. Was that a viable alternative to divorce, she wondered? Certainly, there were times when Marty was terrible, but it wasn't all bad. There were those occasions when flashes of the old Marty would appear as if by magic. He would be sweet and kind and attentive and sexy. Rarely . . . but there were times.

And then she remembered the words of Father Cassidy. He'd said she was unmarried in the eyes of the church. Living in sin, in fact. What would he do if she failed to seek an annulment?

"Ann?"

It was Marty again, sitting by the door as he had, off and on, for the last three nights, talking to her, trying to reason with her, apologizing, cajoling, sometimes begging.

"Just leave me alone, Marty." she said softly.

"You can't stay in there forever," he said. "I know how hurt you must be, and I'm sorry. But I have some good news."

Good news? What possible good news could he have?

"I talked to a specialist today," he said. "A doctor by the name of Colton. He says there's an operation that might reverse the effects of the vasectomy. It's not successful that often, but it's worth a shot, and I'll do it, Ann. I'll do anything to make you happy. I love you. The thought of losing you is killing me. Won't you please come out and talk to me?"

She didn't answer.

"Ann," he continued, "you're a fair-minded person. If I've wronged you, and I know I have, I can only apologize and try to make it up to you somehow. You have to give me that chance."

Still, she didn't answer.

"All right!" he cried. "I lied to you about the vasectomy. I had no right to do that. But I was coming off a bad marriage and I wasn't thinking properly. When I didn't tell you right off, I was trapped. That makes me a shit, and I won't pretend otherwise. But I can't undo what's been done. All I can do is try. You have to give me that chance. You hear me?"

"I hear you," she answered weakly.

"Well, then, what about it?"

"I'll think about it," she said.

"Ann," he went on, "I love you. I can't live without you. If we don't patch this up, I don't know what I'll do. You've got to give me a chance."

Throughout the night, she thought about that grand gesture—the operation—and about Marty. Yes, he was weak. Yes, he was a liar. But she loved him. What he had done should have destroyed her love, but it hadn't. She didn't understand why it hadn't. Was it because he needed her? Was it because he was vulnerable? Was it because she needed him? Or was it fear of a future without him? She had no answers, just questions.

The next morning, exhausted from lack of sleep, debilitated from pain and sorrow and vacillation, Ann finally capitulated.

When she opened the door, Marty was sitting on the floor in his pajamas and robe, a cup of coffee in his hand. He looked dreadful, almost as awful as she did.

"Can I get you some coffee?" he asked.

"Don't bother," she said. "I'll get it."

"It's all ready," he insisted. "Won't take a minute, really."

She walked slowly into the kitchen and sat down. Marty placed a mug of hot coffee in front of her and took a seat. His hands—cold, clammy hands—reached out and took one of hers.

"Ann," he said, his eyes filling with tears, "I'm so sorry. So terribly sorry. Just tell me what you want, give me a chance to make it up to you. I'll do anything. Anything. I can't live without you, Ann. I just can't!"

She was drained. There was no fight left in her. "It's all right," she said, her voice barely above a whisper. "I'm not leaving you."

His face brightened perceptibly. "You'll never regret it," he said, getting to his feet, bending over and kissing her forehead. "Never. I'll make it up to you, Ann. Just tell me how. Do you want me to have the operation?"

She looked up at him and nodded. "I think that would be a good start, Marty."

"You got it. I'll phone the doctor and make the appointment. What else can I do?" he asked.

She looked into his eyes. "Just be honest with me from now on. No more lies, Marty. Be fair and be honest. That's all I really want. Can you do that?"

"Of course," he said. "No problem."

"You must understand something, Marty," she said, tearing her gaze away from his face.

"What?"

"This is going to take some time," she said. "Perhaps a lot of time. I just don't know at this point. I don't want you to push me, okay?"

"Sure," he said, patting her on the head, kissing her

on the cheek. "Whatever you want, Ann. No problem at all."

Three days later, Ann was walking slowly along the winding road that meandered through the complex, looking at the stars and the moon, still trying to come to grips with her decision to stay with Marty. In two weeks, he was to enter the hospital for the operation that might restore his ability to have children. The doctor had said the chances were slim, but Marty, by making the gesture, had won back some of her trust. Still, she wondered if she'd made the right decision.

"Ann?"

She recognized the voice immediately, but in the darkness it startled her. She whirled around and saw Bill, casually dressed, his hands stuffed in his pockets.

"I'm sorry. I didn't mean to scare you. I was just out for a walk and I saw you, and I thought I should at least say hello. How're you doing?"

She hung her head. "I'm fine, I guess."

"You guess?"

"I'm a bit embarrassed," she explained. "You must think I'm a terrible fool. After coming to you and telling you everything, and then not following through. I can imagine what you must think."

He was close now, close enough for her to smell his pleasant aftershave. In the soft light cast by the glow of the yellow streetlamp, his face seemed smoother, much less rugged than before.

"Ann," he said, "you mustn't think I'm critical of your decision to stay with your husband. Your decision was made out of love and forgiveness, and there can be no finer virtue in any human being. Besides, what you do with your life is no one's business but your own. You must never apologize for your feelings or your actions. Never."

She let out a deep sigh. "But you said I should divorce him. Don't you think—"

He held up a hand to silence her. "You asked me what I thought you should do and I told you. But, that's what *I* would do, and that isn't necessarily what's best for *you*. I don't have the compassion you have. I was looking at things from my own viewpoint.

"Only you can live your life, Ann, nobody else. What I think means nothing. What's important is what *you* think. That's all that's important. Love is precious, Ann. Very precious. I know."

There was such melancholy in his voice, she remembered what someone had said about him. "You . . . lost your wife, didn't you?"

"Yes," he answered.

"I know it's none of my business," Ann said, "but what happened?"

Bill stared at the ground for a moment. "Vivian died of cancer. She was seven months pregnant at the time. They knew she wouldn't be able to carry the child full term, so they took him early—it was a boy—but he never made it. Vivian died on the table."

Ann covered her mouth with her hands. "Oh, Bill. How awful. I'm so sorry."

He shook his head. "We thought we'd wait a few years before we had children. Isn't that a bitch?" He turned away for a moment, wiped his eyes with a handkerchief, then said, "She was one hell of a woman." His voice was wistful, filled with pain. "She was beautiful, intelligent, compassionate, loving—everything a man could ask for. We were only married six years, and every day of every one of those years, I would wake up in the morning and pinch myself, thanking God for such incredible luck. I guess He heard me and decided I had too good a deal. He sure as hell evened things out."

His voice had turned harsh, filled with bitterness. Aware of the sound of it, he looked away for a moment, then turned back to face her, a thin smile on his face. "I don't know what she saw in me, but whatever it was—"

"You must miss her terribly."

"I do," he said. "It's been a long time, and she's never really out of my thoughts. I guess that's bad, in a way, but I can't help it." He sighed, then looked directly into her eyes. "I'm sorry. I'm prattling away like—"

"It's all right, Bill," she said.

"Ann," he said, the melancholy gone now, his voice strong and sure, "you must never doubt yourself, understand? Always do what you think is right and then put it behind you. The hell with what anyone else thinks. That's the only way to survive in this crummy world."

"You're very understanding," she said.

"There's nothing to understand," he said. "You're a woman. Women have an enormous capacity for devotion and commitment, unlike most of us men." He turned and started to walk away, then stopped. Facing her again, he said, "I wish you all the happiness that life can provide, Ann. Good luck."

"Thank you, Bill. You're very kind."

"And remember, if ever you need a friend, I'm there. Okay?"

"Okay," she answered.

"You won't forget?" he asked, smiling broadly.

"No, I won't forget," she answered.

Experiencing Bill Connally's loneliness only solidified Ann's resolve to make her marriage work, no matter what it took.

Bill Connally looked at the tricky, sloping green 158 yards away, bent down, and picked up a handful of cut grass, which he threw in the air. The wind—what little there was of it on this hot, muggy day—was almost directly behind him. Satisfied, he went to his bag and pulled out his six iron. Setting himself, he addressed the ball, then struck it. The ball seemed to leap from the ground as it began its high arc toward the green, then curled left, eventually burying itself in one of the large bunkers guarding the green.

One of his playing partners, Les Phillips, another lawyer, chortled. "Goddam!" he said. "I think you're gonna make me rich today, Bill."

Bill threw him a quick glare, wiped the dirt from his club, and put it back in the bag. "Today's your day, Les."

Both men climbed into the electric cart and drove toward the green. Bill was driving, and Les, the passenger, was rubbing his hands together in glee. "There *is* justice, after all," he said. "I was beginning to think I'd never take money from you this year, Bill."

Bill snorted. "You may take money from me, Les, but don't ever think there's such a thing as justice."

Les frowned. "Oh-oh, the voice of doom. What's buggin' you today, Bill? Don't tell me one of those sleazeball clients of yours is actually innocent."

Bill laughed and shook his head. "It's got nothin' to do with business, Les."

"What then? You haven't been yourself all day. You've been preoccupied with something, that's for sure."

"It shows?"

"When's the last time you hooked all day long?" Les said.

Again, Bill laughed. "I guess you're right."

"So?" Les insisted. "What is it?"

Bill looked straight ahead. "Anybody ever tell you you're a nosy son of a bitch, Les?"

Les grinned. "Just you. So give. What's the problem?"

They reached the green, parked the cart, and selected their clubs for the next shot. For Bill, it would be a sand wedge. Les, delighted at being on the green, made a big deal of removing his putter from his bag. Bill leaned on the cart and said, "It just pisses me off, is all."

"What pisses you off?"

Bill didn't answer. Instead, he climbed down into the deep bunker, dug his feet into the sand, and swung at the ball. It soared, flying entirely over the green, finally coming to rest in the deep rough some thirty yards behind it. Bill waved a hand in the air. "That! That's what pisses me off."

Les grunted. Obviously, whatever was bugging Bill today would remain a secret. Too bad. There were times when Bill would talk about his clients, without using their names, of course. The stories were often hair-raising and never dull. Today he seemed especially upset. This story had to be a pip.

CHAPTER

7

THE OPERATION TO REATTACH MARTY'S VAS DEFERENS failed. Ann was discouraged by the news but heartened by his dramatic and sudden change in attitude. It seemed that Marty, having come perilously close to losing Ann, was determined to ensure that their marriage regained its lost luster. He was caring, unselfish, and considerate.

Initially, Ann suspected that the new Marty was putting on an act, but when he brought up the subject of adoption, her doubts about him were swept away.

"Let's look into it," he told her. "I know how much it means to you, and I'll do whatever it takes to make you happy."

Ann and Marty talked to the agency responsible for arranging adoptions. Ann was stunned to learn that the waiting list for newborn white children was upwards of four years. There were other ways to adopt, private placements, but she was dubious about that, having read a number of horror stories. Together, Marty and Ann reconsidered the idea of adoption. Their many conversations were rational and totally free of the anger that had characterized earlier discussions of children. In the end, they decided against adopting a child.

Ann, buoyed by Marty's new persona, accepted with apparent equanimity the reality that she would never be a mother. It was a decision they'd made together, not something shoved down her throat.

Her attitude on a host of other things changed as well. Where once she'd attended mass and gone to confession regularly, she now eschewed both. At her lowest moment, she'd sought help and received nothing she considered worthwhile. She attended mass a few times, but the spiritual comfort she'd felt in the past was gone. Sometimes, on the way home from work, she'd enter the church alone, light a candle, and pray, but not often. Religion, at least on the surface, had ceased to be a major part of Ann's life.

She'd seen Bill Connally several times, sometimes at meetings, other times when they'd bump into each other at the supermarket or the club. Each time they met, he'd been warm, friendly, and compassionate. She could tell he genuinely liked her, and there was never a hint that he thought less of her for rejecting his advice. For that, she was grateful.

Bill was becoming famous. Ann had seen him interviewed on television often in recent days, both locally and nationally, discussing a case he was involved in, and she was happy for his sudden success. Although the cause of the attention, Bill's defense of a vicious killer, was something many might consider in a negative light, Ann's respect for Bill remained undiminished.

Bill was still single, and she'd heard he was a terrible rake, but that didn't alter her respect for him either, and one day, when he made a good-natured pass at her, it pleased rather than offended her.

It had happened as they were sitting by the bird sanctuary on a beautiful Saturday afternoon. Marty was pitching some potential investors and Ann had wanted to get out of the house, so she'd walked to one of her favorite places, sat on a bench, and watched the colorful menagerie with intense interest.

Bill had been jogging and, covered with perspiration, took a seat beside her.

"They're beautiful, aren't they?" he said.

"Yes, they are," she answered. "I love to come here and watch them. The egrets, especially. They're so . . . stately, the way they walk."

"Do I smell okay?" Bill asked.

"Pardon me?"

"I'm sweating like a horse. I can't tell if I'm offensive or not. Am I okay?"

She laughed out loud. "You're fine, Bill. Just fine. By the way, I saw you on television last night."

He beamed. "You did, eh? So what did you think? Did I come across all right? I didn't seem too cold, did I?"

"You were just fine," she said, "although I don't think the man you're defending deserves you."

"Frank Peters? He does look a little scuzzy, doesn't he."

She put a hand to her mouth in surprise. "That sounds strange, coming from you. He's your client."

Bill laughed. "Just between you and me, you understand. But that doesn't mean he's guilty. Some of the best-looking people in the world are rotten to the core. You know what they say: you can't tell a book by its cover."

"What's it like, defending a man . . . like that? I mean, isn't it hard just being physically close to him?"

He pursed his lips, thought for a moment, then said, "It's just a job, Ann, like anything else. In this country, everyone is entitled to a defense, be they guilty or innocent. That's what makes America great. I'm just performing a necessary function to the best of my ability."

"And I'm sure you do it well," she said.

"I try," he said. "By the way, did you hear I'm moving?"

"No. Where?"

"I bought a house on Lake Tarpon. I've always loved the water, and now I can finally afford to live right by it. I move in a week."

"We'll miss you," Ann said.

"I'll miss you too, Ann." Then, changing the subject, he said, "So, how're things?"

"Things are fine," she said. "Marty's been wonderful these past few months."

"I'm very happy for you, Ann. You deserve the best."

"Thank you, Bill. Obviously, you're doing well as a lawyer, but how's your social life?"

He shook his head. "Terrible. My love life is a shambles, what with this AIDS thing. No more single women for me.

From now on I'm concentrating on married women. *Happily* married women."

He was being outrageous, but it was good fun, and he made her laugh. It seemed that every time he talked to her, away from his office, of course, he made her laugh. "You're terrible," she said, but her eyes were flashing.

"I know," he answered. Then, turning to face her, he said, "Look, why don't we have an affair?"

She looked at him in astonishment. "What?"

"I mean it," he said, looking at her out of the corner of his eyes. "Marty works late a lot, so you have plenty of opportunity. Aside from being a good lover, if I do say so myself, I'm a hell of a cook. When I move into my new house, we'll have a housewarming, just the two of us. I'll prepare a gourmet dinner, take you for a boat ride, then we'll make love by the light of the moon. We'll have a wonderful time. It'd be great. Whaddaya say?"

She laughed again. "You're simply impossible. I have enough trouble with one relationship. I don't think I could handle two."

He hung his head in mock dismay. "Well, if you ever change your mind, let me know." Then he grinned at her, stood up, said goodbye, and jogged away.

Ann had watched him disappear and, for a moment, wondered what it would be like to make love to Bill Connally. She felt a sudden stirring within her that brought a blush to her cheeks. His gentle pass had flattered her. Though he was kidding around, she sensed he found her desirable. As she found him, if she dared to admit it. Quickly, she stood up and headed home, chastising herself for thinking such things.

It really was a home now. Ann and Marty had lived in Florida for almost five years. It hadn't been nearly as bad as she'd imagined it might be. She enjoyed her work and the many friends they'd developed, both as a couple and as individuals.

For the next three years, Ann's life seemed full. She felt renewed, vibrant, and optimistic about the future. There were times when Marty was a complete boor, but she wrote them off to the pressures of business. His income varied, but one year it had soared to over a hundred thousand dollars. Their savings, managed by Ann, were mounting.

Marty was still a driven man, working too hard again, but it wasn't like before. Whenever he was going to be delayed, he'd call and let Ann know. Like tonight, when he'd called and told her he would be tied up with clients for much of the evening. She was to eat alone. As Ann prepared dinner for one, she counted her blessings.

It was midnight when she heard the front door open and close. Marty entered the room, undressed, and crawled into bed without turning on the light, which wasn't like him. Normally, when he got home this late, he was on an adrenaline high and would sit up in bed and give her a blow-by-blow account of his exciting day.

But not tonight. Tonight, he undressed in the dark and crawled into bed without his pajamas, lying flat on his stomach, the covers pulled up to his neck.

Ann, alarmed, snapped on the light. Maybe he was ill.

"Are you all right?" she asked.

"I'm fine," he growled. "Turn out the light. I want to sleep."

She could smell the booze on his breath. And the perfume on his neck.

"Marty! What is it?"

As she said it, she pushed back the covers, revealing his naked back and buttocks, both covered in angry red welts.

He rolled over on his side, removing his back from her view, and snarled at her. "Nothing!" he said. "I was looking at some property in the goddam dark and accidentally backed into some wire. That's all. Go to sleep."

Ann, still stunned, switched off the light. As she lay in bed, the image burned into her retinas danced before her eyes, and the smell of the perfume lingered in her nostrils.

She turned the light back on, got out of bed, and padded over to the closet. She went directly to his suit rack. Marty was very careful about his clothes and changed his suits on a daily basis. He had an even dozen of them. The suit he had worn today was hung at the left of his closet rack. The suit to be worn tomorrow would be positioned to the right. Once each suit had been worn twice, the entire wardrobe would be taken to the cleaners for attention. It was strange, almost a fetish, just another in a long list of quirks. The only time Marty ever wore a sports jacket and slacks was the day his collection of suits went to the cleaners.

She took the suit he'd worn today from the rack and looked it over. The strong smell of the same perfume she'd noticed on his neck assailed her nostrils. The suit was unharmed. Anything strong enough to cause the welts she'd seen on his body would have certainly made tears in the fabric. Yet there were none. Which meant—

"Satisfied?"

She whirled to face him, the suit still in her hand. He was nude, except for the medium-thick glasses he always wore.

She stared at him in shock. "You said you backed into a fence, but your suit is fine."

"Happy now?" The look on his face was positively evil.

"Happy? Marty, for God's sake. What's going on?"

"You really want to know?"

"Yes! I really want to know."

He turned away from her, yanked his robe from its hanger, put it on, and stomped out of the bedroom.

When she caught up to him, he was in the living room, pouring himself a straight Scotch. "You know," he said, as she entered the room and took a seat in the yellow chair, "you're responsible for this."

Speechless, she just stared at him.

"Yeah," he went on, "you. Good old Ann, the perfect woman. Forgiving, loving. Such crap!"

"What on earth are you talking about?"

"I'm talking about you," he said scornfully.

"Me?"

"Yes, you."

"I don't understand," she said.

"The vasectomy!" he shouted. "You bitch. For four long years you've never let me forget that I lied to you. You've made me feel like the lowest of the low."

Her mouth dropped open in shock. "That's not true,"

she protested. "I . . . I've forgiven you. That's been over for years."

"No, it hasn't. I see the look in your eyes every goddam day. You say you forgive me, but you haven't, not really. You make me feel as though I'm the worst kind of slime. So from time to time I like to be punished. Somehow, it makes me feel better."

"Punished?" She could barely utter the word. "It makes you feel better? I don't understand."

His lips were curled in a sneer. "You don't understand? Bullshit! You're no goddam saint. You know what this is about."

At last, reality struck her like a hammer blow. "You mean, you're into—"

"Yes!" he said, wild-eyed. "Go ahead, say it! I'm a masochist, thanks to you and your fucking gift of guilt. It's the only way I can live with myself."

She felt physically ill. With her hand covering her mouth, she blurted out, "Marty, that's sick!"

He shook his head. "Sick? It's not sick, it's just different, that's all. I went to a shrink, and he agrees with me."

"I can't believe I'm hearing this," she said. "You went to a shrink? When?"

"Four years ago. After the operation failed."

"And he told you this was okay?"

"Yes."

"And you expect me to believe that?"

"You think I'm lying?"

There was a look of defiance in his eyes that signaled his desire to fight. But Ann, heartsick, didn't want to fight. She wanted to understand. Her mind raced, and then she remembered articles she'd read about such people. She'd read enough to know that sexual deviancy almost always manifested itself at an early age. It wasn't something that was suddenly triggered by guilt later in life.

And then she saw the real Marty for the first time. The mystery of Marty—almost from the moment she'd met him—was mystery no more. Things that had confused and troubled her for years were now explained. She saw him for what he was, for what he had always been. He was sick. Sicker yet for trying to blame her for his deviancy. The carefully constructed layers of deceit had finally been stripped away.

"Oh, Marty," she cried, "you're such a liar. This isn't about me, is it?"

Some of the defiance left his eyes. There was no answer.

"You've always been this way, haven't you," she said. It was a statement rather than a question. Again, there was no answer.

Ann shuddered. "Do you . . . make love to them?" she asked quietly. "Or is it just the humiliation you crave?"

"You don't understand," he said, his voice almost a whine. "It's a need I have. I can't help it."

She believed him. "You didn't answer my question. Do you fuck them, Marty?"

Startled by her use of a word he'd never heard her utter before, he said, "It's not what you think."

She didn't want to hear any more. Disgusted, repulsed, she ran back to the bedroom. This time, she wasn't about to hide in the guest room. She wanted to get dressed, to get out of this house. To get away from this hideous nightmare.

"Ann!"

He was behind her, his strong arms grabbing her by the shoulders, spinning her around. Her hands turned into fists and she tried to hit him. But he held her fast.

"Ann, hold on! All right. Perhaps I do have a problem, but I love you. I'll see a shrink if you want. I'll work on it. I promise. I love you. You mustn't leave!"

She tried to blink back the tears, but couldn't. They coursed down her cheeks in a zigzag pattern as she shook her head violently back and forth. "No, Marty. I'm leaving. I have to get out of this house, right now!" She tore out of his grasp.

Marty stood by silently as Ann dressed quickly, threw some things in a bag, and left.

She spent the night in a motel, feeling more alone than she'd ever felt in her life.

The next morning Ann called Norma Wells, her gynecologist, and asked her for the name of a good psychiatrist, preferably female.

"Is this for yourself or someone else?" Norma asked.

"It's for me, Norma."

For a moment there was silence. Then Norma asked, "What's the problem? Are you depressed?"

"I'm depressed," Ann said, "but that's not the problem. Norma, I can't really discuss this with you, not right now. I just have to talk to someone who knows ... about certain things."

Norma cleared her throat. "I recommend Judy Wallace

quite highly. She keeps herself current, she's very sharp, and she's easy to work with."

Norma gave Ann the telephone number, and Dr. Wallace, perhaps sensing the panic in Ann's voice, said she'd see her that very afternoon.

It was a large office, with soft brown furnishings, most of them leather and oak, a surprisingly masculine office for such a feminine psychiatrist. Dr. Wallace was a woman in her early forties, tall and thin, with large, warm green eyes and a ready smile. Her long blond hair hung down to her shoulders. She had a fine figure, which was further enhanced by the soft blue silk dress she was wearing. Her husband of many years was also a psychiatrist, who shared the two-office building they owned. They had three teenage daughters who were now in high school. If the combination of being a full-time professional and a mother was stressful, it never showed. Judy Wallace looked content and relaxed, as though she were on her way to nothing more strenuous than lunch.

Ann laid her head back in the soft leather high-backed chair. Dr. Wallace, seated in an identical chair immediately facing Ann, leaned forward. "What's troubling you, Ann?"

Ann's thoughts tumbled out like prisoners escaping from jail. The hurts, the disappointments, the humiliations, the fears, all gushed forth in a steady stream of release. For thirty minutes she talked nonstop, and when she was finally spent, she brought her head forward, put her hands over her face, and wept unashamedly, making no effort to wipe her tears away.

Dr. Wallace put down her note pad and handed Ann

a box of tissues. "Here," she said. "I know it must seem hopeless, but it isn't. As difficult as this is, I've heard much worse."

Ann wiped her face, blew her nose, and sighed. "I don't know, doctor. This is pretty awful stuff."

"I agree," Dr. Wallace said. "Let's try and sort it out together. But before we do that, I need to know more about you. The more I know, the easier it will be for me to help you."

"You mean analysis?"

Judy laughed. "I mean understanding what makes you tick."

"Won't that take a lot of time?"

"I don't think so. You're very articulate, and you're able to verbalize your thoughts quite well. I don't think it will take long at all." Then she added, "You're trying to make a decision, aren't you?"

"Yes."

"And you want that decision to be right, true?"

Ann nodded. "I'm forty-two years old, doctor. I feel my time is running out."

"You've been married for twelve years, you said. Will a few weeks make that much difference?"

"Not really, I guess."

Dr. Wallace smiled. "All right. Let's set up a program. For the first few weeks, I'll see you once a week, if you can manage. After work is fine. Does that sound all right?"

"Yes."

"Good. Between now and our next talk, I want you to consider this. You already have a good grasp of what's involved here. You said you feel Marty's sexual disorder has nothing whatsoever to do with you. You're quite right about that. Which leaves you with two options. The first is that you remain with your husband and learn to accept him for what he is. Even if he does seek help, he won't be changing overnight, and there's a good chance he'll never change. Major sexual disorders are among the most difficult to treat, and the success rate is abysmally low. Having said that, let me also say that there can be successful marriages where the partners have different sexual mores.

"On the other hand, if you feel unable to accept Marty the way he is, you are left with option number two, which is to live away from Marty. As harsh as that sounds, there are no other viable options. You either learn to live with Marty the way he truly is or you leave. Anything else would be destructive.

"Whatever you ultimately decide, you'll have to accept your decision as being the right one for you. Whether you leave or stay, to spend the rest of your life feeling guilty would also be destructive. We want to avoid destructive behavior.

"What we will try to do, together, is to find out what's best for you. Right now, you're all that's important. That may sound selfish, but it's not. We'll let Marty worry about his own problems, okay?"

"Okay," Ann said softly.

For three months, while Marty saw his doctor and Ann consulted with Dr. Wallace, they were like strangers living in the same house, each going a separate way. They'd agreed not to discuss the matter until after the therapy sessions had concluded. Ann slept in the guest room and prepared meals for herself while Marty ate out.

At first, Ann was earnest and forthcoming in expressing her feelings to Dr. Wallace, but six weeks after the sessions began, Ann, through a friend, discovered that Marty, despite his big show of seeking help, was seeing a woman named Elizabeth Winters. In an uncharacteristic fit of rage, Ann confronted the woman and did something incredibly stupid. She threatened her. Later, ashamed and upset, she decided never to tell Dr. Wallace, either about her knowledge of the woman's existence or about the confrontation. What was the point? Nothing would change, and she would accomplish nothing except to make herself look foolish in the eyes of the doctor.

After another six weeks of therapy, Ann was ready to accept the inevitable with very little guilt. Marty would never change; Ann knew she could never accept his sexual deviancy.

She decided to do what was best for her. She called Bill Connally's office and made an appointment to see her old friend.

She would divorce Marty. Tonight she would tell Marty to his miserable face.

PART TWO

Every murderer is probably
somebody's old friend.

Agatha Christie

CHAPTER

8

CATHY POLLARD HUNG UP THE TELEPHONE AND SHOOK her head in utter frustration. It was the third time she'd called Ann that morning and there was still no answer. Each time she'd called, she'd gotten the damn answering machine.

Hello! Marty and Ann are unable to come to the telephone at the moment. If you'll leave your name, number, and the time you called when you hear the beep, we'll get back to you as soon as possible. Thank you.

It all sounded so cozy. Marty and Ann indeed. Christ! If people only knew.

Three times Cathy had left a message. "Ann, it's Cathy. If you're there, please pick up the telephone. I just got a call from Lou and I have to talk to you before work."

It wasn't true. Lou Holt was their boss at the accounting firm of Tilbey & Company, but Cathy, not knowing what had happened after she'd left last night, was afraid that Ann and Marty were having some sort of terrible confrontation.

God! What a night. The very day Ann had decided to divorce the sick sonofabitch.

They'd talked about it until one in the morning, when Ann, concerned about Cathy, had almost forced her from the house. And now there was no answer to her repeated telephone calls. What did it mean? Had there been a confrontation when Marty finally arrived home, stinking of the fat woman's perfume, with more angry welts on his ass? Had Ann left in the middle of the night?

Cathy's imagination was running wild. She decided to go over there before work. She had to learn for herself what was what. She toweled off, dressed in a hurry, and ran to the car.

Cathy's heart raced as she drove up to Ann's house. There were two green-and-white Pinellas County sheriff cars parked near a stand of pines, not forty feet from the entrance. Two uniformed deputies stood by the front door, staring off into space. On the street, some eight or nine people were gathered, talking among themselves.

Cathy parked the car at the curb and ran toward the crowd. She saw Gina Rizzo, one of Ann's friends and neighbors, looking bewildered. Cathy grabbed Gina's arm. "Gina! What happened?"

Gina turned, her shock-widened eyes recognizing Cathy, and said, "Cathy! The cops won't tell us anything, other than that Ann's not home. Neither is Marty. But something happened. They took all our names and addresses and said they'd be talking to us later."

"You don't know what happened?"

Gina shook her head. "I haven't a clue. Ann's car is still there in its stall but Marty's is gone. The cops have been here since before sunup. I saw them when I went out to pick up the morning paper. There've been a bunch of them, coming and going. Nobody will tell us anything."

Cathy's hand flew to her mouth. "Oh, my God!" she exclaimed.

"Do you know something?" Gina asked, her eyes even wider.

Cathy could feel the adrenaline pumping through her veins, pounding through her temples. "Oh, my God!" she said again.

Gina squeezed her arm. "What? What?"

Cathy started to answer, then stopped. She pulled away from Gina and walked quickly toward the front door of Ann's house.

"I'm Ann Cohen's friend," she explained to one of the cops guarding the door. "I was with her last night. If something's happened, I want to know about it."

The cop, a lanky six-footer, looked down at her. "You were with her last night?"

"Yes."

He motioned for her to stay put. "Just a minute."

The cop went inside the house and then came back with a short, bald, hefty black man, somewhere in his forties, dressed in a rumpled dark-blue suit. The man looked at Cathy for a moment. "You were with Mrs. Cohen last night?"

"Yes."

"Would you come in, please?"

Cathy walked past him into the house.

The living room was being examined by three men, one using a small hand-held vacuum cleaner, the other two wielding what looked like a large gun of some kind, one that emitted not bullets but a soft green light.

The man motioned to a chair in the kitchen. Cathy sat. He pulled his badge from his jacket pocket and displayed it to her, then put it back. "I'm Lieutenant Luther Jackson, Pinellas County Sheriff's Department. What's your name?"

"My name is Cathy Pollard. I'm a friend of Ann's."

Jackson was making notes in a small notebook he'd taken from his inside pocket. "Where do you live, Miss Pollard?"

"Mrs. Pollard," she corrected. "I live at twenty-four-eighty-eight Country Place Lane, in Pasco."

"When did you last see Mrs. Cohen?"

It seemed so strange to be sitting in Ann's kitchen, the house filled with cops and Ann nowhere in sight. She felt that Ann's house was being violated by these people.

Unable to contain her curiosity any longer, she blurted out, "What happened? Did she kill herself?"

Jackson looked at her oddly. "Kill herself? What makes you think she killed herself?"

Cathy exploded. "Stop being coy. Just answer the goddam question. Is she alive or not? She's my friend, you asshole!"

Jackson looked at her for a moment, considered answering in kind, and then changed his mind. "Take it easy, Mrs. Pollard. Your friend is very much alive."

The relief washed over Cathy like a cold shower. "Thank God! Then what is this all about?"

Jackson hesitated for a moment, then said, "*Mr.* Cohen has been murdered."

Cathy was stunned. For a moment, she couldn't speak. Then, gasping for air, she stammered, "Marty? Murdered? How? Where? Here?"

The cop stared at her. "I thought maybe you could tell me what happened."

"Me? What are you talking about?"

"You said you were with her last night."

"Yes ... I was." Then it dawned on her. The cop was implying *they'd killed Marty!* "Are you crazy?" she cried. "You think Ann and I killed Marty?"

"I didn't say that. You said you were with her last night. Why don't you tell me what happened?"

Could Ann have ... ? No! Cathy told herself. Impossible. Ann wasn't the kind. Ann couldn't. Not ever.

"Mrs. Pollard?"

Cathy stared blankly into the detective's dark eyes, holding her breath, then exhaling. "Ann! Oh, God! This is terrible. How did this happen? When?"

The cop leaned forward, his breath heavy with the smell of onions. "Mrs. Pollard, right now I'll be the one asking the questions, and you'll be the one giving me the answers. Have we got that straight?"

"I guess."

"When did you last see Mrs. Cohen?"

"Here. At the house. I left about ... I guess it was one o'clock."

"In the morning?"

"Yes."

"Are you sure about the time?"

"Yes. It was one o'clock. I remember Ann saying I had to get home. She was concerned that she was messing up my sleep. That's the way she is, always worrying about everybody except herself."

"You were together before that?"

"Yes."

"Where?"

"Here."

"Here? Just the two of you?"

"Yes. We were alone."

"Alone?"

"Yes."

"What were you doing here?"

"Ann . . . Ann was upset."

"Why?"

Cathy thought about what she was going to say. The thought frightened her even more. "I can't tell you that."

"Why not?"

"I can't! That's all. I just can't!"

Luther pulled a package of cigarettes from his shirt pocket, selected one, and put it to his lips.

"Would you mind not smoking?" Cathy said softly.

"Whassamatter? You some kinda health nut?"

"Not really. Cigarette smoke makes me sick. I'm allergic."

Luther glared at her, then put the cigarette away. "All right, so what was Mrs. Cohen upset about last night?"

Cathy remained mute.

Luther slammed his notebook on the kitchen table and leaned back in his chair. "Mrs. Pollard," he said harshly, "you can either answer my questions now, here, or we can go downtown. If you don't answer the questions downtown, you'll be subpoenaed and end up in front of a judge. If you don't answer the questions there, you'll go to jail. So let's save us both a lot of trouble and just answer the questions right now. Okay?"

"You don't understand," Cathy protested.

"I don't have time for this," he snapped. "This is a murder investigation, understand? You're a material witness. That gives me the right to ask you questions. I'm a police officer, lady, and you're beginning to piss me off."

Cathy glared at him. "You really think she killed him, don't you? That's what this is about."

"I didn't say that."

"But you're thinking it. That's why you're here. Well, you're wrong. Ann couldn't kill Marty! She couldn't have!"

Again the cop leaned forward, the smell of the onions almost making Cathy gag. "Why do you say that?"

"Because Ann's not a violent person. She just isn't. She's one of the sweetest, kindest people you'll ever meet. Where is she?"

Luther shrugged. "I don't know. I thought you might be able to tell me."

"You mean she's disappeared?"

Again, he shrugged. "What were you doing here last night?"

Cathy took a deep breath, then told him, haltingly but completely. He listened carefully, made copious notes, then asked several more questions.

"It was your idea to drive over to the woman's house?"

"Yes," Cathy said. "Ann had already decided to divorce Marty, but she thought that by actually seeing what was going on, it would give her some added motivation. That's all it was. Damn!" She buried her face in her hands.

Luther kept at her. "You could see through the window, even though the blinds were drawn?"

"Yes," Cathy mumbled. Then, raising her head, she said, "They weren't completely shut. We looked in the side, at the corner. It's one of those long windows that covers the entire wall. We could see clearly."

"And you say this has happened before?"

"Yes. I don't mean we were ever there before, just the part about Marty having done this kind of thing before. The first time was about three months ago. Marty came home with marks all over his backside and told Ann what he was into. He didn't seem to think there was anything wrong with it. He told Ann he'd been seeing hookers. Ann was just sick about it. She didn't know what to do. She was shattered."

"But it wasn't hookers, was it?"

"No."

"It was the same woman? This—" he consulted his notes "—Elizabeth Winters?"

"Yes. As far as I know, anyway."

"How did Mrs. Cohen find out about the woman?"

"I don't know," she said. Then she corrected herself. "No, I remember. Ann found out from Betty at the tennis club."

"Explain that to me."

Cathy ran a hand over her mouth and said, "Betty Crawford runs a small flower shop in Palm Harbor. She also plays tennis in Ann's ladies' league. Marty didn't know Betty, or the fact that Betty knew Ann. He sent some flowers to this bitch of his a few weeks ago. Betty told Ann about it."

The cop took a deep breath. "Let me get this straight. The woman with the flower shop, a Betty Crawford, told Mrs. Cohen that her husband had sent flowers to Mrs. Winters. And that was a few weeks ago."

"Yes."

"Did Mrs. Cohen ever talk to the Winters woman?"

Cathy hesitated. "I don't know," she said.

It was a lie. She did know. She'd been there, all right.

Luther looked at her for a moment and then nodded. For the next half hour, he asked seemingly innocuous questions, wrote down her answers, and then finally closed his notebook. "Just one more thing, Mrs. Pollard. You said that you left your friend at about one o'clock, because you were sure she was going to be all right. Is that correct?"

"Yes, but I was wrong. If she's gone off somewhere, I must have been wrong."

He shook his head. "That's not really important. What's important is how you saw things at that time, the point when you left. Mrs. Cohen was quite rational, correct?"

"Rational? She was devastated. I mean, she wasn't acting crazy or anything, but I knew how hurt she was."

"Hurt? Why should she be hurt? She'd already decided to divorce the guy, according to you. You mean angry, don't you?"

"Well, of course she was angry," Cathy replied, her frustration mounting. "If you'd just seen your wife in bed with another man, you'd be angry too."

"Let's keep my wife out of this, okay? She was angry, right?"

"Of course."

"But you left because you thought she'd be okay, right?"

"That's right, but—"

He stood up. "You've been a big help, Mrs. Pollard. I'll have one of the officers take you downtown and you can sign a statement."

"I thought you said if I answered your questions I wouldn't have to do that."

"I'm sorry. I did say that, but your information is too important. It won't keep. We need to get it on paper right away."

Cathy shook her head. "I can't right now. I have to be at work." She looked at her watch. "Oh, I'm already very late."

The detective sighed. "I don't think they'll mind, Mrs. Pollard. This is a murder investigation. We really need you to sign that statement. I'll call your boss and explain, if you like."

Cathy shook her head. "No. I'll call the office myself. God! They'll be wondering about both of us."

He nodded and handed her the phone.

Cathy made the call. When she hung up, Luther sat down again, put his face close to hers, and said, "Look, Mrs. Pollard, I know you're a real pal of Mrs. Cohen's. And that's fine. You want to help your friend, don't you?"

"Of course."

"Good. Then let me give you a piece of advice."

"About what?"

He lowered his voice. "She told you about seeing the woman, right?"

"What?"

"The Winters woman. We know Mrs. Cohen threatened to kill her. We know about that scene at the Winters house, and we know she had a friend with her. From the description, I figure you were that friend. When I asked you earlier if she'd ever talked to the woman, you said no, but I knew from the look on your face you were lying. You were trying to protect your friend, and that's understandable."

He stood up and his voice got louder.

"My advice is this. Don't try to be cute. You're not a very good liar. Don't get mixed up in something that can cause you a lot of trouble. Understand? Tell us the truth. That's always the best thing."

Cathy scowled. "Did she tell you, that pig Winters?"

Luther stared at her for a moment, then shook his head. "No," he said softly. "Elizabeth Winters didn't tell us anything. Elizabeth Winters is dead."

CHAPTER

9

THE LAST IN A SERIES OF VICIOUS NIGHTMARES CAUSED
Ann Cohen's eyes to snap open again at 8 A.M. She jerked
upright, bathed in cold sweat, her chest heaving as she
gasped for air. Her eyes wide open, she looked around
the room for a moment, then closed them again as the
room began to swirl.

What she had seen was enough. She recognized that
she was in a hospital room with a single barred window. She tried to force herself to think clearly, but it
was impossible. Again, she opened her eyes, but the
movement of the room nauseated her. She shut them
and gripped the edges of the high, narrow bed, as if that
might slow things down, but it was a fruitless effort.

Small bits of memory came and went. Strange, non-
sensical images. She'd been at home, alone, drinking,

waiting for Marty to come home so she could tell him she was leaving. She'd gotten drunk waiting so long. She was in a hospital. Was that the reason? Had Marty found her passed out and brought her in?

No. That wasn't it.

Her head throbbed unmercifully. Her entire body was a temple of pain. Her mouth and throat were dry and foul-tasting. Even her teeth hurt.

She lay back on the bed and tried to focus on the upper corner of the room. She remembered seeing Marty lying on that woman's bed, face down, his hands and feet bound, being whipped. She clutched the side of the thin mattress, just as she'd clutched Cathy's arm there at the Winters house. But the visions persisted. She saw Marty again, this time lying on some sort of table, his face marred by two small, round holes. Had it been a dream? A nightmare?

She shook her head, trying desperately to rid herself of the terrible images. Then she heard the metallic, grinding sound of the locked door being opened. A thin white-haired nurse came in, accompanied by a fullback-sized policewoman, who held a long black stick in her meaty hands.

Police!

Policemen had been in her kitchen. They'd talked about Marty being dead and about a gun—her gun—and they'd taken it away and said she should tell them. . . .

She looked up at her visitors. Their eyes were saying the same thing the policemen had said: You killed Marty.

"Hello, Mrs. Cohen," the policewoman said. She slapped the nightstick into her left palm. The sight and sound of it triggered something in Ann's brain. It wasn't a nightstick, it was a whip. And the fat policewoman wasn't a cop anymore, she was Elizabeth Winters, bringing the whip up high. . . .

Ann brought her hands up to cover her face. At the same time, she brought her knees to her chest, cowering.

"Mrs. Cohen?" She heard the nurse say. "It's all right. No one is going to hurt you."

Slowly, Ann removed her hands from her face and stared at the two women standing by the bed. "Where am I?" she asked.

"You're in Morton Plant Hospital," the nurse said. "As soon as the doctor checks you out, this policewoman will be taking you to jail."

"Jail?" That meant it was true. They thought she'd killed Marty and were taking her to jail. She was so confused. Try as she might, she couldn't get her brain to function. She felt divorced from reality.

"I didn't kill Marty," Ann croaked, her hands clutching the smock she wore. "I swear to God!"

"That's all right, lady," the policewoman said. "You don't have to say anything right now. We'll get you properly booked and then you can call your lawyer."

Ann looked down at herself. She was dressed in a short green backless hospital gown and nothing else. What was happening? This couldn't be real! It had to be some awful hallucination. Marty couldn't be dead. He couldn't! But she'd seen the bullet holes. And now she was on her way to jail.

Her body started shaking uncontrollably and her stomach heaved again. She staggered to the bathroom and leaned over the toilet bowl. Exhausted, she slipped to the cold tile floor as the tears began to flow again.

What happened next was almost a blur. She was vaguely aware of a doctor entering the room, giving her a cursory examination, and then talking with the policewoman.

"You can have her," she heard him say. "I'll sign the release." She was told to get dressed.

They gave her fresh panties and a new brassiere and a pair of orange coveralls that had PCJ stenciled in big black letters on the back. They gave her plastic slippers for her feet. The vomit-soaked clothes she'd worn the night before, along with her handbag—all of it encased in a sealed plastic bag—were handed to the policewoman, who placed them in a paper sack.

Once dressed, Ann, still unsteady on her feet, felt her arms being placed behind her, the cold steel of handcuffs being snapped on her wrists, and strong arms leading her from the room to a waiting van. The door slammed shut with a terrible bang.

At the county jail, she was escorted to a windowless room with a small table, where a fortyish black man dressed in civilian clothes was seated. He rested both hands on top of a manila file folder and intoned, "Mrs. Cohen, you are under arrest. You're charged with two counts of first-degree murder. You have the right to remain silent. You have the right to an attorney. If you cannot . . ."

Although Ann heard "two counts," the number didn't register with her. She was still in a state of shock. She was hearing something she'd heard a hundred times, on television or in the movies, but this time it was real. The man was directing the words at her. They were accusing her of killing Marty. It was impossible. "Do you understand these rights as I have explained them to you?"

She mumbled her assent.

"Do you wish to talk with an attorney?"

"Yes!" she said, bursting into tears again. "Oh, my God! Yes!"

The policeman turned away from her. "Book her and let her call her lawyer."

"Yes, sir."

Again, in a fog, Ann felt herself being led through a series of small rooms, where she was fingerprinted, photographed, and taken to a phone. She was shaking so hard it was impossible for her to press the buttons. Besides, she didn't know either of Bill Connally's telephone numbers. She turned to the policewoman and said, "I don't know his number."

"Who?"

"My lawyer. William Connally."

"Connally?"

"Yes."

The policewoman's eyebrows went up. She consulted a small book beside the telephone and said, "The number is 645-9388."

Ann lifted the receiver from the telephone and tried to press the numbers, but her hands were shaking so hard she kept making mistakes. She turned to the policewoman and pleaded, "Could you?"

The policewoman grunted, punched the buttons herself, then nodded at Ann, who put the receiver to her ear. She could hear a woman's voice, obscenely pleasant, saying, "Good morning. Wilson, Smith and Connally."

"I need to talk to Mr. Connally," Ann said, her voice wavering.

"Mr. Connally is in conference. Could I have him return the call?"

"No! I must speak to him now!" She knew her voice had become loud, but it didn't matter. The panic would add impact to her words. "I'm in jail," she added.

"Could I have your name, please?" The voice said, not missing a beat, as though this was an ordinary occurrence.

"My name is Cohen. Tell him it's Ann Cohen!"

"One moment, please."

After what seemed like an eternity, Ann heard Bill's familiar voice on the telephone.

"Ann? Is that you?" he asked.

Again, the tears surged down her face. She was almost incoherent, but managed to tell him enough for him to say, "I'll be right there."

After making a follow-up call to a contact in the Sheriff's Department, Bill Connally put down the phone and, for a moment, leaned back in his high-backed leather chair, staring off into space. Then, galvanized into action, he bolted upright and walked quickly out of his office. He stopped at his secretary's desk and snapped instructions.

"First, I want you to cancel everything I've got for the next four hours. Then call Rex Kelsey and tell him I want to see him right away. Then—"

As he continued to reel off the orders, Hugh Smith, one of the firm's three partners, walked slowly out from his office across the hall and listened. When Bill was finished, Smith asked, "What's up?"

Bill turned to him and said, "Ann Cohen's been arrested."

Hugh remembered the woman's name. Earlier today, Connally had briefed him on her pending divorce. Hugh had scheduled a meeting for the morning. Hugh's eyebrows arched. "For what?"

"Murder. Two counts."

A look of horror washed over Hugh's face. "It's not—"

Bill nodded. "It sure as hell is."

"Who besides her husband?"

"The girlfriend."

"Oh, my God!" Hugh exclaimed. "I don't believe it."

Bill gritted his teeth. "She came to me. I pawned her off on you. I never should have done it."

"Bill, surely—"

"I was a fool," Connally continued. "I should have looked after it personally, even though you're the divorce expert in this firm. I thought I was doing what was best for her. Damn!" He threw his hands in the air in disgust.

Hugh rubbed his chin. "You can't blame yourself for this, Bill."

"But I do. When I told her I thought you should handle it, I could tell she was disappointed. I told her I'd help out too, but it didn't register. I should have known."

Bill walked back to his office with Hugh in tow. "She's a friend, Smitty. By suggesting she see you instead, I effectively turned my back on her."

"Bill, will you knock it off? You're busy as hell. You have no time for divorce cases. Surely you told her that."

"I did, but she didn't understand. She just thought I didn't care."

Hugh shook his head. "Jesus, what a mess. Why the hell did she do it?"

Bill whirled, his eyes blazing. "Don't ever say that again, you understand? Not ever!"

"But you said—"

Bill didn't let him finish. "I said she'd been arrested, that's all. Ann Cohen is incapable of murder." He turned back to his desk and shuffled some papers. "I have no idea why they arrested her, but I'll find out soon enough. In the meantime, I want everyone in this office to understand that Ann Cohen is an innocent woman. Got it?"

Stunned by the intensity of his partner's feelings, Hugh Smith simply nodded his head, remaining silent as he watched Bill throw some papers into a briefcase.

The man was really something, Hugh thought. When Bill had first joined the firm three years ago, he'd had an easygoing, shy sort of charm about him that was disarming and endearing. Now his ego was fully developed, bordering on arrogance, and he was a holy terror when he didn't get his way. But Bill Connally contributed more than his share to the bottom line, and Hugh Smith and Jack Wilson were more than happy to have him as a partner.

Bill grunted something and was gone. Hugh sighed and returned to his own office. Although the name of the firm was Wilson, Smith & Connally, in reality Connally was now running the show. Some partners were more equal than others.

An hour after she'd made the call to Bill, Ann was led into a small room where he stood waiting for her. At the sight of him, she threw herself into his arms, almost collapsing from the fear and anguish, the combined physical and emotional hangover. Never in her life had she felt so utterly helpless. The smell of Bill's cologne, the strength of his arms, all served to ease a fraction of the pain that threatened to overwhelm her. He would set the police straight. He'd correct this terrible mistake. She knew it.

He was holding her in his arms, whispering assurances into her ear as she continued to weep. She felt she could no longer control her emotions at all and feared she was on the very edge of insanity.

"Don't worry, Ann," he said soothingly. "I know how idiotic that must sound to you, but you have to pull yourself together. I need your help if I'm to clear this mess up."

He directed her to a chair, one of two that braced a small, square plastic table. They both sat down. Ann looked into his eyes, then stared at the table. "I must look terrible," she said, running a hand through her tangled hair.

"Ann," he said, ignoring her remark, "I've had only the briefest discussion with the police. They've told me that Marty and this woman he's been seeing are both dead and that—"

Ann stared at him. "What did you say?"

Bill seemed confused. "They didn't tell you?"

"She's dead? Elizabeth Winters is dead?"

Bill hesitated for a moment and then said simply, "Yes."

Ann's hand flew to her mouth. "Oh, my God! I thought it was only Marty!"

"I'm sorry."

She stared at him in dazed bewilderment. "They think I killed them?"

He nodded. "I'm afraid so."

Ann brought the other shaking hand to her mouth. Bill chewed on his lower lip for a moment. "Later I'll have an opportunity to review what evidence they have," he said. "But for the moment, I want to concentrate on what you can remember. Let me say at the outset that I offer you my deepest sympathy. I know how hard you've worked to keep your marriage alive. I can understand what a blow your husband's death is to you. After what you've been through, to find yourself charged with his murder must be an unbearable experience. However, as painful as it is, I must know what happened last night. I want you to tell me everything."

Ann hadn't heard a word he'd said. She was staring at the wall, numb with pain and anguish, still trying to make her mind work. "They were both killed?" she gasped.

Bill, usually an impatient man, looked at Ann with eyes that expressed his empathy. "Yes," he said softly.

"Where did this happen?"

"At the woman's house, about two this morning. Someone shot them both to death while they were in bed."

"And they think I killed them? My God! How can that be? How could they think such a thing?"

Bill took a deep breath, exhaled, and then said, "Ann, this has been a terrible shock, I know. But I must know what you did last night if I'm to help you. Please try to remember."

She rubbed her temples with the tips of her fingers, then wrapped her arms around herself to control the shaking, as best she could, and tried to speak. She couldn't.

Bill squeezed her shoulder comfortingly. "I realize how frightened and confused you are, but you must do this. I need to know everything, no matter how insignificant it may seem. I want to impress upon you that the earliest recollections of events are often the most reliable. So, please, even though this is a terrible situation, help me to help you. All right?"

"I'll try," she said weakly.

"Good." He paused for a moment, took another deep breath, and then said, "Keep this in mind. No matter how things look, no matter how depressed you are, remember this: I know you didn't do it. You couldn't have, and I'm going to save you from this, no matter what it takes. I'll stop them from making a horrible mistake. I believe in you. Totally. I'm not just saying that, I mean it. Try very hard to have faith in me. Will you do that?"

She dropped her hands and nodded.

"Good. Now, what happened last night?"

Ann tried to gather her thoughts together. Most of what she remembered was murky. "Last night, I followed him," she said.

"You followed who?"

"Marty. Cathy and I did."

"Cathy? Look, start at the beginning, please. I realize this is difficult, but I need to understand exactly what happened, and I need it in some sort of chronological order. Let's start at the beginning. You said you followed Marty. Where? Why? What caused you to do that?"

She started to tell him everything. About halfway through, he held up a hand. She noticed for the first time that he had been recording their conversation on a small portable tape recorder. He took a moment to flip the tape, then said, "Okay. Go on." Finally, she finished her story.

"Tell me again what happened when you got home the first time."

"Cathy stayed with me for a while, but I felt awful involving her in this. I urged her to go home. She finally did. Then . . . the house was so . . . empty. I felt terrible. Totally alone. I got in the car and drove around for a while. Just to be away from the place."

"Do you remember what time that was?"

"No."

"And when you arrived back home?"

"I sat in the kitchen and drank. I was waiting for Marty to show up so I could tell him to his face I'd decided to—" She began to cough.

"Divorce him?" Connally asked, finishing the sentence.

"Yes. I never had the chance. The police came."

"During the time when you were at the woman's house, did you see anyone? Anyone who might have recognized you?"

"I don't know. I don't think so."

"And when you leaned against the house to look in the window, you put your hands on the window?"

"Yes."

"But you never went inside the house?"

"No."

"Okay. Later, when you were out driving around alone, did you see anyone? Stop for gas? Have a drink at a bar?"

"No," she said. "I don't even remember where I went."

"Were you drunk then?"

Ann shook her head. The motion made her momentarily dizzy. She waited for the feeling to subside and then said, "No. I was sober. I didn't start drinking until I got back home."

Bill looked upset. "You must remember where you drove. It's very important. Try!"

The urgency in his voice filled her with a sense of panic. "I can't!" she cried. "I just can't!"

"Yes, you can!" he insisted. "Think! When you came out Clusters Drive, did you turn left or right?"

"I—I turned left. Yes! I drove up to Tarpon; then I just kept going right up Nineteen. I don't know why."

He patted her hand. "That's better. You're doing fine, Ann. Okay, you went up Highway Nineteen. Then what?"

Ann rubbed her forehead as she tried to think. "I got all the way to Weeki Wachee before I realized how far I'd gone. Then I turned around and came home."

"Okay, did you see anybody? Stop at a friend's? Anything?"

"No. It was the middle of the night."

"Could you have gone back to the house? The woman's house?"

Ann stared at him. "What are you trying to say, Bill?"

"Don't get upset. I just want to have everything clear in my mind. I want to rule out every possibility."

"No. I'd had all the humiliation I could stand for one night."

"You're sure you didn't go back?"

"I'm sure."

"Good."

A flash of anger made her eyes sparkle. "Don't you believe me?"

"Of course I believe you. But I have to be able to tell the police something. Could anyone have seen you when you went on this drive?"

"Not that I know of. You sound like you think I could have done it!"

"Of course you didn't do it. I know that. But the police must have something, or you'd never have been arrested. I'm just trying to get the facts together so we can make our presentation and get you the hell out of this place. I realize how difficult this is for you, but it can't be helped."

"I'm sorry."

"Don't apologize. You have every right in the world to be upset." He took her hands in both of his and squeezed them. "You're doing fine, Ann. It's going to be all right."

She tried to smile but simply nodded.

"Now," he said, "according to what you've told me, you were at the Winters house earlier in the evening; you went home; then you went for a drive alone. You didn't encounter anyone. Later, you returned home and got drunk. In fact, you don't really have an accounting for your time, other than your recollection. We need some corroboration. That's what I'm trying to latch on to. You understand?"

"Yes."

"You see how it looks?"

"Yes."

"Good," he said. "And you're sure you didn't take the gun?"

"Yes. I'm sure. That I'm very sure of, because when the police came I told them where the gun was. When they went to get it, it was still there. I saw them take it away."

The blood seemed to drain from the lawyer's face as he listened to Ann's explanation. "Let's talk about that," he said. "When the police came to the door of your house, what exactly did they say? Every word is important."

Ann tried to concentrate. She told him as much as she could remember, but her memory was hazy.

Bill turned off the tape recorder, leaned forward, and said, "Now, let me get this straight. Did the police ask you about the gun before they gave you some papers to sign?"

"I told you, I'm not sure."

"But you were pretty drunk, you said. Could it have happened that way?"

"I guess so."

"Could they have asked you about the gun, had you sign the papers, and *then* tell you that Marty had been murdered?"

Ann shook her head. "I'm not sure. I can't remember. All I remember is some papers and the gun and—"

"But it might have been the way I've described?"

"Yes."

He smiled. "I want you to concentrate very hard. I think that's the way it happened, and that's the way I want you to remember it. Will you do that for me?"

"I'll try," she said.

"Good."

He turned on the tape recorder. "The police asked about the gun, then they gave you some papers to sign, and then they told you Marty had been killed. Is that what happened?"

"I . . . think so," she said.

"How did you feel when they told you Marty had been murdered?"

She stared at him. "How did I feel? I was stunned! As drunk as I was, I could hardly believe it. It seemed impossible."

"How long was it, after they asked about the gun, before they told you about Marty?"

"I don't know. Right away, I guess."

"They were in your kitchen?"

"Yes."

"And you were drunk."

"Yes. Very."

"But you willingly signed the papers?"

"Yes. They said . . . that it was routine. Oh, God! Why didn't I call you? I was so stupid! They kept giving me papers to sign. They said it was for bookkeeping purposes. Maybe they knew I was an accountant. For some stupid reason, I thought it important that I help them with their bookkeeping. Isn't that the craziest thing you've ever heard?"

Her face was contorted with pain and anguish. Realizing she was near the edge, Bill smiled and said, "All right. I have only a few more questions, and that'll be it for now." He drummed his fingers on the table for a moment. "They used the words 'It's only for bookkeeping purposes' when they got you to sign the papers?"

"Yes, that's what they said."

"And did they ask you if you'd killed Marty?"

Ann thought about it for a moment, running a hand through her hair. "I remember they kept telling me I'd feel better if I told them all about it, but I didn't know what they were talking about until finally they told me Marty was—murdered."

"They didn't specifically ask if you'd killed him?"

"No."

"But they made it sound like you were a suspect?"

"Oh, yes. They thought I'd done it, all right."

He switched off the tape recorder, patted her on the arm, and said, "That's enough."

"Why are you looking like that?" she asked.

For a moment, he just stared at her, the expression on his face impossible to read. Then he said, "Ann, you didn't do anything wrong. You were terribly upset for good reason. There is nothing—nothing—you could have done any differently."

"I should have called you as soon as the police came to the door. I never should have let them in the house."

He shook his head. "It's all right."

"I was drunk!" she exclaimed, still trying to explain. "I'd just seen my husband engaged in sick sex with a disgusting pig of a woman. What the hell do they expect of me?"

Again, he took her hands in both of his and spoke softly. "I realize you're still in shock from everything that's happened, and I know in my heart that you did not kill your husband. In this case, we have a break. The police screwed up. I think we have a small chance of getting this quashed in a hurry."

A flicker of life danced through her eyes. "You do?"

"Yes. I don't want to give you false hope, but there's a chance. However, even if this idea doesn't pan out, I want you to remember that, in the end, everything will work out, because you just didn't do it. Sooner or later, I'll find the evidence to prove that."

"What happens next?"

"Well, you'll need to tell the police what you've just told me. But before you do, I want to get your statement clear in both our minds. I'll be with you during that interview to ensure that you don't say anything you shouldn't. I want you to promise me you won't say a single word to anyone—and I mean *anyone*—unless I'm there with you. Understand?"

"Yes."

"Good. After we speak to the police, I'll have a talk with the prosecutor who's been assigned to the case. Once I've seen what he's got, I'll file a motion to suppress. I'm talking about the gun here. I don't think they handled that properly. There's a possibility I can get a judge to grant a motion prohibiting the gun from being introduced as evidence. I'm guessing that the gun is the key piece of evidence here. Without the gun, they don't have much of a case."

Ann wasn't sure what it all meant. "What happens now? Right now?"

He paused for a moment. "Most first appearances are held in the mornings. Since this is a murder charge, nothing can be done, in terms of getting you out, until after your first appearance. That's where we'll hear the charges for the first time, and that's where we get the chance to talk about bail. As I told you, I'm going from here to talk to the prosecutor. In all likelihood, the original charges will be reduced. Bail will be set and we'll get you out of here. That's number one. Then we'll take it from there."

"How long do I have to stay here?"

"Probably until sometime tomorrow afternoon." He stopped talking and tapped his fingers on the table for a moment. "The way first appearances are held is with you in a special room inside the jail here, and me over in the court. Everything is done with the use of a TV system."

"You mean you won't be with me?"

"Not physically, but that's okay. You don't have to say anything. The prosecutor, myself, and the judge do all the talking. You just have to stand there."

A vision entered Ann's consciousness. "Will I be dressed like a prisoner? In handcuffs?"

"No. Where are the clothes you were wearing last night?"

"I was sick," she said. "They gave them back to me in a plastic bag. They're ruined."

"Where are they now?"

"They took them somewhere. I don't know."

Bill smiled. "That's all right. I know where they took them. We'll want fresh clothes anyway. I'll bring you some and some makeup items tonight when I come to see you. And tomorrow, when you have your first appearance, there'll be no handcuffs. You can count on that."

Ann's head dropped. "They think I did it. It's so unbelievable." Then she looked up into his eyes. "You talked about bail. How will I raise the money?"

Bill patted her hand. "Leave that to me. Try not to dwell on the mechanics of this, as frightening as they are. Try to concentrate on where you went last night. As the shock wears off, you might recall things a little better. Leave the rest to me."

"How . . . how am I going to pay you?"

"We'll worry about that later," he said.

"Could you contact my father?"

"Of course."

"And my boss. I was supposed to work today."

He nodded. "I'll look after all of that. First I'll call your father. Do you have the number?"

She recited it to him.

"Okay. What about Marty's family?"

Ann took a deep breath. "Yes. His mother. The address is in the little black book underneath the phone stand in the kitchen. Will you call her?"

"Yes."

"And the kids, of course. You must explain to them that I didn't do it. His mother will be calling them. She'll be sure I did it. She never liked me, ever."

"That's the least of your concerns," Bill said. "Now, I'll need to get into your house also to look over a few things." He pulled out a sheet of paper from his briefcase and handed it to her. "This is a power of attorney. It gives me permission to enter your house. It also gives me the right to take care of your affairs, should this thing take a little time to straighten out. You understand?"

"Yes."

She signed the paper and handed it back to him.

"Would you ask Gina to water my plants? You know Gina."

"You'll be out tomorrow. The plants will be fine."

She started to cry again. "Arrangements have to be made . . . for the funeral. Marty was Jewish. He'll have to be buried tomorrow, at the latest. What can I do?"

"Leave that with me for the moment." He rubbed his jaw, took a deep breath, and then asked, "Ann, do you know what a polygraph is?"

"Yes. A lie-detector machine."

"Right. If I could get the prosecutor to go along, would you have any objection to taking a test?"

Some more life came into her eyes. More hope. "No, not at all. I'd welcome it! Oh, Bill, I'd gladly do that."

"Okay," he said, "I'll see what I can do. Have you considered who might have killed them?"

She was thunderstruck. The thought had never entered her mind.

"I have no idea," she said numbly.

CHAPTER

10

BILL CONNALLY SAT IN THE BROWN LEATHER CHAIR IN the anteroom of the office of Assistant State Attorney Jeff Smylie, making good use of his time. He perched his briefcase on his knees and extracted some papers, then placed the papers atop the case.

The briefcase held more than papers. Inside, there was a portable telephone, a small tape recorder, and a tiny lap-top computer in which were stored the records of a number of special clients.

He scanned the preliminary police report he'd just picked up from the sheriff's department: a seven-page report that detailed the events leading to the arrest of Ann Cohen. He glanced at his watch and cursed under his breath.

He hated to be kept waiting. As a young lawyer working for peanuts in the Public Defender's office, and later, when he'd hung out his own shingle, he'd had to take it. Now, some twenty-two years later, netting over half a million a year, he found being kept waiting almost intolerable. In his personal life, he no longer stood for it. Restaurants that refused to seat him and his party immediately failed to keep his business, as did anyone else who wasted his valuable time. Those who wished to do business with Bill Connally soon learned that his interests came first.

Thanks to the Peters case and the best-selling book he'd written about it, his appearances on fifty-three radio and television shows, and the subsequent speaking tour, he was fast becoming nationally known. That gave him great satisfaction. The outline for another book was being drafted by a ghostwriter at this very moment, and Connally fully expected the book would do at least as well as the first. If it did, he would have another million dollars to play with. There was even talk of a television series, but it was just talk at this point.

Bill Connally also despised people who found it difficult to make quick decisions. Being involved in the criminal justice system only exacerbated his intolerance because, as just another lawyer, he was forced to endure the inevitable, regular delays. And there were those, aware of his impatience, who perhaps were jealous of his success or simply didn't like him, who enjoyed making his life as difficult as possible. They had the power to keep him waiting as long as they wished. Many stretched it to the limit. And he had to take it.

Again, he glanced at his watch. He was about to reread the prelim report when he heard the receptionist say, "Mr. Smylie can see you now, Mr. Connally."

He looked up, smiled at her, put away his papers, and strode into the austere office of the prosecutor.

Smylie was standing in the center of the room, his arm extended, his long dark hair carefully blow-dried, his boyish face wreathed in the phoniest of smiles.

"Good afternoon, Bill. How're things?"

Bill's face reddened at the appellation. He preferred to be addressed as *Mr.* Connally, especially by a thirty-five-year-old prosecutor still wet behind the ears. Of course, he reminded himself, there was a certain merit in having an opponent who was young and inexperienced, even if annoyingly cocky. After all, he could have drawn a more seasoned prosecutor, one whose arrogance had some foundation. You had to count your blessings.

"Good afternoon, Jeff," he said, as he shook his opponent's hand. "I understand you and Ted Leland have drawn the Cohen case. I'd like to talk to you about it."

"Sure," Jeff said, grinning. "Have a seat. I heard you were handling the defense. I had no idea your client was mobbed up."

Bill took a seat and crossed his legs. "Mrs. Cohen is a friend of mine," he retorted, "and I resent the implication. It makes you a small man, Jeff. I thought you'd have grown some by now."

It had started, this war of egos.

Jeff looked surprised. "A friend of yours? Really? Well, this just landed on my desk. Leland doesn't even know he's on it yet. He's up in Atlanta taking depos. Have you had a chance to read the police report?"

"Yes, I have."

"I'd say it's a pretty tight case, Bill."

There it was again. Bill. These youngsters had no respect for anything anymore. It was a changing world. In a few years, Bill Connally fully expected to see attorneys wandering around the courthouse in blue jeans and T-shirts.

"Ann Cohen is no killer," he replied.

"Come on, Bill. You know as well as I do that anyone is capable of murder given the proper circumstances." He was grinning confidently again, practically gloating. "You said you'd read the police report. Are you sure we're both reading the same one?"

Bill's eyes narrowed into small slits. "Have you received the forensics report?"

"Just the prelim."

"Did it confirm the murder weapon?"

Jeff blushed. "Not yet, but we know it was a thirty-eight. And your client owns a thirty-eight. One that had recently been fired, as a matter of fact."

"Big deal!" Bill snorted. "There are probably five thousand thirty-eights within twenty square blocks of this building. As for Ann's gun, there could be a number of explanations why it was dirty."

"I kinda like mine," Jeff answered, a twinkle in his eye. "There's also some other stuff, stuff that isn't in the police report."

"Such as?"

"Well, we have a witness who saw a woman leave the murder scene shortly after the shots were fired. We have three witnesses who have identified a car leaving the scene as being the same make and color as one owned by your client." Smylie clasped his hands behind his head. "And we have evidence that your client knew her husband was screwing around, so we have motive, a possible murder weapon, the opportunity, and some witnesses. All less than twenty-four hours after the commission of the crimes. I'd say once we really crank this thing up, your client is in deep doo-doo."

"You have the car's tag number, of course."

"It was dark."

"No shit!" Bill snapped. "You know what you got? Zip! You have to kick her loose."

"No way."

"Listen to me," Bill said. "Mrs. Cohen, along with a friend of hers, *was* at the Winters house earlier that night, but neither one of them went inside. It was hours before the killings took place. I don't need to remind you, of all people, that witnesses are notorious for getting things wrong."

It was a reference to three years ago, a reference that removed the grin from Jeff's face. Smylie had been the prosecutor on the Peters case, and he had come out second best.

Frank Peters had been—and still was, for that matter—a professional killer for the mob. In the old days, he would have been referred to as an enforcer. Three years ago, Peters had killed a man in front of three witnesses, a rare mistake. The witnesses had fingered Peters in a lineup and agreed to testify in court. Bill, hired to defend Peters, had, in effect, put the witnesses on trial, and it had worked beautifully. Peters had been acquitted and

Smylie, outraged, hungered for an opportunity to even the score.

Well, he was about to get it.

"While she was there," Bill went on, "she looked in the bedroom window and saw her husband engaged in sexual misconduct with another woman. She was traumatized by that experience, which made her unable to give informed consent to search when the deputies came to her door, which makes all that careful paperwork your policemen prepared not worth squat. They should have had her identify the body, period. They should have gotten a search warrant to look for the gun. What you've got is illegal search and seizure, plain and simple."

The prosecutor didn't bat an eye. "Well, if you see it that way, you're free to take it in front of the judge, but it won't fly. We have a witness who's already given us a statement to the effect that Ann Cohen was in good shape two hours after seeing her husband's frolic in the hay."

Bill stiffened. "Cathy Pollard?" he said, trying to look unsurprised but wishing he'd had the chance to prime her first. "I haven't had the opportunity to talk to her yet, but I'm sure that won't wash. She's no shrink. It won't hold up."

"Neither are you!" Jeff snapped.

"I may not be a doctor, Jeff," Bill said smoothly, "but I do have years of experience in this business. You think you got a case? Okay, we'll see what develops. In the meantime, let's talk about bond."

"No bail."

"No bail? Are you nuts? Even if she were guilty, which she isn't, the best you've got is second degree. First is crazy! Why are you being so goddammed hard-nosed on this? You still nursing a grudge from three years ago?"

Jeff laughed. "It has nothing to do with you and me, Bill," he said. "This is business. Jesus, you should hear yourself! You admit she was there and saw them in bed together. I don't think it's very complicated. She came back later and blew them away, that's all. Later! If she'd done it as soon as she saw them in bed, it would be different. We'd probably look at it as an act of passion. But that's not what happened. That alone makes it first degree, and we have some other stuff that just locks it up."

"Like what?"

"Like the fact that your client threatened to blow Elizabeth Winters's head off two months ago, to name one small item. I have no doubt she threatened her husband as well."

"Who told you that?"

Jeff picked up the folder, looked inside, then threw it back on the desk. "Woman named Gloria Simmons. We have her sworn statement. Elizabeth Winters told her about it when it happened."

"I want a copy of that statement."

"All in due course. I'll have the entire package for you at first appearance." He leaned forward with a look of triumph and said, "Tomorrow morning at eight. I'm asking for Murder One. Two counts. No bail. That's the way it's gonna be."

Bill shook his head. "So Elizabeth Winters was threatened by my client. Big deal! If everybody who's ever threatened to kill someone carried out his threat, the population of this country would be about ten thousand people. Come on! Hearsay may have allowed the officers to consider my client a suspect, but it's no damn good at a trial."

Jeff was about to retort, then stopped himself.

"You have no witnesses to the murder, and you've got no evidence that puts her inside the house," Bill added.

Jeff's eyebrows arched. "How can you say that? You don't have the complete forensics report. Neither do I. It isn't ready yet."

"I don't need the report. She never *was* inside that house. Never! You won't find anything to indicate otherwise."

Smylie was grinning again. "Because she told you? How very interesting." The smile turned into a sneer.

Bill chewed on his lower lip for a moment, then sighed. The bravado of a few moments ago was gone. Now, suddenly, he looked worn and worried. "Look, Jeff," he said, the previous edge in his voice replaced by practiced sincerity, "I've known this woman for years. She's a fine person." He paused. "With what little you've got, you shouldn't be averse to reasonable bond."

Jeff shook his head. "I'm sticking to my guns."

Another sigh from Bill. "Have we drawn a judge yet?"

"Yeah. Sam Clark."

Shit! Bill thought. Clark was one of several judges who did not approve of William Connally. "Did you do a paraffin test?" he asked.

"No. She blew away any chance of that by pissing all over her hands when she got sick in the can. I think she did it on purpose."

"Oh, come off it. She was drunk. If she was that clever, she sure as hell wouldn't have allowed the cops to walk in her house and grab the gun. It doesn't make any sense."

Jeff shrugged. "It may not make sense, but in my experience—although it pales in comparison to yours, of course—I've learned that nothing these people do ever makes any sense." He fingered some file folders on his desk. "I've got a guy offing his wife because he wanted to watch football and she wanted to watch something else. I've got a woman blowing her husband's head off because he forgot to buy some lotto tickets on Saturday night. She said she had a vision that Jesus was giving her the numbers. Jesus! The whole world is fucking crazy!

"As for your client, we've got her at the scene, we've got what could be the gun, we've got—oh, the hell with it. You know damn well I've got more than enough. I expect that by the time we finish the investigation, we'll have what we need. It's Murder One."

He paused to light a cigarette, then continued.

"I'll be frank with you, Bill. Based on what I've been hearing, I get the feeling that her husband was a true-blue asshole. Okay, you want to talk second degree, I'll give it serious thought, but you'll have to work with me. If you plead her second degree at the arraignment and save us all a lot of trouble, I think I can get Telfer to go along. Think about it."

Bill stared at him, then shook his head. "You haven't been listening, Jeff. She just didn't do it." He stood up, thrust his hands in his pockets, stared out the window for a moment, and then returned his attention to the still-gloating prosecutor. "She's willing to take a polygraph exam. Under your supervision and mine."

"No way, Bill. You know how to beat that box. If we give her the test and she looks good, we're in trouble, 'cause you'd make sure the press found out. If she looks bad, we have to keep our mouth shut, and we can't use it in court. It's a lousy deal. No way."

"What if I signed an agreement that the results would be kept secret?"

The young attorney shook his head. "No. No way."

"You don't trust me?"

"I didn't say that. It's a no-win deal for me. I won't do it. Period."

Bill glared at him for a moment. "Very well. Have it your way. We'll see you in court." He picked up his briefcase and stormed out of the room.

Outside the courthouse, Bill sat in his car, punching buttons on his portable phone.

"Wilson, Smith and—"

"Mary, it's Mr. Connally. Get me Smitty right away."

Hugh Smith was on the line in seconds.

"Smitty," Connally said, "I need a brief prepared immediately. Motion to suppress. The judge is Sam Clark. I'll give you the details in a minute, but first I want someone to contact a woman named Cathy Pollard. She works at the accounting firm of Tilbey and Company. I want her brought here to the courthouse, along with the brief. I'm at the Pinellas Criminal Division. I'll be on the fourth floor. Got it? . . . Good. Now, as for the brief. . . ."

Two hours later, as Bill waited in the hallway leading to the judges' chambers, one of the junior attorneys arrived with the brief. Bill looked it over, grunted, and asked, "Where's Cathy?"

"We just located her," the associate said. "She wasn't at work, and she wasn't at home. We didn't know where she was until she finally showed up at work and answered our call. She should be here any minute."

And she was. Connally looked up and saw her hustling down the long hallway of the fourth floor, her arm held by another of the young attorneys who worked for the law firm. He went forward to meet her.

"Mrs. Pollard," he said, his face pinched with concern, "we need to talk."

He looked around and pulled her into a small room used by witnesses waiting to appear in court. At the moment, it was empty. The two young attorneys waited outside.

"Cathy—may I call you Cathy?" he asked, fighting to control the timbre of his voice. She nodded. "What have you told the police?"

She seemed to be in shock. "Just what happened last night. It's a bit complicated. I was with her—"

"I know."

She looked astonished. "You do?"

"Yes. I've talked to Ann at some length."

"You have? Then she's all right?"

"In a manner of speaking."

Cathy almost wilted with relief. Connally pressed her arm. "Listen to me," he said. "Did they ask you about Ann's state of mind when you left her last night?"

"Yes. They spent a lot of time on that."

"And what did you say?"

"Just that I'd made a terrible mistake. I thought she was all right. You see, we were over at—"

"I know. Just tell me what you said."

She told him. When she was finished, he asked, "And you signed a statement to that effect?"

"Yes. What else could I do?"

He shook his head. "You could have called *me*, dammit!" He waved a hand in the air. "All right, what's done is done. What else did the police do?"

"They called my husband to see what time I got home."

"And when was that?"

"It was a quarter after one in the morning. We had a big argument, but—"

"Never mind that," Connally snapped. "Anything else?"

"Just that—well, I had the feeling the police think Ann and I had something to do with Marty and that . . . slut! They think Ann did it, don't they? That's why you're here, right?"

"I'm afraid so," Connally said. "She's been charged with both murders."

"They *charged* her?"

"Yes."

Cathy's face went from ashen to ghostly white. "Where is she?"

"She's in jail."

"Jail? Then they knew where she was all the time?"

"What are you talking about? Who knew what?"

"The police. They told me they didn't know where she was."

"They did *what*?"

Cathy told him about the interview with Luther Jackson. When she was finished, Bill was beaming. "All right. I want that included in your statement to us. I'm waiting to present a brief to Judge Clark that might get Ann out of jail, but I need another statement from you. I'm going to have one of the boys write it out. You look it over, and if you think it's right, sign it, okay?"

"The bastards!"

Bill nodded. "Now you're beginning to see what we're up against."

Cathy gritted her teeth. "I'll sign whatever you want."

CHAPTER 11

"YOU'VE REDECORATED," REX KELSEY SAID, AS HE hung his large frame on one of two Eames chairs that fronted the massive mahogany desk bearing the engraved brass nameplate of William Connally.

In his forties, Rex was a tall, muscular ex-cop, six years retired after twenty years on the Baltimore police force. Never married, he'd always been a loner. Now he worked as a private investigator, mostly for attorneys who couldn't afford their own investigative staff.

He had a bland, unremarkable face. His small myopic eyes were a little too close together, a feature exaggerated by his flat, broad nose. The face, along with his short, curly red hair and the large glasses he always wore, gave him a kind of schoolteacher look, which served him well. He wasn't often taken for what he was. He looked more like a man who'd be employed as a bus driver or short-order cook or in some other unexciting job. But he was an investigator—and a good one, when he wanted to be. He worked when he felt like it, thanks to his generous police pension, and spent his free time fishing, gardening, and reading mysteries.

Rex only wore a tie to funerals, and today he was dressed in his usual fashion: white Dockers, a plain blue shirt open at the collar, and Nikes. A Timex graced his wrist.

He'd worked for Bill Connally most often right after he retired. In those days, Bill was just another criminal lawyer, defending a number of nondescript sociopaths unable to pay a fee. But now, most of Bill's work involved clients who were linked to organized crime. Rex definitely had a problem with that. Independent hoods he could abide; organized crime was something else. But still, he couldn't help liking Bill as a person, so they'd remained in contact.

Rex's built-in bias against organized crime figures precluded the chance of his working on any cases that involved such people. Consequently, Bill gave him routine stuff—divorces, insurance claims—plodding, semiautomatic work, work that, because of the new nature of Bill's career, had been nonexistent for some time.

"You like it?" Connally asked, following Rex's eyes around the office.

"I guess! It's very impressive. How 'bout you?"

"I'd better," Connally said. "It was my idea. The partners weren't all that wild about spending the money, but I like to live in style."

It was a sumptuous office indeed, large and uncluttered, with thick beige carpet, grass-cloth wall coverings, large serigraphs on the wall, and expensive pieces of sculpture on marblelike pedestals.

Kelsey grinned. "It wasn't always that way. I remember when you drove a Ford, lived in an eighty-thousand-dollar condo, and had a small office in an industrial complex. Now you live in a custom house on the lake, you drive a Mercedes, and your office is worth more than my house. All in three years. You've come a long way, Bill. Fast."

Bill opened his desk drawer, removed a long black cigar, the only one he'd allow himself all day, played with it awhile, chopped off the end, and then lit it. He leaned back in his leather chair and stared at the ceiling. "Yeah," he said. "I really have."

"You've never looked better, either," Rex said. "Money obviously agrees with you." He crossed his legs and picked at some lint on his white Dockers. "So why did you call me? It's been awhile."

"I know. And I apologize for that. But you're the guy who wants to be independent. We have six full-time company investigators. You could have been one of them."

Rex grinned again. "I know. It's like you said. I like my independence. So how come you called?"

"Because this one's special. A personal friend. I want the best. The very best. My guys are okay, but they're busy as hell on a number of things. I want you because you can devote all your energies to this case."

Ignoring the subtle slur, Rex played with his glasses for a moment. He smiled. "Well, I appreciate the business. You know I've always enjoyed working with you . . . to a point. What case?"

Bill stood up and walked to the large window of the eleventh-floor corner suite, which overlooked Tampa Bay. From where he stood, on the west side of the water, he could see much of the bay area and beyond, from MacDill Air Force Base to Tampa International Airport and everything in between. On this bright hot July day, the view was arresting, with the usual thunder clouds starting to form in the north, twisting and turning as the natural energy built, leading to a series of violent electrical discharges.

Thunderclouds were a lot like human brains, Bill mused. A buildup of pressure, a release, a period of calm, and then the rebuilding of pressure.

He turned away from the window and took a seat in the other Eames chair, clapping a hand on Rex's arm.

"This one's really important, Rex. A very dear friend of mine has been arrested for killing her husband and her husband's mistress while the two were in bed together. The police found what could be the murder weapon in my friend's house. They have her prints all over the gun. They have her at the murder scene less than two hours before the hit. To make matters worse, she had motives galore and she has no alibi for the time of the killing."

Rex let out a low whistle. "Is that the one in Palm Harbor? Ann Cohen? Is that her name? I heard something about it on the car radio."

"The same."

"Looks tough. She do it?"

Bill shook his head. "No."

The investigator raised his eyebrows. "Is this the party line, or is that really the way you see it?"

"She didn't do it. She was framed, pure and simple. It just isn't something she's capable of. I know all that crap about people being pressed beyond their limits. Fact is, she's a gentle person, no more capable of killing than the Amish. Besides, if she was going to off the bastard, she would have done it a long time ago."

"But if they found her prints—"

Bill stood up and paced the floor. "I know. It's like I told you. She was framed. She really was." He waved a big hand in the air. "Imagine! After years of defending the guilty, I'm faced with the awesome responsibility of defending someone who's actually innocent. Scary!"

Rex was unconvinced. "Are you sure about this?" he asked. "You must have something more than just feelings."

The lawyer stopped pacing and rubbed his chin. "Not a hell of a lot," he said. "Not at the moment, anyway. If Ann Cohen killed those two, I'll—well, the fact is, I've never been more sure of anything in my life."

"So what do you want from me?"

"Everything you've got and then some. I want you one hundred percent on this one. I'll give you three hundred a day plus expenses. I want you to interview everyone at the condo complex where she lives. Place called the Clusters. You know it?"

"Sure. That's where you used to live."

Bill grinned. "Of course. You were there, weren't you. I guess I'm getting old. I forget things. Anyway, I want you to talk to everyone there. See if anyone had an ax to grind with Ann. That's the key. Then you'll need to talk to friends at her clubs, friends outside the complex—she had plenty—and those at her office. You'll also have to interview all the friends of the mistress, Elizabeth Winters.

"She and Ann's husband were both kinky, into S and M. That was the attraction, I guess, since she was certainly nothing to look at. I figure the hit came from her end. I want you to concentrate on that angle, especially Winters's other boyfriends, of which she had several. Maybe one of them got jealous and decided to lay it on Ann because she was the most logical choice."

He looked at his notes. "Winters had a best friend named Gloria Simmons. She told the police about a threat Ann made a month or so ago, which really meant nothing, but the prosecutor thinks it's a big deal. Both Simmons and Winters worked at the same place as waitresses, and both have been busted for prostitution. There might be an angle there.

"Then you'll need to work on Ann's husband's pals. Anybody and everybody who had contact with Ann, her husband, and the woman. Somewhere, we have to find a hook."

He took a deep pull from the cigar and exhaled the purplish smoke.

"But first, before anything else, I want you to survey every store that was open at one in the morning last night, from Alderman right up to Highway Fifty."

Rex frowned. "What?"

Bill shoved his hands in his pockets and rested his rear end on the edge of the desk. He explained what Ann had told him about the trip to the Winters house earlier in the evening. He added, "Ann was devastated by what she'd seen. She drove up U.S. Nineteen all the way to Weeki Wachee and then back again. She says she was alone and didn't talk to anyone. Maybe she did and just can't remember. Let's face it, she was pretty shook up. In any case, she took the drive while the murders were being committed. So you can see why we must come up with someone who saw her. It's vital!"

"Bill, I can't handle this alone. I'll need a small army. And they'll have to be paid. I'm not trying to hold you up here, but—"

"Take it easy," Bill replied. "You can handle it. Take the Weeki Wachee road first. If we come up with someone who can testify they saw Ann thirty miles from the scene of the crime when it was taking place, we don't need much more. If we do go to trial, it won't be for at least six months, so that gives you plenty of time.

"I realize it's a lot, but I trust you. I know you'll be thorough. The important thing is that we cover all the ground. I'm going to a meeting tonight with some of her friends to talk about bail money. I'll take you with me. At least that will break the ice with them. They'll know you're working for me."

Luigi Martino looked around the baggage claim area as he waited for his suitcase. Near the far wall, he saw a man holding a cardboard sign with Luigi's name on it, so he walked over to the man and stuck out his hand. "Mr. Connally?"

The man shook hands and said, "No, Mr. Martino. My name is Bannister. I just work for the firm. Mr. Connally asked me to come and get you."

"I appreciate that. How's my daughter?"

The man shook his head. "I'm sure she's fine. I haven't talked to her myself, but Mr. Connally has. He'll be able to bring you up to date. Did you have a pleasant flight?"

Annoyed by the stupid question, Luigi stared at the man for a moment without speaking, then turned and went back to the carousel. In a few moments, his old, badly marred leather suitcase appeared. He grabbed it and headed back to Bannister. "Let's go," he said curtly.

Thirty minutes later, he was ushered into the office of William Connally. "Mr. Martino, I'm Bill Connally," Bill said, extending his hand. "I'm sorry we had to meet under such terrible circumstances. I've known Ann for some time. She's a fine woman. Can I get you a drink?"

"No. How's my daughter?"

"She's doing very well, considering. Naturally, she's deeply shocked, but she'll be fine. As soon as I can, I'll arrange a meeting for you."

"Where is she?"

"At the moment, she's being held at the correctional center. She's being isolated—which is, quite frankly, amazing when you consider how crowded they are down there. At least she won't be mixed in with the usual vermin."

Luigi took a seat and shook his head. "You've talked to her?"

"Yes, of course."

"Tell me what happened."

Bill told him. When he was finished, Luigi shook his head again. "Terrible. Just awful. I never liked that man, not from the first moment I laid eyes on him. I was astonished when he actually started to make money.

I didn't think he had the capability. He was a restless, selfish person. A poor choice.

"When my wife died—Ann's mother—she'd been ill for some time, and the last few weeks were very hard. Ann flew up to Chicago and stayed with her. Not once— not once did that selfish son of a bitch show his face. Not until my wife was dead. Then he came for the funeral. But for three weeks he left Ann to bear the burden alone. Said he was busy. Busy! What kind of man leaves his wife to face the death of her mother like that? Cruel!"

Bill nodded his head in agreement. "You're an attorney, I understand."

"Yes. I did family work. I'm retired now, of course. But in my younger days, I did a little criminal work, mostly court-appointed cases. In those days, we did a little of everything. Things are different now. Everyone's a specialist like you. Ann mentioned you some time ago. You're neighbors, aren't you?"

"We were a while ago. I've moved."

"She said you were a very good lawyer. Didn't I see you on Donahue about three months ago?"

The celebrity beamed. "Yes, that was me. I was pushing a book."

Luigi nodded, then ran a stubby hand over his face. "I can't believe what's happened. You say it was her gun?"

"We're not sure. But, from what I've heard so far, it probably is. The bullets were hollow points. The gun had to be sent to the FBI lab in Washington for analysis."

"How can that be? Ann would never—"

"I know. To put it simply, I think she was framed."

Luigi slammed a hand on the arm of the chair and

cursed in Italian. Then he asked, "Who would do this to Ann?"

Bill patted the old man's shoulder. "We'll find out, Mr. Martino. As I said, we have an investigator working on this case. A top man. If we need more, we'll hire them. Sooner or later, we'll get to the bottom of it, I promise you."

Luigi exhaled deeply. After a moment of silence, he asked, "What about your fee?"

"We needn't discuss that at the moment."

"Look," Luigi said, "I'm a lawyer. I know how these things go. Let me pay you a retainer. I can afford it. How much?"

Bill smiled appreciatively. "Let me think about it, do some figuring, and I'll let you know, okay? We'll play it by ear from this point."

"All right. Just let me know. What about bail?"

"Ann's first appearance is tomorrow. We'll know better then. If bail is refused, I have a hearing the next morning. I expect bail will be allowed at that time. However, it's likely to be steep."

"What sort of hearing?"

"A motion to suppress. Ann waived her right to an attorney before she told the police about the gun. I'm going to claim the consent was uninformed due to emotional trauma. It might work."

"And the hearing is in two days? So soon?"

"I got lucky." Bill smiled. "Judge Clark had an unexpected continuance and we got the slot."

The old man nodded. "You *are* good," he said. "As for bail, I could raise about two hundred and fifty thousand if need be."

"That's good. But I expect it to be higher than that. I'm having a meeting tonight at the home of Gene and Della White to discuss this very thing with some of Ann's friends. Do you know the Whites?"

"Yes. They're Ann's neighbors."

"The meeting is at eight o'clock. Will you come?"

"I'll be there," Luigi said, as he rose to his feet. "I feel very tired. I'd like to go to my daughter's home."

"Of course. I'll have Mr. Bannister drive you."

"You'll call me as soon as you've arranged for me to see her?"

"Yes."

"Fine."

Bannister drove Ann's father to the house. When they arrived, Luigi Martino got out of the car, pulled his suitcase from the back seat, thanked the young lawyer, then walked slowly toward the front door. As he reached the front step, he leaned over a flowerpot, lifted a ceramic butterfly, and picked up a key partially stuck in the earth. He put the key in the lock and opened the door.

A creature of habit, his daughter. The key was always there, to be used by friends to come in and water the plants when she and Marty were away, although that hadn't happened in some time. She had told her father about it in case he ever wanted to visit and forgot his own key. The last time he'd been here had been four months ago.

He went inside and closed the door behind him. Slowly, he walked around, noticing the disruption caused by the police during their search for additional evidence. Clothes were piled everywhere. Drawers were sitting on the floor, their contents spilled on the thick carpet. The place was a mess.

Luigi took off his jacket and threw it on the bed. First, he thought to himself, he would call Ann's brother, Paolo. Paolo was a busy lawyer in Seattle who went by the name Paul Martin—the boy's eschewing his heritage had brought pain to his father—and hardly had time to visit anymore. Well, this was important. His sister was in trouble. In mourning *and* in trouble. Paolo, no matter the difficulty, would have to take the time.

Then, after talking to Paolo, he would start putting things away. He was a fastidious man. So, he knew, was his daughter. Soon she would be home, if all went well. He didn't want her coming home to a dirty house. She had enough on her mind.

At eight o'clock that evening, Bill Connally stood in the middle of Gene and Della White's living room, the villa immediately adjacent to Gina Rizzo's. The room was filled with neighbors, all of them Ann's friends. As promised, Luigi Martino was there as well, looking tired and drawn. There were twenty in the room, eyeing Bill intently.

Rex Kelsey watched them just as intently. Connally, having once lived in the Clusters himself, *knew* these people. On the drive over, he'd taken the trouble to give Kelsey a thumbnail sketch of each of them. Now Kelsey tried to match the faces with the names and burn them into his memory.

Gene and Della White. He was a district sales manager for a Japanese electronics company; she worked as an operating room nurse. They'd been married for ten years, both for the second time. Gene was a friendly, hard-working, sometimes bombastic man, tall and muscular except for a slight potbelly. He had three passions: beer, college football, and Della. Della was a tiny, quiet, handsome-looking woman whose interests were more aesthetic. An ardent pacifist, she had the soul of a saint. The pending death of her fourteen-year-old poodle was breaking her heart. Gene and Della seemed like opposites, but the marriage was solid.

Kelsey's gaze fell on Anita Phillips, middle-aged but still stunning. Once, according to Connally, she'd been married to an industrialist who'd made big bucks. He'd left her to marry some bimbo, but it had cost him dearly. The cash settlement alone was over ten million. Connally knew all about it because his partner Hugh Smith had handled the divorce. The billing had been close to a quarter million dollars. Smith had practically kissed Bill for bringing in the business.

Anita had, at Smith's suggestion, stashed the cash and moved into the Clusters, taking a four-bedroom unit. Smith had told her that while things settled down she shouldn't make any sudden decisions. She hadn't taken his advice. She'd plunged into the business world on her own, buying a statewide chain of video stores. Even though the market was already saturated, her thirty-four-store chain was emerging as a leader in the field as a result of her hard-driving, promotion-oriented marketing skills. Some said her success was due to things she'd learned from her ex-husband through osmosis. It wasn't true, according to Connally. If anything, it had been the other way around. *His* success had been largely due to her behind-the-scenes counseling.

While she stayed at home and raised three children, he'd gone forth, carrying the spear. But almost every night, he'd sought out her excellent advice. Eventually successful beyond his wildest dreams, he'd found it difficult to accept the fact that Anita had been in some way responsible. The marriage had foundered on the rocks of a bruised ego.

Now she was on her own, her drive fueled by the need to show the world who really had the smarts. Even a successful business career wasn't enough. Anita, Connally had said, had a ravenous sexual appetite. There would be no more marriages for her. Just a series of one-night stands with handsome men dazzled by her power, success, and beauty. She would do the choosing; she would decide when and where. To her, men were nothing more than animated dildos.

Yeah, Rex thought, looking at her now, her eyes sparkling as she took in every nuance; he could certainly see it.

Then there was Gina Rizzo, the seemingly dumb blonde from California. In some ways, Connally had said, she was dumb, all right, but in money matters she wasn't. In the late fifties, before rock had taken over the music business, she'd been a pop singer, one of the best. She'd taken every nickel she earned and invested it in California real estate. She'd been clever in other ways as well. While on top, she'd stayed in California, even though her husband had wanted to move to New York. When he finally walked out, it had cost him dearly, thanks to California's community property laws. The property settlement included almost a million in cash. Gina had put that in California real estate as well. Although she was loaded, Gina had taken the opposite route from Anita. Whereas Anita had thrown herself into life, Gina had retreated from it.

Two women, both discarded by their husbands in the prime of their lives. Both beautiful, both wealthy. One had gone forward, one backward. The contrast was thought-provoking.

Kelsey continued to search the faces of the group as Connally made his pitch.

"I thank you all for coming," he said. "I'm here tonight to talk to you about several things. But before I get too far along, I'd like to thank the Whites for being kind enough to offer their home as our meeting place." He nodded in their direction. "Next, I'd like to introduce two associates of mine. The first is Lee Ogden, an associate attorney with our firm."

Lee Ogden stood up and took a short bow. Then Connally pointed to Kelsey.

"I'd also like to introduce you to Rex Kelsey. Rex is a private investigator who will be heading up the investigation we'll be conducting. During the next few weeks, Rex will be contacting all of you. He'll be asking you questions about anything and everything you know relating to this case. It's important for you to understand that in order for me to mount a proper defense for Ann, we're going to need every piece of information, no matter how insignificant it may seem."

Rex stood up and nodded at those in the room.

"Our investigation," Connally continued, "will be done

with a view to determining anything that will give us a
lead on the real killer. Since we all know Ann didn't do
it, there has to be someone else. Perhaps, if we really
put our minds to it, we can gather some information
that will point us in the right direction. To be blunt,
the quickest way to get Ann off the hook is to hand
the police the real killer."

Connally shoved his hands in his pockets and stuck
out his jaw. "Ann didn't do this. Whoever did knew about
Marty and the woman. They also knew that Ann and
Marty owned a gun, and where it was, which points
to someone who knew a lot about them. Someone
who managed to gain entry to her house, take the
gun, commit the murders, then put the gun back. All
without Ann's knowing about it. It might even have
been one of you—her friends."

The room erupted. Connally held up his hand for quiet.

"I know it sounds terrible," he said, "but those are
the facts. I can't ignore the possibility that one of you
is involved. If you're not, and you cooperate, we'll soon
be able to eliminate you. But I'd be lying to you if I
didn't let you know that all of you are suspects until
we have the killer in our grasp."

There was a further murmur of conversation. Connally raised his hand again.

"You all know Ann," he said, smiling, trying to take
the sting out of it. "You all knew Marty. You all, with
the exception of Mr. Martino, know me. I know Ann did
not do this. Right now she's in jail, charged with Marty's
murder and the murder of his mistress. She's enduring
it well. To give you an idea of the kind of woman she

is, her immediate concern is to see that Marty receives a decent burial."

"You can forget about that," said a voice from the back of the room. It was Gina. "I talked to a friend of mine in the sheriff's office. He says Marty's mother flew in earlier in the day. She told him she's gonna go to court and have the body released to her. I think she plans to bury him back in Chicago."

Connally shook his head. "Don't worry about that. I'm aware of the effort, but the body has not been released. It probably won't be for at least two days, and I'll make sure it stays here."

He took a deep breath.

"My main reason for being here tonight is to let you know where we stand. And to talk about bail. As you know, Ann has been charged with murder in the first degree. Tomorrow, she goes before a judge for the first time. The prosecutor has indicated that he'll oppose any request for bail, but I think we can fight that successfully. However, if bail *is* granted, it's likely to be quite steep. I would guess that it will be in the half-million to million-dollar range."

Another swell of conversation.

"Now, the way bail works is this. The court will accept cash or a bank check, which, if the defendant appears for trial, is then returned. If property is used, we have to go through a bail bondsman, who charges ten percent, which is not returned. Ann's assets cannot be used, because everything she owns was jointly owned by Marty. That means it all stays frozen until this thing is resolved. So, I need to turn to you, her friends. Are you prepared to put up her bail?"

They all looked at one another for a moment. Then Anita stood up and said, "We'll raise it."

Connally looked relieved. "That's wonderful. I'd like all of you to make whatever arrangements you can tomorrow morning. As soon as you do, call Lee at the office and let him know the amount you're prepared to post. He'll coordinate everything and tell you what the next steps are. I know that Ann will be forever grateful."

He smiled warmly. "I realize that some of you are shocked by what I've said tonight—about being suspects. In my heart, I know you had nothing to do with this. But I wouldn't be doing my job properly if I didn't play it by the book. I hope you understand."

As some of them mumbled to one another, Kelsey smiled to himself. Connally was a master manipulator. First, he'd made them squirm a little. Even if they had nothing to hide, they'd squirm. No one likes to think he's a suspect in a murder case. Connally's whole purpose in putting them on edge was to make sure they'd dig deep enough to come up with the bail money for his client. Yeah, Connally was a master. It was nice to be working with him again. Except for one thing.

After thinking about the case for the past few hours, Rex was convinced that Ann Cohen was the killer.

CHAPTER

12

PETER QUILL STRETCHED HIS WEIGHT LIFTER'S BODY, threw the sheets back, got up from his bed, and stumbled into the bathroom. It was five in the afternoon and the house was empty. In a few moments, Connie would be home after leaving work and picking the kids up at the day-care center. He always liked to be up and around when they got home. It was the least he could do.

He and Connie had agreed that while the kids were young, at least, they'd try to spend as much time as possible with them, even though both of them worked. Connie worked as a secretary and Peter, a Pinellas County sheriff's deputy, had the midnight-to-eight shift every third month. On those days when he drew the night shift, he would usually arrive home after Connie and the kids had left, crawl into bed, and sleep. Then he'd get up, dress in civilian clothes for their arrival, play with the kids for an hour, eat breakfast while they had dinner, and help Connie put them to bed. Then, he and Connie would watch a little TV, or make love, or sometimes just talk.

Quickly, he showered, shampooed his short blond hair, dried off, and brushed his teeth. As he shaved, he looked at himself in the mirror and smiled. Even without the uniform, he looked like a cop. Just like his father, and his father before him. Why was it that the Irish were so often cops?

He wiped the shaving cream off his face, applied deodorant and cologne, and got dressed. He chose the old blue jeans and a matching denim shirt, with the sleeves rolled halfway up his powerful arms. He heard the front door open and hurried into the living room.

"Hi, Daddy!"

"Hi, Daddy!"

"Hi, Daddy!"

Three voices: two children, one adult—all happy to see him.

He picked up one child in each arm, three-year-old Jennette in the left, four-year-old Erica in the right. Then he leaned forward and gave Connie a kiss. To his surprise, he felt her tongue dart quickly into his mouth. He grinned at her.

"You've been thinking about the same thing I've been thinking about," he said.

The look in her green eyes was positively lascivious. "Whatever gave you that idea?"

Laughing, he whirled the kids around for a moment and then said, "Okay, let's all go outside and play while Mommy makes dinner."

"Yay!"

Later, they all sat down to eat in the kitchen, while the local newscast was beginning on the small television set next to the stove. As usual, the top item was a murder, a common occurrence in the violence-ridden Tampa Bay area.

Peter picked at his food in silence. Connie, ever conscious of his moods, looked at him quizzically. "Did this happen on your shift?"

Peter nodded. "We'll talk about it later."

He continued to eat, though his appetite had diminished.

Later, after the kids were asleep, he lay in bed with Connie and stared at the ceiling. Earlier in the day, he'd wanted to make love, but now the mood had passed.

"What is it, Pete?" she asked softly, as she played with the blond hair on his chest.

He rolled on his side and looked into her beautiful, concerned green eyes. "The woman didn't do it."

Connie immediately sat up in bed and stared at him. "Why do you say that?"

He took a deep breath and let it out slowly. "Weber and I were the ones who discovered the bodies. It was a real mess. One of the worst I've ever seen. I'll spare you the details; it looked like the work of someone who was filled with the most incredible hate imaginable. But I don't think it was. I think it was a professional hit."

"Why?"

He shook his head. "I don't know. At first, I thought it was just anger. That's what I said to Weber and he agreed. But after having slept on it, I don't think so. It was so cold-blooded." He rubbed his eyes and went on. "Anyway, after the crime unit arrived, we were told to see the woman—the wife—and bring her down to ID the body. When we got to her house, Weber checked her car and noticed that the hood was still warm. It was almost four in the morning and she was still up. She was so drunk she could hardly stand."

"And?"

"Well, we asked her if she owned a gun. She said she did and told us where it was. She let us pick up the gun without a murmur. Signed a consent form and everything."

"So?"

"The gun had been fired. I guess ballistics has confirmed that it was the murder weapon and that's why they arrested her."

Connie shook her head. "I don't see the problem. If it was her gun and she was still up—drunk—I would think that would be all you'd need. What makes you think she didn't do it?"

Peter rolled on his back and stared at the ceiling. "I guess it was the look in her eyes when we told her that her husband had been murdered. It was as though someone had turned off a light. She seemed to die right there. She was completely surprised. Completely! She was too drunk to fake it. This from someone capable of such a cold, calculated murder? Hardly.

"When we asked if she had a gun, she admitted it right off. She told us where it was. She was drunk, and yet she told us where it was!"

Connie looked confused. "I still don't understand why you think she didn't do it. If she was drunk, it was probably because she'd just killed two people. She probably realized that it was all over. She didn't know where to run."

Peter shook his head. "No. She had no reason to think that her gun was involved. There was no pretense at all. Someone who'd just blown away her husband and his girlfriend wouldn't act like that. Either they'd still be high on rage, in which case they'd do something really stupid, or they'd blab a confession the moment they saw us. Or if they were really cold and calculating, they'd have thrown the gun away. These things follow a pattern."

"A pattern?"

"Sure. Pop used to talk about it all the time. Most killings are done on the spur of the moment. You know, people argue, lose their cool, and bang! It's done. They either fall apart afterward or try to cover up. Either way, they usually don't carry it off well.

"The psychos are different. They're the ones who really think it out. They plan ahead and carry it out. They usually cover their tracks pretty well. That's why we catch fewer of them. But this woman—if she'd done it in a rage, she wouldn't have reacted the way she did when we told her her husband was dead. She would have reacted to us as soon as we got there. I mean, she would have been on guard or something. And as drunk as she was, how could she put on a performance like that? She was really shook about her husband being killed. I know it! And the gun! If she'd planned to do it, she wouldn't be stupid enough to put the gun back in her night table."

"But you said she was drunk. People who are drunk do crazy things."

"I know they do, but not that kind of crazy. It just doesn't fit."

"Pete! Listen to me. You said this was one of the worst you'd ever seen. Don't you think your reaction could be due to that? Maybe you're suffering from shock, or something. People just don't get arrested without a whole lot of evidence, especially these days. Maybe when you go to work and see what else they've got, you'll feel better. But whatever you do, you need to deal with this right away. Remember what your father said. You have to leave work at work. Otherwise you'll go nuts."

"I know." He rose from the bed and started to get dressed.

"Where are you going?"

"To work. I'm going to take your advice. I want to find out what else they've got. You don't mind?"

She reached up and pulled his face to hers, then kissed him deeply. "No, I don't mind. I love you. The sooner you put this to rest, the better you'll feel. Maybe, if you see what they've got, you can come back home. You still have two and a half hours before you have to report. You've got me primed and ready. It would be such a waste."

Peter ran a hand along her cheek and stared into her eyes. "God! You are something! If more guys had wives like you, there'd be a lot less screwing around in this world."

She kissed his hand and said, "If there were more men like you, there'd be more wives like me. Hurry home."

"Yeah."

When Peter arrived at headquarters, he went directly to the detectives' floor. Lieutenant Luther Jackson looked up from his desk. "What you doing here?"

Peter sat in a plastic chair beside the desk. "I just wanted to ask you a couple of questions about the bust last night."

"You and Weber were on that, right?"

"Yeah."

"Whaddaya wanna know?"

"Well . . . "

Luther grunted and leaned back in his chair. "Whaddaya worried about, you think you won't get credit? Weber signed the report but your name is on it, too. Whatsa matter? You think Weber's tryin' to hog the glory? He's not that kinda guy. Matter of fact, he said it was you who asked if she had a gun. Weber's a stand-up guy, Quill."

Peter shook his head. "I'm not questioning Weber's character."

"Then what?"

"I was curious, that's all. She—the woman—didn't seem to be the kind to . . . well, I was just wondering. Did the gun check out?"

Again, Luther grunted. "Oh, yeah. You been in bed all day. I forgot. Ballistics can't confirm it, so they sent it up to the FBI. But I'd say it looks pretty good. Six empty shells still in the gun match the type, at least. Hollow points. She started screamin' for her lawyer as soon as she sobered up. Nice-lookin' piece, too. Too bad. Looks like her husband was some kinda sicko. A real shame to throw your life away like that, but it happens all the time, man."

Peter looked shaken.

"Whassamatta with you?" Jackson asked.

"Nothing. I'm just surprised. I figured they had something or they wouldn't have busted her. But I'm still surprised."

"Surprised? Why? Because she's a great-lookin' piece? How long you been a cop, Quill?"

"Two years."

"Two years? Listen. Give it another three or four and you won't be surprised by nothin'. Lemme tell ya, the things that people can do to each other, there's no limit. This your first homicide?"

"No."

"No?"

"No. I've had six."

"Six. You get a few more under your belt and you won't be surprised at nothin'." He scratched his forehead. "I had a deal once where this asshole killed a little boy, then sat down and ate him! Can you imagine that? A fuckin' animal! But when we talked to him, he seemed like a choirboy. The only time he came apart is when we showed him pictures of his dead mother. Crazy bastard. The worst fuckin' kind.

"I've had sweet little old ladies slit their husbands' throats, saying it was some burglar who did it. Old ladies in their eighties! Tired of living with a sick, dying man. And the kids! Jesus Christ! We got fourteen-year-olds on crack who'll kill anybody for ten lousy bucks! The whole fuckin' world is crazy, Quill. You start trying to figure it all out and you'll be out on your ass faster'n shit through a puppy. Don't waste your time, man."

Peter stood up and nodded his head. "I guess you're right, Luther. I was just curious, that's all."

"Don't worry about it."

"Listen, could I have a copy of the reports? Just for looking at?"

Luther stared at him for a moment and then said, "You want 'em, you got 'em. But I get the feeling you aren't really listening to me. Why is that?"

Peter held up both hands in mock surrender. "I hear you. Really. I just—well, one of these days, I want to be a homicide detective. The more I learn about these things, the sooner I'll get the chance. Just a favor. I'll owe you one."

Luther shrugged, removed some papers from the file, made copies of them, and handed them to Peter. "Here you are," he said. "But keep it quiet. Not a word to anybody, hear?"

"I hear ya."

"She got to you, huh?"

"Who?"

"The Cohen broad."

Peter shrugged. "I wouldn't say she got to me. It's just this feeling I have. I really don't think she did it."

"Look, man. This is all in the hands of the state prosecutor now. Put it out of your mind. Let them worry about it. Besides, she did it. No fuckin' doubt about it."

Jeff Smylie ran a hand through his carefully blow-dried hair and tried to concentrate on the Cohen case. It was becoming increasingly difficult. In three days, he was due in court for the start of another murder case, a relatively simple one, it seemed, of a drug deal gone bad. One man dead, two wounded, one seriously enough that he'd never walk again. And within the next two months he was scheduled to appear in court to prosecute two more murder cases.

Smylie shook his head as he ran the figures through his head. This year the killings were running seventeen percent ahead of last year's many thousands of homicides; it was almost out of control. The prisons in Florida—and in the entire nation—were filled to overflowing. Even killers were being freed years ahead of time, on orders from federal judges, simply because of overcrowding in the facilities. And still the cases mounted. More and more men and women were being sentenced to occupy the cells vacated by other men and women who had no business being on the streets. Many would commit other crimes within days of their release. What was the point of it all? he wondered. Who were they trying to kid? Why was it so goddam difficult to get the money to build more prisons?

Jeff looked at the stack of files on his desk. The most serious ones, the capital crimes, were tagged with red markers. He had four of those. Then there were the yellow tags: second-degree murder, manslaughter, attempted murder. He had thirty-six of those. There were ten different color codes. Blue tags were given to major felonies, such as assault with a deadly weapon, rape, conspiracy. Burglaries and lesser felonies got a green tag. The colors went from red down to innocuous white, the tag for a misdemeanor. Almost a trifle, but it still had to be prosecuted, taking up precious and already limited court time. As a specialist, Jeff was only given cases with red and yellow tags. There were more than enough.

He sighed and let his thoughts swing back to the Cohen case. It was by far the one that interested him most, not because of the circumstances but because he'd be facing William Connally. Jeff wanted to win this time. He *had* to win this time. Connally was pulling out all the stops, moving to suppress evidence already. It would only be one of many moves the wily attorney was bound to make, so Jeff would have to be on his toes. He'd have to give this case his full attention, close everything else out of his mind.

During the last few hours, reports from the ongoing investigation had landed on Smylie's desk. Some of the news was welcome, some not. There'd been a witness; a man had seen a woman leaving the murder scene shortly after the shots were fired. He read the statement. The man said it had been dark, so he couldn't identify the woman's face, but he did describe what she was wearing and the car she was driving. Jeff picked up a copy of the police report, compared the facts with the statement, and placed it back on the desk. Then he read the statement taken from Cathy Pollard. Something didn't fit.

He put her statement aside and read some others. Three witnesses had spotted a car leaving the murder scene. One had identified it as a beige Mercedes 560 SEL, the other two just knew it was foreign. Ann Cohen owned a beige Mercedes 560 SEL. That was good. They had the Cohen woman's fingerprints on the outside of the bedroom window. Very good. But Cathy Pollard's prints were also found on the window. Not so good. It backed up the story that they were there together. But then again, that only accounted for the first time Ann was there.

The Cohen woman's prints were on the gun, and it had recently been fired. Excellent! But her prints had not been found inside the Winters house, just as Connally had predicted. Strange. If she was careless enough to leave them on the gun, why wouldn't she leave them in the house too?

He stood up and walked over to a corkboard on one wall of his office. Carefully, he extracted sheets of paper from the file folder in his hand and stuck them to the corkboard with push pins. He stood back and looked at the sheets pinned to the board, all arranged in chronological order. One contained a heading that said *1:00 a.m.* Underneath the heading was written, *Ann Cohen alone*. Immediately beside that piece of paper was another marked *1:38.* Underneath was written, *Shots fired*. Beside that was another marked *1:55*. Beneath it, *Weber arrives*.

He walked closer to the board and studied each piece of paper carefully. Then, he shook his head, untacked the papers, and returned them to the file folder. He picked up his telephone and punched a two-digit number.

"Mr. Telfer's office," a secretary answered.

"Hi, Peggy. This is Smylie. Is His Nibs still around?"

"Doesn't look too good, Jeff," Telfer's secretary said. "He's trying to get home before midnight tonight. How long do you need?"

"About ten minutes."

"I'll see what I can do. You in your office?"

"Yes."

"I'll get back to you."

"Thanks, Peggy."

He hung up the telephone and sat behind his desk. What an outfit, he thought. You had to make an appointment with your boss, through his secretary, to see him for a lousy ten minutes. It seemed so stupid, and yet there was a reason for it. The office was so incredibly busy, with everyone wanting to talk to Telfer about their innumerable cases, the man had to resort to time rationing, in an almost futile effort to bring his workday down from eighteen to sixteen hours.

It was a half hour before Peggy called back and said the boss would see him. Jeff was there in fifteen seconds.

Lionel Telfer was, as usual, sitting behind a desk cluttered with manila file folders. Even at this late hour, he looked fresh. A portly man, he disguised his girth by wearing a carefully tailored pin-striped suit, the vertical lines deceiving the eye. His thinning hair was coiffed weekly, the hair at the sides left long and swept over his round skull to minimize the baldness. His moon-shaped face was a soft white, caused mainly by the workaholism that kept him indoors most of the time.

Without looking up, he said, "So?"

"It's the Cohen case, sir."

"What about it?"

"I have a few problems."

"Such as?"

"Well, for one, there's the clothing thing. That really bothers me."

"The clothing thing?"

"Yes. According to one of the witnesses, Mrs. Cohen was wearing a white blouse and black slacks at one in the morning, just before the killings. She was also wearing low-heeled shoes. The police report says she was wearing the same thing when they picked her up at four. But the only witness who saw anyone leaving the house claims she was wearing a skirt and high heels."

"So?"

Jeff grimaced. "It seems strange that she would get all dressed up to commit two murders."

"Why?"

"It just doesn't seem logical. Connally will jump all over that. I'm worried that the jury will be impressed with what I think he's sure to say."

Telfer looked up at him for the first time. "Don't you have a motion to suppress coming up fast?"

"Yes, sir."

"Well, I'd sure as hell be concerned about that before I started worrying about what some goddam jury might or might not think six months down the road. If Connally suppresses your evidence, you're up shit creek unless you find some better evidence."

"I realize that, sir, but there's nothing I can do about it. I've prepared my argument, I have my witnesses, I've got case law ready. There isn't much else I can do."

"So you're looking ahead?"

"Yes, sir."

Telfer pursed his lips. Then he asked, "What else has you concerned?"

"The gun."

"What about it?"

"Well, it seems strange to me that a woman who took the trouble to change her clothes would forget to ditch the gun. If her mind was functioning that well, it seems to me her first concern would be the gun."

Telfer frowned. "Are you telling me you think this woman is innocent?"

Jeff held up a hand. "Not at all. I'm just concerned about how it looks. Some of it doesn't make a whole lot of sense."

Telfer dropped his pen on the desk, put his arms behind his head, and gave Jeff his full attention. "Well," he said, "you have a point. I think what you have here is a very calculating killer. She's an accountant, is she not?"

"Yes."

"Accountants work with numbers. People who like to work with numbers have very precise, orderly minds. They tend to be perfectionists. Consider this: Ann Cohen has been married to a man who cheats on her for twelve years. She'll claim she didn't know, but they always know. Her husband likes kinky sex; she doesn't. She could divorce him, but she doesn't. Why? Because she's been looking over all sorts of income tax returns and is pissed that she's getting paid forty grand a year to help all these people who are making ten and twenty times that much money. If she divorces her husband, she ends up with maybe a hundred thou. But if she kills him and gets away with it, she gets everything, plus a— what was the value of the insurance policy?"

"Five hundred thousand."

"Taken out when?"

"Three years ago."

"Three years ago. How interesting."

"Sir?"

Telfer stood up and walked to the window. "You know, Jeff, sometimes the obvious is what fools us. It's right there in front of our noses and we can't see it." He turned and faced his subordinate. "The Pollard woman mentioned a big fight the Cohens had three years ago, right?"

"Yes. But she didn't know what it was about."

"Find out. Now, the insurance policy was taken out three years ago. That also happens to coincide with the Peters case."

Smylie was baffled. "The Peters case? What's that got to do with it?"

"Everything."

"I don't understand how that case—"

"If you'll shut up for a few minutes, I'll tell you."

Jeff sat down. Telfer hooked his thumbs into his belt and leaned back on the desk. "William Connally became a major player after the Peters case. He was a neighbor of Ann Cohen. And the Peters case hit the media at the same time as Martin and Ann Cohen had their big battle. The Pollard woman doesn't know what the battle was about, but supposing it was another woman? It might be reasonable to assume that Ann Cohen got her husband to take out a new life insurance policy as part of a deal to keep the marriage together. Already, she's thinking ahead.

"She says to herself, 'Hey! I know a really good defense attorney if I ever get in trouble. Like, if I knocked off my asshole husband and the bitch he's been screwing.' So she takes three years to think about it and plan it. In the meantime, Connally keeps getting his name in the papers by winning cases.

"When she finds out that her husband is still seeing this woman, Ann Cohen goes down there and sees them together. She's really pissed because the threat didn't work. In a fury, she decides to kill them both. But she's cool. She's thought about this for three years. This is no act of passion. This is a carefully conceived execution.

"But after she blows them away, something short-circuits in Ann Cohen's brain. She remembers some things but forgets others. She's in such a fog she doesn't really know what she's doing. She ditches the clothes but puts the gun back in the bedroom. Then, aware she's really messed up, she decides to get stoned, thinking, in the back of her mind, that no matter what happens, her friend Connally, being the perfect lawyer, will get her off. The main things to remember are these: she knew Connally personally, she knew he was a good lawyer with a terrific record, and she hated her husband. She had both a financial motive and a revenge motive.

"She probably planned on ditching the gun but simply went to pieces after she killed the two of them. Her mind drew a blank from the shock of what she'd done. She had the presence of mind to change her clothes but not to ditch the gun. I think you can find a shrink who will testify that it could have happened that way."

Jeff's face was beginning to brighten. "You know, you could be right."

"Could be? I *am* right. And you have to prove it."

"Yes, sir."

"Good. Now get to work, because I have a hunch Connally's motion may fly."

Jeff was shocked. "You do? Why? The deputies played it by the book."

"I know they did. But Sam Clark is a pain in the ass about no-warrant searches. If Clark thinks there's the slightest chance that Ann Cohen's rights were violated, he'll pounce on it. And you can't appeal. Which means the gun is out. Without the gun, you'll have a hell of time."

Smylie could feel the sweat starting to bead on his forehead. As he walked toward the door, he wondered how Lionel Telfer managed to make himself aware of the details of some hundred cases going on in any given week. It was astounding. It explained why the man was where he was.

"Remember what I told you," Telfer said, a chill in his voice. "You lose this one and you're back to prosecuting people for spittin' on the sidewalk."

"I remember."

Telfer watched his man leave. Had choosing Smylie been a mistake? Telfer had figured that giving Smylie a case against Connally would spur the prosecutor to work his ass off, just to beat Connally, if nothing else. But the young attorney was obviously running scared.

Telfer picked up the Cohen file and began to leaf through the pages. Despite his ebullience of a few moments ago, he too felt there was something odd about this case.

CHAPTER

13

PETER QUILL, FRESH FROM DUTY AND STILL DRESSED in his policeman's uniform, parked his car in the golf course parking lot and walked to the maintenance shed, looking for his father. He saw Rusty, one of the other workers at the golf course, leaning over a golf cart, tinkering with some wires.

"Hi, Rusty."

The old man looked up and grinned. "Hi, Pete. How's crime?"

"Still as bad as ever. You know where my dad is?"

"Yeah. He's taking soil samples on the back nine. Somewhere between the fourteenth and the eighteenth. We got some fungus or something eatin' away at the grass. You want to drive out take number forty-five over there."

"Thanks, Rusty."

Peter sat behind the wheel of the golf cart, turned the ignition key on, and guided the cart out of the shed and onto the course.

It was only eight-forty-five in the morning, but already the heat was intense. He drove toward the tenth hole, then down the cart path, past golfers teeing off, and headed for the fourteenth hole, keeping his head down as he bumped along in the rough beside the fairway. At this time of year, a lot of the members of this small course started their round of golf as close as possible to the break of dawn, because by noon it was too hot to play.

He found his father at the sixteenth green, using a boring tool to take a ten-inch plug of soil from the edge of the green.

"Hey, Dad!"

His father looked up and motioned to the maintenance cart. "Put on a hard hat, son. You're liable to be conked on the head."

Peter took a red hard hat from the cart, removed his brown straw deputy's hat, and replaced it with the plastic one. Then he joined his father at the edge of the green.

"You just get off duty?"

"Yeah."

"Must be important."

"Not really. I just wanted to talk to you."

"How's Connie and those fine-lookin' grandkids of mine?"

"Great. Just great."

His father stopped working and leaned back on his

haunches. "So what's the problem?"

Peter talked as his father returned to his work, continuing to take samples while still listening carefully. That was one thing Peter always appreciated about his father and mother: they listened. Not many people, parents or otherwise, listened anymore.

When Peter had finished, the elder Quill said, "You're this upset because of her *eyes*?"

Peter shook his head. "It's not just that. It's—well, call it an instinct. You always told me I had to trust my instincts. You said good cops have good instincts."

His father grunted. "Yeah. I said that. And it's true, far as it goes. But you're talking about something else. Your job is to be a cop. You let the lawyers decide on guilt or innocence. That ain't your job. Hell, you've been a cop for two years. If you start getting personally involved in cases, you're gonna be a burned-out wreck in no time. You can't do it, son."

"But—"

"No buts," his father said, as he put three core samples in plastic containers, marked them, and stored them on the maintenance cart. "Come on. Follow me in, and we'll talk some more."

Peter climbed into his cart and followed his father back to the shed. The breeze, while warm, still felt good against his cheeks. Once they reached the shed, Peter's father placed his collection of samples in a cardboard carton and then put the carton up on a wooden shelf. "We've got some whiz kid from the university coming over this morning to look at these. Then maybe we'll be able to figure out what to use. Nothin's worked so far." He clapped a hand on Peter's shoulder. "Come on,

I'll buy you a cup of coffee."

They went into the small employees' lounge, where the elder Quill poured some coffee into foam cups. They both sat down on two vinyl benches that had once adorned golf carts.

"Pete," his father said, staring into his coffee cup, "the fact is, you can't really tell about people. I've seen things with my own eyes that I still don't believe. I mean, I saw it, and still it don't make any sense. You can't make a judgment on anything except hard evidence in a case like this.

"According to the newspapers, they've been able to determine that this woman was at the scene of the killings. That right?"

"Yeah."

"They say her fingerprints are on the gun you found and that they're pretty sure it's the murder weapon. She had a hell of a motive, if what I hear is right."

Peter sighed and nodded his head. "Well, her husband was screwing another woman. And I guess they were both into kinky sex. Not his wife, but the other one."

His father grunted. "I see that William Connally is representing her, so she's already got a top-notch lawyer. How'd she manage to get him? I thought he worked for the mob."

"They used to be neighbors," Peter said. "I guess he's just helping an old friend."

His father nodded. "If there's something to find, I'm sure he'll find it. I don't know why you're wasting your time."

Peter sighed again. "I don't know either. I've never felt like this before. I talked to Luther Jackson and he's satisfied. Weber, my sergeant, he's satisfied. I don't understand it. To be honest with you, it bothers me that it bothers me. That ever happen to you?"

His father grinned as he looked up at his son. "Sure. About three or four times. I was positive the detectives were wrong. I was positive I *knew* the suspect was innocent. Damn, I was sure. But I was wrong, each and every time.

"I tell ya, people today are all stressed out. Everybody's workin' their ass off to keep their heads above water. It's tough out there, son. Sometimes I think that's why we're growin' more crazies all the time."

As Peter sat there, lightly tapping his forehead with his knuckles, his father got up and threw his empty cup into a small garbage pail. "Don't feel bad, Pete. It happens. But you need to put it out of your head. Forget it. Whatever it is that's buggin' you, let the detectives and the lawyers take care of it. Chances are she's guilty as hell, but if she isn't, there isn't a thing you can do anyway. Not if you want to keep your job. Sheriffs kinda frown on deputies running around trying to make them look bad, you know?"

"Yeah, I know."

Jeff Smylie parked his car in the special section reserved for prosecutors and walked toward the Pinellas County Criminal Courthouse, which houses the Sixth Judicial District. The building, a bleak, four-story, gray concrete structure located about a mile from the Clearwater–St. Petersburg Airport, stands adjacent to the Pinellas County Jail. Most of those who work within the building dub it the no-frills courthouse: no majestic marble columns, no brass plaques on the walls, no statues, no inscriptions above the entrance.

To Jeff, it looked like an office building, a low-cost office building. Inside, the austereness was even more apparent. The fourth floor, where most major felony cases, like Ann Cohen's, were heard, held four rather small courtrooms, each almost identical in appearance. Unadorned beige walls, beige carpets. From four to seven rows of spectator benches, depending on the size of the room, sat behind a rarely polished brass rail. Low ceilings with indirect lighting made the room appear to be nothing more than a conference room at some airport hotel. The U.S. flag hung forlornly on a pole near the front wall to the right of the judge. To the judge's left, an identically sized pole held the flag of the State of Florida.

But Jeff wasn't headed for the fourth floor. He got off the elevator at the second, where first appearances were held in a small courtroom. Since the law requires that all arrested persons must appear before a judge within twenty-four hours of the arrest, this courtroom was open 365 days a year. In the interests of time, the defendants took their position in a small room at the jail. Their images appeared on three television screens located in the courtroom, some thousand yards away. Defendants watched the proceedings on another television screen mounted on the wall of the room in the jail.

As Jeff entered the courtroom, Ann Cohen sat in a room next to the small jail courtroom and waited for her name to be called. Much to her surprise, in view of Bill's assurances to the contrary, she was handcuffed.

Her wrists ached. At least they had allowed her to wear the clothes Bill had brought for her the night before.

She looked around the small room, crowded with women waiting, like her, for their first appearance before a judge. There were about twenty of them, some black, some white, some dressed in street clothes, others wearing prison smocks. All were handcuffed. They looked like the dregs of society: hookers, drug addicts. One woman kept talking to herself. As they had been assembled earlier this morning, Ann had heard someone say she'd hacked her husband and three children to death the night before.

Ann shuddered. She'd started shaking again about fifteen minutes ago. The terrible hangover was gone, but her body still ached unmercifully. She knew she was running on pure adrenaline, because she'd had so little sleep.

She'd been alone in her cell, away from these people who made her skin crawl. One of the jailers had said they always kept murderers in isolation the first night. In the jailer's mind, she was guilty, period. They all were. The police never made mistakes.

She'd spent most of the night on her knees, praying, asking a God she'd previously abandoned for help. She'd prayed for Marty's soul, and for the soul of Elizabeth Winters, for she felt no joy in knowing the woman was dead. She'd asked for strength and for a renewal of her lost faith. She wondered if God was listening.

When she'd slept, it had only been for minutes at a time. Whenever she closed her eyes, the images would return: Marty standing in the living room, telling her bald-faced lies, Marty being whipped, Marty being shot. In her mind, she could see the bullets strike his face, feel his pain. Each time, she'd jerk awake, bathed in sweat, unsure whether she'd screamed out or not, to return to her knees and ask God to please—this time—help her get through the night.

One by one the women were taken out, and as each one left the intensity of Ann's present agony increased. Finally, she heard her own name being called. A policewoman came over, removed the handcuffs, and escorted her into a small room next door.

Heart pounding, body shaking, hands and feet as cold as the cement floor of her cell, Ann's eyes turned to the television monitor showing the inside of the courtroom. Instantly, she was able to pick out Bill, as he stood in front of a lectern. It was eerie, seeing him on the television screen, along with a number of other people moving in and out of the room. It made her feel detached from her own life, like an observer watching a news broadcast: another day, another crime. She shuddered.

Connally, upon seeing her face on the television screen in front of him, turned toward the camera and gave her a thumbs-up sign. Her own thumb felt too cold and heavy, as if it were encased in a block of ice and weighed against her side, to return the gesture.

Bill studied Ann's face on the television monitor. The terror was there for all to see. Her bloodshot eyes were wide, the lids blinking erratically. She'd developed a tic at the corner of her mouth. Clearly, she was on the edge of a breakdown and he wondered for an instant if he'd made a terrible mistake in judgment. Perhaps she was too consumed with fear and misplaced guilt to see this through. He'd cautioned her against such negative thinking, but—

No, he thought, as he tore his attention away from the monitor. She'd make it. With his encouragement, she'd be fine. She had to be fine.

Judge Priscilla Walton looked down from her large desk and nodded. "Mr. Smylie?"

They were ready to go.

Jeff Smylie stood up, tapped an index finger on his desk for a moment, and then said, "Your Honor, the State moves for pretrial detention at this time. The defendant is charged with two capital offenses, with special circumstances on both counts. The evidence in this case is overwhelming. Both murders were committed in a brutal and violent fashion. Both victims were made to suffer excruciating pain before the final shots were fired. This was not a crime of passion. It was a premeditated, vicious execution.

"The defendant has the financial capability to leave this jurisdiction, and the State believes she may well do so. With that in mind, we ask that bail be denied."

The judge made a notation and directed her attention to Bill. "Mr. Connally?"

"Your Honor, the defendant will plead not guilty to both charges at her arraignment. She will do so not because she is exercising her rights but because she just plain didn't do it. While I've had less than twenty-four hours to review the case, I'm already convinced that my client will soon be cleared.

"As for the overwhelming evidence—well, it isn't quite so overwhelming as Mr. Smylie might wish. The murder weapon has not been positively identified. Witnesses have sworn to seeing a car at the murder scene similar to one owned by the defendant, but no tag numbers were taken down. The State's major piece of evidence consists of the defendant's fingerprints being found on the *outside* of the bedroom window of the home where the murders took place. That's true, and she can explain it. No evidence of any kind has been offered to indicate that my client was ever *inside* the house."

He scratched his chin for a moment.

"There's no question that my client had a motive. We won't argue that. But given the opportunity, I will present twenty character witnesses who will swear that they have never seen my client commit an act of violence of any kind, even when greatly provoked, in the many years they've known her. All in all, I'd say that the police have moved much too quickly on this one."

Smylie wanted to interrupt but held his tongue. The threat made by Ann Cohen against Elizabeth Winters was an act of violence, all right, but at this first appearance, in effect a bail hearing, knowledge of the threat was inadmissible because of hearsay rules.

"The defendant has lived in the community for over eleven years," Connally continued, "and she has ties here. She's a professional, a CPA, and has worked for a local accounting firm for the same period of time. She's never been arrested and is a member of several civic groups. She's a pillar of the community.

"The defendant made no effort to flee, Your Honor. She was approached by the police while in her home and allowed them to enter voluntarily. After a search

was conducted, she offered no resistance when requested to accompany the officers. As for the evidence that
led to her arrest, it is our contention that it was illegally
obtained, and we have filed motions to that effect. We
ask that the defendant be released on her own recognizance."

Judge Walton turned to Smylie. "Mr. Smylie, do you
have some evidence to support your concern that the
defendant may fail to appear?"

The hell with it, Smylie thought. It was worth a try.
He stood up and said, "We have a deposition from a
witness, Your Honor, that indicates the defendant had
threatened one of the victims—"

The judge held up a hand. "You know what I want,
Mr. Smylie."

Smylie stiffened. "No, Your Honor."

"Very well. Arraignment is set for July sixteenth. This
being a capital case, bond is set at five hundred thousand dollars."

Connally smiled.

A thousand yards away, Ann Cohen almost fainted.

And in the back of the courtroom, Peter Quill made
some notes and left quickly.

Five hours later, Ann's father and friends had posted
her bail. When Bill escorted Ann from the jail, they
were all waiting for her, and she almost threw herself
into their welcoming arms. They were immediately surrounded by an army of screaming reporters from both
the print and electronic media, hurling questions like
heavy stones.

"Why'd you do it, Ann?"

"You gonna plead temporary insanity?"

"How'd it feel to pull the trigger?"

The questions went unheard and unanswered. Nothing was registering. It was simply a cacophony of sound. When Bill finally got her into the car and away from the crowd, she was so overwhelmed with relief and gratitude that she was unable to speak for a full fifteen minutes.

She could only place her head on her father's shoulder and weep.

CHAPTER

14

IT WAS THE MORNING AFTER THE MORNING AFTER. ANN was being escorted by Bill to the courtroom for another confrontation with the criminal justice system. As was his custom with first-time clients, he'd brought her to the courthouse very early, to acquaint her with the building, the courtrooms themselves, and the mechanics of courtroom procedures, so she would feel as comfortable as possible under the circumstances.

They were on the fourth floor. Still numb and feeling weak, Ann gripped his arm tightly as he walked down the hallway that led to the various courtrooms.

The previous night, he had carefully explained the procedures that would be followed inside the courtroom. He wanted her to know exactly what would be happening, but Ann had had difficulty understanding what he was telling her. So this morning he was trying again.

"At the back of this room, behind these windows, is space for two television cameras, one live and one spare. If the judge allows the cameras to record a trial, the stations take turns as to which one will do it, then share the tape with their competitors."

Ann blanched. "Will we be on television?"

Bill put his arm around her and patted her shoulder. "The hearing won't. But if we go to trial, it might be. Clark, the judge, is a bit of a ham. He likes to see himself on television. For that reason, and because the press is showing an inordinate amount of interest in your case, this will probably be the trial room."

"Why?"

"Because you're a beautiful woman involved in a murder case. There are elements of sex, violence, betrayal—all the good stuff. But don't worry about that. If we get a break, this may never get to trial." He smiled hopefully at her. "For now, Ann, our hearing is down the hall." He led her away and down the hallway until they faced another set of double doors. "This is Division M," he said, "where our motions will be heard."

The door was unlocked. The only person inside was a bailiff who looked up as they entered the room.

"Mr. Connally?" the bailiff asked, surprise written all over his face.

"Hi, Phil. I know. We're early. I just wanted to have my client get the feel of the place. Okay?"

"No problem, Mr. Connally."

It was a much smaller courtroom than courtroom A, which they'd just visited. The room was no larger than forty feet by thirty feet. But the color scheme and the layout were almost identical. Four rows of benches occupied the rear of the room. There was no provision for television cameras. Bill squeezed Ann's arm gently. "Not so scary, is it?"

"Not when I see it like this," she answered.

He grinned. "That's why we're doing this. Come on, let's go downstairs and have some coffee. I want you to understand exactly what we can expect."

An hour later, they were in the courtroom for real. The clock on the wall behind Connally showed it was 8:02. He placed one of Ann's ice-cold hands in both of his and rubbed it. "You going to be all right?"

Her face was ashen, her eyes bloodshot and rimmed with red. "I'm scared to death," she whispered.

"Try not to worry," he said. "The wheels of justice grind slowly, but they do move. Have faith in me. This may not work, but it's only the first shot."

She took a deep breath and said, "I do have faith in you, Bill. My life is in your hands."

Jeff Smylie was already seated at the prosecutor's table, a small stack of file folders piled up in the wire cart sitting beside his table. The clerk was in position, as were the two bailiffs. The court reporter sat on a small chair, her tiny machine propped on a portable wire stand. In the rear of the room, a dozen reporters, all with note pads in hand, sat on the spectator benches. The jury box was empty, this being a hearing, not a trial.

"All rise."

Everyone stood up as Judge Clark entered the courtroom and took his position at the slightly raised bench.

Sam Clark was a seasoned jurist, having served on the bench for over eleven years. Now in his early sixties, he looked the part, with his heavy thatch of silver hair. Bushy eyebrows extended over large, clear brown eyes. His slightly jowly face seemed pleasant enough, but when he was angry, everyone knew it. His Crosby ears would turn blood red. Veteran attorneys had learned to monitor the hue of the judge's ears and take heed. Even when the judge was smiling, if his ears were red, it was time to speak softly. He had thrown his share of lawyers into jail on contempt charges.

"Everyone here?" he asked of no one in particular.

"Yes, Your Honor," Connally said.

"Ready, Your Honor," Smylie said.

"All right. Tempus fugit. Let's go, Mr. Connally. It's your show."

Connally walked from his position behind the desk to the lectern in front of the empty jury box and opened a loose-leaf binder. Gripping the sides of the lectern with both hands, he said, "Thank you, Your Honor. Your Honor already has my motions in writing. And the prosecution has agreed to argue both—"

The judge tapped a finger on the bench and said, "Yes, yes, Mr. Connally. The record will show that you are moving to suppress and claiming lack of probable cause. Call your first witness."

Connally gritted his teeth. It had scarcely begun and Clark was already on his ass. "Call Ann Cohen," he said.

Ann stood up and walked toward the witness box. The clerk nodded at her. "Please raise your right hand."

She stopped, raised her right hand, and was sworn.

Then she completed the short journey to the witness chair. As she sat down and stared at the spectator section, she looked for a face she could recognize, but they were just strangers. All there, for some reason she couldn't understand, to see this woman accused of killing her husband and his lover.

Bill had explained that he had requested her father and her friends not attend the hearing. He said that because of her father's age, he didn't want to subject him to the shock of seeing his daughter in court. Not yet. Not while there was a chance this whole thing could be stopped and not until Connally had had time to prepare Ann's father for what he was to see. Even though Mr. Martino was an attorney himself, he would have to be conditioned before seeing his only daughter as a defendant in a murder case.

As for the friends, he wanted to keep them in reserve, for a time when they would really be needed. If the case ever went before a jury, the sight of Ann's friends in the spectator section—well-dressed, good-looking friends, en masse—could do nothing but help.

It made sense, and it reminded Ann of just how thoughtful Bill was, concerned about her feelings and her father's as well. How refreshing.

Her eyes locked on Bill's as he stood at the lectern, facing her and the judge, leaning forward and smiling slightly with his eyes and lips.

Bill would save her. She knew it. Last night and again this morning, he'd told her what to expect. He didn't want to get her hopes up, he'd said, but there was a chance that this hearing would stop the police in their tracks. Then, he hoped, the police would spend some time trying to find the real killer. He'd cautioned her on what to say and what not to say. He'd made her aware of what Smylie would attempt to do: confuse her, make her look guilty. "Smylie is your enemy," he'd said.

Connally glanced at his notes and lifted his head. "For the record, would you state your full name and your present address."

"Ann Marino Cohen, 605 Bent Tree Drive, Palm Harbor."

The sound of her own voice startled her. It seemed to echo in the courtroom. Once again, she was aware of the strangers seated in the rear, staring at her, making notes.

"Mrs. Cohen, would you tell the Court what happened on the night of July seventh and the morning of July eighth, to the best of your recollection."

Ann gave her story. She kept her voice calm and sure. She kept her chin up and only cried once, when she mentioned what she'd seen through the partially drawn blinds. She talked about Cathy, the drive to Weeki Wachee, the drinking, and the confusion.

When she finished, Connally asked, "Now, at the moment you looked in the window of the house located at 1184 Felcher Avenue in Palm Harbor and saw your husband tied to the bed, being whipped, what was your reaction?"

Smylie was on his feet. "Objection! Irrelevant."

Judge Clark gave the prosecutor a sharp look. "Overruled." Then he tapped a finger on the bench. "Mr. Smylie, there's no jury to impress here today. Just little old me. And I'm not going to be impressed when you object to questions that you know deal with state of mind. That's one of the reasons this hearing is in progress. So let's not make this more difficult than it needs to be. I'll allow you sufficient leeway when your turn comes. All right?"

"Yes, Your Honor."

The judge swung his chair around, looked at Ann, and said, "You may answer the question, Mrs. Cohen."

"Yes. I was . . . I felt physically ill."

Connally asked, "Anything else?"

"Yes. I was shocked. Saddened. I realized at that moment that my marriage was truly over."

"Were you angry?"

Smylie had his hand in the air. "Objection," he said softly. "Leading." This time, the judge simply nodded.

"Withdrawn," Connally said. "Mrs. Cohen, what were your feelings toward your husband at that moment?"

Ann thought for a moment. "I was very sad. I saw him as a sick man, a man I could no longer stay married to. I thought of him as . . . a stranger, in a way. Someone I thought I knew but really didn't. I felt no anger toward him, only pity."

"How long had you been married?"

"Twelve years."

"Would you characterize your marriage as a happy one?"

Ann took a deep breath. "Yes. Until the last three months."

"What happened three months ago?"

She fought back a sudden impulse to cry again. "That was when I first discovered Marty's predilection for sexual deviancy."

"What do you mean by deviancy?"

"He was a masochist."

"Objection!" Smylie was on his feet again. "The witness is not a psychiatrist, Your Honor. She—"

Judge Clark gave Smylie a sharp stare that stopped him in his tracks. Already, the enormous ears were turning a soft pink. "Mr. Smylie," he said, a note of frustration in his voice, "we're here to determine whether or not certain evidence was legally or illegally obtained, among other things. While it is true that the witness is not qualified to determine, in legal or medical terms, the true nature of her husband's alleged mental disorder— if indeed one existed—it really doesn't figure in what we're doing today. So let's just worry about those things that are important to us, all right? Otherwise we'll take a week to do what should take less than a day. Can you live with that, Mr. Smylie?"

"Yes, Your Honor."

"Thank you. Mr. Connally, would you please proceed?"

Connally nodded. "Mrs. Cohen, did your husband ever express to you his sexual interests?"

"Yes. He told me that he . . . enjoyed being beaten."

"In what way?"

"He told me that he enjoyed being whipped . . . on his behind."

"How did that come about? His confession, I mean."

"He came home one night with welts on his back and buttocks. I asked him what had happened. We argued. Finally, he told me that they'd been caused by someone hitting him with a whip . . . at his own request."

"And what did you say to him when he confessed this to you?"

"I begged him to seek professional help. I told him I loved him and didn't want to lose him. I told him I would be supportive if he would see a doctor."

"And did he?"

"He went on three visits I know of, but I don't think he was serious."

"Objection!"

"Sustained." Judge Clark leaned forward and said, "Mrs. Cohen, you may only testify to what you know to be the facts. You may testify that your husband saw a doctor three times if you know that to be true. But your comments as to his intent are opinion. We deal only with facts here."

"I'm sorry, Your Honor."

"That's all right. Continue."

Connally rubbed his chin for a moment and then said, "You have testified that on July seventh, at approximately eleven-thirty in the evening, you and Mrs. Pollard were standing outside the bedroom window of a home located at 1184 Felcher Avenue in Palm Harbor. You have testified that you saw your husband being beaten in a manner consistent with what he confessed to you three months ago. You have testified that it upset you. Were you still upset when the police arrived at your door later that night?"

"Of course."

"What was your state of mind at that time?"

"I was confused. I was also drunk."

"You were drunk. You'd started drinking at about one o'clock in the morning, right after your friend Cathy Pollard left, correct?"

"Yes."

"Why did you wait until Cathy Pollard left before you started drinking?"

"I didn't want her to see me like that."

"Why not?"

"I was . . . I knew that she was concerned about me. I didn't want to burden her with my problems any further. So I told her I was all right."

"Were you?"

"No. I was upset. I was waiting for my husband to come home so I could tell him to his face that I was divorcing him."

"I see. And when the police officers arrived, you were drunk and very depressed by what you had seen earlier—your husband."

"Yes."

"Did you understand what the policemen were saying to you?"

"Not really. I was shocked when they arrived. I thought at first that I must have committed some traffic violation and they'd followed me home. I know it doesn't make sense, but I wasn't thinking clearly."

"What happened when you answered the door? What did they say and what did you say?"

"They asked if they could come in and I said they could. They asked if I owned a gun and I told them I did. I told them where it was and they went and got it. I didn't think I had anything to hide. I was trying to be helpful."

"But you didn't really understand what was—"

"Objection. Asked and answered."

"Sustained."

Connally stepped out from behind the lectern and

leaned against it. "Why did you sign the forms that were presented to you?"

Ann took a deep breath. "Because the officer said it had something to do with keeping the books straight. I'm an accountant, and I know how important it is to keep proper records. I had no idea what was happening, but by force of habit I thought it was important that I help him."

"So you signed the forms as a sort of reflex action?"

"Objection!" Smylie cried. "Leading."

Judge Clark shook his head. "Come on, Mr. Smylie, she said 'force of habit.' Same thing. You're beginning to give me heartburn. The objection is overruled."

"Go ahead, Ann," Connally urged.

"Yes, it was just a reflex action. I was so upset, I didn't know what I was doing."

"What was on your mind?"

"I was still thinking about what I'd seen earlier. Marty and . . . that woman."

"Did the police officers tell you that you had the right to refuse to answer any questions?"

"Not that I can remember."

Connally smiled, removed a blank sheet of paper from his binder, approached the witness chair, and said, "Would you sign your name on this piece of paper, please?"

Ann signed her name and handed the paper back to Connally, who said, "Defense exhibit one, Your Honor."

Judge Clark nodded to the clerk, who stamped the paper and left it on his desk. Connally said, "I have nothing further, Your Honor."

The judge turned and looked at Smylie. Smylie stood

up and walked to the lectern. Reaching it, he shook his head, a wry look on his face, and asked, "Mrs. Cohen, when the police officers came to your home, they asked for your permission to come in. Isn't that true?"

"Yes."

"At no time did they force their way in. Isn't that true?"

"Yes."

"They didn't search your home, did they?"

"I don't know. I was in the kitchen."

"But isn't it true that to the best of your recollection the only thing you saw them take was the gun, after you voluntarily told them where it was located."

"Yes."

"And before they asked you if you owned a gun, they advised you that you had the right to refuse to answer. They told you that you had the right to call an attorney. Isn't that true?"

"I can't remember them saying that. All I remember is that they told me they wanted to see my gun and I said it was all right. I told them where it was. I remember that, but I can't remember exactly what was said."

"But your recollection is that no force was used and that you were trying to be helpful, to keep the books straight, as you testified."

"Yes."

Smylie pulled some papers from his file folder and walked towards the clerk. "I'd like to present state exhibits one, two, and three, Your Honor."

Judge Clark nodded. The clerk stamped the papers and then handed them back to Smylie, who approached Ann in the witness chair. "I show you State's exhibit number one, a Consent to Interview form." He handed her the paper. "Do you recognize the signature?"

Ann looked at it for a moment and then said, "Yes. It's my signature."

Smylie showed her two other papers she'd signed, asked the same question, and received the same answer. Then he said, "You have testified that the first time you were aware of the fact that your husband enjoyed being beaten was three months ago, when he confessed to you, correct?"

"Correct."

"So you've known about this for three months."

"Yes."

"And you decided to go to the house on Felcher Avenue on the night of July seventh because you thought he was engaging in the same type of activity again. Is that not true?"

"Yes."

"And when you saw what they were doing, it was as you'd imagined it, wasn't it?"

"In a way, yes."

Smylie smiled, then said, "The fact is that you expected to see it when you looked in the window. Isn't that true?"

"I wasn't sure what I would see." Ann looked at Connally, then back at Smylie. "I was curious. I didn't expect I would see him being beaten. I just wanted to know if he was seeing that woman again."

"But you saw his car in the driveway. Wasn't that enough?"

"Objection!" Connally said. "He's badgering the witness."

"Overruled," the judge snapped.

Ann put a hand to her mouth and then said, "I wanted to see what they were doing because I'd made a decision to divorce my husband. I thought that seeing them together would give me the resolve I needed. I was aware that my husband was a very manipulative man. I wanted to ensure he could never talk me out of divorcing him. It was important to me."

Smylie threw his hands in the air. "I have nothing further, Your Honor."

Judge Clark nodded at Ann Cohen. "You are excused, Mrs. Cohen. Call your next witness, Mr. Connally."

"Call Catherine Pollard."

Cathy Pollard was brought into the courtroom, sworn, and directed to the witness chair. Connally asked her a number of questions, most of which were designed to corroborate what Ann had said about the two of them going to the house on Felcher Avenue. Then he asked, "When you and Mrs. Cohen looked through the bedroom window and saw Mr. Cohen on the bed, what was Mrs. Cohen's reaction?"

"She just sort of wilted right there. She looked like someone had kicked her in the stomach."

"Did she appear angry?"

"No. She seemed devastated."

"And when you took her home, what did she do or say?"

"She just sat at the kitchen table and stared at the wall. She didn't say much. After half an hour or so, she told me she'd be fine, thanked me for being with her, and said I should go home. I didn't want to leave."

"Why not?"

"I was concerned. She was so depressed. I even thought she might try to kill herself."

"But you did leave. Why?"

Cathy wrung her hands as she sat in the witness chair. "Because we talked, and Ann assured me that she was fine. We talked about her depression, which was natural under the circumstances. I thought . . . I thought I would do more harm than good if I stayed. Ann told me that Marty had hurt her enough. She wasn't going to kill herself. She'd already called a divorce lawyer. She had an appointment to see him in the morning. She seemed quite determined. In the end, I decided that while she was depressed she was not about to do anything stupid."

"Did she express anger at any time?"

"No. She just said it was time to get the divorce. It was obvious Marty would never change, and she had to get on with her life."

Connally nodded. "What happened later that morning?"

Cathy recounted the events of the following morning.

"And what was your reaction when Lieutenant Jackson told you he didn't know where Ann was?"

"I was very confused. Then he told me Marty had been killed and implied that Ann had done it."

"What time of day did this conversation take place?"

"It was approximately eight-thirty in the morning. On the eighth."

"Did you at any time consider that Ann Cohen had been responsible for the death of her husband?"

"Objection! Irrelevant."

"Sustained."

Connally glared at Smylie for a moment and then said, "When you left Ann Cohen that night, you were concerned that she might kill herself. Is that your testimony?"

"Yes."

"And your first thought when you arrived back at her house the next morning was that she had done so. Is that true?"

"Yes."

"Then it would be fair to say that she was pretty shook up, wouldn't it?"

"Absolutely. And brokenhearted."

"But not, in any way, murderous."

Smylie groaned, held a hand out to the judge, who nodded. "Objection sustained. Move along, Mr. Connally."

"I have no further questions, Your Honor."

Judge Clark nodded at Smylie, who took his place at the lectern. "Mrs. Pollard," Smylie began, eyeing his notes, "approximately six weeks ago, you and Mrs. Cohen paid a visit to Mrs. Elizabeth Winters at her home located at 1184 Felcher Avenue in Palm Harbor, isn't that true?"

Connally was instantly on his feet, his hand in the air. "Objection! Improper cross!"

Smylie couldn't help it. A look of triumph appeared on his face as he gripped the lectern tightly. "Your Honor, may we approach the bench?"

Judge Clark motioned both men to come forward. They were joined by the court reporter and her small shorthand machine.

Judge Clark looked at Smylie. "Okay, what's on your mind?"

In almost a stage whisper, Smylie said, "Your Honor, the defense has brought this witness forward to bolster his contention that the officers had no probable cause for asking the defendant if she owned a gun. However, the witness has given a sworn statement to the effect that she has personal knowledge of a threat made against one of the victims. At the time the officers were instructed to visit the home of the defendant, they were aware of that threat, having been given that information by another witness.

"Knowledge of the threat's being made is at the heart of the State's contention that the officers had probable cause to ask the defendant if she owned a gun. This witness, having direct knowledge, should be allowed to testify, since it relates to the motion. I realize that my cross-examination is outside the normal bounds, but we can, if necessary, call the witness later to testify on behalf of the State. I'm just trying to save us all a lot of time."

Judge Clark nodded, made a note, and then looked at Connally. "Mr. Connally?"

Connally was livid. "Your Honor, the State has not provided us with a copy of this mystery witness's statement. That's a direct violation of—"

Smylie cut him off. "Your Honor, we've had less than forty-eight hours to prepare for this motion. Copies of evidence pertinent to the hearing are still being prepared. It was my intention to present a copy of the witness's statement to Mr. Connally prior to our calling this witness for the State. I didn't realize he was going to put her on so early. I'll be happy to withdraw the question until such time as Mr. Connally has had an opportunity to examine her statement."

Judge Clark gave Smylie a hard stare, then turned to Connally. The defense attorney seemed unusually agitated. "Your Honor," Bill said, "what happened six weeks ago is irrelevant. Even if a threat were made, it matters little. The witness should be confined to answering questions brought up on direct at this point. If the State wants to present the witness as its own at another time, they have that right, but not until I've had an opportunity to examine the statement."

Judge Clark tapped a finger on his desk, then said, "All right! Enough! We'll take a ten-minute recess. Mr. Smylie, you'll have a copy of that statement in Mr. Connally's hands within ten minutes. When court resumes, you will confine your cross to subjects brought up on direct. You'll have to call the witness back later." He banged his gavel on the desk and said, "Recess, ten minutes."

Everyone stood as the judge left the room. Then Cathy was led back to the witness's waiting room. Finally, Connally turned and stared at Ann, eyes blazing.

"What's wrong?" Ann whispered.

"Your friend Cathy," he rasped. "Jesus Christ! She never told me she was with you when you made that threat! Nor did you! Dammit! You were supposed to tell me everything!"

Ann was stunned by his first display of hostility toward her. "I . . . don't know. I thought I did."

"You thought you did? Never! You never mentioned her name! I assumed you were alone. That's why it wasn't important. There were no witnesses. I remember asking you specifically. You said you were alone."

Ann could feel the anxiety building within her. It had been such an incredibly stupid thing to do, the threat. Impulsive and stupid. But she was sure she'd told Bill about Cathy being there.

"I'm sorry," she said, her lips quivering. "I haven't been thinking properly lately."

The anger left his face almost as quickly as it had appeared. "It's all right," he said. "I'm sorry I barked at you. It was uncalled for. I was just surprised. I hate to be surprised in court. There's no real harm done. This motion to suppress is just a shot in the dark anyway."

When court resumed, Connally had his copy of Cathy Pollard's statement. It seemed to take some of the wind out of his sails. Smylie finished his cross-examination of Cathy and sat down, looking pleased with himself.

Connally stood up and said, "I call Sergeant James Murray to the stand."

"Call Sergeant James Murray."

Once Murray was sworn and seated, Connally seemed to turn his energy up a notch. His voice boomed, its timbre senatorial, as he stood stiffly at the lectern and hurled his questions at the policeman.

"Sergeant Murray, you were the officer who directed Sergeant William Weber and Deputy Peter Quill to interrogate the defendant, were you not?"

"There were no instructions to interrogate," Murray snapped.

"What exactly did you say to the two deputies?"

"I told them that, based on the evidence we had seen and heard so far, they were to call on the defendant, read her her rights, ask her if she wanted a lawyer, and, if she did, bring her in."

"They were not to question her?"

Murray squirmed in his seat for a moment. "They were to ask some questions, yes, but they were to make sure it was done properly."

Connally leaned forward. "Was it your idea that they not tell her about the death of her husband until after a search had been conducted?"

Murray shook his head. "I did not give specific instructions as to the form. I simply told them that some evidence indicated she was a suspect and they were to be very careful."

"What evidence?"

"Well, one of the cars in the driveway was registered to Mr. Cohen. Two witnesses at the murder scene made statements to the effect that they had seen a car leave the scene shortly after the sound of the gun being fired. They both said it was a beige-colored vehicle. I checked and discovered that Mrs. Cohen owned a beige Mercedes. We also had a statement from another witness who said that one of the victims, Mrs. Winters, had been threatened by Mrs. Cohen."

"Who was this witness?"

"Miss Gloria Simmons."

"What did she tell you?"

"That Mrs. Winters had talked to her about six weeks ago. That Mrs. Simmons was afraid Mrs. Cohen might kill her for messing with Mrs. Cohen's husband."

"And that was the extent of it?"

"Yes."

"So, on the basis of hearsay record of this conversation, you assumed you had probable cause to consider the defendant a suspect."

"Not exactly. I told you. I had two witnesses who saw a beige car leave the scene right after the shots were fired."

"But, in fact, your main reason in seeing her was to advise her of the death of her husband. Isn't that so?"

"No. We did need an identification, but at that moment my main concern was in locating Mrs. Cohen."

Connally frowned, looked at the judge, and said, "I have no further questions of this witness, Your Honor."

"Mr. Smylie?"

Smylie walked to the lectern and leaned on it. "Sergeant, you were concerned that the defendant might flee, were you not?"

"I was indeed."

"When you gave instructions to your deputies, you told them to read the defendant her rights, isn't that true?"

"Yes."

"I have nothing further, Your Honor."

Connally stood up and said, "I call Sergeant William Weber."

Sergeant Weber was called and sworn. He took his position in the witness chair and waited.

Connally asked him a number of questions, but the sergeant was unyielding. He had arrived at the home of Mrs. Cohen, he said, had noticed that her car, identified by tag number, had been recently driven. Aware that a felony had occurred, aware that she was a suspect, he had read her her rights, had her sign a waiver, had her sign a Consent to Search form, and had finally told her about the death of her husband. He had then brought her to the morgue to identify the body.

"Isn't it true," Connally asked, "that the defendant was drunk when you arrived at her home?"

Weber hesitated for a moment, then said, "I wouldn't say she was drunk."

"No? What would you say?"

"I'd say she was a little tipsy, that's all."

Connally almost laughed out loud. "A little tipsy? How quaint. How long have you been with the department, Sergeant Weber?"

"Ten years."

"In that time, how many people have you arrested for driving under the influence?"

"I can't really say."

"No? Well, according to your record, the number is three hundred and sixty-four. That sound right to you?"

"Objection!" Smylie was on his feet. "The sergeant's record is not at issue here. Besides, the defense has not introduced the sergeant's record as evidence."

Judge Clark looked at Connally, who said, "I withdraw the question, Your Honor."

He turned his attention back to Weber. "Isn't it a fact, Sergeant Weber, that you have a lot of experience in determining whether or not someone is intoxicated?"

"Yes, you could say that."

"And your testimony is that you didn't think the defendant was drunk?"

"That's right. I didn't think she was. She was coherent and ambulatory. She knew what she was doing."

"I see. Are you aware that a blood test taken at the hospital after the defendant went into an alcohol-induced coma, approximately four hours after she was arrested by you, measured a blood-alcohol content of point eighteen?"

"Objection!"

This time, Connally was ready. He held a piece of paper in his hand and said, "I introduce the medical report as Defense exhibit two, Your Honor."

"Objection! No foundation!"

Clark's ears were turning bright red. "All right! Both of you come to the bench."

The two lawyers stood in front of the judge, the court reporter perched her little machine on the edge of the bench, and Clark said, "Look, Mr. Smylie, have you seen this medical report?"

"Yes, Your Honor."

"Is it legit?"

"The report is legit, but we have the right to question its accuracy. If the defense would lay the foundation for the report's introduction, we would have the opportunity. This way, we don't. That's unfair."

Clark turned to Connally. "Mr. Connally," he snarled, "as I see it, you are bound and determined to prove that your client was drunk when the police arrived. Am I right?"

"Yes, Your Honor."

"Very well. Mr. Smylie, why don't you stipulate that she was drunk and save all of us a lot of time. As far as the law is concerned, drunkenness alone is not going to have a bearing on my ruling."

Smylie had heard what he wanted to hear. Suppressing a grin, he said, "So stipulated, Your Honor."

The lawyers walked back to their respective positions. Once again, Connally addressed Weber.

"You knew that she didn't understand a word of what you were saying to her, didn't you?"

"No," he answered firmly. "She understood what she was doing."

Connally scowled, then bored in. "You knew her husband was dead but you didn't tell her that until after you'd questioned her. Isn't that right?"

"Yes."

"Why didn't you tell her that her husband was dead the moment you arrived at her door?"

Weber almost sneered. "Because I was sure she already knew it."

"I see. Is it your experience that killers voluntarily give up the murder weapon upon request?"

Smylie had his hand in the air again. "Objection, Your Honor. Counsel is attempting to turn his motion into a trial. We're here to determine if the evidence should be suppressed."

"Your Honor," Connally said, "we're trying to determine if the officers considered the defendant a suspect at the time of her interrogation. That's all."

Judge Clark nodded and said, "You may inquire, counsel, but keep it to that. The objection is sustained."

Connally turned his attention back to Weber. "You considered her a suspect, didn't you?"

"Yes."

"Therefore, you had an obligation to make sure she fully understood her rights, but you didn't carry it out. Isn't that true?"

"No. I read her her rights."

"You read her her rights *after* you found the gun, isn't that so?"

"No."

"When you finally got around to the papers you wanted her to sign, she didn't know what you were talking about, isn't that true?"

"Objection!" Smylie said. "Asked and answered!"

"Withdrawn," Connally said, waving a hand in disgust. Then he said, "If you considered the defendant a suspect, Sergeant Weber, why were you so hesitant to tell her that her husband was dead? Isn't it true that you were afraid that if you told her the facts of her husband's death, she'd be in shock? Isn't that what you really were worried about?"

Smylie was screaming. "Objection!"

Connally waved a hand again and said, "Withdrawn. That's all I have for this witness."

Smylie stood up, chewed on his lower lip for a moment, then said, "I have no questions."

The judge turned to Connally, who said, "We call Deputy Peter Quill, Your Honor."

A very nervous Peter Quill was brought into the courtroom. He hadn't heard what had transpired previously, but he knew he would be asked some very pointed questions by William Connally. Weber had discussed it with him last night.

Quill had been told what he must say.

C H A P T E R

15

REX KELSEY LOOKED AT GINA RIZZO'S CLUTTERED
living room and shook his head. There was hardly room
to move around. Boxes were stacked everywhere. Small
mountains of clothes, ranging from expensive cocktail
dresses to designer jeans, were stacked on top of the
boxes, the sofa, the chairs, some tables, and the few
open spaces left. Other bric-a-brac was piled on top of
the mountains of clothes. It was impossible to determine
what color the carpet was, such was the chaos.

"You just move in?" he asked.

Gina shook her full mane of golden hair. "Well, not
really. But I've been busy, you know? I work five days
a week, and what with the tennis and the aerobics and
everything else, there isn't much time, you know?"

"Yeah," Rex said.

"Would you like a cup of coffee?"

"Sure, that would be fine."

He took a seat at the kitchen table—the kitchen being the only room in the house where you could sit down—and appraised Gina as she prepared the coffee. She was fifty-six, Connally had said. That was a bit of a surprise. She didn't look it. More like forty-six. He looked for signs of a lift but saw none. The facial skin was too loose. No lift. Genetics. And careful avoidance of the sun. There were some wrinkles around the eyes, chin and neck, but the face was surprisingly youthful. Her wide eyes were carefully made up, and her body seemed firm and supple.

She wore a half-dozen gold chains around her neck. One of them held a thick gold crucifix. Another held a golden charm in the form of a tennis racket, a small pearl imbedded in the center. Three chains held nothing, but the last, the shortest, almost a choker, displayed a diamond—or was it a cubic zirconia?—that looked to be at least three carats. Had to be fake. Nobody would be dumb enough to wear a three-carat diamond around her neck on a small chain that could be ripped off with a single sharp tug.

The fingers of both hands displayed a variety of colorful rings that ranged from a large blue stone of some kind to a thin gold band nestled next to a diamond ring with a solitaire that looked to be as large as the stone around her neck. Clearly, the woman liked jewelry. Maybe they *were* real. Connally had said she owned a ton of California real estate. He'd also said she'd contributed a hundred grand toward Ann's bail within an hour after the banks opened.

She was loaded. But she worked as a saleswoman at a department store selling women's fashions for five bucks an hour plus commission. Maybe, in spite of everyone's claim to the contrary, her singing voice was gone, but a department store? Five bucks an hour?

Rex had decided to talk to some of Mrs. Cohen's friends today because she was in court. Her friends had wanted to be there, but Connally had insisted they stay home. This, he'd explained, was a motion, not a trial. Ann was pretty upset, he'd said, and he was afraid she'd come totally unglued if she saw friends and family in the courtroom. Maybe he was right.

Rex had hired two men to do the other legwork that was immediately required, the checking of every store along the route that Cohen had taken on the night her husband was killed. Connally was sure there would be someone who would have seen her, despite her claims to the contrary. Rex was just as sure the opposite was true and, not wanting to waste his time, had given the job to some other investigators he worked with from time to time, leaving himself the opportunity to talk to people who might really know something.

The coffee was ready. It was the instant kind. Gina put the cups on the table and stared at Kelsey.

"I appreciate your taking the time to talk with me," he said.

"It's okay," Gina said. "I don't go in until one. I want to help Ann in whatever way I can."

"You realize why I'm here?" he asked.

"Why you're here?"

"Yes."

"I think so. You want to know if I saw or heard anything that night that might help Ann. And, I suppose, to see if I had anything to do with Marty's killing. At least, that's what I gather after that wonderful little speech by your boss. Jeez! Give me a break! Why would any of us do such a thing? It's really crazy."

Rex smiled. "Did you see or hear anything that night?"

"I wish I did, but I was asleep. I never saw either of them."

Kelsey nodded. "What kind of guy was Marty?"

"Marty?"

"Yeah."

"He was a real—pardon the expression—shit. There's no other word for it. He treated everybody as though they didn't have a brain in their heads. He was an arrogant man. Really arrogant."

"Did you know he was kinky?"

"Kinky?"

"Yeah, kinky. Sexually. Did Ann ever talk to you about it?"

"Talk about it?"

Rex shifted in the chair, impatient with her nervous habit of repeating questions before answering them. He could understand why she was still single.

"Yeah," he said.

"Why do you want to know from me? Why don't you ask Ann?"

Rex sipped the coffee for a moment and then tapped a finger on the table. "Gina, if Mr. Connally is going to do the best for Ann, he needs to know everything there is to know. That's why he hired me. I ask a couple thousand questions, a lot of which might seem unimportant, and then he and I sit down and try to figure it all out.

It's a long slow process, but it works. So help me out, will ya?"

She stared out the window for a moment. Finally, after thinking it over, she said, "Yes, she talked about it. Just once. She loved that bastard and he was stringing her along like crazy. He knew which buttons to push, and he did it all the time. You know what really pisses me off?"

"What?"

"The goddam cops! They still haven't asked me a thing. You know why? They don't give a shit. They figure Ann did it and that's that. If they'd talk to people, they'd realize she couldn't have killed him. Jesus! If she was going to do it, she'd have done it three months ago."

"So she talked to you about it?"

Gina stared at him for a minute. "Are you really a detective? You sure don't look like one."

Kelsey grinned. It wasn't the first time he'd been asked that question. "I really am," he said, as he pulled out his credentials and showed them to her. "I realize most people think detectives all look like Tom Selleck, but the fact is, they don't. If you want the sad truth, most of us are fat, dumpy little guys who smoke cheap cigars and wear thick glasses. An ugly lot."

"I didn't mean to say you were ugly."

"I know. So Ann Cohen talked to you about Marty?"

"Marty? Yes."

"What did she say?"

"Say? Well, when Marty came home with marks all over his back, she was really in a bad way. I mean, she'd been married all that time and he'd never done anything like that before. It was really a hell of a shock."

"Did she ever express anything but shock?"

"Shock? What do you mean?"

"Did she ever express anger?"

"You mean like was she angry?"

"Yeah."

"Sure she was angry. What do you expect? But being angry and killing someone are two different things."

"Did she ever threaten to kill him?"

"Of course not! What's the matter with you? Are you working for her or against her?"

Rex waved a hand in the air. "Take it easy. I have to ask these questions. Sooner or later, the police will get around to asking them too. We don't want any surprises."

"Well, she never threatened to kill Marty. Ever! Like I told you, she loved him. Why, I'll never understand."

"What about the woman? The Winters woman. Did Ann ever threaten to kill her?"

Gina shook her head. "You just don't understand Ann. Ann would never threaten anyone. She isn't the violent type."

"She went down there one night. Did you know that?"

"Where?"

"To the Winters woman's house. She went down there and told her she'd kill her if she didn't stop seeing Marty. Did you know that?"

"That's bullshit! Ann would never do that."

Rex shifted the conversation to a different subject. "You said Marty was a shit. Can you give me a little more?"

"More? How much time do you have. A week?"

"That bad?"

"That bad. He was the worst!"

"Give me just a couple of examples."

"Examples? Well, he was always putting her down, you know? Like she was a real dummy. She's no dummy. Neither am I. But women get treated like that all the time, especially if they look good. What is with you guys anyway? Where did you get taught that beautiful women are stupid? Do they have a special course for men that we don't know about?"

"Not that I know of. So he treated her like she was a dummy?" He almost bit his tongue. He was starting to talk like Gina.

"Yeah," she said. "He'd do it in front of us, too. Sometimes we'd all get together—me, Della and Gene, Anita—we'd get together for dinner once in a while, usually at Della's place because she likes to cook, and Marty would get up as soon as he'd finished dinner and say he hadda go somewhere. He'd leave Ann there by herself, looking like an idiot. He did that a lot. He wouldn't ever enter into the conversation, you know? Like we were too boring. And when he did, it was just to tell us that we were all full of shit."

"Anything else?"

She hesitated for a moment. "Well, is this gonna come out in court?"

"What you tell me right now is off the record. Later, we'll decide what we need to put down. We'll ask you to sign what they call a deposition."

"Deposition? I know all about depositions. Jesus! Try getting a divorce in California. You'll know from depositions."

"You're from California?"

"Not originally. I was brought up in New York."

He'd had a hunch she would say that. He sipped the coffee, played with his glasses for a moment, and then said, "Anything you don't want to come out will stay secret, unless we all agree that it will help Ann." It seemed to satisfy her. She looked at the rings on her right hand for a moment, sighed, and then said, "Well, Marty was a real hustler, you know?"

"In what way?"

"What way? In every way. Besides his regular business, he was always working some real estate deal on the side. And he came on to every woman he met, including me."

"He did?"

"Yeah. Lots of times. When he was hot for someone's bod, he could be a real charmer. That was the only time he ever smiled, when he was on the make. He told me— it was up at the club; he was real smooth—he talked about how rotten my ex was for leaving me like that, and how beautiful I was, and how I turned him on."

"So what did you say?"

"What did I say? I told him where the truck stopped, that's what I said. Ann's my friend. I wasn't about to sleep with her husband. Jesus! Give me a break here! Besides, he was a shit. Even if I didn't know Ann from a hole in the ground, I wasn't about to sleep with Marty Cohen. Jesus!"

"Did you tell Ann?"

"Ann? No. What am I going to say? Hey, Ann! Your husband wants to sleep with me. Besides, you guys are all the same. Your boss is no better on that score."

Rex's eyebrows rose. "Mr. Connally?"

"Sure. He made a pass at me, once or twice."

"Really? And?"

"And? What do you mean and? He isn't married. I'm not married, so what difference does it make?"

"Anybody else know?"

Her face reddened slightly. "No. I didn't talk about it to anybody. Or about Marty either. I was afraid, at least in the case of Marty, that it might get back to Ann."

"And you had no idea he was kinky? Marty, I mean."

"Not until Ann told me."

Rex shifted in the wooden chair. "Can you think of anybody who would have a reason to make Ann look like she did it? Anybody here have a beef with her?"

"Ann? No way. She's one of the most caring people you'll ever want to meet. She's really sweet. She cares about everybody. She's on the board of directors of the homeowners association here, you know. There's no money in it, she just does it because she gives a shit. That's all. God! When I first moved in here five years ago, she came over and made me feel like a friend right off."

"You've been here five years? In this house?"

She realized what she'd said and blushed more deeply. "Okay, so I'm a little slow getting things put away. As soon as I have some time, I'll get around to it."

Rex waved a hand. "Hey," he said, "I'm not here to give you action. You can do whatever you want. So you can't think of anyone who had a beef with Ann."

Gina shook her head. "A beef with Ann? No. No one. There'd be no reason to. The only person that ever gave Ann a hard time was her asshole husband."

Kelsey ran a finger over his lips for a moment and

then said, "Okay, Gina. You've been a big help. If I need to talk to you again, I'll let you know."

"Any time."

He got up and headed toward the front door. Then he turned. "By the way, I have five of your albums. They're just about worn out. They ever gonna reissue your stuff on compact disk?"

She positively glowed. "Oh, you have my albums? Well, I don't know about them being reissued, but I can lend you some tapes sometime if you want to make some dupes. I have lots of tapes."

"I just might do that," he said, as he went out the door.

If Gina Rizzo was ostentatious, Anita Phillips was just the opposite. She wore no jewelry other than a simple thin gold necklace. The Ten Million Dollar Woman, Connally had called her. She was attractive, bright, pleasant, and cooperative. Her villa was furnished tastefully but inexpensively. If you didn't know, you'd never guess that this woman had money. She greeted Kelsey warmly and showed him to the living room. In the distance, the investigator could hear the sound of a man snoring. Anita heard it too and explained.

"That's an old friend of my father's who just happened to be in the area. I'm afraid he had a little too much to drink last night."

Rex smiled, nodded, and opened his notebook. "I appreciate your seeing me this morning, Mrs. Phillips. I know you have a company to run, so I'll keep it as short as possible."

"Please, call me Anita. We're all very concerned about

Ann. Whatever we can do to help, we'll do. It's terrible what the police have done. Just terrible. Ann's not capable of murder."

"That's what I hear from everyone. She seems well-liked."

"For good reason. She's a sweetheart. Just a sweetheart."

"Did you see or hear anything that night?"

She shook her head. "No. I normally work long hours. When I get home, I usually retire quite early."

Not always, he thought, listening to the snores in the background. "Can you think of anyone who might have a reason to kill Ann's husband?"

"I can think of quite a few," she said without hesitation. "He was a liar and a cheat. He cost a lot of people a lot of money."

Rex was immediately interested. "How so?"

"Well, Marty was a developer of structured retirement centers. His specialty was forming limited partnerships, buying the land, getting the necessary zoning approvals, then selling the entire project to established organizations, sometimes for a profit, sometimes at a loss. It didn't matter to Marty. As a general partner, he took his cut off the top.

"He sold limited partnerships to a couple of young hustlers who were new at the game. The property they were going to develop was restricted use! Practically useless. He got the suckers to sign a waiver he'd prepared. A disclosure notice of some sort. In any case, when they found out they were use-restricted, they sued, but they lost. They've been a little upset ever since."

"Upset enough to kill him?"

"Possibly."

"Do you know their names?"

"I did, but I can't remember them now. You could find their names in the court records."

"How do you know all this?"

She laughed. "Because Marty tried to involve *me* in that deal, for six hundred thousand dollars. I didn't even look at the papers, just gave them to my attorney, who immediately noticed the waiver. When I confronted Marty, he said he was unaware of either the restrictions or the waiver. Of course, he was lying through his teeth.

"When a friend of mine told me about the two rich youngsters who'd been taken, I almost volunteered to be a witness for the plaintiffs, but because he was Ann's husband I demurred. Pity. Marty should have lost that case. He was a crook."

"Your attorney—was that Mr. Connally?"

"No. I used his firm for my divorce, but they're too expensive for routine stuff. My attorney is a man named Bruce Graham. You know him?"

"No, I don't. How long ago was this?"

"About two years ago."

Rex made a note. Then he said, "You said you could mention a number of people. Who else?"

She shrugged. "I'm sure if you go over Marty's files, you'll find any number of people who had an ax to grind with Marty. He was *not* a nice person. How Ann put up with him, I'll never know. People are amazing, especially women. They let themselves be trampled. I just don't understand it."

"Did Marty ever make a pass at you?"

She seemed unsurprised at the question. "Marty was a sexual jock. He made a pass at me more than once. I think he tried to bed every woman in the complex at one time or another. We used to laugh about it."

"Seems he was taking a chance. Did you mention it to Ann?"

"No. Ann seemed oblivious to Marty's deceit, but I think she really knew what he was about. There was no point in rubbing her nose in it. As for Marty, I think he was aware of Ann's self-deception and gambled that she would refuse to believe anyone who tried to enlighten her. He was probably right. Ann's one of those poor, religiously inculcated women who still live in another century, believing that marriage is forever. Such drivel!"

"You don't?"

"Of course not. My husband was a power-hungry egomaniac who treated me very badly. He was the one who wanted the divorce, not me. He wanted to be a kid again. At first I fought it, but now that I'm on my own, I realize what a favor he did me. I like it this way. If I ever get married again, it will be to a sweet, understanding, loving, considerate, sensitive man who couldn't care less about money and power. And if he ever pulls any of this macho crap on me, he'll be out on his ass. I have no illusions. I won't waste my time on men who are seduced by their own self-importance. I've got enough money, and I don't need the crap that goes along with the successful man. Not now, not ever."

Rex scratched his head for a moment. Then he said, "I can't figure out whether you're a fan of Ann's or not. Mr.

Connally said you put up a hundred and fifty thousand of her bail money, but you've indicated that you think she's—"

Anita cut him off. "Don't put words in my mouth. I would have put up the entire amount, except for the fact that my doing so would have put some noses out of joint around here. As for Ann, I love her dearly, but that doesn't mean I'm blind to her faults. Nobody's perfect, Rex: not you, and not your esteemed boss, either."

"Mr. Connally?"

"None other."

"Why do you say that?"

She sighed and shook her head. "No reason. I just don't particularly like him, that's all."

"May I ask why?"

She grinned. "He's just another egomaniac."

Rex closed his notebook and stood up. "I appreciate the time, Anita. If I have anything else, I'll be back."

"I hope so," she said. "I look forward to seeing you again, Rex."

She held out her hand. Rex took it and shook it gently. It was a warm hand, and dry. The index finger was massaging his wrist. Just as her eyes were massaging his face.

Anita Phillips was one hot lady.

Rex spent the next few hours talking to various other members of the Clusters community, with much the same result. They all thought the world of Ann and despised Marty. Lots of possible suspects, but why would anyone who liked Ann want to frame her for her husband's murder?

Seeking a change of pace, Kelsey drove to the home of Gloria Simmons, Elizabeth Winters's friend. She wasn't home.

He consulted his notebook, then drove to Clyde's Place, a gulfside restaurant where Winters had worked with her friend. Clyde's was an old barnlike building close to Clearwater Beach and, like most places on the beach, catered to a younger crowd. They were there in force in their bathing suits, their bodies trim and tanned, drinking beer and eating hamburgers.

The guy standing behind the cash register looked like a wrestler, complete with long, curly golden locks that almost covered his face. "I'm looking for Gloria Simmons," Kelsey said.

"What for?"

"I'm a friend of her brother up in Jersey. He said I should say hello."

Gorgeous George pointed to the salad bar. "She's over there fillin' up the trays. Make it fast, pal. She's got a lot to do."

"Right."

Gloria Simmons could have been Elizabeth Winters's sister. They were both very large ladies.

"My name is Rex Kelsey," he said, as he stood beside her, displaying his two-hundred-watt smile.

"What can I do for you?" she asked, not looking up.

"I'm a private investigator," he said, "working for William Connally."

That got her attention, fast. "You get out of here," she yelped.

"I just want to ask you a couple of questions," Rex said. "It won't take a minute."

"I've got nothin' to say to you, asshole," she said, her face red with anger.

"Hey!"

It was the wrestler, moving toward Kelsey with catlike grace. Gloria Simmons looked over Kelsey's shoulder and said, "Clyde, this asshole's a private cop workin' for the bitch that killed Liz. Throw him the hell out of here, will ya?"

Rex turned to face the man. He held up his hands and said, "Take it easy, friend. If Gloria doesn't want to talk, that's fine with me. Let's not get excited."

"Out!" the man ordered.

Maybe Connally was right, Rex thought, as he fired up the car and pulled out of the parking lot. Connally'd said he figured the hit came from the Winters side of the equation. Nah! That was crazy. It had to be the Cohen woman.

There was another person he wanted to see, the man who had encouraged Marty to move to Florida, and since the office was only a few blocks away, Rex decided to drop in on Andy Duggan, now vice-president of Exclusive Properties, Inc.

Duggan greeted him warmly and showed him to a seat in his large office. "What can I do for you, Mr. Kelsey?"

Rex handed Duggan a business card. "I'm a private investigator looking into the Marty Cohen murder. Since he worked here, I thought maybe you could—"

Duggan started laughing before Rex could finish. "Marty? Marty hasn't worked here for over two years."

"I beg your pardon?"

Duggan laughed again and leaned back in his chair.

"Marty was a hustler, you know? A born hustler. He left us two years ago and went out on his own. Oh, he worked a few deals with me every year"—his eyebrows rose—"solid stuff, you know? We don't play the kind of games Marty played."

"Why would he deal with you if he was on his own?"

Duggan shrugged. "This isn't for publication, and if you try to make me repeat it I'll deny it, but—"

"Yes?"

"I think Marty was conning everybody, including his wife and the IRS. On paper, he wanted it to look like he was still working for us. I don't know how he handled his own stuff, and I don't wanna know, but I know he was doing it."

"Did he have a partner?"

Duggan shrugged. "I don't know for sure, but I think he worked alone. He had to have had a lawyer, but I don't know who it was. He never said."

"How much did he put through you?"

Duggan opened a file drawer, removed a folder, and glanced at it. Then he turned and said, "Last year we paid him ninety-four thousand bucks."

"And he was making more on his own?"

"He sure as hell was," Duggan said. "He was a slick one, Marty was. I taught him the business. He used to be an accountant, did you know that?"

"Yeah."

"Well, he was a fast learner. I could never have pulled the shit he did. I don't have the balls for it. Marty was different. A real true-blue prick, but one helluva sales-man."

CHAPTER

16

"DEPUTY QUILL," WILLIAM CONNALLY SAID, "WILL you tell us exactly what happened on the morning of July eighth when you visited the home of the defendant?"

Peter Quill cleared his throat for a moment, glanced at Ann, and said, "Yes. Sergeant Weber and I arrived at Mrs. Cohen's home just before four in the morning. We noticed that the lights were on inside. We also noticed that her car had recently been driven. Having been told by Sergeant Murray that she was considered a suspect, we were very careful. We knocked on the door. When she answered, she was fully dressed.

"Sergeant Weber asked her if we could come in and talk to her. She gave her permission. Then he read her the Miranda card and asked if she understood it. She said she did. He got her to sign a waiver and started to question her. Then—"

Connally cut him off. "Your testimony is that he Mirandized the defendant before questioning her?"

"Yes, he did."

"How did the defendant appear to you?"

Quill hesitated for a moment, then said, "She seemed a bit drunk."

"Anything else?"

"I don't know what you mean."

"Well, was she angry? Upset? Confused? Happy to see you two handsome men? What?"

"She seemed upset. I figured it was because she'd just killed her husband."

Connally cursed under his breath and said, "Motion to strike, Your Honor."

Judge Clark nodded, made a notation, and said, "Just answer the questions, Deputy Quill."

"Yes, Your Honor."

Quill's hand was beginning to tremble slightly. In order to steady it, he placed it on the barrier in front of the witness chair. Connally stared at the hand for a moment, made a note in his loose-leaf binder, then asked, "When did you tell her that you wanted her to identify the body of her husband, before or after you questioned her?"

"After."

"Why?"

"Because she was a suspect."

"If she was a suspect, why didn't you just Mirandize her, tell her she was a suspect, and take her to the police station?"

"I don't know. You'll have to ask Sergeant Weber."

"I'm asking you, Deputy!"

Quill looked increasingly uncomfortable. "Sergeant Weber was in charge. I was just there. I don't know why he did it."

Connally took a step toward the witness chair, then stopped. "Isn't it a fact that you wanted to question her first because you knew that once you advised her of the death of her husband she'd be too upset to answer any questions?"

"No. Besides, I wasn't making the decision."

"But you were there."

"Yes."

"Tell the Court exactly what the defendant did or said when she was told that her husband had been murdered."

Quill looked at Ann again, then tore his gaze away. "She seemed surprised."

"Surprised?"

"Yes."

"What did she say?"

"She said we were crazy, I think."

"And then you took her downtown?"

"Yes."

"I have no further questions, Your Honor."

Judge Clark looked at Connally in surprise. Then, the judge turned to Smylie, who simply shook his head.

"You're excused."

Quill got up and walked quickly out of the courtroom. Connally's eyes never left him until he was out of sight. Finally, the lawyer turned back to the judge and said, "Call Robert Post."

A short, thin, bearded man was brought into the courtroom, sworn in, and directed to the witness chair. Connally, his knuckles white from gripping the lectern so tightly, said, "Mr. Post, tell the Court exactly what you do for a living."

"I'm a professional graphologist. A handwriting expert."

"Thank you. You've testified on behalf of the State in many trials, is that not true?"

"Yes, I have."

Connally turned to Smylie and said, "Will the State stipulate that the witness is an expert in handwriting analysis?"

Smylie frowned, rose slowly to his feet, and said, "So stipulated, Your Honor."

Connally walked to the clerk's desk and picked up several pieces of paper. "With the Court's permission, I would like to show the witness Defense exhibit one and State's exhibits one through three, Your Honor."

"Go ahead."

Connally folded the first of the papers so that only the signature was visible, then held it in front of the witness. "Mr. Post," he said, "have I asked you prior to this hearing to give an opinion on any handwriting samples?"

"No."

"I have shown you no samples whatsoever?"

"That is correct."

Connally handed the paper to Post. "I want you to examine the signature on this paper and explain what it says about the person who wrote it."

Post looked at the signature and said, "It's too small

a sample to give you much of an opinion. I'd need a lot more."

"I understand. Just do what you can with what you've got."

Post shrugged and said, "I can see that it is the signature of a woman. That's obvious."

"What can you tell us about that woman?"

"Not much. She seems to be a bit nervous from the looks of this. Frightened, I'd say. The way the 'h' is collapsing, and the lack of smooth lines—"

"That's fine." Connally took the paper from the witness and said, "The analysis refers to the signature I asked the defendant to make earlier this morning. Now," he continued, "please look at the other three signatures." He folded the other three documents—the documents Ann had signed at the time of her interrogation—the same way as the first one and handed them to Post. Post looked them over.

"What do they tell you?" Connally asked.

"They are very different. I mean, different from the first one you showed me. These are all similar to one another, but not to the first one."

"Are they signed by the same person?"

"I'd say they were."

"What do they tell you."

"Offhand, I'd say that the person who did this was really quite intoxicated, or possibly under the influence of drugs."

Connally beamed. "Would you say the person who wrote those signatures was in full control of her faculties?"

"I can't say that. Certainly, there is evidence of impairment. I can only say that there is no form to the signatures. They were done hastily, with no attention to accuracy. The signer was clearly in a hurry."

"You said that the signatures were made by a woman. You also said that she was either drunk or under the influence of drugs. If that is true, she wouldn't be in control of her faculties, isn't that so?"

"Objection! Leading!"

"Withdrawn. Mr. Post, surely you can be a little more specific. You've testified that the signatures were done in a hurry, by a woman who was either drunk or under the influence of drugs. Can you be a little more specific as to the woman's mental state?"

Post hesitated for a moment, then said, "I'd say that the woman who signed these was pretty confused."

The glow on Connally's face got brighter. "Thank you, Mr. Post." He turned to Smylie and said, "Your witness."

Smylie shook his head. "We have no questions, Your Honor."

Connally said, "We have no other witnesses, Your Honor."

"Mr. Smylie?"

"We call Mrs. Catherine Pollard to the stand."

Cathy Pollard was brought back into the courtroom. Smylie took his position and said, "Mrs. Pollard, on the night of May twenty-fourth, you and Mrs. Cohen paid a visit to Mrs. Elizabeth Winters at her home, located at 1184 Felcher Avenue in Palm Harbor. Isn't that true?"

Cathy looked distraught. In a voice filled with anguish, she said, "Yes."

"And on that visit, you and the defendant talked directly with Elizabeth Winters, isn't that true?"

"Yes."

"Tell the court what was said."

"I don't remember exactly."

Smylie moved from behind the lectern to the left of it and leaned casually against the jury box. "Isn't it true that you signed a statement on July eighth to the effect that you had witnessed the defendant making a threat on the life of Elizabeth Winters?"

Looking for a hole to crawl into, Cathy slowly nodded her head. "Yes."

"Do you want me to get the deposition to refresh your memory?"

Cathy shook her head. Tears were beginning to spill down her cheeks. "No," she said. "I remember."

"Please tell the Court what you remember."

Cathy told them, slowly, agonizingly. Ann had been told her husband was messing around with Elizabeth Winters and had decided to confront the woman. Cathy had gone with her to provide moral support. Ann had told the woman that if she didn't stop seeing Marty she'd kill her.

When Cathy was finished with her testimony, she looked dreadful. Then it was Connally's turn.

"Mrs. Pollard," he said softly, "before the defendant made the actual threat, did she discuss what she was going to say with you?"

"Objection," Smylie said quietly. "Irrelevant."

"On the contrary, Your Honor, it goes to the intent of the threat."

Smylie was on his feet. "Your Honor, the fact is, the

threat was made. Whether or not the threat was intended to be taken seriously has no bearing. The police acted on the knowledge that a threat had been made, and that is all we have to prove."

Judge Clark nodded. "Objection sustained."

Connally took a different tack. "Isn't it true that after the threat was made there were more incidents involving Martin Cohen and Elizabeth Winters?"

"Objection," Smylie repeated. "Again, no relevance."

"Sustained."

Connally tried again. "Did the defendant say anything to you about the threat at the time it was made?"

"Objection!"

"Sustained! Mr. Connally, move along." Judge Clark's ears were becoming quite red. Almost as red as Connally's face. The lawyer noticed it immediately. It was time to quit. There was no point to going any further. Whether or not his motion was upheld, there was no point in intimidating the judge to the point where it might affect a trial that would be heard before the very same man. And he had learned something. Peter Quill's shaking hand indicated that the young cop had lied on the stand, which could prove useful. "Thank you," Connally said. "That's all I have for this witness, Your Honor."

Judge Clark looked at Smylie and asked, "Do you have another witness, Mr. Smylie?"

"No, Your Honor."

"Very well. You want to sum up, Mr. Connally?"

"Yes, Your Honor. I move that the Court suppress any and all evidence obtained during the search of the defendant's home. The search was illegal on two counts.

In the first place, there was no probable cause to conduct a search of the defendant's home. Notwithstanding the fact that a reading of rights may or may not have been carried out, it is moot, since the defendant should not have been approached at all. The police officers should have simply advised the defendant that her husband had been murdered and taken her downtown to identify the body.

"The lack of a search warrant renders the evidence gathered inadmissible. We further contend that the defendant was traumatized earlier in the evening, making her unable to give informed consent to anything, and her alleged consent to search is invalid as a result of that traumatization. She was legally incompetent to give permission to search. Again, that makes the search an illegal one. The evidence found is inadmissible.

"I would like to point out that the evidence found during the search is key. Without it, the subsequent arrest of the defendant is not likely to have occurred. I therefore ask for suppression of the evidence and a dismissal of the charges against the defendant. My case law is attached to the motion."

The judge nodded to Smylie, who stood up and walked toward the lectern, passing Connally on the way.

"Your Honor," he said, "the motion before you is frivolous at best. It is simply an attempt by counsel for the defendant to muddy the waters. The officers arrived at her home at three-forty-seven on the morning of July eighth and examined evidence that was readily available. Her car, sitting outside in the open, was found to have been recently driven, even though the hour was late. When the officers arrived at the defendant's home, they were cognizant of the fact that two felonies had been committed. The officers had the right to ask questions of the defendant. The defendant was found dressed and awake. The officers took reasonable and prudent care to ensure that the defendant's rights were protected. They asked for and received permission to enter the defendant's home. They asked for and received permission to ask questions. They advised the defendant of her rights and she signed a waiver to that effect. They asked about a gun and secured the defendant's written permission to examine it. They determined that the gun had been recently fired. That's all. There was no search.

"The defendant was well aware of the sexual activities of her husband. Therefore, she could not have been traumatized by what she saw through the window. If she was confused, it was because of her drunkenness. The defendant was not arrested until after evidence, voluntarily provided after a reading of rights, was examined. At the time of her actual arrest, she was again read her rights and expressed her desire to consult with an attorney, and all questioning stopped.

"The evidence should not be suppressed. The police acted with all due and reasonable care. The motions should be dismissed. I also have case law to support our position."

Smylie handed his papers to the clerk.

Judge Clark leaned forward and said, "I'll reserve judgment on this until I've had a chance to review the submissions. My decision will be posted with the Clerk of the Court as soon as I have made it. You have another motion, Mr. Connally?"

"Yes, Your Honor. We move that bond be reduced. Preferably that the defendant be released on her own recognizance until such time as you have made your ruling."

Judge Clark looked at Smylie, who said, "The State requests that present bond be revoked, Your Honor. The defendant is charged with two counts of first degree murder. We seek pretrial detention."

Judge Clark looked at some papers for a moment, then said, "I'll wait until the grand jury makes its decision. Bond is continued at five hundred thousand dollars. Court is adjourned."

An hour later, Ann and Bill were sitting in his magnificent office, sipping white wine and discussing what had taken place earlier in the day. As they talked, Bill glanced through some papers that had been placed on his desk. His eyes grew cold as he gave his attention to one particular page. Impulsively, Ann got up from her chair, walked over to him, and kissed him on the cheek. "Thank you, Bill. Thank you so much."

He looked up into her eyes. "It's just begun," he said gravely, patting her lightly on the cheek. "I think Judge Clark will rule against us, but we still have a lot of things in our favor. The grand jury, the preliminary hearing—all of it takes time, and time is on our side. My investigator is hard at work, and he's making some progress. I'm sure he'll turn up something significant quite soon. Make no mistake, Ann. I will save you from this. Trust me."

She smiled wanly. "I do trust you, Bill. And I know you'll save me. I don't know what I'd have done without your help. To go to a stranger ..." Her voice trailed off as she stood by the window looking at the panoramic view.

"Ann," he said softly. She turned and faced him, noting his face pinched in pain. "What is it?" she asked.

"While we were in court today, my associates were making arrangements for Martin's funeral."

A look of agony clouded her eyes. "Oh ... yes."

"The body has finally been released. We've managed to stop Martin's mother from taking his remains back to Chicago. We also talked to Rabbi Markowitz, and he's assured us that no special dispensation needs to be granted to allow the funeral to be held tomorrow morning, right here in Palm Harbor. You'd said you wanted it private but available to his ... friends."

"Yes."

He sighed. "Well, it's all set," he said. "We've gotten an order requiring the press to stay at least five hundred feet away, but that only applies to private property, the cemetery itself. We can't keep them away from public property."

"I understand."

"I'm not sure you do," he said. "The press has taken an inordinate interest in this case. Martin's mother has been saying things that are—well, unconscionable."

Ann removed a small white handkerchief from her handbag and dabbed at her eyes. "She never liked me," she said. "She always insisted that I was the reason Marty divorced his first wife. She always thought—a thought freely expressed on a hundred occasions— that I seduced Marty while he was a happily married man. It wasn't true, of course, but nothing Marty or I said would ever change her mind. I can imagine what she has to say."

Connally sipped his wine for a moment. "In any case, I can't keep her away from the funeral."

"I wouldn't want you to."

"I know. I just want you to be aware that there's likely to be a nasty scene. Martin's mother strikes me as being emotionally unstable. The press will be there in force, using telephoto lenses to take photographs from outside the grounds."

Ann smiled at him. "You're really trying to protect me from everything, aren't you? That's very sweet, Bill, but I'll be all right. I really will."

"Well, I just—"

"You're not suggesting that I not attend?"

He waved a hand in the air. "Not at all. You must attend. That's just it."

"I understand, Bill. I really do."

He gave a deep sigh. "Good."

Ann turned and looked out the window again.

For a few minutes neither of them spoke. Finally, Bill asked, "What are you thinking?"

Without turning her head, Ann said, "Thinking? I had a vision of Marty sitting in front of the television set, watching some baseball game. I remember how I used to resent it. I could take it now, him sitting there in front of the television. It would be better than—"

"Ann!" Connally exploded, slamming his hand on his desk with such force that it made her snap her head around. "Cut it out! You're romanticizing a marriage that never existed. This may not be the right moment to tell you this, but I can't help it. In truth, your husband was a terrible, terrible man. You've got to accept the reality of that fact."

Stunned by his sudden outburst, Ann simply stared at him.

"This may sound harsh," Bill said, continuing, "but whoever killed Marty did you a favor."

She stepped back as if he'd slapped her in the face. "Bill," she said, her face contorted by shock, "you mustn't say such things. Marty was sick. He—"

"Listen to me!" he thundered. "You're all wrapped up in grief over a man who cheated on you in every imaginable way. You think that Marty was involved exclusively with Elizabeth Winters. Well, he wasn't. He had a score of girlfriends. My investigator has discovered that Marty was screwing women all over town. He even made passes at your closest friends."

Ann's eyes widened. "They never—"

"Mentioned it to you? You're right. They never said a word because they thought you knew what Marty was all about. That isn't the worst of it, though. Forget for a moment that Marty betrayed your trust by his sexual exploits. Forget that he was a degenerate. He was worse than that. He was a thief. He robbed you!"

Ann's face was contorted by confusion.

"How much money did Marty earn last year?" Bill asked.

"What?" Ann couldn't get her brain to function.

"How much money did Marty earn?" Bill repeated.

Ann tried to think. "It varied. I think last year . . . I think he made just under eighty-four thousand. It wasn't a very good year."

"Wrong!" Connally said, picking up some of the papers

from his desk and waving them in front of her. "My investigator has turned up evidence that Marty made at least two hundred and fifty thousand dollars last year, and we haven't talked to everyone yet."

Ann's eyes widened in shock. "That can't be right."

"It *is* right," he said. "Marty was cheating you financially as well as sexually. He's been a compulsive gambler for years. Most of the money he earned was never reported to the IRS, and since you signed the goddam income tax forms, if there's ever an audit you'll be on the hook for hundreds of thousands of dollars. You're an accountant, so I don't have to brief you on how that little game goes. Marty may have destroyed you, Ann, without your even knowing it."

Bill slammed his hand on the desk again.

"He doesn't deserve your grief, Ann. He never deserved your love. You've got to see him for what he really was. A selfish, grasping, greedy maggot. You understand?"

She stared at him in stunned silence. The lawyer's face was red, his eyes cold and harsh, his hands formed into fists. Then, quickly, the anger faded away and he rose to his feet.

"I'm sorry, Ann. I shouldn't yell at you. It's just—well, you must accept the reality of what's been going on. You've been throwing your life away for nothing. You have to stop feeling sorry for a man who tried to ruin your life."

"No one ever told me about any gambling . . . or extra income. Marty always let me manage the money. He said I was so good at it. I . . . I had no idea. Are you sure?"

"Positive."

"I—" She found herself unable to speak.

The anger in Connally's face was completely gone now, replaced by a look of deep concern. "You deserved better, Ann," he said softly. "Much better. That may sound cruel right now, but it's true. The sooner you face reality, the better off you'll be. The days ahead will be tough, really tough. You'll need to be tough to get through them. I only mean to help you, Ann. That's all I'm trying to do." The smile was back on his face. "You understand?"

"I'm not sure," she said, in a voice that was barely audible.

Bill ushered a very shaken Ann slowly out of his office, arranged for Bannister to take her home, then went back to his office and grabbed the phone. He placed a call to Rex. Rex wasn't in. Bill told Kelsey's service to beep the detective. Three minutes later Kelsey returned the call.

"How'd it go in court?" Rex asked.

"Not good," Bill answered, "but you're moving right along. I read your notes. Terrific stuff."

"Thanks."

"I want you to do something."

"Yes?"

"There was a cop. One of the arresting officers. Deputy named Peter Quill. He lied his head off in court today. I just know it. I think he was coerced. I want you to lean on him a little."

Rex sounded unenthusiastic. "If he lied in court, he sure as hell won't tell me about it."

"Maybe, maybe not," Bill countered. "He seems like

a rookie. I think he could be an ally. I don't want you to confront him, I just want you to make him a friend. You're good at that kind of stuff, Rex."

Kelsey laughed, then said, "I'll see what I can do."

"Good. Let me know as soon as possible."

"I will."

Bill hung up the phone, leaned back in his chair, and looked out the window. He thought about Ann and the call he'd received from her the day before the murders. She was ready to institute divorce proceedings, she'd said. Fat chance. Marty would have talked her out of it somehow, the bastard.

It was going well, he thought.

All of it.

CHAPTER

17

AS HER TIRED FATHER SNOOZED IN THE GUEST BED-
room, Ann Cohen sat at the kitchen table, a cup of coffee
in her hands, and watched the squirrels as they cavorted
in the trees, oblivious to her mountain of misery.

The funeral was over, thank God.

It had been awful. As the limo had entered and left the
grounds, an army of reporters and photographers had
almost blocked it, a mob screaming garbled questions
at her as she sat in the back seat, hidden behind heavily
tinted glass.

At graveside, Marty's mother had created her expected
scene. She'd rushed toward Ann with her hands raised in
the air, yelling at the top of her lungs, "Murderer! Killer!"
before she was pulled away by Marty's children.

The children were grown now. All three, bless them,

had made a point of telling her they knew she couldn't have murdered their father. She suspected Susan had put them up to it, Susan being the one she'd always been the closest to. No matter. She'd found strength in their words. And she'd gained additional strength from the support she'd been given by her friends: Gina, Della, Anita, Cathy, and the rest.

Poor Cathy, she thought. Still filled with shame for having seemingly become a Judas. It wasn't so, Ann had told her again today, but the self-imposed guilt weighed heavily on Cathy's narrow shoulders.

None of Marty's so-called friends had attended the funeral except for Andy Duggan, who went around slapping people on the back and smiling as though this were some sales conference. He'd given Ann his condolences with a hearty handshake and a bright smile, in the manner of a co-conspirator.

Ann's brother had been there too. Paolo, the aloof one, had arrived the night before. At first, he'd been sympathetic, but at dinner, with just Ann and her father, Paolo had acted like a prosecutor, hurling a barrage of insensitive questions at Ann until her father had told him to shut up. He had, but the look in his eyes betrayed him. No matter his protestations to the contrary, it was clear to Ann that Paolo thought her guilty. When he'd flown back to Seattle immediately after the funeral, she'd felt relieved.

The next few days flew by until over a week had passed since the events that had irrevocably altered the course of Ann Cohen's life. For Ann, it had been a week of mind-numbing shock, terrifying encounters with the criminal justice system and spirit-draining exposure in the media.

Judge Clark had made his ruling on Bill's motions. As Bill had cautioned, both had been denied. Yesterday, Ann had stood in court yet another time, as the actual charges had been entered by Jeff Smylie and Ted Leland. Smylie was first among equals on this two-man prosecution team aligned against her. Smylie was the talker, Bill had said; the taciturn Leland was the strategy man, the legal eagle, the man who would tell the bellicose Smylie when to make his moves.

Bill had waived the reading of the charges, but Ann knew what they were. Eight separate charges, the most severe of which were the first-degree-murder charges. The others were just fluff, designed to encourage Bill to seek some sort of accommodation with Smylie.

Bill had pleaded her not guilty and again asked for bond to be reduced. Smylie had countered with a request that bond be revoked. In the end, Judge Clark had continued the bail at five hundred thousand dollars.

One more skirmish. One more exposure in front of an increasingly obstreperous and growing phalanx of unfeeling media vultures.

Ever since her arrest, Ann had been plagued by nightmares, often waking up in the middle of the night sweating profusely, her body rigid with fear, trapped in that tiny moment when the unconscious mind has not yet yielded to the reality of consciousness. In a matter of seconds, she would realize that she was experiencing yet another nightmare, but for long agonizing minutes the terror of the hallucination—the physical pain, the pounding heart, the shortness of breath—would keep her immobilized, lying stiffly in bed, wondering if it would ever end.

There were times when her cries brought her father on the run from the guest room. He would wake her, hold her in his arms as he had done so often when she was a child, brush her sweat-dampened hair with a large but gentle hand, and whisper words of endearment in her ear. "It's just a dream, baby. You're having a nightmare. You'll be all right." He'd stay with her until she'd calmed down.

Now she faced another critical moment. The grand jury was examining the case, making a decision on whether or not to indict her for murder. If they did, it could mean a return to jail. Bill had again cautioned her that the indictments were all but a certainty, but he also said he doubted bail would be revoked. There was no cause, he'd said.

While waiting for the grand jury to decide, Ann thought it would be wise to return to work. Perhaps, she thought, the concentration required would force her mind to travel other paths. Paths filled with columns of numbers. She could lose herself in numbers. It would be the best therapy she could imagine.

So ten days after the murder of her husband, Ann Cohen rose early and took a long, hot shower. She spent a full half hour drying and setting her hair, another half hour dressing and applying her makeup.

When she was done, she looked in the mirror and was pleased with what she saw. The makeup, skillfully applied, covered many of the deep furrows in her brow, and drops had brought some sparkle to her eyes. Even her father seemed pleased. As she left the house, she was relieved to find that the reporters had finally departed from the entrance to the Clusters compound, after hanging around for an entire week.

When she arrived at the office, Cathy hugged her and told her how wonderful she looked. Most of the others greeted her warmly as well, but Ann could detect a new remoteness. The smiles were there, but they were the kind of smiles that were given clients, not the smiles that were reserved for friends.

She placed her purse on her desk and headed for the office of Lou Holt, managing director of this ten-man satellite office. Ann rapped on the glass door and smiled. As usual, Holt was seated stiffly at his desk, sipping coffee and looking over a stack of computer printouts. She'd called and told him she was coming in. He expected her.

"How are you?" he said, as he shook her hand and gestured to a chair in front of his large oak desk.

"Still a little shaky," Ann said candidly.

"I can imagine."

She crossed her legs and took a deep breath. "You know, for years, I've been in the habit of reading the morning paper before coming to work. Every day, there've been reports of murders and other crimes. I've seen a thousand faces staring out at me from those pages, and I've wondered what makes those people do such things. And then, one day, you look at the paper and you see your own face looking back at you. And you realize that people are looking at your face and wondering the same thing.

"It's almost unbearable. I feel as if I want to take out

a full-page ad and tell everyone I didn't do it. But even if I did, they probably wouldn't believe me. That's what I find so hard to take. The assumption by most people that I'm a killer." She shuddered. "Thank God, most of my friends have stood by me. But there have been others who look at me in a new way. I can almost read their minds. It's . . . awful."

"I'm sure it is," Holt said.

He removed his glasses and rubbed his eyes for a moment. Then he took a deep breath, looked at a painting hung on the wall, and said, "Ann, I'm sure you know I don't think for one minute that you had anything to do with any of this. It's a most unfortunate situation. I'm sure it will be cleared up eventually. But in the meantime, I've had some discussions with Atlanta. It appears that they have some concerns—"

Immediately, she was alert. "Concerns?"

Holt squirmed in his high-backed chair. "Well, there's been a considerable amount of publicity. The name of the firm has been mentioned a number of times. Atlanta feels that . . . "

"Yes?"

"I don't really know how to tell you this," Holt said, his voice strained.

Ann felt her cheeks redden in anger. "Let me try," she said. "They feel I'm an embarrassment to the firm. They want me out of here until I'm completely cleared. Is that it?"

Holt shook his head. "Worse than that, I'm afraid."

She looked at him in shock. "You mean I'm fired? Permanently?"

He looked at her sadly and nodded. "I argued quite

strenuously, Ann. I want you to know that. I find their actions unacceptable and reprehensible. But we are but a minor cog in the scheme of things. They insisted.

"I have negotiated, on your behalf, a rather generous severance settlement," he continued. "A full four months. That's three months more than is required. I realize it's little solace, but my hands are tied."

She stood up. "So . . . I'm fired."

He stood up. "I'm truly sorry, Ann. I wish I could—"

"Has my check been prepared?"

"Yes. I have it right here." He reached in his desk drawer and removed a white envelope, which he handed to her. "I can't tell you how much this distresses me, Ann. I—"

"Why did you let me come in to hear this? You could have told me on the telephone. A goddam letter would have been better. Damn you!"

She didn't wait to hear what else he had to say. She was already on her way down the hall. When she reached her desk, she opened a drawer, pulled out two long manila envelopes, and started filling them with her personal things. Cathy saw her through the glass in her own office and came running out. "What happened?"

"I've been fired."

"What?"

Ann continued stuffing the envelopes. "It figures, doesn't it?"

"Not to me. I'm going with you."

Ann grabbed her arm. "Cathy! Don't be silly. I realize you're trying to be a friend and I appreciate it. I really do. But you mustn't. This has nothing to do with you."

Cathy, her eyes blazing, pulled her arm away. "Yes,

it does. I have the right to work for whomever I want. There are lots of openings for a good accountant. You wait. We'll walk out of here together."

Before Ann could say another word, Cathy stormed off in the direction of Lou Holt's office. Everyone in the office could hear her voice. "You spineless jellyfish. Take this job and stuff it!"

Cathy returned, looked at Ann triumphantly, and threw some things in a small cardboard box. "Ready?" she said, her eyes still flashing.

Two hours later, Ann, Cathy, and Ann's father were sitting around the kitchen table, letting off steam, when the doorbell rang. Luigi said, "I'll get it." A moment later, he returned and asked, in a low voice, "Do you know a Clive Bennett?"

Ann looked at Cathy in surprise. Cathy answered for both of them. "He's—was—one of our biggest accounts," she said. "Ann and I did most of the monthly reports— and the annual statement, of course. He's here?"

"Yes," Luigi said. "He wants to talk to Ann. You want to see him?"

Ann shrugged. "He probably wants to offer his condolences. It's okay, Daddy. I'll see him."

She got up from the table and went to the door. The white-haired president of Bennett Industries, one of the county's largest commercial contractors, smiled at her. "Hello, Ann. May I talk to you for a moment?"

"Of course. Please come in."

She led him into the living room and showed him to a seat on the sofa.

"You're very kind to come by." He'd been a client for six years. A self-made millionaire, he'd started out laying stone and pouring "mud," as he called cement. He'd never finished high school, but he'd listened and learned and worked hard, and at age thirty-two he'd started his own company. That was thirty years ago. Now, despite his incredible success, he was the same man inside, more comfortable in boots and jeans than in expensive suits, happier discussing politics than debits and credits. He was one of Ann's favorite people, with his good humor, good ol' boy charm, and old-fashioned values.

Bennett leaned forward, patted her on the hand, and said, "I've been wanting to come by for a week, ever since I heard about the ... trouble, but I figured you'd had enough of people. It's a terrible thing, Ann. Just terrible. My heart goes out to you, it really does."

Again, Ann said, "You're very kind, Mr. Bennett. Thank you for taking the time to come by."

He made no move to leave. "I called you at work about an hour ago. Talked to Holt. He said you'd been let go. He said that Cathy walked out with you. Is that true? Is she here?"

"I'm afraid so," Ann said. "But there are a lot of good people left. I'm sure your account will be properly serviced."

Bennett shook his head. "Not by them, it won't. What are your plans?"

"My plans? What do you mean?"

"Where are you gonna work? You're still gonna work, aren't you? You're too good an accountant to give it up."

"I don't know," Ann said. "I haven't had a chance to think about it."

He was beaming. "Well, I have a suggestion."

"A suggestion?"

"Yes," he said. "Look, you and Cathy worked well together. You're a CPA. You probably know my business better'n I do. You've done one hell of a good job for years. I don't want to lose that. I'd like to see you hang out your own shingle. I'll be your first account. It ain't all you'll need, but it'll pay the light bill until you really get rolling. I'll even give you a retainer in advance, if it'll help."

She was stunned. "Mr. Bennett," she said, "I don't know what to say. I'm—well, frankly, I'm floored. Under normal circumstances I'd give it serious consideration, but the fact is I'm still under a very large cloud. According to my attorney, I will be facing a long trial in a few months. It's even possible I'll have to go to jail soon. If I did this, and there was—"

He held up a hand and cut her off. "Let's have none of that kind of talk. In the first place, you're no more a killer than I am. There's no way on God's green earth they're ever gonna find you guilty. In the second place, even if you have to take time to get this trial over with, Cathy could do the work, unless there's some reason why you wouldn't want to have her working for you."

"No, of course not. But—"

"Hey, Cathy!" Bennett yelled. "Come out here a minute."

Cathy and Ann's father came into the living room. Bennett stood up and shook hands with Ann's father as he was introduced. Then he shook hands with Cathy.

"Listen, Cathy," he said, as excited as a kid, "I been telling Ann I'd like to move my account. I'd like to see her and you get together and start your own business. That okay with you?"

Cathy looked as shocked as Ann. "I . . . it's not for me to say, Mr. Bennett. I mean, it would be up to Ann."

Bennett scowled. "I know that. I just want to know how you'd feel if she said it was a good idea."

Cathy, still taken aback, said, "I think it would be wonderful!"

Bennett turned to Ann. "Then there's nothing left to talk about. So your maiden name's Martino?"

"Yes."

"Good. With the publicity and all that, I don't think you want to be using the name Cohen. Why not use your maiden name? Call it Martino and Associates. Soon as you're set up, call me, and I'll get a check over to you. Don't take longer than a week. We got a lot to do."

"I don't know what to say," Ann said.

Bennett gripped her shoulder and squeezed it. "Say yes! That's all!"

Ann couldn't help it. Her face broke into a big grin. "All right. I'll say yes."

Bennett stood up and stuck out his hand. "Great. And congratulations. If you have any trouble finding a good office, you let me know. I have lots of friends in that business."

Luigi Martino shook Bennett's hand. "Mr. Bennett, I imagine you have friends in every business. Would you do me the very great honor of allowing me to buy you a drink?"

Bennett grinned. "You bet your life, Mr. Martino. Like I say, it's always five o'clock somewhere in the world."

CHAPTER

18

CONNIE QUILL WAS JUST FINISHING THE DINNER dishes when she heard the doorbell ring. Being a cop's wife, she didn't immediately open the door. Instead, she looked through the little peephole and saw a man she didn't recognize. "Who is it?" she asked.

"My name is Rex Kelsey," the man said. "I'd like to talk to Peter Quill if it's possible."

"What do you want?"

Rex smiled. The Quill kid may have been a rookie, but he'd trained his wife well. "I'm a private investigator, Mrs. Quill. I'm working on a case that involves your husband. It'll only take a minute."

"Why don't you see him at work? This is his home."

"I realize that," he said, "but I thought he'd want it this way. Why don't you ask him?"

Connie left the door locked and went out to the back yard where Peter was rolling on the thick grass, roughhousing with the kids. He looked up she approached. "What's up?"

"There's a man at the door. He says he's a private investigator. He says he wants to talk to you about a case he's working on. I told him to see you at work, but he insisted I tell you."

Peter stood up and brushed himself off. "It's okay. I'll talk to him."

"Why don't you do it at work? You shouldn't let these people bug you when you're at home. You work hard enough."

Peter didn't answer. Instead, he kissed his wife on the cheek and went inside the house. He removed a small .22 caliber handgun from a locked cabinet in the kitchen, then slipped the gun in his pocket. He strode to the front hall, looked through the peephole, then opened the door and stepped outside, letting the door lock behind him. "I'm Peter Quill," he said.

Rex stuck out his hand. "Rex Kelsey. I'm a private cop. Right now I'm working for William Connally on the Cohen case. I'm sorry to bother you at home, but I thought it might be better this way."

Peter appraised the unremarkable schoolteacher face for a moment, then asked, "You carrying?"

"Sure," Kelsey said, "but I've got a permit."

"Give me your piece."

Reluctantly, Rex took the Colt from its holster and handed it to the young cop, butt first. "I'll be back in a minute," Peter said.

"Where the hell you going?"

"I'm going to lock up your gun. You'll get it back later."

Rex waited as Peter went inside. When the deputy returned, he said, "Let's take a walk."

"Fine."

"You got some ID?"

Rex showed Peter his ID as the two men walked down the street. The policeman grunted, "What's on your mind?"

"Well," Rex said, "as you know, Mr. Connally is going to be taking a deposition from you in a few days, but he asked me to talk to you before that."

"Why?"

"Because I was a cop for twenty years, up in Baltimore. I know how it is."

"How what is?"

Rex looked at him through his thick glasses, smiled once more, and said, "How it is to be a cop in court. A lot of times we're forced to say things we know aren't right, but we can't help it. We have bosses or buddies that need to be protected and sometimes it just isn't worth telling the truth. We end up in deep shit while some sleazeball walks free. For what? What did we accomplish? Zip! I know about that stuff."

Peter stopped walking. He stared at Kelsey for a moment, then said, "I don't know what the hell you're talking about."

"Sure you do," Rex said. "But before you get all bent out of shape, let me tell you something. I've been going over this case in my mind for days now, and I don't see any way she didn't do it. So even though I'm working for the guy who's trying to get her off, it's just a job, that's all. I'll do it, the best I know how. As for Connally, he's a pretty shrewd character. He figures you lied at the hearing. He wants to go after your ass real hard. Weber's too. You should know that."

Peter leaned against a car parked in the street and crossed his thick arms in front of his chest. "Don't jive me, Kelsey. What the hell are you doing here?"

Rex shrugged and stuffed his hands in his pockets. "I'm not jiving you. I'm telling you the truth." His gaze met Quill's for a moment, and then he said, "Look, like I said, I was a cop for twenty years. There were some things I was proud of and some things I wasn't. But all in all, I did a good job. How long you been a cop?"

"Two years."

"How do you like it?"

"Some parts I like, some I don't."

"Let me guess. You're a cop because it's a family tradition. That's the way it was with me. But it isn't like the old days. Especially now, when the system is so totally screwed up. Take this Cohen broad, for example. Her husband is screwing around, so she kills him and his girlfriend. But because she's got a friend who happens to be one of the best criminal attorneys in the country, she'll probably get off. He'll pull every trick in the book, if I know him. By the time he's through, he'll have the jury so goddam confused, they won't know what to think."

Peter snorted. "If you're so convinced she's guilty, what are you bugging me for?"

"I told you. It's a job, that's all. Connally pays well, and the woman is entitled to a defense. I have no problem with that."

"What makes you so sure she's guilty?"

"Like Joe Friday used to say, just the facts. The gun you guys found was recently fired. I'm sure that when the FBI gets through checking it out, they'll be able to prove it was the murder weapon. She admits she was there earlier that night. She doesn't even deny it, or the fact that she'd threatened the Winters woman. You've got witnesses who saw a car just like hers leaving the scene. You said she'd been driving the car not too long before you went to her house. She stands to make a half million on the insurance. She can't account for her time. Hell, man, what else is there?"

Peter remained silent for a moment. Then he unfolded his big arms and said, "You mind if I pat you down?"

Kelsey's eyebrows shot up. "What for? You already took my gun."

"You wearing a wire?"

"A wire? Hell, no! Why would I be wearing a wire?"

"Mind if I check it out?"

Rex looked up and down the street. It was empty of people. He looked at the windows of the houses crammed close together in this rather new development. "Here?"

"Yeah."

"You pat me down here in the street, and anybody looking out their window is gonna think we're a couple of faggots."

"I'll take the chance."

"Suit yourself."

Rex turned and placed his hands on the hood of the car, then he spread his legs apart. In seconds, Peter had run his hands up and down the detective's body, checking everything. He found no recording device. "Okay, you're clean," he said.

Rex straightened up. "You want to explain what that's all about?"

"Let's walk some more," Peter said.

They walked about a quarter of a mile until they came to a small park. The sun had just disappeared over the horizon, and a group of kids were making their way home before darkness fell. Peter pointed to a bench and the two men sat down.

"I think you're wrong," Peter said.

"Wrong? About what?"

Peter took a deep breath. "I'd like to tell you some things, but I don't want it getting back to Connally. Not yet, anyway. If I find out you told him, I'll deny it. It's just your word against mine, and without witnesses you're up the creek. You understand?"

"If that's the way you want it. What's on your mind?"

Quill seemed anxious to get something off his chest. He took another deep breath, then started talking rapidly, his voice low, his hands cutting through the air as he emphasized his points. "As far as what went on at that hearing," he began, "my story won't change. Not ever. I'm not all that crazy about what I'm doing right now, but someday I want to be a detective. I have to pay my dues first, so that's what I'm doing. I don't care what Connally does, he'll never get me to change what I said. You got that?"

"I got it."

"Okay. But I'll tell you something. I don't think she did it."

Rex laughed. "You realize how crazy this is? I'm working to keep her out of jail, and I think she did it. You're working to put her in jail, and you *don't* think she did it. Is that nuts, or what?"

Peter started laughing as well. "You're right. It's crazy."

"So tell me why you don't think she did it," Kelsey said.

Peter thought about it for a moment, then nodded his head. "Just remember. This conversation never took place."

"Deal."

"Well, the first thing is, I've been thinking about this ever since it happened. When we went to talk to her, she was so drunk she could hardly stand up. We talked to her a bit, and then Weber told her about her husband being murdered. Okay, I haven't been a cop that long, but I can tell you, I never saw anyone react like that. She was totally blown away. It really surprised her. There's no way she was acting. She was too shit-faced to pull that off."

"Really?"

"Really. And I'll tell you something else. The prosecutor has to turn everything he's got over to Connally sometime before the trial, right?"

"Yes, he does."

"Well, make sure he does. I don't think they'll hold back because, the way I hear it, Telfer just won't abide anyone messing with evidence. But the empty casings in the gun we found—"

"Yes?"

"They had no prints. The gun itself had her prints all

over it, but the shells inside were clean. That make any sense to you?"

"No."

"Another thing. When we brought her in to ID the body, she really freaked. I've seen that before, but it's usually when somebody sees a loved one who got killed in a traffic accident. Killers, especially the domestics, are kinda quiet when you show them the body. They don't know what the hell to do. They're afraid of looking guilty, you know? You were a cop. You know what I'm talking about."

Rex nodded. "What did she do, exactly?"

"She was screamin' and yellin' and beatin' on his body with her fists. She was cursing him for dyin'! I've never seen anything like it. Right after that, she passed out. The detectives took her over to the hospital. While she was being looked at by the doctors, the detectives checked out the clothes she was wearing. No blood anywhere. They were the same clothes she was wearing when her friend left her earlier in the evening, which were different from the clothes one of the witnesses says he saw her wearing.

"I also heard that when the crime team checked her house out, they found nothing that would tie her in except for a box of Winchester hollow points. There were forty-four rounds in the box. Thirty-eights. Six missing. Same shells we found in the gun. But get this. Neither the box nor the rounds had any prints on them. None at all. They used the laser to try and find some old prints. Nothing. That means that the rounds were washed with alcohol. The same with the empty casings they found in the gun.

"So," he continued, "the woman takes the trouble to alcohol-wash the box of shells, puts on her gloves, then loads the gun. She takes the gloves off to do the killings, then brings the gun home, gets drunk, and gives us the gun as soon as we ask for it." He spit at the grass. "That makes no sense at all. She would be that careful with the rounds and not the gun? No way. If she was that cold-blooded and careful, there's no way we'd have found the gun in the first place. This whole thing sucks. I think she was set up. I really do!"

Rex was astonished by what he was hearing. "Let's suppose for a minute that you're right," he said. "Someone killed those two and set Ann up. Who? Why? If Ann was framed to draw suspicion away from the killer, that would mean it has to be an amateur, because you and I both know that professionals don't work that way. They just kill and walk away. This is too slick to be the work of an amateur. It's either Ann or a pro, which brings us full circle."

"I know," Peter said, throwing his hands in the air. "That's what's driving me nuts. I know what I saw, but I can't make sense of it. Remember, I was with Weber when we discovered the bodies. The hit on those two looked like a professional job, made to look like a sex thing. I'm sure of it."

Kelsey shook his head. "The only way this could be a frame is if somebody hired a professional to kill those two and set Ann up. That's so far out it's not even in this galaxy."

"That's it!" Peter shouted suddenly.

"What?"

"That has to be it," Peter repeated. "It's the only thing that makes sense."

"You call that making sense?"

Peter shook his head in frustration. "You don't understand. I know what I saw. Ann Cohen couldn't have done the killing. I'm convinced of that."

Rex stared at Peter for a moment. "You really are, aren't you?"

"Yes."

"You really think someone hired a professional to do this?"

"Yes."

"It would have to be someone who hated them all with a passion," Rex said, thinking aloud. "I know Marty was a shit, and the Winters broad was no prize, but I haven't found anyone who even dislikes Ann Cohen, let alone hates her."

"You have to keep looking," Peter said evenly.

For a few moments, neither man spoke. Then, for the next half hour, they compared mental notes, carefully reviewing each scrap of information. When the conversation was finally over, the sky was black and the air was thick with moisture. As they started walking back to Peter's house, Rex said, "Peter, if I'm going to break this thing, I'll need your help—on the QT, of course. I don't have to tell you that helping me could get you into a lot of shit, but I'm gonna ask you anyway. Will you help me?"

Peter hesitated only for an instant. "Yes," he said. "I'll help you."

Rex let out a deep breath. "You're crazy, you know that?"

"Maybe," Peter said, "but I have to live with myself."

The next morning, Rex was at the county courthouse, checking on the tip he'd received from Anita Phillips. Buoyed by what Quill had said, he was looking at things with a new enthusiasm. Once certain that Ann was just another guilty person getting the full William Connally treatment, he was now beginning seriously to consider the possibility that she was innocent.

Anita Phillips had said somebody had sued Marty Cohen over a business deal gone bad. A possible lead. What that would have to do with Ann was uncertain, but it was worth looking into. It didn't take long for the clerk to find the records. Rex paid the seven-dollar fee for a copy of the documents and then had a thought. "Is that the only suit filed against Martin Cohen?" he asked.

"That's all I have. There could be something in another county."

Rex started to leave, then paused. He went back to the clerk. "What about real estate transactions? Can you look up any property transfers between Martin Cohen and anyone else?"

"Certainly. It'll only take a minute."

She was almost right. In less than three minutes, she was back. "I have three," she said. "Do you want copies of all of them?"

"Yes."

"Okay."

Three more minutes, a payment of twenty-one bucks, and the copies were in Kelsey's hands. He looked through them quickly. There was a record of land that Marty had sold to a woman from Oregon. He didn't relish the idea of traveling to Oregon, but he could if he had to. Then there was an office complex that had been sold to a local couple. It would have to be checked out. The third document almost took his breath away.

Rex stared at it, feeling the adrenaline surging through his body. The document was evidence that, eighteen months ago, Gina Rizzo had bought five acres of land from Martin Cohen for $400,000. She'd never mentioned it.

He shoved the documents into his briefcase and got into his car.

Bill Connally parked and walked briskly to the not-yet-opened offices of Martino and Associates. It was on the second floor of a brand-new complex less than a quarter of a mile from US Highway 19, the main drag in Pinellas County.

The door to the office was open. Carpet layers were busy installing a lush light-brown floor covering. Ann and Cathy were standing by the window, leaning against the sill, watching their dream take shape. They both smiled as Bill stepped inside and hopped over the roll of carpet.

"Good morning!"

"Good morning."

"We don't have a coffeemaker yet," Ann said, "but there's a machine downstairs. Can I get you a cup?"

"No," he said. "I don't have the time. I just wanted to come by and tell you that the grand jury is going to look at your case in four days. I just got the word."

Ann's face fell.

"I didn't mean to spoil your day," Bill said, "but I wanted you to know. I'm due in court soon, and I expect it will take most of the day. Why don't we discuss it tonight? Look, why don't we have dinner together? Maybe some good food and quiet surroundings will make it a little easier."

"That sounds good to me."

"I'll pick you up, say, eight o'clock. That fit in?"

"Yes," she said. "That'll be fine."

"Good. I'll see you then. Nice to see you again, Cathy."

"And you," Cathy said to the departing lawyer.

"I'm so lucky," Ann said, looking out the window at Bill getting into his car.

Cathy glanced at her in surprise. "Lucky?"

"Yes, lucky. I know I've been having a rough time, but can you imagine where I'd be if I didn't have him in my corner?"

Rex Kelsey glowered at the real estate agent and tried again. "Look," he said, "you're not listening to me. Let me try one more time. I know the property isn't listed, but I know the owner. If I like it, I'm sure she'll sell, and you'll be sure to get the deal. All I'm asking is for you to take me out there and show it to me. Then I want it appraised. I'll pay for the appraisal. Once I know what I'm dealing with, I'll be able to make an offer."

The real estate agent, a short, thin, nervous man in his fifties, was still reluctant. "I understand what you're saying Mr. Kelsey, but what I'm trying to get across to you is the fact that we have several parcels of land that are available within this office. The listings we have are already appraised and are for sale. Why would you want to run around on a possible wild goose chase when I can show you property more suitable? Why would you be interested in land you've never laid eyes on?"

"Because I'm weird, that's why," Rex said, as he got up and stomped out of the office.

Five minutes later, he was sitting in front of another agent, this one a little more gullible. Smiling and nodding, the agent went through some documents, located the property on a map, and suggested they drive out in his new Cadillac. Kelsey appeared eager to do so.

It was a piece of land within smelling distance of the county waste treatment plant. A pungent odor hung heavily in the air as the two men walked about the property.

"I know it don't look like much, but it's zoned light industrial. The only problem, other than the location, is the county easement on four of the acres."

"Easement?"

"Yeah. You got five acres here," the agent explained, "but you can only use one. The other four are reserved for possible later expansion of the treatment plant, which is probably a certainty, given the growth in the area."

"So what we really have is one acre?"

"That's right, and only a forty-foot frontage at that. Now, I know that looks bad, but you could put up a small factory in forty feet if you set it back far enough from the road."

"Yeah, I could at that," Rex said. "What do you figure this property is worth?"

The real estate man scratched his head for a moment, then said, "Well, don't hold me to it, but I wouldn't figure it was worth more'n, say, forty thousand."

"Forty thousand?"

"Somewhere in there. You said you knew the owner and she wanted to sell. You got any idea what she paid for it?"

"No."

"Well, we could look it up."

"Don't bother," Rex said. "She'll tell me. Okay, you've been a big help. We can go back now."

An hour later, Rex stopped by Ann's office. The carpet layers were just finishing up, and Ann and Cathy appeared excited. They both recognized Rex immediately. "Hello, Mr. Kelsey," Ann said, extending her hand. "Nice to see you again."

He shook Ann's hand and then Cathy's. "You two look like you're settling in. When does the furniture arrive?"

"It's due this afternoon."

"Well, it's quite a day."

The smile left Ann's face. "It is, to a point. Bill was just here. He says the grand jury is going to look into our case in four days."

"I'm sorry," Rex said, "but I'm sure Mr. Connally told you that grand juries, at least the ones in Florida, pretty well follow whatever the prosecutor says. It's tradition, you might say. I wouldn't put much stock in what they do."

Ann smiled weakly. "Yes. Bill told me that."

"Good. I just stopped by because I have a couple of questions." There was no place to sit, so they all stood, leaning against the wall. "When we talked in Mr. Connally's office a while ago," Rex began, "you were telling me about that night. I hate to rake this up again, but it's important."

"It's all right."

"You said that Marty called you at seven-thirty. Then you called Cathy, who got to your house about nine. You said you didn't remember talking to anyone else. Now that you've had a few days to think it over, are you really sure about that?"

Ann looked at Cathy for a moment, then back at Kelsey. "I'm sure. There was no one else." Kelsey seemed disappointed. "Why do you ask?" Ann asked.

"Oh, it was just something I was wondering about. I've been talking to some of your neighbors, asking if they saw anyone near your place that night. You all seem pretty close. I thought maybe one of them had dropped by, just for a moment."

Ann looked as if she'd been struck by lightning.

"What is it?" Rex asked.

"I just remembered," she said. "Gina came by. I guess it was about eight. I was crying, and she asked me what was the matter. I don't normally discuss my problems with Gina because she's so depressed most of the time. She starts to talk about her own problems. I've heard the same story so many times."

"How long was she there?"

Ann chewed on her lower lip for a moment. "I guess it was maybe fifteen minutes. No more." She shook her head. "I can't imagine why I forgot about it, but it can't be important. Gina's a little crazy, but she's a friend. She couldn't possibly have anything to do with any of this."

"I'm sure you're right, but we need to know everything that happened anyway. You told her what was going on with Marty?"

Ann nodded. "I was really upset, and I told her I thought Marty was at it again. Then she started talking about her ex-husband, and I told her I really didn't want to hear about it, so she left."

"Where did this conversation take place?"

"In the kitchen, why?"

"Did she go anywhere else in the house?"

"What do you mean?"

"Well, did she use the bathroom or anything?"

"No. Why would she do that? She lives a hundred feet away."

Rex grinned. "Okay. I just wanted to check."

Ann shook her head. "Surely you don't think that Gina is involved. She couldn't be! She's my friend!"

Rex patted her on the arm. "I know that. Don't be alarmed. We're just checking everything out. It doesn't mean anything. Don't get upset."

He said his goodbyes and then headed back to his car. It was time to have another chat with Gina Rizzo.

CHAPTER

19

WHEN REX KELSEY REACHED GINA RIZZO'S HOUSE, there was no answer to his knock. Remembering what Connally had told him, he realized she'd be at work. A department store, Connally'd said. Rex searched his memory for the name. It wouldn't come. He looked in his notebook and found it.

Fifteen minutes later, he was in the department store searching for Gina. As he entered the women's fashions department, he spotted her showing a blue-haired woman in her seventies the latest creation by some New York designer. Trying to be as unobtrusive as possible, Rex lolled around the upscale department for a while as Gina did her thing. After about five minutes, he heard a female voice behind him.

"May I help you, sir?"

Rex turned and looked into the dark green eyes of a redhead so beautiful he almost stopped breathing. The plastic tag above her left breast said WELCOME TO ROLOFSON'S. Beneath that, the name *Veronica* was embossed. She was in her early thirties and had no business being cooped up in a department store. Her remarkable face and magnificent figure belonged out in the open, where everyone could appreciate her.

"Ahhh . . . I was just looking—well, actually, I—" Rex found himself mumbling. His mouth didn't seem to work anymore. The embarrassment brought a quick blush to his cheeks, a blush that didn't go unnoticed by Veronica. She smiled sweetly and said, "Was it for your wife, or perhaps a friend?"

Perfect teeth. Straight and white.

"Actually, I was—damn!"

She frowned. "I beg your pardon?"

Rex fished through his pocket and withdrew his ID. "I'm sorry," he stammered. "I wanted to talk to one of your employees, but she's busy. I'll have to see her another time when she's not working."

"What's her name?"

"That wouldn't be fair. I don't want to get her in any trouble."

The vision before his eyes studied the ID for a moment. "You're a detective?"

The blush deepened. She'd affected him so much he wasn't acting like one. More like some tongue-tied kid of fourteen. He felt like a complete fool. "There are times when I wonder about that," he said, "but I really am."

"Veronica Hughes," she said, grinning and extending a delicate white hand. "I'm with store security."

Rex almost laughed out loud. "You're the store detective?"

"One of them," she said, a frown again replacing the grin. "What's so funny about that?"

"Oh, it has nothing to do with you. It's just that I feel like such an idiot." He shook her hand and said, "My name is Rex Kelsey. I'm doing my imitation of a detective so well the store detective thinks I might be a shoplifter. Great! That's what's funny. Not the fact that you're—oh, shit!"

She placed her hands on her hips and asked, "What seems to be your problem?"

Rex let out a deep sigh and said, "I'll tell you the truth. There's no use pretending. For years, I've had this fantasy. I'd meet this incredibly gorgeous redhead, we'd fall in love, have six redheaded kids, all future doctors and lawyers, and live happily ever after. When I saw you, I'm afraid my brain started to self-destruct. It's not often one runs into a fantasy he's had for maybe twenty years. I'm sorry. I've been working too hard. I don't normally act like a complete nerd. God, you're beautiful! Are you married?"

The frown disappeared and she began to laugh. It started deep down and finally rolled out through her perfect teeth and past those luscious red lips, a musical, cheerful, magical symphony. "My word! Do you always try to pick women up in the middle of a department store?"

"No. At least, I never have until this very moment. Are you?"

"What?"

"Married."

"No."

"Great! Would you have dinner with me tonight?"

She appraised him openly for a moment, then said, "No."

"I understand," he said, deflated.

"No, you don't," the vision countered. "I have another engagement. How about tomorrow night?"

He couldn't believe his ears. "That would be terrific."

"I'm through at six. Would you like to meet me here?"

"That would be fine."

"Good. I'll see you tomorrow then."

"Yes, yes. I'll be here."

Rex turned and floated out of Rolofson's Department Store. It was ten minutes before he could get the car started and in motion.

Philip Barnes and Louis Cope were two of the many people ripped off by Marty Cohen. They had an office in downtown Clearwater. They were both young, under thirty. Rex wondered where they'd accumulated the money to start Barnes/Cope Investments.

Yes, they said, they'd bought limited partnerships from Martin Cohen. Yes, they'd sued. Yes, they'd lost. Yes, they despised the man, but it wasn't a total loss. They'd managed to get the restrictions lifted and sell the project. They'd gotten their money back, so that part was just fine. They showed him documents that confirmed their story. As for Martin Cohen, they had nothing to do with his murder. They were both in New York the night of the killing. They had six witnesses who could testify to that, one of them a federal judge, Cope's father.

Rex made some notes, thanked them for their time, and left the office. Once back in his car, he checked Gina's schedule. According to Connally, she worked odd hours at the department store. Sometimes she started at one and stayed until nine; other days her shift would run from nine to five. Since she'd started in the morning today, he reasoned she'd be off at five. He drove back to Rolofson's and cruised around the parking lot for a few moments, looking for Gina's car. When he found it, he made a mental note. He'd be there when she got out from work. Right there, in the back seat of her car. In the meantime, he wanted to have another look at her house.

An hour later, dressed in blue coveralls with *Central Air Conditioning* inscribed on the back, Kelsey, disguised in a wig, beard, and dark wraparound sunglasses, used his lock-picking kit to gain entry to Gina's villa.

The place was a joke, with boxes and clothes covering almost every square inch of floor space except for the kitchen, one of the bathrooms, and the bedroom. Especially the bedroom. It seemed almost normal. Rex went through every drawer, every cupboard, every file cabinet, looking for something that might tie Gina to Martin Cohen. For two hours, his search proved fruitless. And then, behind some boxes in one of the hall closets, he found a small safe. It was a real cheapie, the kind they sold at K Mart. He took a stethoscope from his toolbox and placed it against the front of the safe, three inches to the right of the dial. Slowly turning the dial, he listened for the telltale clicks that would signal a tumbler falling into position. Within five minutes, he had the safe open.

He was astonished by what was in it. First, there was over twenty-five thousand dollars in cash. In these days of plastic money, that was unusual. There were some other papers that would normally be kept in a bank safe deposit box, along with some jewelry that certainly should have been. Rex removed a loupe from his tool kit, switched on a flashlight, and examined some of the jewels. They were real.

At the back of the safe was a small strongbox, locked with a padlock. Out came the lock-picking kit again. Once opened, the strongbox revealed nothing more than a few photographs. There were seventeen photos in all. Most of them were of Gina, standing on stage, a microphone in her hand, with a big band backing her up. But one of them wasn't.

It was a picture of Marty Cohen, lying on a bed, naked, his hands and feet bound. It was Gina's bed. Rex whistled softly, removed a Polaroid camera from his tool kit, attached a close-up lens, and made a copy of the picture. Then he put the photos back in the strongbox, closed and locked it, and placed it back in the safe. Reluctantly, he put the money back as well.

After locking the safe, he tidied up his toolbox and headed for the front door. He was halfway to his car when he heard a woman's voice say, "Who in the hell are you?"

He turned and looked into the eyes of Della White. Quickly adopting a good-ol'-boy drawl that suited Alabama more than Florida, he said, "Oh, didn't Miss Rizzo tell y'all?"

"Tell me what?"

"She's been havin' some trouble with her air conditioner. She ast us to come out and take a look. Ain't nuthin' serious. Just a tad low on freon is all. We filled 'er up and it's workin' jus' fine now."

"She never said a thing to me," Della said, obviously perplexed.

Rex shook his head. Impulsively, he said, "You Mrs. White?"

She was taken aback by the question. "How do you know my name?"

"Miss Rizzo tol' me. She tol' me she was gonna leave a key under the mat, but she was afraid she'd forget. So she said if she forgot, I was to go next door to Mrs. White. She said y'all had a key. But, sonofagun, she didn't forget. She left the key, all right, so I was able to get in and do the fix. I'm sorry if I scared y'all. I thought she'd a tol' y'all."

A look of relief came over Della's face. "Oh, well, I guess she forgot to tell me, all right. I wouldn't normally be here, but it's my day off. We're all a little edgy these days. I'm sorry if I bothered you."

"Hey! No problem. Well, I better get goin'. We got us a mess of troubles today. When it's cold, seems like nobody ever wants their air checked and we got nuthin' to do. Then, when it gets hot, all heck breaks loose. Same year after year. I'll see y'all."

Jeff Smylie was leaning over his desk, gathering up materials needed for a hearing scheduled to begin in a half hour, when Lionel Telfer strolled into his office and gently dropped a manila folder on the desk. "I thought you'd want to see this right away," he said, beaming.

Jeff picked up the folder and opened it. It was a three-page report from the FBI forensics lab in Washington. They had taken several bullet fragments removed from the walls, mattress, and bodies found at 1184 Felcher Avenue and subjected them to a series of laser, spectrophometric, and ultraviolet tests. Then the gun found in Ann Cohen's home had been test-fired, with the expended slugs given the same analyses. The results were clear. The three complex tests measured fifty possible areas of similarity. Matching thirty or more areas would signify that the gun found in the home of Ann Cohen was the murder weapon. In this case, even though the slug fragments were small, the wizards at the FBI had been able to identify forty-two areas of similarity. There was no question. The gun found in the home of Ann Cohen wasn't the gun that *could* have been used. It was the gun that *was* used. It changed everything.

Jeff slammed a hand on the desk and exclaimed. "We've got him! This time we've got the bastard!"

Telfer's face clouded over. "Now you listen to me, Jeff," he snapped. "The defendant in this case is a woman named Ann Cohen. William Connally just happens to be her attorney. You start confusing the two, and I'll pull you. I want you focused on the *case*, not Connally."

Jeff took a deep breath and nodded his head. "Sorry, sir. I was just—"

"I know what you're thinking," Telfer growled. "You've had it in for Connally ever since the Peters trial. You better get your damn head straight. I mean it! The grand jury meets in four days. Now that the gun is a given, I expect two counts of Murder One. You got that?"

Again, Jeff nodded his head. "Yes, sir. I understand. I won't let you down."

"You better not," Telfer said, as he turned and walked out of the office. As the door closed behind his boss, Jeff picked up the FBI report and kissed it.

The windows of Gina Rizzo's car were heavily tinted, like most cars in the Sunshine State. It helped to deflect the heat from the sun, but it also prevented her from seeing Rex Kelsey sitting in the back seat as she unlocked the door and climbed in.

"Hello, Gina," he said softly.

Startled, she banged her head on the ceiling of the low-slung sports car. "Jesus Christ!" she yelled. "What the hell are you doing here? You trying to scare me to death? How did you get in my car anyway?"

"Take it easy," Rex said. "I wanted to talk to you, and I thought this was the best place."

"The best place? Jesus! How did you get into my car?"

"I'm a detective. We know how to do stuff like that. Start the car, will ya? It's hot in here."

Gina fired up the car and turned on the air. "You got a lot of nerve. I got a good mind to get out and call the cops."

"Go ahead," Rex said. "And when they show, you can tell them all about you and Marty."

"Marty? What about Marty?"

"Marty sold you a piece of property for four hundred thousand dollars. It was almost worthless. How did that make you feel?"

She turned in the seat and stared into his eyes. "How did that make me feel? Who told *you* about it?"

"I was checking some court records," he said. "Your name came up. I looked at the property. It stinks. Literally and figuratively. How'd a smart girl like you get suckered into a deal like that?"

"A deal like that? You bastard! You have no goddam right! What I do with my money is my business, nobody else's. You can go to hell!"

Rex made a clucking sound with his tongue. "Gina, my dear. You weren't listening the other night when Mr. Connally said all of you were suspects. You are, you know. You all had access to Ann's house. You all knew about Marty and his girlfriend. And you! Marty made a pass at you, and you kept quiet about it. Some friend! Now I find out that you two did business together. Hey! This is a murder case. If it bothers you that your life is under a microscope, tough shit! It's gonna be that way until we find out who killed those two. And the tougher you make it for me, the tougher I'll make it for you. So let's not waste each other's time, okay?"

The air seemed to go out of her lungs. She turned away from him, sagged in the seat, and rested her hands on the steering wheel. "I don't know why I bought it," she said. "Greed, I guess. Marty was smooth, you know. Real smooth. When he showed me that property I thought he was joking. But he said he had some friends in county government. He said they were going to build a new waste treatment plant somewhere else and the existing one would be shut down. Once that happened, the easement would be lifted and the property would be worth twice what I paid for it."

"And you believed him?"

"Believed him? Sure I believed him. The property was real close to a major development already under construction. Marty showed me some documents. He said the people who owned the land on either side of my property were cousins or something of one of the county commissioners. Well, I know how that stuff works. I thought he was on to something. He said he had three other people who were hot for the land but he wanted to do me a favor. So I went for it. Later, I did some checking and found he'd just bought the property himself about two months before for thirty-six thousand. I knew then I'd been had. He told me he'd paid over three hundred thousand for it."

"If the land was so hot, why was he anxious to sell it?"

"He said he needed the money. He owed some people. Marty was a gambler."

"How'd you know that?"

"How do you think? Marty told me."

"When?"

"When? When he talked about the deal."

Talking to Gina was beginning to give Rex a headache, but he pressed on. "So Marty told you he was a gambler. Why would he tell you that?"

"Why would he tell me that? Because he was explaining why he needed to sell the property, that's why."

That angle would have to wait. "So what happened when you found out you'd been cheated?"

Gina let out a deep sigh, then hung her head. "What happened was, I took some steps."

"Yeah? Tell me about it."

"Why should I?"

"Gina, why are you making this so tough? Don't you know what's next? I turn you over to the cops and they check it out. Who would you rather talk to, me or the cops?"

Again she turned in her seat and stared at him. "You think I had something to do with this?"

"Maybe."

"Me? Kill Marty? You're crazy. Sure, Marty was a bastard. But I wouldn't kill him. He was paying me back! Why the hell would I kill him? And even if I did kill him, I sure as hell wouldn't try to make it look like Ann did it! You're—"

Rex was stunned. "Paying you back?" he said, interrupting her. "What the hell are you talking about?"

Gina turned and stared out the front window. "Look," she said, "I could use a drink. It's been a long day. Do you mind if we talk somewhere else? I feel like I'm in a cage here."

He didn't answer. Instead, he grabbed Gina's handbag from the passenger's seat, looked through it, and then put it back. No gun. He'd checked the glove compartment earlier. This was, after all, Florida, where lots of people carried guns, either on their person or in their car.

"Okay, Gina," he said. "There's a bar across the street. Let's talk." His suit was soaking wet. The air was cooler now, with the motor running and the air conditioner blasting away. But sitting in the closed car, waiting for Gina, had been like sitting in a sauna.

Minutes later, they were huddled in the corner of the bar, Rex nursing a Scotch and water, Gina sipping white wine. "I was really upset," she explained, "as you might imagine. So I talked to this friend of mine. A real big guy. He runs a gym on Nineteen where I work out once in a while. Well, I was crying on his shoulder one night and he said he'd help me out. We talked about it and came up with a plan, you might say. I knew that Marty was kinky; hell, we all knew. It was the talk of the neighborhood, but we never let on to Ann.

"Anyway, I figured I could use that to my advantage. I came on to Marty one night when all of us were having dinner at Della's. Nothing really big, just a little squeeze on the arm. Jesus! He just about got off right there! The next morning, he called me at work and said he wanted to see me. I hemmed and hawed a bit, then told him that if he could come over without Ann knowing about it, I'd see him that night. I never let on that I knew about the property being worthless.

"So I got my friend to hide in the bedroom closet while Marty and I went through the usual bullshit. I let on to Marty that I was into whips and chains and all that shit. Jesus! He had his clothes off so fast it would make your head spin. I told him I liked to be the one doing the disciplining and he said that was just fine with him. I tied him up, and then my friend came out of the closet, wearing one of those things skiers put on their heads."

"A balaclava?"

"Balaclava? Is that what you call it?"

"Yeah."

"Well, anyway, my friend came out of the closet—" she stopped talking and started giggling.

"What's so funny?"

She shook her head. "I'll tell you later." Then her face got serious again. "Jesus! I thought Marty was gonna have a heart attack right there. You never saw anybody so scared in your whole life! My friend had this big fishing knife in his hand. He put it in front of Marty's eyes and told Marty that unless he gave me my money back, he'd castrate him right then and there.

"Well, Marty was about to die of fright. I mean it! He said he would pay me back. He said it would take a few months but he'd get me the money. Like I told you, he was a gambler, and those guys do hit it big once in a while. Besides, he was making big money, about half a million a year, I heard. Poor Ann. She thought he was making less than a hundred thousand. What a bastard he was!

"Anyway, Marty swore to pay me back. He said he'd sold me on that deal because he was way behind on some money he owed some very tough customers. Mob guys in Tampa. Anyway, he promised he'd pay me something every month. And he did, every month. Sometimes it was less than a thousand bucks, and sometimes it was as much as forty thousand. The week before he was killed, he gave me twenty-five thousand. It was always in cash. All he owed me was another eighty thousand and I was even. Why the hell would I kill him?"

Rex shook his head in admiration. She was one tough cookie. "You weren't afraid he would kill you to get you off his back?"

"Off his back? No," she said. "My friend never let Marty see his face. Marty didn't know who the guy was, and my friend told Marty that if anything happened to me, Marty was as good as dead. So Marty just did what he was told."

"Can you prove any of this?"

"If I have to. My friend will back me up, I'm sure. I mean, we weren't really doing anything illegal. Just getting back the money that was stolen from me in the first place. It was all a bluff. My friend wasn't really going to harm him. Not really. He's got muscles out to here, but he wouldn't hurt a fly."

"I'm going to need to talk to him," Rex said.

Gina sipped her wine for a moment. "Will you keep it quiet? With the cops, I mean."

"Sure," he lied. "If everything checks out, you've got nothing to fear from me."

"Okay," she said. "His name is Fred Tasker. You can find him at the gym most nights."

Rex made a note. "I guess that's all for now. I'll have a chat with your friend Tasker and see what he says."

Gina grinned. "I hafta tell you something about him, so you won't be surprised."

"What?"

"That's why I was laughing about him coming out of the closet. He's gay. And he has this thing about redheads. He's gonna love you!"

Tasker, about thirty, with a twenty-inch neck and a fifty-two-inch chest, was big, all right. The gym was a male-female operation, and as Tasker promenaded around his domain, his shoulders back and his chest thrust forward, Kelsey could see the adoring eyes of some of the women who thirsted for a drink at his loving cup. Such a waste.

Rex introduced himself and eyed the man warily as he asked a series of questions. The answers confirmed what Gina had said. "I was just doing her a favor," Tasker said, in a voice as rough as sandpaper. "That asshole had it comin'. It's just a shame he got offed before he had a chance to pay back all the money he owed her. Gina's a nice person. We've been friends a long time."

They talked some more, and then Rex thanked him for the information and left. Tasker hadn't made a pass. Rex couldn't decide whether he was relieved or insulted.

Later that night, at almost midnight, Rex was sitting in Bill Connally's office, winding up an oral report. "So, as you can see," he said, rubbing his aching eyes, "I'm like a dog chasing his own tail. Winters and Simmons were both part-time hookers, but very low-end stuff. Both had been arrested before, but I can't find anyone who had a beef with Winters. As for Marty Cohen, he had about a hundred enemies. I just have to keep hitting them, one after the other."

Connally nodded. "You've done an excellent job, Rex. You've covered a lot of ground in a short period of time. I knew I could count on you."

"I appreciate that, Mr. Connally. However, I still haven't found anyone who saw Mrs. Cohen that night. My people have talked to just about every possible person who might have seen her when she took that drive. So far, nothing."

"Keep at it, will you?"

"I will."

"Anything else?"

Rex chewed on his lower lip for a moment. "Well, this is a bit tricky."

"What is?"

"As I told you, Quill is convinced this thing was some kind of mob hit. We know now that Marty Cohen was a big gambler. I was thinking maybe I would have a chat with Johnny Bellesario."

Bill's eyebrows arched. "Really?"

"Yeah. Bellesario handles most of the action around here. I realize he's not about to tell me anything of substance, but I thought if I talked to him I might learn something. Maybe Marty Cohen owed somebody else a lot of money. Since you're Johnny's lawyer, I figured you could get me an appointment with him. I wouldn't bother with it, except it's something that needs checking, don't you think? Maybe he might—"

Bill waved a hand to cut him off. "I'll save you some time," he said. "I'll talk to him myself. But I think you're barking up the wrong tree."

CHAPTER

20

Two months after the deaths of Marty Cohen and Elizabeth Winters, Rex Kelsey was still mired in an investigation that was going nowhere. He'd been to Oregon and California, Illinois and Minnesota. He'd talked to over a hundred people, some several times. Many had good reasons to hate Marty Cohen, some enough to kill him. But there was nothing solid.

As for Elizabeth Winters, she'd been shown to be a woman living on the seamy side of the street. She'd been involved in many things: drugs, prostitution, the lot. She'd been involved with many people, but again, leads that seemed promising petered out quickly. Her ex-husband George was clean. Her other boyfriends looked clean.

Even the mob connection, through Marty's gambling, had led to nothing. Connally reported that he'd talked to Johnny Bellesario. According to the mob's top man in the bay area, Marty Cohen was a gambler, all right, but his account was current when he was killed. There was no reason why anyone in the mob would want him dead. At least, no reason Bellesario could think of.

Rex felt as though he were trapped in quicksand, flailing uselessly, sinking just the same. He'd never had a case with so many dead ends. Now absolutely convinced, after several more sessions with the woman herself, that Ann Cohen was indeed innocent, he felt thwarted. The evidence revealed to Connally by the prosecutor, as the law required—depositions from a score of witnesses, forensic reports, and her own statement, which included the fateful decision to take a drive in the middle of the night—seemed to point directly to Ann's guilt. Connally, genius that he was, would be hard pressed without something to counter the State's case. It was Rex's job to find it. But he hadn't, and it was starting to worry him.

Quill, the young cop, had helped just as he'd said he would. He'd enlisted the aid of one of the clerks in the sheriff's department, a clerk with access to computer files. They'd gone back five years and developed a list of every beige-colored Mercedes or BMW sedan registered within a five-county area. The list totaled over a thousand names. The owner's names were then checked for possible connections to either Marty or the Winters woman. The three of them, Quill, Rex, and the clerk, were halfway through the list. Now, even Veronica Hughes was helping. So far, nothing had been found that might indicate involvement by any of the names on the list that had been checked, but they still hoped that soon something would.

Rex knew that both Quill and the clerk were risking their jobs by doing what they were doing, and he was grateful for their dedication.

The only bright spot in the whole thing was Veronica. Rex and Veronica had found they had more in common than the color of their hair and their chosen profession. Each day they were seeing yet another facet of what was quickly turning out to be a jewel of a relationship. For Kelsey the loner, the man who'd always wanted to keep things strictly physical, it was a new experience, this really caring about someone. He was falling in love, something he'd managed to avoid all his life. It should have frightened him, but it didn't.

For Veronica, who'd also never been married, it was a total change in attitude as well. An ardent feminist, she'd vowed never to become romantically involved with a man. She prized her independence too much to see it subjugated. But Rex, with his offbeat personality, had captivated her. He was like no other man she'd ever met. He was dedicated, but not to the exclusion of everything else. He was charming, in a boyish sort of way. He had a terrific sense of humor and a healthy lust for life, not just work. She found him irresistible, which astonished her.

The first new hints of romance entered Ann's life as well. Having been thrust by circumstances into regular close proximity with Bill Connally, she found herself thinking about him constantly, even when she was working. The interminable numbers that had always commanded her total attention were less demanding now, and she often found her mind wandering. Always a perfectionist about her work, she found the daydreams very disconcerting.

When she and Bill were together, they spent most of their time talking about the case, scraping the bottom of the barrel for other possible ideas that could shed new light on the mystery. But at other times they talked about each other, and it was having an effect on both of them.

To Ann, Bill was attentive, caring, and sensitive. There were occasional bursts of temper, but they didn't last long. She wrote that off to his larger-than-normal ego, an ego born of accomplishment. And he wasn't selfish like Marty. He talked freely about his past and about his hopes for the future. Perhaps most importantly, he treated her as an equal, something she found refreshing, even thrilling.

"I want to tell you something," he said one night, as they sat on an old-fashioned wooden glider positioned on the large rear deck of his home. "You've endured all of this magnificently. You have an indomitable spirit, you know. Tremendous courage. You deserve a chance for happiness."

Ann lowered her gaze, then looked out over the waters of the lake as they gently slapped the shoreline some twenty feet below. It was hot, but the light wind coming in from the north made it bearable by sweeping her long hair away from her face. The full moon was reflected about midway in the lake, the image giving the illusion of two moons in the night. The house was huge, but aside from a live-in maid, they were alone.

"You're very kind, Bill," Ann said. "I don't think I could have come this far without your encouragement and support. When the grand jury handed down that indictment, I thought I'd die. I never thought I would ever be accused of murder, even after you warned me it would happen. I still can't imagine who could hate me so much—to want me to be found guilty."

"Ann," he said, "remember what we talked about. You mustn't think that. Whoever did this was interested only in getting the heat off his own back. Nobody hates you. Nobody could ever hate you." His face clouded. "Which brings me to a problem we must discuss."

"Yes?"

"I find myself drawn to you, Ann. Very much."

She looked at him with misting eyes. "I know that, Bill, and I'm not unappreciative of your feelings. I have feelings, too. I want you to know that. It's just . . . I can't really think about anything until this thing is over. Can you understand that?"

"Of course I can," he said. "That isn't the problem. It's unprofessional of me to even think like this. I've always prided myself on my professionalism, but—"

"It's all right," Ann said.

"No, it isn't," he insisted. "I want you to be aware of my feelings, because they could affect my handling of your case. Try as I might, I find it increasingly difficult to be as objective as I should be." Then he dropped a bombshell. "I want you to consider retaining another lawyer."

Ann was stunned. "Bill, I couldn't. I just couldn't."

"You must consider it," he said. "I'm unable to shut off my personal feelings, and that's a cardinal sin in this business. I could screw up badly because of it. That's not fair to you."

"You can't be serious!" she exclaimed. "You can't quit now. My God. Are we both supposed to stop feeling anything just because you're defending me? What kind of law is that?"

"It's not the law," he said quietly, "it's the ethics of my position. A fine distinction, perhaps, but an important one. When a lawyer becomes personally involved with his client, he ceases thinking as a lawyer and begins to think as a friend, which can be fatal. My obligation to you is to provide the very best defense I can. It's axiomatic that personal involvement dilutes the effectiveness of a lawyer, just as it would a brain surgeon, for example."

"Bill, you're a fine attorney. The very best. Without you, I feel I have no chance. You talked about my spirit and courage. If you make me find another lawyer, I'll lose both. Please don't do this."

He looked at her for a moment, his eyes soft and gentle. Then, sighing deeply, he said, "All right. If you're sure."

"Of course I'm sure. Who else but you would fight for my life like this?"

Three months after the murders, Bill Connally was as frustrated as Rex Kelsey. Rex's people still hadn't found anyone who'd seen Ann during her ill-timed drive. Bill hadn't really expected he would, but it meant there was no one to swear she was thirty miles from the scene of the crime when it took place. For the briefest instant, Bill seriously considered resorting to subterfuge. He knew men who would lie on the stand for a price. That wasn't the problem. The problem was Ann. She'd know it was a lie and that would ruin everything. So he discarded the idea.

There were still a number of inconsistencies in the State's case. He would have to pound away at them. He was convinced he would prevail in the end.

For Ann, there'd been a number of bright spots amid the gloom. She was seriously addressing her emotions, and her irrational feelings of guilt had disappeared completely. She looked at things realistically. She wasn't afraid to admit that Marty had been a total bastard, even though he was dead. To speak ill of the dead, in the case of Martin Cohen, was a healthy catharsis.

The accounting firm was growing, thanks mainly to Clive Bennett. They had five large accounts: Bennett, three of his friends, and Anita Phillips, who'd joined them three weeks ago. She simply walked into the office one morning and announced that she wanted Ann to be her accountant. So at least there was some money. That was a blessing. Everything Ann and Marty had owned together was still tied up.

The news about Marty's secret income and his gambling had come as a shock. The thought that the IRS might someday audit old returns and demand money Ann had never seen made her fearful. It could wipe her out, if what she'd heard was true. But Bill, ever confident, had told her not to worry; he would defend her if it happened. First things first, he'd said.

Her father had gone back to Chicago, but he phoned almost every day with words of encouragement.

And every day, notwithstanding her decision not to become romantically involved until after the trial, she thought about Bill. He was the most fascinating man she'd ever known, and she felt herself drawn inexorably to him, even while fully aware of the dangers.

He'd become quite candid when discussing his feelings toward her, and he'd been open about his feelings on other matters as well, such as the death of his wife and how it had almost destroyed him. She found his ability to express his feelings a welcome trait. And she welcomed something else. After years of being put down by Marty, she was being flattered and courted by a man who was handsome and successful and respected throughout the entire country—no matter that he defended gangsters. It was nice to be flattered by such a man, nice to be told she was intelligent and beautiful and desirable.

The first draft of his second book had been completed. One night he arrived at her door, manuscript in hand, and told her he wanted her opinion on it before he submitted it to his agent.

Her opinion!

It took her three nights to read it, and when she was finished she realized how much she cared about this man, this wonderful, dedicated man who was striving to save her from a system gone strangely berserk.

After reading the manuscript, she invited Bill over for dinner. He accepted eagerly, and now, as they dawdled over coffee in the living room, she said, "I thought the book was wonderful."

"I'm glad you liked it," he said. "Do you think it needs more work, or should I just send it off to my agent?"

"I think it's fine, Bill. I really do. But I'm no literary critic. Do what you think is right. Please don't let me sway you in any way."

He smiled at her. "I want you to sway me. I value your opinion. Do you really think it's all right, or are you just trying to make me feel good? I know I have a big ego, but I'm aware of it. I don't need to be stroked all the time. What I want from you is the absolute truth. Always."

"Bill, I think it's wonderful. Only one thing worries me."

"What?"

"Well, you talk about some of the more recent clients you've worked with. You don't give away any of their secrets, but still, won't they be upset when they read this?"

He shook his head. "No. Not at all. You're talking about people who like being in the limelight. They want to be notorious." He laughed. "Hell, their egos are even bigger than mine."

"Are you sure?"

"I'm sure."

For a moment, neither of them said anything. Then Bill leaned back on the sofa. "Ann, the trial is scheduled to begin in two months. I've already explained to you what that entails. The preparation will be arduous and difficult. In the end we'll win, I know, but it might be nice if you took a few days off, right now, and really relaxed. Or relaxed as well as you can, under the circumstances."

"You mean go away?"

He took her hand and held it tightly. "Yes. Just you and me. Before you say no, let me explain. I own a small villa in Lauderdale. It's right by the beach, part of an enclave that's very, very private. I can get permission from Judge Clark for you to leave this jurisdiction, as long as you're with me. It would be good for us. Especially good for you." He waved his arm around the room. "It would be good to get you out of this house for a while. Everything in this place reminds you of Marty, and that's not good. You're still living your old life, in a way. I think it's time you began to prepare for your new life."

She could feel his eyes boring into hers. "I don't know, Bill. Would you let me think about it for a couple of days?"

"Of course," he said. "And I don't want you to think— well, this isn't a sexual thing, Ann. Certainly, I find you the most desirable woman I've ever known, but . . . how can I explain this?"

She laughed. This man, master of the courtroom, was having trouble expressing himself, like a young boy on his first date. She found it touching. "You're trying to tell me," she said, "that if I don't want to go to bed with you, you still want me to come."

His eyes lit up. "Exactly! I enjoy your company, Ann. I enjoy being with you. But I would never think of putting pressure on you. At the same time, I don't want you to think that—"

Again she laughed. "I understand, Bill. I really do. I'll give it serious thought, okay?"

"Okay," he said.

For the next two days, Ann considered the pros and cons of going away with Bill Connally. She knew it wouldn't take much to fall completely in love with Bill, and that in itself was terrifying in many ways. Just months ago, her marriage had been shattered by the revelations of long-kept secrets, secrets that, now that Marty's activities were being fully investigated, were still being disclosed, like successive layers of paint masking the real image beneath. As each layer was removed, the image of her marriage mutated once more.

She'd never known about the other women, or the money, or the gambling. How could that be? Was she really that naïve? Was the cliché true: the wife was always the last to know? Or was the opposite more real, that the wife always knew? If it was the latter, what did that make her? Was she too trusting? Too stupid?

If she went away with Bill and fell in love, what would the future hold? Would she be crushed again? She already knew Bill was an unabashed womanizer. Everyone knew. Would he change if they became involved?

As a lawyer, Bill represented some of the most unsavory people in Florida. The very nature of his work demanded secrecy. Did that carry over into other areas of his character? Aside from his work, what did she really know about him? She knew he was warm and tender and affectionate. He was considerate, charming, and hard-working. He was also bombastic at times, ego-driven, prone to sudden quick bursts of temper.

On the other hand, what did the future hold without him?

The future. Did she even have a future? What if Bill, no matter his prodigious skills, was unable to convince a jury that she was innocent? It wouldn't be his fault, of course, because he was facing a daunting array of evidence. Certainly, he was confident, but what else could he be? What if her future was compressed to a period of two months? Did it not make sense to have at least two months of happiness before the world came crashing to an end?

She remembered the wonderful euphoric madness of being in love. It was magic. To have Bill hold her close, tell her how much he loved her, to feel his soft hands upon her body, caressing her ... A shiver ran down her spine.

She decided what she would do. If she only had two months of freedom left, she would really live them. There had been enough sadness and despair. Now was the time for some joy and happiness.

She picked up the telephone.

The condo was lovely, located very close to the ocean, the grounds dotted with bougainvillaea, hibiscus, and tall palms. A postcard scene. Inside, the furnishings were sparse, befitting a seldom-used residence, but expensive and comfortable. There were two bedrooms, and Bill made a big production of placing his things in one and hers in the other.

They dined that first night at a small oceanside restaurant and talked about the case. But after dinner they returned to the condo, where he started a small fire in the stone fireplace and switched on the stereo. Motioning to two oversized pillows positioned in front of the fire, he said, "Make yourself comfortable, while I get some brandy."

They chatted for a few minutes, as the fire crackled and the music blended with the sound of the waves crashing on shore. And then he removed the glass from her hand, took her into his arms, and kissed her. She felt herself melt into his strong arms.

His hands reached up and removed a clip holding her hair, letting its full weight fall down to her shoulders. He stared into her eyes, the light from the fire making his own sparkle. "Ann, I've wanted to hold you in my arms for so long," he whispered. He kissed her again, more deeply this time, while his hand cupped her breast.

She felt her own desire overwhelming her. There was no thought of anything but the moment, and she surrendered to that moment. She had a terrible longing, a need to be loved, to give love, unashamedly, unabashedly, unequivocally. Right there, in front of the fire, right this minute. There was no time for ceremony, no time to carefully undress each other or suggest a move to one of the bedrooms. There was only a fierce, overpowering, animalistic need that had to be satisfied . . . now.

She almost tore off her clothes, as Bill quickly slipped out of his. And then they were in each other's arms, his cologne blending with her perfume, her skin on fire from the feel of his lips as they caressed her entire body. They made love with total, sweet abandon, the long-pent-up passion finally released.

Oh, God! she thought, as she rejoiced in the pleasure of the moment. How long it's been since I've felt so totally free! So captivated, so loved! Yes, he loved her. He hadn't said so yet, but she knew he did. She could see it in his eyes, feel it in his touch, hear it in his voice. And his was an unselfish love, not like Marty's.

She shuddered as she responded totally to his lovemaking.

For four glorious days, she let herself go with complete abandon. Bill was simply wonderful: an attentive, tender, and patient companion; a stimulating conversationalist, with surprising depth and knowledge of many things; a terrific cook, just as he'd said; and an energetic, passionate lover. In a way, it was like being released from prison all over again. And when the mini-vacation was over, Ann knew she was very much in love with Bill Connally.

CHAPTER

21

THREE DAYS BEFORE THE SCHEDULED TRIAL DATE, Bill Connally conferred with his client. "We can ask for another couple of months, Ann. There are any number of things I can do."

"Absolutely not," she said emphatically. "I don't know if I can stand another moment of this. The press is gearing up all over again. My picture is plastered all over the country. It's revolting! I want it over!"

"I understand your feelings," he said, "but Rex and the others haven't really found any worthwhile evidence, let alone the real killer. That concerns me. If we take more time, our people may find something. Every extra day gives us that added chance."

Ann was resolute. "No," she said. "I didn't kill them. You know it and I know it. If we can't convince a jury—

well, then we can't. I've lived too long with this hanging over my head, Bill; it's killing me. I can feel it. It's got to stop."

She leaned over the desk and kissed him on the lips. "I have complete faith in you, my love. I know you'll do the best you can. That's all I ask."

"But—"

"No buts! No more delay. I want this trial over and done with."

Bill came around the desk and took her in his arms. "Okay, sweetheart," he said, forcing a confident look to his eyes. In truth, he was anything but confident. He was good, yes, but juries were completely unpredictable. Smylie had plenty of ammunition and knew how to use it.

On the morning the trial was to begin, Judge Sam Clark invited Connally, Smylie, and Ted Leland into chambers. He wanted to set the tone for what was to follow. His brow furrowed, his bushy eyebrows almost obscuring his eyes, he said. "In one hour, we begin a trial that might take two or three weeks. If it takes three, we'll bump into Christmas, and I'd like to avoid that, if at all possible. Juries tend to get a little grumpy when you mess with their Christmas plans.

"You are all experienced trial lawyers. I want it understood that this trial will be conducted with a minimum of histrionics and a maximum of decorum. I want a clean, orderly proceeding, and I won't stand for anything else. If anyone gets out of line, they'll be the poorer for it. Understood?"

The three men nodded. Clark turned to Connally. "I see you've listed twenty people as character witnesses. That's wildly excessive. I want you to cut it down to five."

Connally blanched. "Your Honor!"

Clark held up a hand to silence him. "This trial will last long enough as it is. We've got the media crawling all over the place. Ever since the *Times* ran that story about you and Smylie's personal vendetta, it's been a goddam circus. I don't like that. Not at all.

"As you know, I've given permission for the trial to be videotaped. You know what that means. In the months to come, I'll have a score of appellate judges looking over my shoulder. If your client is acquitted, they'll be looking at the tapes for one reason—considering my future. If she's convicted, appeal is automatic; they'll be looking for reasons to make me look bad. Either way, I'll be under a microscope, so I won't stand for any crap. This one gets played by the book. All the way."

Again, the three men nodded. Clark turned to Smylie. "With regard to your request to show State's exhibit six to the jury, request is denied. It's too inflammatory. You may show the exhibit to the witnesses, but not to the jury. However, you may show exhibit seven."

Smylie said nothing. He'd expected as much. State's exhibit six was a blown-up photo of the bodies as they'd been found. It *was* inflammatory. Exhibit seven was a line drawing of the position of the bodies. It would do almost as well.

The judge gave the attorneys his instructions for another half hour.

Then it was time for trial.

PART THREE

One good turn deserves another.

Gaius Petronius

CHAPTER

22

THE TRIAL OF ANN COHEN OPENED FIVE MONTHS TO THE day after her arrest. As she sat in the courtroom, the big one with the pool television cameras in the back, she looked nervous. Bill had drilled her carefully during the preceding three weeks. One of the things he'd tried to instill in her was the need for her to appear calm and cool. Not remote, but exuding a look that would be perceived by the jury as confident. But she didn't feel confident, not that first day.

She couldn't help it. For five months, she'd agonized over the death of her husband and the fact that their life together had been fodder for the media. Pictures of Marty, Elizabeth Winters, and Ann had appeared in most of the major news magazines, in all the nation's top newspapers, and on every television network—

especially this month, as the trial neared. The truth was bad enough, but the tabloids, with their tendency to embellish and exaggerate, had made it appear that Ann was as depraved as Marty and Elizabeth. Someone from the police department had told one of the reporters about the sexy black lingerie found in Ann's closet, and a model wearing similar attire had graced the cover of one of the tabloids, under the heading SEXY WIDOW FACES CHAIR.

Yesterday, and the day before, and the day before that, Ann had sat quietly as Bill and the two prosecutors picked a jury, the three lawyers and the judge asking scores of questions in the process, first of the group, then of each individual in turn. Bill had wanted as few women on the jury as possible. She was beautiful and successful, he'd said, just the kind of person a lot of women would be jealous of.

But it hadn't worked out that way. The jury pool was weighted in favor of women. After all of Bill's questioning, her jury—the people who would decide her fate—was made up of nine women and three men, with one alternate in case someone got ill—also a woman.

Ann glanced in the direction of the spectators' section. The media people were there in force, but there were others too, thank God. She could see Anita, and Gina, and Della, and Daddy. Oh, Daddy, she thought. You look so worried!

Paolo had remained in Seattle. Too busy, he'd said, when he'd phoned two nights ago. His prayers would be with her, he'd said. Right. Did God listen to Paolo anymore? Did God listen to Ann?

She knew that no matter what happened, she was

now notorious, a person to be stared at and talked about. Her guilt or innocence was almost secondary. Her life would never—could never—be the same. That reality had depressed her, but her growing love for Bill assuaged some of the pall that hung over her. He'd told her he loved her and wanted to marry her right after the trial, and she'd given him a qualified yes.

It made sense. Her notoriety wouldn't matter much to Bill. He was, perhaps, the only kind of man she could have a decent relationship with. But she wondered. Did he really want to marry her, or was he just trying to build her spirits for the arduous days ahead? She'd know soon enough, she thought.

Dressed in a dark blue dress and wearing a single strand of pearls, she stood out in the packed courtroom. She could feel the gazes of everyone in the room drawn to her like a magnet. Once it might have thrilled her to be the object of so much attention. Here it only served to make her more nervous. Never again would she enjoy being stared at.

Jeff Smylie, sitting at a table some fifteen feet away, looked every inch a prosecutor, all six feet of him, from his styled jet-black hair to his gleaming black Italian shoes. He wore an expertly tailored, dark blue pin-striped suit, a plain white cotton shirt, and a blue silk tie that featured a forest of tiny, almost imperceptible images of the Statue of Liberty. He wore no jewelry other than a wide, plain gold wedding band and a gold watch. Beside him, his partner, Ted Leland, dressed in a gray tweed suit, didn't look nearly as imposing.

Bill, always a fashion plate, wore a dark blue Italian

silk, a starched white shirt with French cuffs, a bright red tie, and polished black Bally shoes.

Ann found herself staring at Smylie as court was called to order and everyone stood up. Smylie held his body with an almost military stiffness. His handsome face bore an expression of confidence. He was her enemy, the man who'd determined that she'd killed Marty and that awful woman. It wasn't true, but Smylie, without even knowing her, was trying to destroy her life. Why? What had she ever done to him? Why hadn't he spent some time looking for the real killer? What was it about her that so convinced him she had done it?

Bill had counseled her many times. He'd told her it was the system, she mustn't take it personally, but she found this impossible. It *was* personal. Jeff Smylie wanted her executed! If that wasn't personal, nothing was.

She felt a tug at her arm. It was Bill, motioning her to sit down. She looked away from Smylie.

Judge Clark was seated, court was in session, and everyone was now staring at her as she stood there glaring silently at her nemesis. With a start, she realized what was happening and quickly took her seat.

She stared straight ahead as the judge listened to a series of motions presented by Bill, none of which she understood. He'd taken the time to explain them to her the previous night, telling her they were obligatory requests that the charges be dropped. Then she heard Smylie addressing the jury. Her concentration was immediately focused on him.

"Ladies and gentlemen of the jury," Smylie began, his eyes making contact with each member of the jury in turn, his arms crossed in front of his chest, "you are here today to consider the case that will be presented by myself, my associate, and the attorney for the defendant. My job is to prove that the defendant, Ann Cohen, did, with full knowledge of her actions, murder her husband and her husband's lover. And I intend to prove it to you, beyond a reasonable doubt.

"The early morning of July eighth was a time of tragedy. For on that morning, Ann Cohen"—he paused while he raised his right arm and pointed in her direction—"murdered her husband, Martin, and her husband's lover, Elizabeth Winters, brutally, sadistically, and vengefully." The arm came down, but Smylie continued to stare at Ann. "The facts of this case are simple, and it's the *facts* I want you to keep in mind as you hear the evidence.

"Ann Cohen discovered that her husband was sleeping with Elizabeth Winters on a regular basis. He was more than sleeping with her; he was engaged in deviant sexual behavior with her. Ann Cohen, *by her own admission*, was well aware of her husband's infidelity. On the night of July seventh, Ann Cohen, along with her friend Cathy Pollard, went to the home of Elizabeth Winters just hours before the murders took place. *By their own admissions*, both women looked in the bedroom window and saw Marty Cohen in Elizabeth Winters's bed. *By their own admissions*, both women saw Martin Cohen strapped to the bed and saw him being whipped by Elizabeth Winters."

He stopped and stared at Ann.

"There wasn't much Ann Cohen could do at that precise moment, because her friend was with her.

So she went home, started drinking, and after a few hours, drunk and upset, she returned to the home of Elizabeth Winters, only this time she took a gun with her.

"She entered the front door of the house, which was unlocked, went into the bedroom, and confronted the two with the gun in her hand. She forced one of her victims to tie the other to the bed, and when that was done, she tied that victim herself. Now Martin Cohen and Elizabeth Winters were both lying on their backs, their hands and feet fastened to the bed posts, awaiting their fate.

"Next, Ann Cohen took two small towels from the bathroom. She placed one in her husband's mouth, and the other in the mouth of Elizabeth Winters, to ensure that their screams would be not heard. Then Ann Cohen carefully positioned herself within inches of one victim, the gun in her hands, took aim, and slowly squeezed the trigger.

"We don't know who was shot first, but we do know that the first bullet—a hollow-point slug designed expressly for the purpose of doing terrible damage to human flesh—ripped through her victim's sexual organs and exited near the spine."

There was a gasp from the spectator section. These were details that had never been released to the press. Connally had briefed Ann only a week ago, but now, hearing the words, she felt ill. Bill had warned her she must not, under any circumstances, exhibit any emotion other than sadness when these words were spoken by Smylie. He'd told her any display of emotion would be misinterpreted. Valiantly, she fought the urge to vomit, as Smylie continued to stare at her, an expression of disgust on his face.

Smylie pressed on. "Ann Cohen let her first victim suffer while she turned her attention to victim number two. Again she took careful aim and fired another bullet into the sexual organs of her second victim. For approximately twenty seconds she just stood and watched them as they writhed in pain, bleeding profusely, until finally, pressed for time, she quickly fired two bullets into each brain."

Smylie turned and faced the jury, his voice rising. "She *executed* them: slowly, methodically, and brutally. Then, as a final touch, she moved the dead body of her husband, using the bed sheet for leverage, so that his body was directly on top of the body of Elizabeth Winters. And that's how she left them, face to face, a message of hate and revenge for all to see. Vengeance was done that night."

He placed his hands on the rail of the jury box. "Then Ann Cohen went home and continued drinking, waiting for the inevitable visit from the police. When they arrived at her home around four in the morning, they discovered that her car had recently been driven, and they found Ann Cohen fully dressed and awake, waiting for them."

He took a deep breath and shook his head in assumed sadness. "I've given you the basic facts, the things I want you most to remember as this trial proceeds, because Ann Cohen's attorney will try and obscure these facts by presenting evidence that has no real bearing on this case.

"He might tell you that Martin Cohen was not a nice

man. Maybe he wasn't, but no one has the right to take the life of another. He might tell you that Ann Cohen was drunk. Maybe she was, but drunkenness is no excuse for murder. He'll certainly tell you a lot of other things, none of which really mean anything." He pounded a fist into the palm of his hand. "The *facts* are what count here, the only things that count. And the facts are there for all to see.

"Ann Cohen committed two acts of premeditated murder. She had many motives. She had the opportunity, and she had the means. I will present evidence that will prove that Ann Cohen acted vengefully, and most viciously, as she took away the lives of those two people. She didn't just execute them. She *brutalized* them."

He turned, with his back to the jury, and faced Ann Cohen for a moment. Then, slowly, he crossed his arms over his chest again and dropped his voice about one octave. "I will show you the murder weapon, a revolver that was found in the possession of Ann Cohen. I will produce an expert witness who will testify that the bullets fired from that gun ended the lives of Martin Cohen and Elizabeth Winters. I will produce another witness, also an expert, who will testify to evidence that proves—that *proves*—Ann Cohen was at the scene of the crime. I will present other witnesses who will testify to what they saw and heard on the night of the murders. I will present witnesses who will testify to the many motives for the actions of Ann Cohen.

"And when I am finished, you will have a clear picture of what happened that fateful night. You will, I am sure, be as convinced as I am that Ann Cohen is guilty of murder, beyond any reasonable doubt. I am confident that you will find the defendant guilty of murder in the first degree. Thank you."

It was one of Smylie's shorter opening statements, but its impact was strong. The members of the jury stared at Ann, their eyes wide.

As the young prosecutor returned to his seat, the judge turned to Connally. "Mr. Connally, do you wish to make an opening statement?"

"Yes, Your Honor."

"Proceed."

"Thank you, Your Honor."

Connally rose to his feet, nodded to Smylie, and walked to the front of the jury box. He had to blunt the effect of Smylie's words as quickly as possible. "Good morning," he said, a smile on his face.

Almost involuntarily, there was a murmur as, unconsciously, twelve nervous jurors and one alternate answered him back.

"Ladies and gentlemen," he said, the well-modulated voice strong and sure, "this may well astonish you, but I agree with several things the prosecutor has told you."

He paused for a moment, then continued. "Ann Cohen did indeed have many motives to kill her husband. Many very strong motives. Motives that have led more than a few women to take violent action. And I won't deny that Ann Cohen was at the scene of the crime that night. She was. She won't lie about that, because Ann Cohen isn't a liar."

He turned and walked over to the desk, behind which Ann sat stiffly in a chair. He walked behind her and placed a big hand on each shoulder. Looking at each member of the jury in turn, he said, "As this case proceeds, you will learn a lot about this client of mine. You'll get to know her quite well. You'll hear from a number of witnesses who will testify as to her character, and you'll realize that there are people in this world who are totally incapable of killing another human being. Ann Cohen is one of those people."

He moved back in front of the jury. "Martin Cohen and Elizabeth Winters were brutalized, all right. It was a despicable crime. The prosecutor has described what happened in detail, almost as though he watched it happen.

"But he wasn't there.

"We know that somebody killed Martin Cohen and Elizabeth Winters, but when the prosecutor tells you that Ann Cohen pulled the trigger of that gun, he departs from the facts and resorts to fantasy. There isn't a scintilla of evidence to indicate that Ann Cohen was ever inside that house. Not one single shred of evidence!

"Ann Cohen didn't pull that trigger. I'm not sure who did, and I know the police aren't looking for anyone else because they thought from the very first that Ann was the one. But they were—and are—wrong!"

He paused for a moment, then went on. "In fact, Ann Cohen is the third victim in this case. She not only lost a husband that she stuck with through some pretty horrible times, but she has been accused, falsely, of killing him.

"There's no possible way you could imagine how devastating that's been to her. To have every intimate detail of your life exposed in the public press is horror enough, but to be falsely accused of murder is almost unbearable. It's an experience that will live with her forever, no matter what you decide."

He gritted his teeth. "Unlike the prosecutor, I have two jobs. The first is to prove to you that Ann Cohen is innocent of murder. But that isn't enough. I have to convince you, and everyone else who's ever heard about this case, that Ann Cohen could not possibly have committed murder, because I know in my heart that if there is one person left in this world who even thinks that Ann Cohen killed those two people, she'll never be able to function normally again. Her life will be as good as over. That's the kind of woman she is."

He stopped for a moment, waved a hand in the air, then said, "I know. We're all conditioned to think that if the police arrest somebody for something, that person must have done it. But I'm sure you're well aware that the police can—and do—make mistakes. That's what's happened here, but I don't expect you to accept what I'm saying as gospel just because I'm saying it. That would be silly."

Connally's voice was strong and sure. As he paced in front of the jury box, he was aware that every eye in the room was following him. "My job won't be easy," he said. "You'll hear a lot of things during the course of this trial that you'll find puzzling. If she didn't do it, you'll ask yourself, how come the murder weapon was found in her possession? How come her fingerprints were found on the outside of the bedroom window of the house where the murders took place?

"I intend to answer those questions, and all of the others that are brought forward. I'll explain to you what really happened that night, and when I'm finished, you'll understand, as I do, that Ann Cohen didn't kill anybody. You'll realize that she's a victim of the same ruthless killer who murdered her husband.

"And I know that when all the evidence has been presented and you've listened to Ann's story, a story that will be corroborated by others, you'll find her not guilty. I thank you very much."

Connally returned to his seat. Judge Clark made a note, then turned to Smylie. "Mr. Smylie, you may call your first witness."

"The State calls Lydia Whitcolm."

The old woman walked quickly—surprisingly quickly—into the courtroom, was sworn, and took her position at the witness chair. Smylie leaned on the lectern and said, "Mrs. Whitcolm, where do you live?"

"I live at eleven-eighty Felcher Avenue in Palm Harbor."

"That address is next door to the home occupied by Elizabeth Winters, is it not?"

"Yes."

"Would you tell the Court and the jury what you heard and saw on the morning of July eighth."

Her eyes shining with excitement, Mrs. Whitcolm launched into an explanation of what she'd seen and heard. With some careful prodding by Smylie, she explained that she'd heard gunshots, noted the time, and called the police.

She gave an estimate of the number of seconds between each shot, adding the information that she was quite familiar with the sound of gunfire because her late husband had often taken her on hunting trips. When she was finished, Smylie turned her over to Connally.

"I have no questions of this witness, Your Honor."

"Very well. Mrs. Whitcolm, you are excused. Mr. Smylie, call your next witness."

"The State calls Sergeant William Weber."

Sergeant Weber was brought into the courtroom, sworn, and directed to the witness chair. "Sergeant," Smylie began, "will you please tell the Court and the jury what you saw and heard on the morning of July eighth."

"Yes, sir," Weber said. He pulled out a note pad and placed it in front of him. Reading from his notes, he described how he and Peter Quill had answered a police call, discovered the bodies, and gone to the house of Ann Cohen. He repeated the account of the interview with Ann he had given at the hearing, which ended with taking her to police headquarters.

Smylie walked over to the exhibit table and picked up a gun. "The State wishes to enter into evidence State exhibit number one, Your Honor."

"Mr. Connally?"

"Your Honor, the defense objects to the introduction of this exhibit on the grounds that it was illegally obtained. For the record."

"So noted. Objection overruled. Proceed, Mr. Smylie."

Smylie gave the gun to the clerk, who made a notation, then handed the gun back to Smylie. Smylie walked to the witness stand and handed the gun to Weber. "I show you this gun, Smith and Wesson Thirty-eight Special revolver, serial number C836673. Is this the gun you found in the home of the defendant?"

Weber examined the gun. "Yes. I made a note of the

serial number at the time the gun was found in the home of the defendant. In addition, I made a small mark on the trigger guard. This gun has both the serial number and the mark."

"Thank you." Smylie placed the gun on the evidence table. "That's all I have for this witness, Your Honor."

William Connally rose slowly to his feet and took his position at the lectern. He was smiling. He kept his voice low and smooth.

"Sergeant Weber, you've testified that when you arrived at the home of the defendant, you knocked on the door, is that right?"

"No. I rang the bell."

"I'm sorry. You rang the bell. And the defendant answered the door?"

"Yes."

"Did she open it immediately?"

Weber seemed confused. "What do you mean?"

"Well, did she talk to you through the door first, or did she simply open the door?"

"She opened the door."

Connally seemed surprised. "She did? It was almost four in the morning and she simply opened the door without knowing who was there? Isn't that a little unusual?"

Weber shrugged. "I guess it is."

"You testified that she was dressed. What was she wearing?"

Weber looked at his notes. "She was wearing a white blouse and black slacks."

"What kind of shoes?"

"Ah . . . they were loafers. Black loafers."

"Fine. Now you testified that the first thing you did was to inform the defendant of her rights. In other words, you told her that she was under arrest and—"

"No. I never told her she was under arrest."

"What *did* you say?"

"I told her that she was being questioned and that she had a right not to answer our questions without an attorney being present."

"What did she say when you told her that?"

"She asked what she'd done."

"Did you tell her?"

Weber was starting to squirm a little. "No, I didn't," he said.

"Why not?"

"Because I was interrogating a suspect. I wanted to ask her some questions."

Connally lifted his head and said, "Oh. So you didn't tell her that her husband was dead."

"Not at that point."

"But she was still curious as to why you were there?"

"She didn't seem to be."

Connally's eyebrows rose. "No? It's four in the morning, two policemen come to the door and start reading her her rights, and she's not curious?"

"No, she wasn't. She seemed to know."

"She seemed to know? She was a mind reader?"

Weber sneered. "No. But she knew."

"I see. You're cleverly intimating that she had killed two people and was waiting for you to show up to arrest her."

Smylie was about to object, but Weber spoke before he had the opportunity. "Sort of."

"But when you arrived, she didn't confess to killing anyone, did she?"

"No, she didn't."

"So, it's possible she didn't have the faintest idea why you were there, isn't it?"

"It's possible."

"So you asked her to sign the waiver and she did. Then the other officer asked her if she owned a gun. Is that right?"

"Yes."

"And she said yes, and then you got her to sign another paper, and then you went and got the gun. Is that your testimony?"

"Yes."

"And you were sure she was a killer."

"Yes."

"Didn't it strike you as a little odd that she would be so cooperative?"

"No. That happens lots of times."

"Really? You've been a police officer for ten years, isn't that right?"

"Yes."

"Can you give me *one* instance where a similar thing has happened?"

"Objection, Your Honor." It was Leland, being heard for the first time. "Irrelevant."

Judge Clark glanced at Connally and said, "Sustained."

Connally shifted his weight from his right foot to his left. "Okay. The defendant asked you what your visit was all about. And she asked you why you wanted her to sign the forms, isn't that so?"

"Yes."

"So she was in fact curious."

"Just normal curiosity, that's all. Mostly about the forms."

"And what did you tell her?"

"I told her she needed to sign the forms because it was evidence that everything she was doing was voluntary."

"Didn't you in fact tell her that you needed her to sign the forms in order to 'keep the books straight'?"

"I may have."

"In a deposition taken from you on July twenty-sixth, you admitted that you had used that phrase. Was that the truth?"

"Yes."

"So you *did* say that to her."

"Yes."

"Did you know she was an accountant?"

"No."

"She was totally cooperative, correct?"

"Yes, she was."

"And eventually you did tell her that her husband was dead. What was her reaction?"

Weber shrugged. "She said we were crazy."

"So she *was* surprised?"

"No. She wasn't surprised."

Connally moved from the lectern to a position in front of the jury. Clasping his hands in front of him, he said, "Was the defendant drunk when you called on her at four in the morning?"

Weber hesitated, then said, "Yes, she was."

Connally whirled, strode back to the lectern, then leaned on it. "So. You called on the defendant at four in the morning. She answered the door fully dressed, wearing a white blouse and black slacks and flat black shoes. You told her she could have a lawyer present but she didn't request one. Then she was asked if she had a gun and she told you where it was. So you went and got it. All the time, the defendant, who appeared drunk, cooperated with you, didn't she?"

"Yes."

"She displayed respect?"

"Generally speaking, yes."

"Did she call you names?"

"No."

"Did she struggle with you?"

"No."

"Did she make *any* attempt to run away?"

"No."

"Then you told her that her husband was dead and she needed to come with you. And she said you were crazy. Am I right, so far?"

"Yes."

"She never told you—ever—that she'd done it, did she?"

"No."

"Did you notice any blood on her clothes or person?"

"No."

"Did you examine her hands or clothes for powder marks?"

"No."

"Why not?"

Weber squirmed some more. "I was interested in getting her downtown. I was in a hurry."

Connally sneered at the officer. "The fact is, you *did*

examine her hands and clothes and found nothing, isn't that true?"

"No."

"Isn't it true, Sergeant Weber, that the defendant was drunk and confused and appeared totally unaware of what you were doing at her home in the middle of the night?"

"Objection! Leading!" Smylie barked.

"Overruled. The witness may answer."

Weber chewed on his lower lip for a moment, then said, "She was drunk, yes. I don't know how confused she was."

"Isn't it true, Sergeant Weber, that the defendant's actions throughout the entire time of your interrogation were consistent with the actions of an innocent person?"

"Objection!"

Connally waved a hand in the air. "I withdraw the question. I have no more questions for this witness." Then he strode back to his desk and sat down. He looked into the eyes of each member of the jury, and what he saw warmed his heart. It was as though they were watching a tennis match, even though the game was over for the moment. Their attention went from Connally, to Ann, to Weber, and finally back to Connally again.

Good.

They were already wondering.

CHAPTER 23

SMYLIE'S NEXT WITNESS WAS FRED STONE, ANOTHER neighbor of Elizabeth Winters. "Mr. Stone," Smylie began, "would you describe to the court and jury exactly what you saw and heard on the morning of July eighth?"

Stone leaned forward, his lips almost touching the microphone. "Yes, sir. I was in bed, asleep, and I heard a sound. It woke me up. At first I thought I might be dreaming. I got out of bed, and then I heard another sound. It was a bang, like a gunshot. I went to the window and looked out, trying to figure out where the shots came from. Then I heard some more shots."

"How many shots did you hear in total?"

"I can't be sure. I know I heard five, but there could have been another."

"How long was it between the shots, to the best of your recollection?"

"Well, the one that woke me up, I don't know. It was maybe twenty seconds before I heard the next one. Then I guess it was about another twenty seconds before I heard the rest. They were pretty close together."

"How close?"

"About one or two seconds apart."

"Did you see anything after you heard the shots?"

"Yes. For a while, there was nothing, and then I saw this woman come out of the house across the street, the Winters house. She got into a car and drove off."

"Would you recognize her if you saw her again?"

"No."

"Do you remember the car she was driving?"

"Yes. It was a beige Mercedes four-door sedan. One of the big ones, a five-sixty SEL."

"You're sure about the make, model and color?"

"Yes, I'm quite sure."

Smylie opened his folder and removed a piece of paper. "At this time," he said, "with the court's permission, the State wishes to introduce into evidence State's exhibit number two, a copy of the registration certificate for a beige Mercedes sedan, model five-sixty SEL, owned by the defendant."

Connally was on his feet. "Your Honor, the defense objects to the introduction of this exhibit on the grounds that it is prejudicial to the defendant. We will, however, stipulate that the defendant owns a beige Mercedes five-sixty SEL sedan."

Judge Clark motioned both men to approach the

bench. They did so, along with the court reporter and Ted Leland. Clark, sotto voce, said, "Mr. Connally, it seems to me that you're splitting hairs here."

"Your Honor, it's enough that the jury knows the defendant owns such a vehicle. By introducing the registration, the State makes it appear that this is in fact the vehicle seen by the witness. I don't want that image left in the mind of the jury. The witness has testified that a car similar to the defendant's was seen, but there's no testimony that her car was the actual one involved. There are many similar cars registered in Pinellas County alone."

Clark turned to Smylie, who said, "Your Honor, all we're trying to do is to establish that the defendant owned such a car. The registration proves that she did. We should be allowed to enter the exhibit."

Clark thought about it for a moment, then said, "If the defense stipulates that the defendant owned such a car, that will suffice. The objection is sustained."

As the attorneys returned to their respective positions, the judge turned to the jury and said, "Ladies and gentlemen, the defense has stipulated that the defendant owned a beige Mercedes automobile at the time the murders took place. I have ruled that the stipulation is enough. I caution you that the witness has testified that he saw an automobile similar to the one owned by the defendant. It has not been established that it was—or was not—the automobile owned by the defendant."

Smylie continued to question the witness. "Do you remember what time the shots were fired?"

"Yes. It was a quarter of two. I remember because I looked at the clock."

"Thank you. I have no more questions for this witness."

Judge Clark looked at Connally. Connally nodded and said, "I have a few questions, your honor."

"Proceed."

"Thank you." He walked to the lectern and leaned forward. "Mr. Stone, you said it was a woman you saw leaving the house where you think the gunshots were fired. It was pretty dark. What makes you so sure it was a woman?"

"Well, she was wearing a dress, or a skirt. She had these real high heels on. And she had a purse with her. And she was small, like a woman."

"How small?"

"I couldn't say. Not really. But she wasn't fat, like Mrs. Winters."

"You didn't see her face?"

"No."

"But you're sure it was a woman?"

"Yes."

"And you're sure she was wearing a skirt or a dress?"

"Yes."

"And you're sure she was wearing high heels?"

"Yes."

"Mr. Stone, how old are you?"

"I'm fifty-three."

"How's your eyesight?"

"Pretty good."

"Do you normally wear glasses?"

"Just for reading. My distance eyesight is very good."

Connally smiled. Then he turned his back to the witness and pointed to the rear of the courtroom. "The last row, by the door. Can you tell me if the person sitting on the outside seat is a man or a woman?"

Stone looked at the person and said, "Yes. It's a man."

"Can you describe him?"

"He's about my age. He's got brown hair and dark eyes. He's wearing a brown suit, a white shirt, and a brown tie."

Stone had just described one of the reporters to a tee. Connally, to everyone's surprise, seemed pleased. "Mr. Stone," he said, "you do indeed have good eyesight. Now, just to recap, you have testified that you saw a woman leave the house—the Winters house—not long after you heard the shots fired, and that the woman you saw was wearing either a dress or a skirt and high heels, isn't that so?"

"Yes, sir. That's what I saw."

"Thank you, Mr. Stone." Connally turned to the judge and said, "That's all I have at this time, Your Honor."

Stone was excused.

Smylie called two more witnesses to further establish that a beige Mercedes had been at the scene, then called Dr. Lucas Trout to the stand.

Lucas "Cool Hand Luke" Trout was head of forensics. Of all the witnesses on Smylie's list, Dr. Trout was the one Connally feared most. As he watched the doctor being sworn, he steeled himself for the task ahead. The months of work, the planning, the thinking—everything hinged on how well he blunted the testimony of this witness. He hoped he was ready.

Cool Hand took the stand.

"State your name."

"Dr. Lucas Trout."

Jeff Smylie waited while his witness was sworn and then moved to a position directly in front of the jury. Placing his hands in his pockets, he asked his first question. "Dr. Trout, what is your occupation?"

"I'm a medical doctor and a forensics specialist with the Pinellas County Sheriff's Department."

Slowly, William Connally rose to his feet. "Your Honor," he said, "the defense stipulates that Dr. Trout is a forensics expert." Then he sat down.

Judge Clark nodded. "Very well." The judge turned to face the jury. "Ladies and gentlemen of the jury," he said, "the defense, in stipulating that the witness is a forensics expert, is indicating that they will accept his testimony as it relates to the field of forensics. You may therefore regard such testimony in that light." Turning back to the prosecutor, he said, "Proceed with your witness, Mr. Smylie."

"Thank you, Your Honor. Dr. Trout, how long have you been involved in your present duties?"

"Thirteen years."

"And in that time, how many autopsies have you performed?"

"I have performed over one thousand autopsies personally and have supervised approximately two thousand others."

"I see. And of the autopsies that you have personally performed, how many of them involved gunshot wounds?"

"Approximately half."

"I see. So you have personally performed autopsies on a minimum of five hundred gunshot victims. Is that correct?"

"Yes."

Smylie moved to his desk, picked up three eight-by-ten glossy photos, and turned to the judge, "Your Honor, with the Court's permission, the State wishes to introduce State's exhibits three, four, and five."

Connally stood up and said, "No objection, Your Honor, provided that the exhibits are treated the same as exhibit six."

Clark looked at Smylie, who nodded.

"You may enter the exhibits, Mr. Smylie."

Smylie had the clerk mark the photographs, then handed them to the doctor. "Dr. Trout, I show you photographs of the murder scene, marked State's exhibits three through five, and ask you to identify them. Would you do so, please?"

"Yes. These are photographs taken by the crime unit at the scene of the murders."

"Can you identify the two bodies shown in the photographs?"

"Yes, I can. the man has been positively identified as Martin L. Cohen, of Palm Harbor, Florida, and the woman has been positively identified as Elizabeth T. Winters, also of Palm Harbor, Florida."

"Would you explain to the Court and the jury how, based on your past experience, you think the murders took place?"

"Yes," the doctor said, in a voice seemingly devoid of emotion. It was the voice and the lack of emotion that had earned him the nickname "Cool Hand," not, as some suspected, his ability to carve up bodies without a tremor. Most had never seen him at work. But almost everyone had seen him prowling around the scene of a vicious and sickening death, his face inscrutable, his voice never wavering, his eyes never blinking. To him, it was a quest for truth. The mutilated and mangled bodies he saw day after day were just pieces of evidence.

"An extensive examination has shown that both victims were shot while they were lying on their backs. Then one of the victims, Mr. Cohen, was moved to a position as indicated in the photographs."

"We'll get back to that in a moment. How many wounds were found in each body, and what was their nature?"

"I found three entry wounds in each body, each approximately nine tenths of a centimeter in diameter. I found three exit wounds in each body, ranging in diameter from the smallest, four centimeters, to the largest, which was seven centimeters."

"Seven centimeters? How large is that in inches?"

"Approximately two and three-quarter inches."

"Two and three-quarter inches? That's a very large hole. How do you account for that?"

"The bullets used were hollow points: Winchester thirty-eight Specials, one-twenty-five grain. The bullets are designed to expand rapidly once they come in contact with flesh. The rate of expansion is determined by how much resistance the bullet meets as it travels through the flesh. As a result, the exit wounds are always much larger than the entry wounds."

"Thank you. You said that there were six wounds in all, three in each body. Would you explain where each wound was found and what you believe to be the sequence of events?"

"Yes," the doctor said, his voice still a monotone. "I determined, after careful examination, that Mr. Cohen was shot first in the genital area. The bullet entered the body at a point just above the penis, hit the spine, where it shattered, and exited out the back, three inches above the tailbone, taking some of the bone from the—"

Smylie held up a hand to silence the witness and looked at the judge. "Your Honor, with the court's permission, I would like to present an artist's rendering that would assist the jury in understanding what happened that night."

Judge Clark turned to Connally. "Mr. Connally?"

"If this is exhibit seven, I have no objection, Your Honor."

"Very well."

Ted Leland got up and walked to the exhibit table. He picked up an easel that had been placed near the wall and positioned it so it could be seen by everyone in the courtroom. Then he unwrapped a six-by-three-foot poster that had been placed near the table and put it on the easel.

The poster displayed two artist's renderings in black and white. The first depicted the bed and the two bodies, with both victims shown lying on their backs, their arms and feet bound. Facial features and some of the other detail had been eliminated. The second rendering depicted the scene as the bodies were found, with the body of Martin Cohen lying on top of the body of Elizabeth Winters, face to face, as though still in the act of making love.

"Dr. Trout," Smylie said, "would you step forward and, using this marking pen, indicate the path of the first bullet, making sure to indicate also the distance the gun was from the body at the time the shot was fired."

Trout stepped down, walked to the easel, and drew a line that went from a position about two feet above the bodies, down through the body, and into the mattress. The ink from the marking pen was blood red, a fact not lost on anyone. "Because of the pattern and quantity of powder particles," the doctor said, "we were able to determine that the first shot was fired from close range. I would say less than two feet, and in this direction." His long index finger retraced the line he'd drawn. "The defendant was stand—"

Connally was instantly on his feet. "Objection!" he shouted.

"Sustained!" Judge Clark bellowed. "Strike that!"

Judge Clark glowered at the witness, then directed some remarks to the jury. "The jury is advised to disregard the word 'defendant,' he said. "That is why we are having this trial, to determine if the defendant is indeed responsible." The judge turned his attention back to the witness. As he did so, his ears began to turn pink. "Dr. Trout," he barked, "you know better than that!"

"I'm sorry, Your Honor. I apologize."

"Continue."

"Yes, sir. The murderer took the first shot while standing at the side of the bed. I can't say which victim was shot first, but I can say that the first shots that hit each victim were *not* to the head. After shooting the first victim, the murderer then moved to the other side of the bed and took another shot." Trout drew another red line from a position about two feet away from the body of the woman, a line indicating a bullet entering the body at just to the right of the vaginal cavity and exiting to the left of the tailbone.

"Dr. Trout," Smylie asked, "how are you able to determine that the lines you have drawn are accurate?"

"As I have stated, I made my determination based on the shape and substance of the powder particles found on the victims, the amount of blood found at the scene, and examination of the entry and exit wounds."

"I see. Now, you are testifying that both victims were initially shot in the genital area. Is that right?"

"Yes."

"While they were lying on their backs?"

"Yes."

"And then?"

"The murderer then shot each victim in the head, twice."

"Would you indicate those shots on the rendering, please?"

Trout drew four more lines, two to each body.

"How can you be sure that they weren't shot in the head first?"

"Because the head shots—all four of them—would have caused instant death and the heart would have ceased pumping blood. There was a large amount of blood at the scene. The initial shots, while eventually causing death, would not have been fatal for a number of minutes."

"Now." Again Smylie walked to his desk, picked up two towels, and asked the judge for permission to enter them. It was given. "I show you two towels, marked State's exhibits nine and ten. Do you recognize them?"

Doctor Trout resumed his place in the witness chair

and answered the question. "Yes. These were found at the scene of the murders."

"Did you test these towels in any way?"

"Yes."

"And what did you find?"

"I found that the towel marked State's exhibit nine was spotted with blood that has been positively identified as belonging to both victims. It also contained traces of saliva that has been positively identified as belonging to Mr. Cohen. An examination of Mr. Cohen's mouth discovered fibers from this towel adhering to several of his teeth. As for the towel marked State's exhibit ten, it too was spotted with blood from both victims, as well as saliva positively identified as belonging to Mrs. Winters. Fibers were also found in her mouth matching those of the towel."

"So from your examination, you conclude what?"

"That the towel marked exhibit nine was at one time inserted into the mouth of Mr. Cohen, then removed. The towel marked exhibit ten was inserted into the mouth of Mrs. Winters, then removed."

"In examining the bodies, did you find any evidence that they had been bound?"

"Yes. There were abrasions on both wrists and both ankles of each of the victims."

Smylie picked up a number of four-foot lengths of black velvet rope, had them admitted into evidence, and handed them to the doctor. "I show you State's exhibits eleven through eighteen, eight ropes in all. Can you identify them?"

"Yes. They all have my identifying mark. They were also found at the scene of the murders. Skin samples removed from exhibits eleven through fourteen indicate that they were used to bind the wrists and ankles of Mr. Cohen. Exhibits fifteen through eighteen were used to bind the wrists and ankles of Mrs. Winters."

Smylie took the ropes, showed them to the jury, and then placed them back on the exhibit table. He turned, leaned against the lectern, crossed his arms, and asked, "Based on the evidence, have you formed an opinion as to what transpired on the morning of July eighth?"

"Yes. Based on the evidence, the two victims were tied to the bed hand and foot as they lay on their backs, and a towel was placed inside each victim's mouth. Then a single bullet was fired into each victim, as I've already indicated. After a short period of time, two more shots were fired into each victim's head. Then the towels were removed, as were the bonds, and the body of the man was positioned as depicted in the second graphic."

Smylie turned to the judge. "Your Honor, it is impossible for the jury fully to understand exactly what happened that night by means of this graphic alone. I really need to show them the photographs."

Connally was on his feet. "Objection, Your Honor. We had already agreed—"

Judge Clark held up his hand. "That's enough! Court will be in recess while I see counsel in chambers."

Smylie and Connally glared at each other, then walked quickly toward the front of the courtroom.

In chambers, Judge Clark lashed out at Smylie. "Look," he said, his ears a bright red, "I have already ruled on those photographs. Once I have made a ruling, I expect you to abide by it without further comment. By bringing the subject up in court, you've given those photographs a mystique they don't deserve. You know damn well your witness is quite capable of describing how the bodies were found. It isn't necessary for the jury to see the actual photographs. You're playing games with me, Mr. Smylie, and I don't appreciate it. If you continue this kind of behavior, I'll declare a mistrial and you'll be responsible. Do you understand?"

Smylie wanted very badly to retort, but, knowing the reputation of the judge, he didn't. Instead, he apologized.

Judge Clark looked anything but placated. "All right. I want both of you to cool off. And Mr. Smylie, I want you to consider carefully what I've said."

"Yes, Your Honor."

"Very well. Now get out!"

When court resumed, Judge Clark admonished the jury to forget about any mention of photographs. "You are well aware," he said, "that the police took photographs of the murder scene when they arrived. The photographs have been shown to witnesses, but you have not been allowed to see them yourselves, and you might well wonder why this is so.

"It's quite simple. As a judge, I have the right to determine what you should see and what you should not see. I have ruled that the artist's rendering of the scene is adequate for your understanding of the facts. The photographs themselves are quite gruesome and, in my view, could have an effect on your ability to be completely objective as you hear and see further testimony. Therefore, I want you to put all thought of those photographs out of your mind."

Judge Clark motioned to Smylie to proceed. Smylie again approached Dr. Trout. "Doctor," he said, "you've testified as to how the murders took place, with both victims lying on their backs, unable to move. You've also testified that after the victims were killed, the body of Martin Cohen was moved to a position as shown in the second rendering."

"Correct."

"Why was this done?"

"Objection. Calls for conclusion."

"Sustained."

Smylie walked to the exhibit desk, picked up the gun, and brought it to the witness. "I show you State's exhibit one—"

"Your Honor?"

It was Connally, standing and pointing to the graphic which was still in plain view of the jury. "If the prosecutor is finished with exhibit seven, could it be taken down?"

Smylie held up a hand before Judge Clark could say anything, walked to the easel, and turned the poster back to front. "Will that do?" he snapped.

"That's fine," Connally said, suppressing a smile.

Smylie returned to his witness. "I show you State's exhibit one. A Smith and Wesson Thirty-eight Special revolver, serial number C836673. Do you recognize the weapon?"

"Yes. It has my mark of identification in addition to the serial number."

"Did you find any fingerprints on the weapon?"

"Yes. Using the FBI system of fingerprint identification, I was able to determine that there were enough points of similarity to state categorically that the finger-prints found on the gun were those of the defend-ant."

"Did you find any other fingerprints on the weapon?"

"No. Only those of the defendant."

"Did you examine the shell casings that were found in the gun?"

"Yes."

"Describe them, please."

"They were Winchester Thirty-eight Special hollow points, one-twenty-five grain."

"And were you able to determine if the gun had been recently fired?"

"Yes. Tests that I performed determined that the gun had been fired within a twenty-four-hour period prior to its coming into the possession of the deputies."

"And did you subsequently test-fire the gun to deter-mine if it was indeed the murder weapon?"

"I did. Certain fragments found at the scene and in the bodies were examined and compared to three rounds that were test-fired from the gun while in my possession. I was unable to determine that the spent bullet fragments found at the scene and in the bodies were fired from this weapon."

"Why is that?"

"Because, by their very nature, hollow-point bullets shatter into a number of pieces. They become distorted, and our equipment is not able to make allowances for the distortion of the pieces."

"So what did you do with the bullets?"

"I forwarded them to the FBI laboratory in Washing-ton. Their equipment is much superior to ours."

"And was the FBI lab able to determine if this was the murder weapon?"

"Yes. They submitted a report."

Smylie turned his attention to Judge Clark. "At this time, Your Honor, I would like to enter into evidence State's exhibit eight, the report from the FBI."

"Proceed."

After having the clerk tag the exhibit, Smylie handed the report to Dr. Trout. "Is this the report you spoke of?"

"Yes."

"Would you read the conclusion?"

Trout opened the report, turned to the last page, and said, "We conclude, therefore, that the weapon identified by serial number C836673 is the same weapon that fired the bullets submitted for testing."

"Thank you." Smylie took back the report and placed it on the evidence table. "Were the wounds found on the victims consistent with previous wound patterns where this type of bullet has been used?"

"Yes."

"So, this gun was, without question, the murder weapon."

"Yes, it was."

"And this gun holds six cartridges?"

"Yes."

"And you found a combined total of six entry wounds on the two bodies?"

"That is correct."

"Did you examine evidence found by the crime unit at the scene: to be specific, fingerprint impressions found on the outside of the bedroom window of the Winters home?"

"Yes, I did."

"Were you able to identify them?"

"Yes. One set belonged to the defendant. Another set belonged to Catherine Pollard."

"This evidence would positively place the defendant at the scene of the murders, would it not?"

"Yes."

"So your testimony is that the murderer tied up both victims, stuffed a towel in both of their mouths, then shot each victim in the genital area. The killer allowed them to suffer for an undetermined period of time, then shot them both in the head, twice, removed the ropes and the towels, and moved the body of Mr. Cohen to a position on top of Mrs. Winters. The murder weapon was identified as being the same gun that was found at the home of the defendant. The defendant's fingerprints were also found on the outside of the bedroom window. Is that correct?"

"Yes, sir."

"Thank you, doctor." Smylie turned to Connally and, with a small smile on his face, said, "Your witness."

Smylie took his seat and William Connally slowly rose to his feet. He stood behind his desk, staring at the witness for a moment, then moved to a position in front of the jury box.

"Dr. Trout," he said, the radio announcer's voice calm and even, "your testimony today leaves no doubt but that the murders of Mr. Cohen and Mrs. Winters were carried out in a most heinous fashion. I commend you on your careful examination of the evidence and your attention to detail. Now, you testified that the defendant's fingerprints were found on the murder weapon and the outside of the bedroom where the murders were committed. Is that correct?"

"Yes."

"Are you able to testify as to the exact time this took place, from the fingerprints alone?"

"No."

"So the defendant could have handled the gun and touched the bedroom window hours before the murders, is that not so?"

"Yes."

"Tell me, did you find the defendant's fingerprints anywhere else, either outside or inside the house where the victims' bodies were found?"

"No."

"Just the bedroom window, on the outside?"

"That—and on the murder weapon."

"Oh, yes. When the crime unit examined the murder scene, they went over the place with a fine-tooth comb, is that not so?"

"That's one way of putting it. Actually, they used a number of devices ranging from vacuum cleaners to laser fingerprint detectors."

"Laser equipment was used to ensure that all fingerprints, however faint or old, would be cataloged?"

"Yes."

"How many different sets did you find?"

"They found eleven sets of prints."

"Eleven. But not those of the defendant?"

"Not inside the house, no."

"Eleven sets. Including those of both victims?"

"Yes."

"Which would leave nine sets unaccounted for."

"We have accounted for two sets."

"I see. And the other seven sets: you don't know who they belong to?"

"That's right."

"Now, these prints were all over the inside of the house?"

"Yes."

"Was there any indication that an effort had been made to remove fingerprints from any part of the interior of the house?"

"No."

"I see. And yet the defendant's fingerprints were found *only* on the outside bedroom window."

"That is my testimony."

"Yes. Let's move on. You have testified that you have personally examined over five hundred victims who died from gunshot wounds, is that not so?"

"Yes."

"And you have carried out innumerable ballistics tests. True?"

"That's true."

"Can you tell the Court and the jury the number of those cases where the murder weapon has been identified?"

The doctor leaned forward, his face expressing confusion. "I don't understand."

Connally crossed his arms over his chest. "Let me put it another way. Here, today, we are dealing with a case where we have two victims, each examined by yourself, and a murder weapon, also examined by yourself. How many times have you been involved in a case where you personally conducted the autopsies on the victims and also conducted tests on the murder weapon?"

"Oh, I'd say about a hundred and fifty."

"Fine. At least you could be certain that it was over a hundred and thirty. Is that not so?"

"Yes."

"And of those cases, over one hundred and thirty cases, how many times have you found spent cartridges in the weapon as well as fingerprints on the weapon?"

Trout looked upset. "I don't know."

"Could you give me a reasonable estimate?"

"I would say, perhaps twenty."

"Twenty? Why so low a number?"

"Well, sometimes the gun is located after a long investigation. Sometimes the gun has been wiped clean of fingerprints. Sometimes the casings used at the time of the murder are gone. And of course, the murder weapon in this case was a revolver. Sometime, the murder weapon is a semiautomatic. In those cases, there are no spent shells left in the weapon."

"I see. Well, of these over one hundred and thirty cases where you examined both the gun and the bodies of the victims, you estimate that in approximately twenty cases you found fingerprints on the murder weapon and spent shell casings inside the weapon. Is that correct?"

"Well, yes. I'd say that."

"Twenty times you have been able to examine the gun and the body or bodies and the shell casings?"

"Yes."

"Fine. Now. When you examined the murder weapon in this case, you were able to identify the fingerprints as being those of the defendant. Correct?"

"That's correct."

"You also examined the spent shell casings?"

"Yes."

"And you determined that Winchester Thirty-eight Special hollow-point one-twenty-five grain cartridges were used. True?"

"Yes! I've testified to that."

"I understand. You examined the spent cartridges carefully?"

"Of course!"

"Objection!" It was Smylie, standing up and pointing at Connally. "The witness is being asked to repeat his previous testimony for no purpose."

Judge Clark looked over his glasses at Connally and asked, "Is there a point to this, Mr. Connally?"

"Yes, there is, Your Honor. I was just about to make it."

"Then do so."

"Thank you, Your Honor." Connally turned, faced the jury, and asked, "Did you find any fingerprints on the shell casings, Dr. Trout?"

Trout dropped his eyes. After a moment's hesitation, he said, "No."

Connally whirled and faced him. "None at all?"

"That's right."

"What does that tell you?"

"They had been cleaned."

Moving like a panther, Connally went to stand directly in front of the witness. "Cleaned!" he barked. "Your testimony is that the murder weapon had the defendant's fingerprints all over it—and only hers—and yet the empty shell casings had been cleaned? Is that right?"

Trout gulped once and said, "Yes."

"That would indicate that the murderer used gloves when he loaded the weapon, would it not?"

"Yes."

"I see. Now in these other cases, the twenty other cases where you examined the murder weapon and found identifiable fingerprints, did you examine the shell casings?"

"Yes. All of them."

"And in how many cases did you find fingerprints on the gun but *no* fingerprints on the shell casings?"

Trout shook his head. "I—I'm not sure."

Connally turned, faced the jury and said, "Isn't it a fact, doctor, that in most cases you've been involved in, even when the murderer sometimes took the trouble to wipe the gun, you found *some* fingerprints on the shell casings?"

"Yes, but—"

"Just answer yes or no."

"Yes."

"But in this case, the exact opposite is true, isn't that a fact?"

"Yes."

"And isn't it true that in those cases where the murderer took the trouble to make sure that the shell casings were clear of fingerprints, the murderer also took the trouble to make sure that the gun was wiped clean of prints?"

Trout gulped and said, "Yes. That would be the normal case."

"Isn't it a fact that in all the cases you've been involved in, this is the *only* case where you found a defendant's fingerprints on the murder weapon and *no* prints at all on the spent shell casings?"

Trout remained silent for a moment and then said, "Yes. This is the only time that it's happened."

Connally turned to the judge. "Your Honor, I realize that this is somewhat unorthodox, but the State has other exhibits that I would like to examine while this witness is on the stand."

Judge Clark motioned with his hand for the attorneys to approach the bench. When Smylie, Leland, and Connally stood before him, the judge said, "Mr. Connally?"

"Your honor. The State has a box of cartridges, Winchester Thirty-eight Special, one-twenty-five grain, that they are holding as evidence. It's listed on the State's exhibit list. I know that the box and the cartridges within it have been examined, and I'd like to address the issue while Dr. Trout is on the stand."

The judge turned to Smylie and asked, "What about it?"

Smylie looked ashen. "The State has no objection, Your Honor."

"Very well."

Connally went to the exhibit table and removed the box of cartridges. He had them marked and then handed them to the doctor. "I show you a box of cartridges. Would you identify the box, please?"

"Yes. It is a box of Winchester Thirty-eight Special cartridges, hollow points, one-twenty-five grain."

"Would you explain to the court and jury where this box was found?"

"Yes. The box was found in the home of the defendant."

"How many unspent cartridges are in the box?"

"Forty-four."

"How many cartridges does the box hold?"

"Fifty."

"Would you say that the spent casings found in the murder weapon came from this box?"

"There is every indication that they did."

"Have you examined the box and the cartridges inside it?"

"Yes."

"Did you find any fingerprints on any of the cartridges or the box itself?"

"No."

"None at all?"

"Correct."

"How do you explain that?"

"The box and the cartridges within the box were wiped clean."

"Wiped clean? Isn't it a fact, doctor, that with modern laser equipment, in order for you not to find any fingerprints on either the box, the cartridges inside the box, or the spent casings found in the murder weapon, they all would have had to have been washed with a chemical solution of some kind?"

"Yes, that's true."

"Would it be fair to say that such an action would indicate that whoever did such a thing was a very careful person?"

"Yes, it would."

"And wouldn't it also be fair to suggest that such

a careful person would ensure that his prints were removed from a murder weapon?"

"Objection! Calls for conclusion!"

Connally smiled. "Withdrawn." Then he said, "So your testimony is that the murder weapon found in the home of the defendant was covered with her fingerprints. The shell casings found inside the gun had been cleaned with some chemical solution, as had the box of cartridges found inside the home of the defendant. In addition, the unused cartridges in the box were also cleaned. Someone was very careful. So careful, in fact, that you have never, in your vast experience, seen anything like it. Isn't that true?"

"Objection!"

"I'm just summing up the witness's testimony, Your Honor."

"Overruled."

"Yes. That is my testimony."

Connally moved to the poster still sitting on its easel and turned it so the jury could see it once again. "According to your testimony, and the evidence presented in the form of the photographs, this was a particularly gruesome crime. You testified that blood spots were found on the towels that you say were stuffed in the mouths of the victims. Photographs taken at the crime scene indicate that there are blood spatters on several walls of the room as well as on the sheets and pillows. You have also testified that you believe—and I have no reason to doubt you—that the body of Mr. Cohen was placed on top of the body of Mrs. Winters after they were killed. True?"

"That's right."

"How do you think that was done?"

"The killer used the sheet to roll Mr. Cohen into position."

"I see. Mr. Cohen weighed about one hundred and sixty pounds, did he not?"

"One hundred and fifty-eight, to be exact."

"I see. And you think the killer just moved this dead weight by flipping a sheet?"

"Not flipping. It would take some doing, but it could be done. I was able to re-create the act in my laboratory using a young woman staff member."

"I see. When you reenacted this feat of strength, did you use a satin sheet that was soaked with fresh blood?"

"No."

"How tall was the person you used in your reenactment?"

"About five feet, six inches."

"And what was her weight?"

"About a hundred and twenty pounds."

"Was she able to do this with little effort, or was it something of a struggle?"

"It took some effort, yes."

Connally smiled. "Now," he said, "when the defendant was arrested, she was emotionally upset and placed in the hospital—"

Smylie was on his feet. "Objection, Your Honor. Speaks to facts not yet in evidence. Improper cross."

Connally stood fast. "Your Honor," he said, "the witness has knowledge of evidence vital to the defense. I'm not suggesting that the prosecutor is withholding evidence, but he *is* trying to throw up roadblocks to our getting at the truth. It's not my fault that he has failed to conduct a proper and complete examination of this witness."

Once again, the lawyers were called to the bench. After a short discussion, Judge Clark overruled the objection. Connally, with renewed vigor, said, "Did you examine the clothes of the defendant shortly after her arrest?"

"No."

"Did you examine the clothes of the defendant at *any* time?"

"No."

Connally grinned. "I understand, doctor. Let me ask it another way. Did anyone from your office ever examine the clothes of the defendant at any time?"

"Yes."

"Would you explain the circumstances, please?"

Dr. Trout cleared his throat and said, "When the defendant was taken to the morgue to identify her husband's body, she became physically ill as a result of ingesting an overdose of alcohol. Then she became comatose. She was taken to the hospital, where she was examined and placed in a room. During that time, her clothes were examined by a member of my staff."

"Can you describe her clothes? The ones that were examined?"

"Yes. He examined a white blouse, a dark blue pair of slacks, various undergarments, and her shoes."

"What kind of shoes?"

"They were black leather loafers."

"Was any blood found on any of the items examined?"

"No."

"Was the defendant examined?"

"I just told you that she was."

"Was any blood found anywhere on her person?"

Trout looked past Connally at Smylie, then said, "No."

"None at all?"

"Objection! Asked and answered."

Connally turned to the judge and said, "I'm just trying to ascertain the facts as clearly as possible, Your Honor."

"Overruled."

Connally turned back to the doctor and pressed forward. "You are testifying that not a single drop of blood was found on the clothes of the defendant. Not on her blouse, her slacks, her stocking, her shoes . . . nothing!"

"That's true."

"And yet you expect the jury to believe that she was able to pump six bullets into two people, get blood all over the room, use a sheet to move one hundred-and-fifty-eight-pound body on top of another body, and accomplish all this without getting a single drop of blood on either her clothes or herself?"

"Objection!" Smylie barked. "Calls for a conclusion."

"I'll allow it," Judge Clark snapped.

Trout looked upset. His voice rising slightly, he said, "During that examination we only examined the clothes she was wearing when she was arrested. That was some time after the murders were committed. She had time to clean up and change."

Connally sneered at the doctor. "How interesting. But isn't it true that after the arrest of the defendant, the crime unit went over her house with a fine-tooth comb, to use a cliché, looking for evidence? And isn't it true that they found no traces of either of the victims' blood

on any of the defendant's clothes—or anything else—
found in her house?"

"Yes, but she could have—"

"Hold it!" Connally said. "Your Honor, would you
instruct the witness to answer only those questions
that have been asked? He's throwing suppositions out
here that are completely out of order."

Judge Clark leaned forward. "Dr. Trout, you've been a
witness in this court many times in the past. You know
the rules. I want no more of this."

"I'm sorry, Your Honor."

Connally bored in. "Isn't it a fact, doctor, that the
only physical evidence you have is a gun belonging
to the defendant that has her prints all over it, and the
fingerprints that you found on the outside bedroom
window of the home where the murders took place.
That's all the physical evidence, isn't that true?"

"Well, we have—"

"Yes or no! Just answer the question yes or no!"

"Yes."

"Thank you."

Connally smiled. "Of course. She could have taken
the time to change, and she could have taken the time
to clean the room of any fingerprints as well. But you
say there is no evidence that this was done—"

"Objection! Your Honor, Mr. Connally—"

"Yes, yes. Sustained. Let's not have any speeches, Mr.
Connally."

"I'm just trying to get it straight in my mind, Your
Honor." He turned back to Trout and said, "The only
prints you found belonging to the defendant were those
on the outside window and the gun. A gun she volun-

tarily handed over to the police. Makes a lot of sense to me."

"Objection!"

"Sustained."

"I apologize, Your Honor. I have no more questions for this witness at this time. However, I may have more at another time."

Judge Clark looked at the prosecutor and asked, "Any redirect, Mr. Smylie?"

"Yes, Your Honor."

"Proceed."

Smylie, a scowl on his face, approached the witness. "The fact is, doctor, that the gun, introduced by the State as exhibit number one and found in the home of the defendant, is indeed the murder weapon. Is that not so?"

"Yes is it."

"Without question?"

"Without question."

"Since the attorney for the defendant has discussed the activities of the crime unit that conducted the investigation, let's talk about some other things they found. Was there any evidence that the defendant's home had been broken into?"

"None."

"We heard previously from Sergeant Weber that upon entering the defendant's home, and after having been given permission to look at a gun owned by the defendant, the gun, positively identified as the murder weapon, was found. Did the crime team find any evidence whatsoever that anyone other than the defendant had been in possession of that gun?"

Dr. Trout shook his head. "There was no evidence to suggest that anyone other than the defendant had handled the gun. No."

"Thank you. That's all I have."

Judge Clark turned to Connally, who stood up and said, "Dr. Trout, if someone had a key to the home of the defendant, he would be able to enter at will without leaving any evidence that he had done so, isn't that true?"

Trout hesitated for a moment, then said, "Yes."

Smiling now, Connally said, "So the fact that the crime unit found no evidence of anyone having broken into the defendant's home would be meaningless if, in fact, a number of people had access by the use of a key—"

Smylie was on his feet again. "Objection," he cried, almost purple with frustration.

"Sustained."

Connally sneered at Smylie, turned to the doctor, and said, "Thank you, doctor. You've been a big help." As he sat down, he again looked at each member of the jury. They were still wondering.

It had gone rather well, he thought.

CHAPTER

24

JIMMY GIBBONS SAT ALONE AT THE HUNDRED-DOLLAR-minimum-bet blackjack table in Las Vegas's Caesar's Palace and tried not to show how worried he was. Twenty black checks worth a total of two thousand dollars lay on the green felt table, positioned between the beefy Gibbons and the equally large stone-faced dealer.

Gibbons looked at the two cards in front of him. A five of hearts and a six of clubs. The dealer's cards—the up card covering the down card—lay flat on the table just in front of the dealer's ample apron-covered belly. The up card was a six of spades.

It had been a losing night. All night. But Gibbons felt a change in the wind. He was holding eleven, the dealer six. More than likely, the next card would be a face, giving Jimmy the much-needed twenty-one. Even if it wasn't, the odds were good that whatever came out would be worthwhile. A nine, an eight, even a seven. With the dealer showing a lousy six, he probably had sixteen. The dealer *had* to hit sixteen. The odds were on the player's side.

Gibbons added twenty more black checks to the pile in front of him. By doubling his original two-thousand-dollar bet, he was indicating to the dealer that he wanted a single card. Doubling down, they called it. Four thousand dollars. His last four thousand dollars.

Without hesitation or emotion, the dealer snapped a card, crossways, face up, on top of Jimmy's five and six. A three of diamonds. Shit! In another fluid motion, the dealer flipped his down card over and laid his six beside it. The down card, a four of spades, seemed to be a living thing, mocking Gibbons and his futile attempt to come back from this disastrous day. Almost instantly, the dealer threw another card on the table. A king.

"Twenty," the dealer said, scooping up Jimmy's losing hand—and the four thousand dollars. The floorman standing behind the dealer leaned forward, pencil and paper at the ready. "Marker, Mr. Gibbons?"

Gibbons stared at him, his small round eyes hot with hostility. "What? You don't think you've got enough of my fuckin' money? Twenty-two grand ain't enough for you guys? You want more?" He stood up and pushed the high chair away from him. "Fuck you." Then he stomped away from the table and headed for the bank of elevators. The dealer and the floorman said nothing. They'd heard it all before, from a hundred guys like Jimmy Gibbons.

Most of the high rollers liked "action." Winning or losing wasn't really the thing. It was the excitement of the action, the adrenaline rush they got from dealing with large amounts of money that could change hands in seconds. Sometimes they won, sometimes they lost. But most of them had class. Win or lose, they were gentlemen. But there were always some like Gibbons, who craved money, not action. Winners or losers, they were never gentlemen.

Gibbons went upstairs to his room and threw his considerable bulk on the king-sized water bed, setting off a wave action of major proportions. He was big and fat: six feet three and two hundred and sixty pounds, most of it flab. He smoked three packs of cigarettes a day and was already showing the early symptoms of emphysema. He was forty years old but looked more like a man of fifty. His heavily creased, pockmarked face—the result of childhood chicken pox—was further marred by a score of scars that had been inflicted by a drunken, cruel-hearted father when Jimmy was just a kid. His long, thick nose seemed to hang over thin lips, a small mouth, and almost no chin at all. His forehead, sometimes referred to derisively as a "moonscape," seemed larger than normal. His small beady eyes, sunk deep in their sockets, seemed filled with anger at the best of times.

Even the hookers, at three hundred dollars a throw, tried to do their job and get out of his way as soon as possible. He was not, they said, worth the money.

He was scheduled to return to Tampa in two days. But he was broke, having lost his entire stake in the space of four hours. It was a new record for Jimmy. Usually, when he lost, it would take at least two or three days. The suite they'd given him was free, as were the meals and entertainment. But he felt like a loser, and losers like to get out of Vegas quickly.

He got up from the bed and started packing. There had to be an available airplane seat somewhere to take him out of this rotten town. It was only eight o'clock in the evening.

Desperate men do desperate things. Within two days after returning to Tampa, Jimmy Gibbons was seated on a park bench at high noon, reading the morning paper and waiting for a man he'd finally managed to contact late the night before. The man arrived, took a seat beside Jimmy, and, from beneath a white panama hat, stared at a small sailboat moving slowly across the bay.

Sailboats. He liked sailboats.

"Okay, Jimmy. I'm here. What's on your mind?"

Gibbons continued to read his newspaper. "I need some money," he said. "I thought maybe I could be a mule for a week."

The man in the panama hat said, "You? A mule? That's a little out of your line, isn't it?"

Gibbons was in a hurry. "Look," he said, "don't fuck with me. You got some business for me, great. You don't, then let me run some stuff up north. I don't care where. I'll drive up."

For a moment, the man remained quiet. Then, he said, "You want to handle a shipment to Atlanta?"

"What's it worth?"

"To you? Five grand."

"That's good. I'll do it."

Pedro Sanchez considered the proposition. Jimmy Gibbons was, he knew, connected. A mob minion who sometimes did odd jobs for independents like Sanchez. But not running drugs. Jimmy's specialty was electronics, a trade he'd learned during a three-year stint in the army. Jimmy was a bug man, one of the best. He rarely drank, didn't use drugs, and was considered basically reliable, if a little crazy. But he wasn't stupid, he knew enough to keep his mouth shut, and he wasn't about to rip off ten kilos of Colombian cocaine that needed to be in Atlanta by tomorrow evening.

The outfit Sanchez aws working for had switched tactics in the way they moved cocaine. As a secondary distributor, they no longer moved large shipments, preferring instead to break them down into many smaller lots, using various couriers to move the goods. That way, if one of the couriers got busted, the whole load was not lost. Right now, he could use a man like Jimmy. And clearly Jimmy could use him. Except for one thing: Jimmy's boss, Johnny Bellesario, was a competitor of Sanchez's.

Bellesario was unusual in some respects. He didn't mind independents, as long as they didn't get too big. Sanchez was small in the scheme of things, but getting bigger. Maybe . . . maybe this was Bellesario's way of letting him know that he'd reached the limit of his growth.

"Does Johnny know about this?" Sanchez asked.

Gibbons shook his head. "Fuck, no. He don't want me running that shit. He's got specialists taking care of things like that. Look, I ain't here to fuck with you. If Johnny Bellesario wanted you gone, you'd be gone. He ain't about to send me to set you up. He ain't about to waste his time with that shit. I just need some money."

Sanchez thought about it for a moment, then said, "All right, Jimmy. There's a Chinese restaurant over in Pinellas, just south of Five-eighty-four, on Nineteen. You know the place?"

"No. Just give me the address and I'll find it."

"Okay." Sanchez wrote the address down on a piece of paper. "You meet me behind there at two in the morning."

Gibbons rose from his seat and walked away without uttering another word.

Aboard the sailboat drifting aimlessly in the bay less than half a mile from shore, DEA agent Mark Spencer smiled as he removed the headphones from his ears. For three weeks, he and a special task force of drug agents had been tailing Pedro Sanchez, hoping for just such a break. Now the effort seemed to be paying off. Spencer turned to his companion. "We got it all. It ain't much. I think he's talkin' less than ten keys, but if Pedro shows up himself, it'll be enough to nail his little ass. And maybe we can lean on Gibbons a little. It would be nice to kill two birds with one stone."

At two in the morning, Jimmy Gibbons was waiting behind the restaurant. Pedro, accompanied by two bodyguards, showed up ten minutes late. As soon as the drugs were placed in Jimmy's car, the dark alley behind the restaurant was bathed in bright white light emanating from spotlights temporarily mounted on the roof of the restaurant.

"Freeze! Drug Enforcement Agency! Nobody move!"

.　　　　.　　　　.

One hour later, Rex Kelsey was awakened by a hand gently shaking his shoulder.

"Whaaa?"

"Rex," Veronica Hughes whispered into his ear, "it's Peter Quill on the phone. He says it's really important."

Rex took the phone from her hand, switched on the light, and mumbled into the receiver. "Pete? What is it?"

"Rex," Peter said, "I'm sorry to bother you, but I got something here that's really exciting."

"What?"

"I was in on a drug bust tonight. The DEA had some of us locals doing backup. We nailed four guys, one of them a guy by the name of Jimmy Gibbons. But that isn't the only name he uses. He also uses the name Jimmy Gibson."

"So?"

"So, the list of cars! I've gone over that thing so many times, the names are burned into my memory. We never worried about aliases, because they'd be impossible to check out anyway. But one of the names on that list is James Gibson. I just looked at the list again, and it's the same guy. The address checks out. But here's the real kicker! Jimmy Gibbons, using the name Gibson, rented a beige Mercedes 560 SEL in Tampa two days before Cohen and Winters were murdered. He turned it back in on the morning of the eighth!"

Rex was trying to sort it out in his mind. "Who *is* this guy?"

"That's the best part," Peter said. "He's one of Bellesario's people."

"What?"

"You heard me."

All of a sudden, Rex was fully awake. "Yes, sure! Go on."

"Jimmy is a mob guy," Peter said, the excitement evident in his voice. "He works for Johnny Bellesario. He's an electronics expert, Rex. One of the best."

Rex could feel the adrenaline shooting through his body. "The Mercedes! When did he turn it in?"

"I told you. The day of the killings. July eighth."

"Jesus Christ! Are you sure it's the same guy?"

"Yeah. Wake up, will ya? His ID gives the same address as the one who rented the car."

"Can we talk to him?"

"I dunno. I could ask the DEA guys. It's their case. We were just backing them up."

"Try! Where are you?"

"At a phone booth. I'm still on duty. I snuck home to grab a look at the list."

"Where's Gibbons?"

"I imagine he's at DEA headquarters. They work out of the federal building in St. Pete."

"Yeah. All right, you—"

Quill cut him off. "I can't do anything until I get off shift. That's at eight. Why don't we meet at the federal building then. We'll talk to the feds together."

There was nothing else they could do. "All right, Pete. Hey! You did good!"

"I hope so, Rex. I really do. Time is running out."

Rex hung up the phone, kissed Veronica, and slapped his hands together.

"What is it?" she asked.

"Serendipity, sweetheart. All my life, I've had it. I still

got it. I'm the luckiest guy on the face of the earth. Jesus!"

She was now as wide awake as he. "Well, tell me. What does it mean?"

"I'm not sure," he said. "But we may have a lead. A real one. At least it's something."

"I'm not sure I understand."

Kelsey explained it to her.

25

"**YOUR HONOR, THE STATE CALLS CATHERINE POL-**lard."

It was day four of the trial. For most of the previous two days, Smylie had brought forward witness after witness to bolster his contention that Ann Cohen, alone, was responsible for the brutal deaths of Martin Cohen and Elizabeth Winters. Now he was bringing a key witness to the stand.

Cathy Pollard, her face grim, walked slowly toward the witness stand, moving as though she were facing her own execution. After being sworn in, she took her seat and looked at Ann with eyes that were already rimmed with red. Smylie turned to the judge.

"Your Honor, the witness is a close friend of the defendant and is considered a hostile witness. I would like permission to ask leading questions of this witness."

Judge Clark held up his hand. "I'll reserve a ruling on that until we've heard some of the testimony."

"Very well, Your Honor."

Smylie looked over his notes for a moment and then approached Cathy. "Mrs. Pollard, isn't it true that the defendant has discussed her marital problems with you on several occasions?"

"Yes."

"And isn't it true that she told you she thought her husband was cheating on her?"

"Yes."

"And isn't it true—"

Judge Clark interrupted. "Just a moment. Mr. Connally, the prosecutor is asking leading questions and I don't hear you objecting. Are you aware that I have not as yet ruled on the motion to consider the witness hostile?"

Connally stood up and nodded. "I am aware of that, Your Honor. At this time, the defense has no objection to this line of questioning. In fact, we welcome it. What the witness has to say is the truth, and we are most anxious for the truth to be heard."

Clark gave Connally a sharp look. Clearly, the man was manipulating the members of the jury, but in such a way that there wasn't much the judge could do about it. "Very well. Mr. Smylie, you may continue."

"Thank you, Your Honor." Smylie shoved his hands in his pockets and stared at Cathy. "Isn't it true that the defendant knew of Mrs. Winters and where she lived?"

"Yes."

"Did the defendant ever discuss with you her intention to kill Mrs. Winters?"

Connally was instantly on his feet. "Objection!" he shouted. "I can understand the prosecutor's desire to lead the witness and I have refrained from objecting to his line of questioning to this point. However, I'm sure Your Honor will agree that this exceeds the bounds by some distance."

"Rephrase, Mr. Smylie."

"Yes, Your Honor. Mrs. Pollard, did the defendant ever threaten Mrs. Winters in your presence?"

Cathy glanced at Ann for a moment, then lowered her gaze. "Yes," she said, almost inaudibly.

"I can't hear you, Mrs. Pollard."

Cathy lifted her head. "It wasn't a real threat. She was just trying—"

"Just answer the question yes or no! Did the defendant ever threaten Mrs. Winters in your presence?"

After some hesitation, she said, "Yes."

"She threatened to kill her if she didn't stop seeing Mr. Cohen, isn't that true?"

"Yes."

"And she went to the house on Felcher Avenue and knocked on the door, and when Mrs. Winters came to the door, she told her right to her face, isn't that so?"

"Yes."

"And she said, specifically, that she would blow her head off. Isn't that the phrase she used?"

Cathy shook her head. "I don't remember the exact words."

"You don't remember? Your friend threatens to kill

another human being and you can't remember the words?"

"I was upset. She was upset. It was just to scare her."

Smylie turned to the judge. "Your Honor, I request that the last part of her answer be stricken."

"So ordered. The jury will disregard the reference made by the witness to the effect that the threat was just meant to scare her."

Smylie took a deep breath and then asked, "On the morning of July eighth, you gave a written statement to the police in which you stated that you had heard the defendant threaten Elizabeth Winters. You further stated that she had used the expression 'blow your head off.' Is that not true?"

Cathy squeezed her eyes shut, then said, "Yes."

"Thank you. Now. On the night of July seventh, did you receive a phone call from the defendant?"

"Yes."

"And what was the call about?"

"Ann was upset. She said she'd decided to divorce her husband. She was going to tell him that night. She'd already made arrangements to see a lawyer. She was feeling low."

"Did she mention anything else?"

"Yes. She said her husband had called and told her he'd be very late getting home. She said she was sure he was seeing Elizabeth again."

"At what time did you receive this call?"

"It was about seven-forty-five or so."

"And what did you do?"

"I went over to her house to be with her. We talked

for a while, and then I suggested that we go over to the house and—"

"One moment, please. What house are you referring to?"

"Mrs. Winters. Her house."

"You'd been there on other occasions?"

"Once. You just talked about that."

"Just answer the question. You knew where she lived?"

"Yes."

"All right. You drove together over to the Winters house. What happened when you arrived?"

"We went around to the back and looked in the window of the bedroom."

"What time was that?"

"I don't know exactly. Probably around eleven-thirty."

"What did you see?"

"We saw Marty lying on a bed, face down, with his hands and arms tied to the bedposts. We saw Elizabeth Winters beating him with a whip."

"What did the defendant say at that point?"

"Nothing."

"And later?"

"Nothing."

"Nothing at all?"

"No. She was shocked."

"What did you do then?"

"I drove her home."

"What happened when you arrived at the defendant's home?"

"We just sat and talked for a while. Then I went home."

Smylie walked over to his table, pulled a thick document from the pile on his desk, and again approached the stand. "Isn't it true, Mrs. Pollard, that on July eighth, and again on August eleventh, you gave statements to the effect that you wanted to stay the night with the defendant?"

"Yes."

"But she insisted you leave. Isn't that true?"

"Yes."

"She insisted you leave sometime around one o'clock in the morning of the eighth of July. Isn't that true?"

"Yes, but—"

"That was so she could go back to the house and kill her husband, wasn't it!"

"Objection!"

"Sustained! Mr. Smylie, I'll have no more of this. You have stepped outside the bounds of proper examination of this witness, and you know it. I will not tolerate such behavior. If it happens again, you'll answer for it."

"I apologize, Your Honor."

"So noted. Now sit down for a moment while I talk to the jury." The judge, his ears a bright pink, turned to the jury and said, "Ladies and gentlemen, the prosecutor has made a statement that you could not have helped but hear. Such statements have no place at this stage in the proceedings. Later, in closing arguments, the attorneys may make statements such as the one uttered by Mr. Smylie, but not during the course of examination or cross-examination. These kinds of statements are considered prejudicial because they are designed to make you think the way the attorney making the statement wants you to think. Now, I know that you've heard the statement. If you'll remember, we discussed this kind of thing before this trial began. As difficult as it may be, I want you to put it out of your mind completely. It is improper and prejudicial. Forget it was ever said." Pausing for a moment, he turned to Smylie and said, "Mr. Smylie, continue, but I warn you, I will not tolerate any more of this. My patience is at an end."

Smylie looked grim. Brusquely, he said, "I have no more questions for this witness, Your Honor."

Judge Clark turned to Connally. "Mr. Connally?"

Connally approached the witness chair and smiled at Cathy. "Mrs. Pollard," he said softly, "I know you're a little upset right now, and I can understand that. The defendant is your friend, and you probably think you've done her harm by the testimony you've just given." He shook his head. "The fact is, you haven't done anything of the kind. You've spoken the truth, and the truth is what we're after here. We both know that the defendant did not kill—"

"Objection! Counsel is making speeches, Your Honor."

Clark sighed and leaned forward. "Mr. Connally. You will confine yourself to proper cross-examination of this witness. You understand?"

"I apologize, Your Honor," Connally said. He turned back to Cathy. "Mrs. Pollard, I have only a few questions. You testified that it was you who suggested driving over to the Winters house. Why did you suggest that?"

"Because, even though Ann had told me she was going to divorce Marty, I was afraid she wouldn't. She'd talked to a lawyer, but she'd done that before, and Marty conned her out of going through with it. I thought that if she actually saw him with the woman, she wouldn't let that happen again."

"I see. Now, when the defendant threatened Mrs. Winters, some six weeks before the murders, you were with her, weren't you?"

"Yes."

"Why was that?"

"Because she asked me to come with her. She told me that Marty had been unfaithful and she knew it was with this woman. She asked me to come along to make sure she didn't do anything foolish."

"She said that? Those were her words?"

"Yes. She was angry. She was afraid she might lose her temper. She didn't want to do anything she'd be sorry for afterward. So she asked me to come along."

"Did she take a gun with her?"

"No."

"So, when the threat was made, there was no intention of ever carrying it out?"

"Objection!" Smylie yelled. "Calls for conclusion."

Connally was ready. "Your Honor," he said calmly, "the question speaks to the state of mind of the defendant. Since this witness discussed the defendant's state of mind with the defendant before and after the threat was made, she is in a unique position to testify as to the defendant's true intent."

Clark nodded. "I'll allow it. Objection overruled. The witness may answer."

"There was never any intention to hurt her."

"Thank you," Connally said. "Now, after the threat was made, did the defendant ever express to you the desire to actually kill Mrs. Winters?"

"No. Just the opposite, in fact. She said she couldn't kill anyone, and she was afraid that Mrs. Winters could tell. She was afraid she'd wasted her time."

"So, in actual fact, she made it clear in her conversations with you, both before and after the threat, that the threat was a bluff?"

"Yes. That's all it was ever meant to be."

"Objection!"

Clark shook his head. "Overruled."

"Did the defendant, at any time, suggest that she wanted to see Mrs. Winters dead?"

"No."

"I see. Now, going back to the night the murders took place, when you went over to the house, you looked in the bedroom window, correct?"

"Yes."

"Did you touch the window?"

"Yes. We both touched it when we leaned forward."

"So that's how your prints were found on it?"

"Yes."

"Did you ever—at any time—enter the house?"

"No. Never."

"You went immediately back to the home of the defendant?"

"Yes."

"When you arrived back at the home of the defendant, did she express any desire to kill anyone?"

"No."

"What *did* she say?"

"Not much. She cried a lot and said she was going to tell Marty—her husband—to his face that she was divorcing him. That was about it."

"Did she seem angry?"

"No. She seemed depressed."

"Objection!"

"Your Honor, again, it speaks to the state of mind of the defendant. This witness was the last to see the defendant before the arrival of the police."

"Overruled."

"When you say depressed, what do you mean?"

"She just sat there staring at the table. She seemed totally depressed. I was very worried about her. I suggested I stay the night and she said no. *She* was worried about *me*. She said she was going to tell Marty as soon as he got home, and she knew it was going to be a bad fight, and she didn't want me to have to witness it."

"Did she ever mention anything about a gun?"

"No."

"I see. Now, one last question. What was the defendant wearing when you left her . . . in this state of total depression?"

"She was wearing a white blouse and a pair of black slacks. And loafers. Black loafers. It was the same outfit she'd worn to work."

"Thank you, Mrs. Pollard. I have no more questions."

Cathy started to get up from the witness stand, but Smylie was on his feet. "Redirect, Your Honor."

Cathy sat down.

CHAPTER 26

THEY'D BEEN WAITING TO TALK TO SOMEONE FROM THE DEA since eight, when Peter Quill got off his shift. Now, at nine-thirty, they were still cooling their heels in the cramped reception area of the federal building. Rex Kelsey was becoming increasingly agitated. Once again, as he had just ten minutes ago, he got up and walked over to the young woman seated behind a curved reception desk.

"This Collins character," Rex said. "Is he just screwing around or is he really going to see us?"

The receptionist gave him a bored look. "Agent Collins is very busy. I told you that earlier. You don't have an appointment. You'll just have to wait until he has a moment."

"I'm tired of waiting," Rex snapped. "You federal peo-

ple are all the same. Doesn't matter whether it's the
DEA, the IRS, or whatever. You just go through the
motions, don't you? Nobody gives a shit. Well, as far
as I'm concerned—"

"You wanted to see me?" Rex turned around and
stared into the eyes of a big hostile-looking man with a
full beard and oversized black-rimmed glasses. Young.
Too damn young. "Yes," Rex snapped. "We've been here
since eight."

"So, here I am. What's your problem?"

Rex was joined by Peter, who was still in uniform. "I
was in on a bust last night," Quill said. "You arrested a
guy named Jimmy Gibbons. We'd like to talk to him."

Collins eyed Quill for a moment, noting his lack of
rank. "Obviously, this is unofficial. What's your interest?"

Rex took over. "My name is Rex Kelsey. I'm a private
investigator. I'm involved in a case that Gibbons could
be tied into. We just—"

"Well, let's not clutter up the reception area." He
waved an arm. "We'll talk in my office."

It took them ten minutes to give Collins the entire story. When they were finished, he shook his head. "Something doesn't fit here."

"Like what?" Rex asked.

Collins lit a cigarette and inhaled deeply. "You say
you're working for a lawyer named Connally?"

"Yes, that's right."

"William Connally?"

"Yes."

"Then why don't you talk to him about this?"

"For one thing," Rex said, "he's in court this morning.

For another—" He stopped. "What's Connally got to do with this?"

Collins shrugged. "You don't know?"

"Know what?"

"Connally is Gibbons's lawyer. As soon as Gibbons was busted, he started screaming for his lawyer. Connally was down here about four this morning. Right now, he's got some assistant looking after things. Guy named Bannister. I expect he'll have Gibbons out on bond in about two or three hours. If you want to talk to Gibbons, all you need to do is talk to Connally. Since he represents him, he can give you the full scoop. Gibbons isn't likely to talk to you anyway. He's mobbed up. Those guys usually keep their mouths shut."

Rex was stunned. He stared at Peter as he tried to sort it out in his mind. Then he turned back to Collins. "Yeah. That's a good idea. We'll do that. Thanks."

The two men left the DEA office and headed quietly back to their respective cars. When they reached Kelsey's, the detective turned and said, "Are you thinking what I'm thinking?"

Peter shook his head. "I don't know. You never talked to Connally about this, did you?"

"I never had the chance. You called me in the middle of the night. He was due in court at nine, and you and I were going to meet here at eight." He paused for a moment and said, "I'm not surprised that he's Gibbons's lawyer. After all, he does a lot of work for Bellesario. So if Gibbons is tied to Bellesario, that makes sense."

"Something's bugging you," Peter said. "What is it?"

Rex shook his head. "Collins said that Connally was down here in the middle of the night. That's strange.

Really strange. I've known Connally for years. He hardly does that for anybody! And Gibbons? He's just a minor cog in the Bellesario organization. Why would Connally come down here personally? It doesn't make any sense. Especially now, when he's in the middle of a major trial. He needs all the sleep he can get. I just don't—" Rex stopped talking and stared straight out into space.

"What is it?" Peter asked.

Rex was breathing hard. Very hard. He just stood there.

"What is it?" Peter asked again.

Kelsey turned his head and looked into Peter's eyes. For a few seconds, he just stared. Then he said, "Pete! We need to see some phone records."

"Phone records?"

"Yeah, phone records. Sweet Jesus! You have any connections?"

"You mean to get a court order?"

"Hell, no. There's no way we could ever get a court order. I mean, do some of your pals have a connection on the side?"

Peter shook his head. "I can't think of anyone. Well, there's a detective named Luther Jackson, but he's no friend. I hardly know the guy. Besides, he was one of the police investigators on this case. I don't think he'd—"

Kelsey cut him off. "We have to take the chance. We've got to talk to him. Will you take me in there?"

"Sure, but I don't—"

"Come on, Pete! Let's talk later. I'll follow you in my car."

CHAPTER

27

GLORIA SIMMONS LOOKED MOST UNCOMFORTABLE. FOR five months, she'd dreaded the thought of appearing in court and having her personal life exposed for all to see. When she originally talked to the cops, they assured her she wouldn't have to come to court, but that had been a lie. She'd almost expected it to be. Nevertheless, when the subpoena finally arrived, she'd called Luther Jackson and chewed him out. He'd been totally unsympathetic. He told her flatly that if she failed to appear, she'd end up in jail. Again. Only this time, it would be for more than simple prostitution, as it had been five years ago. This time, he warned her, she'd really suffer.

So here she was. About to face a prosecutor named Jeff Smylie, which didn't concern her all that much. It was the other one, the bitch's attorney, Connally. He was the bastard who'd rip her apart, try to make her look bad, cause her name to be splashed all over the newspapers and her face exposed to millions of television viewers. All because of some sexless bitch who couldn't stand the idea of her husband having some fun. It just wasn't fair.

Jeff Smylie moved to the lectern and asked his first question.

At almost the same moment, Peter Quill and Rex Kelsey were at the Pinellas County Sheriff's Department, talking to Luther Jackson. They'd just finishing making their pitch. To their chagrin, Jackson was unimpressed. "I warned you, Quill," the detective said, pointing a finger at the deputy. "I warned you five months ago. I told you then you should never get involved in these deals. It never works out. All it does is make you look bad. Maybe someday you'll learn."

Peter was about to respond, but Rex grabbed his arm. "Lieutenant Jackson," Rex said sharply, "when I first got involved in this case, I was sure that Ann Cohen was as guilty as they come. And if I was sitting where you are, I'd probably still feel that way. But the fact is, after busting my ass on this thing for five months, I've come to believe she isn't. Right now, she's on trial for two crimes she damn well didn't commit. I'm just as sure as Peter is. If there's the slightest chance that Peter and I are right, you should damn well give us a shot."

Luther snorted. "Where you from, Kelsey? Mars? Listen, we did our investigation and we turned what we had over to the State's Attorney. From then on, it was his baby. That's it. If I get involved in this bullshit, and Smylie finds out that I'm working to blow his case, I'm outta here. All these years go down the toilet. For what? I'll tell you. For nothing! Besides, you guys got nothin'!"

Rex shook his head. "It's not nothing. Look! Jimmy Gibbons is an electronics expert. We all know that. He works for Johnny Bellesario. We know that too. We know that Bellesario runs gambling throughout the central Florida area, and we know that Marty Cohen was a gambler."

"I don't know nothin' about Cohen bein' no gambler," Luther retorted.

"Well, I do," Rex insisted. "You would have found that out if you'd dug a little deeper, but you guys were too sure it was Cohen's wife. Dammit, man, if Gibbons is tied into this, it could mean Bellesario is tied into it. Doesn't the idea of nailing his ass to the wall give you some sort of incentive?"

Luther shook his head. "Johnny Bellesario is the problem of another jurisdiction—Hillsborough County, to be exact. I start messing with this and all I do is turn over what I've learned to them. I get nothing out of it."

Peter's anger, which had been building steadily, bubbled over. "Damn it, lieutenant," he snapped, "we're supposed to give a shit about the law. It sucks that you just want to sit there while an innocent woman gets put away."

Luther leaped to his feet. "So *you* say. You say she's innocent. You said that the day we busted her. You've had that idea stuck up your candy ass from the first day! You got no facts, no evidence, just a bunch of crazy ideas. And let me tell you, deputy, I don't like young cops talking to me like I just got off the fucking boat. I earned this position through a lot of hard work and by paying my dues. You got a long way to go. So don't start talking to me about the law and what's right and wrong. You're still wearing diapers when it comes to being a cop. Don't be laying any trips on me."

Rex tried to calm both men. "Look, we're getting nowhere here. Let's get to the point." Glaring at Jackson, he said, "All we're asking is that you check a few phone records. That's it. If nothing jibes, we'll drop it. What the hell harm is there in checking a few goddam phone records?"

Again, Luther shook his head. "Lots of harm. In the first place, I got a hundred things to do that are more important. In the second place, this is all speculation. Smylie will throw a shoe if he finds out."

"So make sure he doesn't."

Luther let out a sigh of exasperation. "What is it with you guys?"

Rex tried again. "Lieutenant, be straight with me. Doesn't it seem odd to you that Jimmy Gibbons rented a beige Mercedes two days before the killings, and turned it in right after they took place? I checked. The guy owns a Cadillac. If something was wrong with his car and he took it in for repairs, they'd probably give him a loaner. Maybe they didn't have a loaner available and he hadda rent his own car. Another Cadillac I could understand, but a *Mercedes*? All right, maybe he wanted to be a real big shot for a while, but why a *beige* one? That seems more than coincidence, doesn't it?"

"I'll give you that," Luther said.

"According to the rental outfit," Rex went on, "he put less than two hundred miles on it, so he wasn't on any big trip. If Gibbons was just your ordinary guy, I wouldn't be worrying about it, but he isn't. There's a thread connecting him to Marty Cohen. A thin one, I'll grant you, but a thread nevertheless. Cohen was a gambler, that I know. Bellesario runs gambling in the bay area. And Gibbons works for Bellesario. Surely you can see *some* connection."

Luther didn't answer. Instead, he stared at the two men who were ruining his morning. Of course, he could stop it at any time by throwing them out, but something was nagging at him, a small kernel of truth in what they were saying. Finally, very slowly, he sat back down in his chair and picked up the phone. He punched a few numbers and said, "Mary Brown, please."

Peter and Rex held their breath.

"Mary," Luther said, "this is Luther. I need a favor. Off the record, you dig? Okay. Cat's name is Jimmy Gibbons, aka James Gibson. I have an address in Tampa and I need to know if he has a phone. . . . Yeah, I'll wait."

Luther continued to glare at his two antagonists, neither of whom was saying a word. After almost a minute, Mary was back.

"Yeah," Luther said. He seemed a touch more interested. "Okay. Will you take a little stroll through your computer and see who he talked to from, say, mid-June to July eighth? . . . Yeah, this year. . . . I *know* it's a pain in the ass." Then, after a moment, "Dinner at Tio Pepe's? Yes! . . . And dancing? Yes! Jesus! You're gettin' bad, y'know? . . . Thanks, doll. . . . Yeah, I'll wait."

In a few minutes Luther was talking to the woman again, only this time he was making notes. Peter and Rex heard him ask some questions. Then more questions. When he'd finished, he hung up the phone, pushed his chair away from his desk, and said, "Hold on."

Luther's fingers danced through some file folders in a drawer of the green steel cabinet that stood near the wall. He found what he was looking for and made some more notes. Then he came back and resumed his seat at his desk. "All right," he said, letting out another deep sigh, "don't let's get excited, but there's a lot of shit here that needs to be checked out, and one name does stand out."

Rex and Peter were all ears.

"First of all," Luther said, "Gibbons has two phones, a regular one and one of those portable cellular jobs. There's some stuff on his regular phone, but none of the names mean shit to me. I'll check them out later if I get time. But using his portable phone, Gibbons called a guy named Frank Peters at three-fourteen P.M. on June twenty-third."

Rex almost leaped out of his chair. "Frank Peters? The hit man?"

Luther seemed surprised. "You know him?"

"Not personally, but I know who he is."

"How?"

"Connally defended him three years ago. It was a very big case. So big it made Connally."

Luther frowned. "Well, it's the same guy, all right. I just checked the address against the one Mary gave me. He's still living in Tampa. Now, that doesn't mean all that much, because we know that Peters and Gibbons both work for Bellesario. So, in itself, it ain't all that terrific. But there's more."

"More?"

"Yeah. The next day, Gibbons called Peters again, at eight-oh-five in the morning." He looked at his notes. "Then, we have Gibbons making a call to a pay phone located at a Seven-Eleven on Tampa Road, about a mile east of Nineteen, at ten-thirty-five P.M. That was July fourth. On July seventh, he made two more calls to the same pay phone, one at seven-fifty P.M. and another at eleven-twelve."

The three men stared at each other for a moment as their brains tried to sort it out. Rex had it first. "Those times!" he exclaimed. "Ann Cohen got a call from her husband about seven-thirty on the seventh. Then, later, sometime around eleven, she and her friend went over to the Winters house."

He stood up and started pacing the floor, thinking out loud.

"We know Gibbons is a bug man," Rex went on. "Let's suppose, just for the sake of discussion, that Johnny Bellesario wanted Marty Cohen knocked off for some reason. Bellesario gives the project to Peters, who hires Gibbons to bug Marty's house *and* the girlfriend's house, seeing as Marty spends as much time there as at home. Peters, being a pro, wants to know as much about the man he's been hired to kill as possible. You with me so far?"

"It's your story," Luther said, a bored expression on his face.

"Stay with me here," Rex said, his excitement mounting. "Peters wants to know where Marty is at all times, because he isn't quite sure where he wants to make the hit. So Gibbons bugs both places and monitors the bugs around the clock for maybe a week or so, during which time he reports back to Peters on everything he hears—"

"You're reaching," Luther said, interrupting. "Really reaching. Why would either Gibbons or Peters set up Ann Cohen? Why would Bellesario set her up? She's nothing to any of those people. And why would they take so long to plan it? If Bellesario wanted Marty Cohen hit, he'd just get it done. And Gibbons is a bug man. Why would he be the one renting the car?" He scratched his head and stared at the wall. "This is much too elaborate. They could have blasted Marty anywhere! Why kill the woman?"

"Because," Rex answered, "it makes the frame complete, that's why. Because they made this thing look like the work of a crazed, jealous wife. What better way to set it up? You guys just assumed she had to be the one. You were manipulated, don't you see? They never do it this way, and that's what threw us all off. It's perfect because it worked."

Rex paused and took a deep breath.

"You've got to take another look at this thing, don't you think?"

Luther just stared straight ahead for a moment, then glared at Rex and nodded. "Jesus! What a mess." He slammed a hand on the desk. "All right! No promises, but I'll see what I can do. I'm not going to kick it upstairs until I have a little more. In the meantime, you see what you can dig up."

Peter was on his feet again. "Why can't you kick it upstairs?"

Luther let out another frustrated sigh. "Because this case is over, as far as we're concerned. It was over as soon as we gave it to the State's Attorney. Christ, man! The trial is going on right now. We don't have enough new evidence to justify going to Smylie. Not yet."

Peter was incensed. "So we just sit on our asses and let an innocent woman be convicted of two murders she didn't commit? Is that what we do?"

Luther groaned, then shook his head. "God! The innocence of youth. I don't want to hear any more of this crap. I want you both out of my sight. Now!"

Peter held his ground. "Tell me, lieutenant, just so I know. Are you completely satisfied that Ann Cohen murdered her husband and Elizabeth Winters? Because if you are, I'll drop this thing right now. I have nothing but respect for you, as a man and as a cop. If you're one hundred percent satisfied that she acted alone and none of this has anything to do with it, I'll be satisfied as well."

Luther just stared at the young cop. Finally, the veteran detective lit another cigarette and shook his head. "I told you I'd do some checking, and I will. If you want to go over my head, feel free. But let me warn you, the moment you do, you're through as a cop. Not because of me, but because of the system. Now, instead of runnin' up and down my back, why don't you talk to some people yourself? Bring me something I can really use. We just don't have enough."

"You'll keep looking into it?"

"Yes! I just said that, didn't I?"

Peter's face broke into a smile. "Thanks, Luther. I really appreciate it."

Luther waved a hand at him. "You're gonna get us all in deep shit. I just know it. I'm gonna curse the day I ever laid eyes on you, Quill. Damn sure. And it's *Lieutenant* Jackson. Get that through your thick head."

Peter looked at him carefully. Yes, he was frowning. But the eyes were smiling.

The cross-examination of Gloria Simmons was even more brutal than she had feared. By the time he was through, Connally had destroyed her credibility and that of her friend Elizabeth Winters. Through his probing, Connally had made it appear as though both women were demented, sex-crazed, drug abusers, the dregs of society. At that point, he'd had the jury in his pocket. But in his zeal he'd taken it a step too far. He'd continued to question the witness mercilessly for another full hour. In doing so, he'd exposed her every flaw, the minor ones as well as the major ones. When he was finished, he'd ripped her completely apart, leaving her a quivering, whimpering wreck. Now, in the eyes of some of the jurors, Gloria Simmons was to be pitied. Connally had actually managed to make her an object of sympathy. Finally realizing his mistake, he brought his cross-examination to a belated halt.

Judge Clark called a lunch recess.

As Bill escorted Ann out of the courtroom, Rex Kelsey was waiting for them. "We have to talk," Rex said, his eyes alive with excitement.

"You've found something?"

"Yes."

Bill turned to Ann. "Look, I have to talk to Rex for a few minutes. Why don't you have lunch with your father in the cafeteria? The media aren't allowed to bug you there."

Anita Phillips pressed forward. "I've got a better idea," she said. "I brought the motor home down. I have lunch for all of us. It's ready and waiting. We can sit there and relax."

Ann, her father, and her friends headed for the parking lot, while Rex and Bill went to the cafeteria on the second floor. Sitting in the corner of the cramped lunchroom, Bill ruefully contemplated the tuna fish sandwich in front of him and asked, "So. What have you got?"

Rex was eager to tell him, but first he needed some answers. "Mr. Connally," he said softly, "I know you have to maintain confidentiality with your clients, but what do you do when there's a conflict?"

"Conflict? What conflict?"

"Well, as you know, Peter Quill has been really working hard for us. He's been going over the records of the thousand or so people that might have been driving a beige Mercedes or BMW that night. He finally got a match. It turns out that one of your clients could be involved in the killings."

Bill looked stunned. "One of my clients? Who?"

"Jimmy Gibbons."

Bill was about to take a bite out of the sandwich. He stopped, his mouth open, and slowly put the sandwich back on the plate. "Jimmy Gibbons? What the hell are you talking about?"

Rex took a deep breath and said, "Gibbons rented a

beige Mercedes Five-sixty SEL two days before Marty Cohen and Elizabeth Winters were killed. He returned it the day of the murders."

Bill shrugged. "I know that."

Now it was Rex's turn to be shocked. "You do?"

Bill bit into his sandwich, chewed on it for a moment, then swallowed. "When Gibbons called me from the DEA offices, I went down there personally, because I realized the same thing Quill did. I've probably looked over those lists as many times as you two. I knew that Gibbons uses the name Gibson, but I'd never connected it before. This time, it jumped out at me.

"I went down there in the middle of the night to satisfy myself that Gibbons's reasons for being in a beige Mercedes that night had nothing to do with Ann. I talked to him. If his answers had been unsatisfactory, I would have resigned as his attorney right then and there."

Rex was astonished. "You talked to him about the car?"

Bill flushed. "I just said that. Why the hell else would I go downtown in the middle of the night? I don't do that for common criminals. I can't discuss the conversation, but I can tell you you're barking up the wrong tree. I realize there are certain coincidental facts that seem to point in his direction, but that's all they are. Just coincidence."

"Well," Rex said, choosing his words carefully, "it turns out that Gibbons had some telephone conversations with Frank Peters. Did you know that?"

Bill was chewing his food again. He simply shook his head. Rex continued to talk. "Two of the calls came at very interesting times. One was made to a pay phone on

July seventh, just after Ann received the call from Marty that he would be late. Another was made just after Ann and Cathy took off to go down to the Winters house. Same pay phone."

Bill continued to chew.

"As you know," Rex went on, "Gibbons is an electronics specialist who works mainly for Johnny Bellesario. Peters—we don't have to talk about him. It's starting to look—to me, at least—like Johnny Bellesario is involved in this. You representing Gibbons on the drug beef makes it a little complicated. You see the problem?"

Bill nodded. "I see the problem, all right. The problem is you're jumping to conclusions. I can't discuss with you—or anyone else—what Gibbons was doing that night, as you well know. But I can say this. Gibbons is not involved with the murders of those two. That I'm sure of."

Rex looked crestfallen. "Mr. Connally, the calls to Frank Peters—that's just too much!"

Bill's face seemed pinched. "Look," he said, "I can't discuss with you what I've learned. In that respect, you're right about a conflict. But having said that, I can assure you that Jimmy Gibbons is not involved. Naturally, you'd jump to conclusions, especially when it turns out that he made calls to Frank Peters. I have no idea what those calls mean, but since both men work for Bellesario, it's not so surprising. There are all sorts of things that are ongoing, and I'm sure you'll find all kinds of calls going back and forth between people who work for the same organization."

"But you know Peters," Rex protested. "The man is

five feet five! He weighs about one-twenty. Don't you see? He could have dressed like a woman that night!"

Bill nodded. "He could have, but he didn't." He patted Rex on the shoulder. "I can understand how you feel," he said sympathetically. "Too many things seem to add up. The fact is, I had Bannister check out Gibbons's story this morning, and it's real. He's not involved. If I thought for one moment that he was, or that Peters was—or that Bellesario was, for that matter—I would drop the lot of them. But you're talking about two different cases.

"I talked to Bellesario some time ago, you remember? He told me, off the record, of course, and I expect you to remember"—he looked hard at Rex, who nodded—"that Marty Cohen was a gambler, but at the time he didn't owe Bellesario a thing. There'd be no reason for Bellesario to be involved in anything having to do with his death. As for Peters, I'll ask Bellesario about that. I'm certain it's all coincidental, but I'll check it out, just to be sure."

Rex played with his sandwich for a moment. "Mr. Connally, what if they're lying to you? All of them? What if they're feeding you a bunch of crap?"

Bill almost laughed out loud. "Rex, you're good. But so am I. I've saved their asses a number of times. I get a healthy retainer every month. They know the moment they start lying to their attorney, I'm through with them. They need me a lot more than I need them."

Three hours later, Lieutenant Luther Jackson was standing inside the garage area owned by the Regency Rent-a-Car agency on Kennedy Boulevard in Tampa. He was looking at a beige Mercedes 560 SEL sedan. "You're sure this is the car you rented to this James Gibson for three days in July?"

"That's the one," the manager said. "What's the problem?"

The man with Jackson was a Hillsborough County sheriff's deputy named Gallagher. Gallagher said, "We just want to check it out a bit. How many people have used this car since Gibson had his hands on it?"

"I'd have to check, but I can tell you it's quite a lot. We rent this car to big shots coming down here from the north on so-called business trips. They like the nicer things in life, you know? Even at a hundred twenty a day plus mileage. What do they care? They all have big expense accounts."

Gallagher looked at his old friend from across the bay and said, "Well, whatcha think? A waste of time?"

Luther shrugged. "Probably, but let's give it a go. You brought the portable laser and the camera?"

"Just like you asked."

"Great. I owe you one, Jack."

"You owe me more'n one, shmuck."

Jeff Smylie stood tall and straight behind his table. During the last few hours, he'd presented a number of witnesses. The insurance salesman who'd sold Ann Cohen a $500,000 life insurance policy on her husband three years ago. That had gotten the jury's attention. And Connally couldn't even think of a thing to say to the guy. That had been a kick. Then he'd brought in two more witnesses who'd claimed Ann had once expressed terribly angry thoughts about her husband. They hadn't fared too well under Connally's cross. He'd made it seem they were simply jealous of her, lying to make her look bad. Now he'd come to the end of his list. There were no more witnesses. In a clear voice, he said, "Your Honor, the State rests."

Immediately Connally was on his feet with the obligatory motion to dismiss. "You Honor," he said, "I move that all charges as listed in the information be dismissed. The State has failed to prove that the defendant murdered anyone."

Judge Clark shook his head. "Motion denied. Are you ready with your first witness, Mr. Connally?"

"Yes, Your Honor. We call Ann Cohen to the stand."

That was what the media people had been waiting for. They braced themselves as Ann walked toward the center of the room, took the oath, and then moved to the witness chair. They didn't want to miss a thing, not a word.

But they were to be disappointed. As soon as Ann was in the witness chair, Judge Clark motioned for the attorneys to approach the bench. Once in position, the judge said, "Mr. Connally, how long do you expect your direct examination will take?"

"I expect it will be a number of hours, Your Honor. The defendant has a story to tell, and I want the jury to hear it all."

"I'm sure you do. Well, since it's almost five, I'm going to adjourn until nine tomorrow morning. That okay with you, Mr. Smylie?"

"Yes, Your Honor."

"Very well."

Ann Cohen would have to wait one more day to tell her story. As she walked out of the courtroom, Bill on one arm, her father on the other, with friends flanking the trio on both sides, she knew she would be forced to walk the gauntlet of reporters again tomorrow.

Would they ever leave her alone? she wondered. If she was found guilty, it wouldn't matter much. But if she was acquitted, how many would think it was because of her attorney? And later, if she married him, would they think it some sort of reward for saving her? Would they think it was her only reason for falling in love with him?

And then she was seized by another fear. Was it indeed?

CHAPTER

28

THE DIRECT EXAMINATION OF ANN COHEN TOOK EX-
actly three hours, winding up at the lunch hour, just as
Connally had planned. At the beginning of her examination, he had asked her, "Did you kill Martin Cohen
and Elizabeth Winters?" to which she had answered,
"No," in a strong, clear voice. For the remainder of the
examination, Connally had carefully, patiently drawn
from her almost every detail of her life with Marty
Cohen, as well as her recollection of what had happened
that terrible night.

She had answered each and every question as she
had the first one, holding her head high, unafraid to look
at the jury, as she carefully explained the reasons for
her every action. Again, at the end of his examination,
Connally asked her the very same question that he'd

started with. "Once more, I ask you, Ann Cohen: Did you kill Marty Cohen?"

And again, she answered in the same strong voice, "No, I did not."

"Did you kill Elizabeth Winters?"

"No, I did not."

Connally smiled and, with his lips, formed the words *Well done*. A silent message from Bill to Ann, congratulating her for following his instructions to the letter.

In their seemingly endless practice sessions conducted before the trial, Bill had played himself, then taken the part of Smylie, firing hostile questions at her like missiles. He'd explained the need for such rehearsal, telling Ann she had to be fully prepared for Smylie's cross-examination.

At first, she'd broken down and cried as the questions became increasingly brutal. Bill would tell her when it was all right to cry and when it was not. Then the questions would be fired at her with even more force. She had to stand up to Smylie, Bill had warned. It wouldn't be easy. So he would go over the anticipated questions time after time, pounding away, sometimes yelling, until he was sure she wouldn't be taken by surprise. Now, as he turned to Smylie and said, "Your witness," he hoped he'd covered them all.

Judge Clark called for a lunch recess.

After lunch, Smylie nodded at his wily opponent, stood up, and walked to the lectern. In his hands, he held a thick file folder, which he opened and placed on the lectern. For a moment, he said nothing as he leafed through its pages. Then, lifting his head and staring directly at Ann, he asked his first question.

"Mrs. Cohen, you've testified that you first considered divorcing your husband three years ago, is that correct?"

"Yes."

"You consulted an attorney?"

"Yes."

"Who was that attorney?"

"Mr. Connally," she answered calmly.

"I see. But you didn't go through with the divorce, did you?"

"No."

"Why not?"

"I've already testified to that."

"I know. I just want to make sure I have it right."

Ann looked at Bill, who nodded, then back at Smylie. "I was hurt. My husband had lied to me about something very important. I considered divorce, yes, but after Marty was operated on in an attempt to reverse the effects of the vasectomy, I decided to stay with him, because I realized how much I loved him."

"But you did manage to get your husband to take out an additional five hundred thousand dollars in life insurance, didn't you?"

"No. The policy was Marty's idea."

"Of course. You testified that he wanted to prove to you how much he loved you. The fact is, it was your idea, wasn't it?"

"Objection!" Connally called. "Asked and answered."

"Sustained."

"And then," Smylie continued, "three months before the death of your husband, you discovered that your husband was seeing another woman, but instead of divorcing him, you consulted a psychiatrist. Isn't it a fact that you consulted a psychiatrist because you wanted confirmation of something you already knew? That your husband was a sexual deviate and would never change? That he would always be unfaithful to you?"

"I wasn't sure," Ann replied calmly. "I consulted a doctor to try and understand why he was . . . sick."

"Why didn't you immediately seek a divorce?"

"I have testified to that."

"Yes. You said that your husband was seeking professional help himself. You said you thought there was a chance he would change. But that isn't true, is it?"

"Yes, it is."

"You made an appointment with your attorney to discuss divorce on July seventh, three months after you discovered your husband had been unfaithful to you. Isn't it a fact that you had already decided to kill your husband and Elizabeth Winters?"

"No."

"You threatened to kill Elizabeth Winters, didn't you?"

"Not really. I was just—"

"Please, Mrs. Cohen. Just answer my questions yes or no. Did you threaten to kill Elizabeth Winters, yes or no?"

"Yes," Ann answered, her voice filled with anguish.

"You threatened to kill your husband, didn't you?"

"No!"

Smylie looked through his papers and withdrew a yellow sheet. "Allow me to read to you the testimony of Gloria Simmons, who swore under oath that she heard Martin Cohen specifically state he was worried you might kill him."

Connally was on his feet again, his face livid with rage. "Objection!"

"Sustained!" Judge Clark bellowed. "Mr. Smylie, you're well aware of my ruling on the admissibility of that testimony. I have ruled it as hearsay. It's been stricken from the record. Take your seat."

"I apologize, Your Honor."

While a seemingly chagrined Smylie took his seat, the judge again cautioned the jury to disregard that portion of Gloria Simmons's testimony. Then he said, "Recess, ten minutes. Counsel in chambers."

In chambers, Clark said, "Mr. Smylie, I am very close to declaring a mistrial here. At the very least, I'm preparing charges of professional misconduct."

Smylie was ashen-faced. "I'm sorry, Your Honor, it was a mental error. I did not mean to ignore the ruling."

"One more time, Mr. Smylie, and this trial is history. Do I make myself clear?"

"Yes, Your Honor."

Back in court, a slightly subdued Smylie resumed his cross-examination. "When did you first learn that your husband was a heavy gambler?" he asked.

"Not until after his death," Ann answered. "Mr. Connally's investigator discovered it."

"I see. You had no idea that your husband was making a lot more money than he claimed until after his death?"

"I had no idea."

"And you, being an accountant, scrutinized your own tax returns carefully, did you not?"

"Yes."

"Being an accountant, you would be aware of the fact that you would be liable for unclaimed income, since you had signed a joint return?"

"Of course. But I never—"

"Just yes or no, Mrs. Cohen."

Ann fought to control herself. Despite the repeated rehearsals, it was all starting to get to her: the battle of wits between Bill and Smylie, the admonitions of the judge, the constant interruptions. It was as though she was just a cog in the mighty machine that was the criminal justice system. "I'm aware of the law," she said.

"Let me take you back to the night of the killings," Smylie said. "You testified that you and your friend Catherine Pollard went to the home of Elizabeth Winters, looked through the partially closed blinds covering the bedroom window, and witnessed your husband involved in sadomasochistic activity with Elizabeth Winters. You say you both left, and then, around one o'clock in the morning, you took a drive alone. But you are unable to present a single witness to corroborate that story. Isn't it possible you went back to the Winters house?"

"No."

"Isn't it possible that you changed your clothes, killed two people, went home, changed clothes again, and waited for the police to arrive?"

"No."

"Isn't it possible that you put the gun you used to kill your husband back in the night table because you knew it would appear suspicious if it wasn't found?"

"No."

"Isn't it possible that you cleaned the shells simply to confuse the issue?"

"No."

Smylie scratched his head for a moment. "You've known Mr. Connally for some time, haven't you?"

"Yes."

"You've consulted with him about divorcing your husband on at least two occasions, haven't you?"

"Yes."

"And you always knew that if you were ever in serious trouble, he'd be at your side, isn't that true?"

"Objection! Irrelevant!"

"Your Honor," Smylie cried, "I'm trying to establish motive and state of mind of the witness at the time of the murders."

"Overruled."

Smylie moved a few steps toward Ann. "Isn't it true, Mrs. Cohen, that you and Mr. Connally are now romantically involved?"

"Objection!" Connally shouted.

"Overruled," Judge Clark said.

Ann looked at Bill and said, "I care for Mr. Connally very much. He's been a friend for a long time."

Smylie shook his head. "You didn't answer my question. Are you romantically involved with Mr. Connally?"

"Yes, but—"

"That's fine," Smylie said, cutting her off. "The fact is, Mrs. Cohen, you're in love with Mr. Connally, isn't that true?"

Very softly, Ann answered, "Yes."

"Is he in love with you?"

"Yes."

"Isn't it true, Mrs. Cohen, that you and Mr. Connally have been romantically involved for a number of years?"

"No."

"Isn't it true, Mrs. Cohen, that you and Mr. Connally were romantically involved prior to the death of your husband?"

"No!" she shouted. "It's only been the last few months."

"I see," Smylie said. "Isn't it true that you knew divorcing your husband was out of the question for financial reasons?"

"No."

"No? Isn't it true that in a messy divorce action, it was quite possible that all the details of your husband's financial dealings would be brought to light? That might have meant you would be left penniless. Your only way out was to kill him and collect on the insurance. So you killed your husband, and you seduced one of the best criminal attorneys in the country to ensure that—"

"Objection!" Connally screamed, his face red with anger.

"Sustained," Clark said.

"Let me rephrase, Mrs. Cohen. Isn't it true that you were the one to make overtures to Mr. Connally?"

"Objection," Connally yelled.

"I'll allow it. Overruled."

"No," Ann answered firmly. "It was a mutual thing."

"Oh," Smylie said, smiling at the jury.

Ann, feeling that terrible shortness of breath again, closed her eyes for a moment, mouthing a silent prayer.

They were huddled in the corner of a small coffee shop in downtown Clearwater: Kelsey and Quill and

Jackson. Peter and Rex were drinking coffee and trying to understand why Luther had called this midday meeting. Luther was munching a hero sandwich as he talked, his eyes bright with excitement.

"First off," Luther said, using his spoon to disperse the blob of imitation whipped cream floating on top of a steaming cup of hot chocolate, "I want to hear what Rex has to say while I finish my lunch."

Rex shrugged and said, "I told you both on the phone last night. I talked to Connally and he says he talked to Gibbons about the car. He's satisfied there's no connection. He can't tell me what was discussed, naturally, but he had access to the guy. If he's satisfied, who the hell am I to argue with him?"

Luther put down his sandwich and grinned. His gleaming white teeth were covered with bits of cheese and meat. Not a pretty sight. "I've been thinking about that ever since you talked to me last night," he said. "And you you know, it really got me to thinking."

"About what?" Peter asked.

"About this whole thing. I'll admit that when you two jumped all over me, I was as sure as anyone that you were just a couple of cowboys trying to make waves. But things have changed a little."

Rex looked surprised. "Changed? How? You said last night you came up empty."

"I know. I was less than truthful about that."

"Why?"

"Because I wanted to check a few things out before I mentioned what I found."

"You found something?"

Luther looked smug. "You have to understand," he

said, "that all this is strictly off the record for now. We can't go to a judge and get a court order, because this information was obtained outside normal channels. We don't have probable cause to check this stuff. Not really."

"So what did you find out?" Rex asked impatiently.

Luther lit a cigarette, took a deep drag, exhaled, then said, "Well, for one thing, I got an old buddy to help me with the car Gibbons rented. We checked it out yesterday. Found about twenty clear latents on the inside of the trunk lid. Thank God they never clean that part of the car."

Rex shrugged. "You already had a record of Gibbons renting the thing. So what's the big deal?"

Luther smiled, the movement crinkling his eyes, which almost danced with merriment. "We didn't find Gibbons's prints. But we did find three that belong to Frank Peters."

Rex almost leaped out of his chair. "Jesus! He was in the car? Then, he *did* make the hit!"

Luther puffed some more on the cigarette, then said, "Maybe. What we got is no proof of anything except that he stuck his left hand on the inside of the trunk lid."

"You're a hard man to convince," Peter said, trying hard to keep his anger in check.

"And you don't know when you're ahead. You managed to get me working on this thing. A simple 'thank you' wouldn't break my heart."

"You're right," Peter said, hanging his head. "I'm sorry. Thank you."

Luther appraised Peter for a moment. "There's more."

They waited. Luther seemed to be enjoying himself.

Now that he'd been drawn back into the investigation, he was relishing the fact that he'd discovered something. "You guys," he said, "keep talking about the connection between Peters, Gibbons, and Bellesario."

"It makes sense, doesn't it?" Rex said. "You know as well as I do that Bellesario is the common denominator here."

Rex smiled. "There's one other common denominator you keep overlooking."

"Like what?" Rex asked.

"Not what. Whom."

"So whom?"

The grin widened. "William Connally," Luther said.

Rex and Peter were too stunned to speak. While they stared at him, slack-jawed, Luther explained. "I started thinking about it last night. Matter of fact, it kept me up most of the night. Then, this morning, while I was doing some more checking on phone records, I thought I might as well run a check on some calls that were made from Connally's office. As I said, he's a common denominator too. An even bigger one than Bellesario, when you get right down to it."

"Connally?" Rex finally croaked. "How would he figure in this?"

Luther gave him a hard stare. "You were the one who told me Gibbons screamed for Connally as soon as he was arrested, right? And you said that Connally went down to the federal building in the middle of the night. You also said it was a very unusual thing for him to do. Connally told you it was because he remembered seeing Gibbons's aka on those records you guys had."

"Right."

"So Connally's had those records for months. He's also defended Gibbons before. He *knew* where Gibbons lived. He *knew* that Gibbons often used the name Gibson. He should have noticed that name right away, not after the guy calls him in the middle of the night. Connally's blowing smoke in your face, Rex."

Rex just sat there.

"The DEA tells me," Luther continued, "that Connally's man had him sprung in the morning. Gibbons hasn't been seen since. I thought it was worth a look-see. It turns out that big Bill did make a call to Gibbons, at two-fifty-eight on the afternoon of June twenty-third. On the surface, that's no big deal. Connally has acted as Gibbons's lawyer on other occasions, and the call could have nothing to do with this case. But you might remember that about fifteen minutes later, Gibbons made his first call to Peters."

Peter and Rex simply stared. "Connally?" Rex gasped. "I don't get it."

"I didn't either," Luther went on. "Not at first. But it all works. You guys kept telling me that Bellesario was involved in this. The fact that Gibbons and Peters are both on his payroll had you going in that direction. But I couldn't understand why Bellesario would make such a big production out of the hit. It just isn't his style. Besides, why the hell would he want to frame the Cohen woman? That's what was driving me crazy. So I started looking for someone who might have a reason to kill those two *and* set up the Cohen woman. Only one person fills that bill. Connally."

"But—"

Luther held up a hand for silence. "For one thing," he

said, "Connally's acted as the attorney for both Peters and Gibbons. For another, he used to live in the same complex as Ann and Marty Cohen, so he knew both of them. He was aware that Ann owned a beige Mercedes and he was probably aware that she kept a key to her house under some little thing stuck in a flowerpot. In checking the phone records, I discovered that Connally made another call to Gibbons, on May twenty-ninth, a few days after Ann Cohen threatened Elizabeth Winters.

"Since Connally and the Cohen woman were friends, I figured she got nervous after making the threat and wanted to check with Connally to see if she was in trouble. Sure enough, the records show she called him the same day she threatened Winters. So Connally knew she'd made the threat. I think that's when he first got the idea and called Gibbons."

Kelsey and Quill looked at each other in shock.

"What I got is mainly guesswork," Luther continued, "but it could have happened this way."

They waited.

"Connally lived in the same complex as the Cohens for a long time," Luther began. "When I interviewed Gina Rizzo, she mentioned that Marty Cohen was a real stickman. She also mentioned—in passing—that Connally was as well."

"It's no secret that Connally likes women," Rex chimed in. "He's never made a secret of that."

Luther rolled his eyes skyward. "Let me finish, okay?"

Rex nodded.

"Connally was screwing a lot of the women in the complex," Luther continued, "but I don't think he got into the Cohen woman's pants before the killings. Nobody ever gave me that impression. What about you, Rex?"

Rex shook his head. "No way. All I ever heard from anyone was what a great person she was. If she was screwing around, she sure as hell kept it quiet."

"All right," Luther said. "We know that Connally and the Cohen woman are now an item, as they say, because he had to get the judge's permission to take her to Lauderdale. You can be sure that wasn't strictly business. So, if we assume, just for the sake of this discussion, that Connally has had the hots for this woman for some time, it *really* starts to come together. Supposition, sure, but that's what makes it fit. The missing link, as they say."

He took a deep breath.

"When Ann Cohen found out about her husband's vasectomy, she talked to Connally about a divorce. Suppose Connally checked out Marty and discovered a lot more, like the gambling and the broads? Suppose he tells Ann about it, but she doesn't believe him. When Ann decides to stick with her husband, Connally gets pissed. Maybe he hits on Ann a few times and when she turns him down because she's true blue to her husband, Connally, with his king-sized ego, gets even more pissed. He starts brooding about it.

"Let's say he starts to fall in love with her. Not your normal healthy love but some sick, possessive thing. Hey, we all know there are people like that. It's driving him crazy. When he starts to make it big and moves out of the complex into a big house by the lake, he tries to forget her, but he can't.

"Then he gets a call from Ann. Ann tells him about

Winters and the threat. Connally suggests divorce, but she says she's seeing a shrink instead. Connally flips out. He decides to make things happen."

Rex and Peter looked at each other again. It was starting to make sense.

"Connally hires Gibbons to bug her house," Luther continued, "and the Winters house as well, knowing Marty spends a lot of time with this woman. He talks to Frank Peters, a guy he's defended in the past, about a possible hit. Peters agrees to make the hit, but Connally wants it done a certain way."

"You mean, to frame Ann," Rex interrupted. "Why the hell would he do that?"

"I'm coming to that part," Luther said. "It's the thing that I couldn't figure out until now." He stopped for a moment, then said, "Both houses are bugged. Peters is figuring out the best way to do it. On the fifth, Gibbons hears Marty make a date with the broad for the seventh, so they set that night for the hit. Gibbons rents the car, then turns it over to Peters and with Ann Cohen's gun. He probably snatched the gun when he went inside to plant the bugs.

"Connally tells Peters to make the hit on Marty and the woman look like a hate thing. Revenge. Very sexual. That's why they were shot in the genitals first. That's also why Marty's body was placed on top of the woman's.

"While Peters is in there, he pulls out all the bugs that Gibbons had put in. That's why he stuck towels in both their mouths. He needed to keep them quiet while he pulled out the bugs, because once the gun went off, things would start happening. Then he kills them and beats it back to meet with Gibbons somewhere. They change cars again, and Peters gives the gun back to Gibbons.

"Gibbons then goes over to Ann Cohen's house to pull the bugs out of her place and put the gun back. This he's gotta do before the cops show up to tell her her husband is dead, but he knows he's got at least an hour. Plenty of time for him. He probably figured she'd be asleep.

"Anyway, Gibbons gets to the Cohen house and she's gone! He can hardly believe his luck. He uses the key in the flowerpot to get in, just like he did the first time. He pulls out the bugs and puts the gun back, along with that box of unused shells." He leaned back in his chair, lit another cigarette and asked, "How's that all sound?"

Peter and Rex were totally shocked. Rex was the first one to speak. "It all makes sense, except for one thing. Why frame Ann? Why not just kill Marty?"

Luther grinned. "That's the cute part," Luther said, enjoying himself immensely. "Ann and Connally knew each other for years, right? If she gets arrested for murder, who the hell do you think she'll turn to? Some stranger? No fucking way. She's gonna turn to her old friend, one of the best in the business. This is not a stupid woman! So Connally is going to save this poor woman from the criminal justice system, and while he's at it he'll charm the shit out of her. Why not? He knows she's emotionally fucked up. She'd fall in love with any guy who's gonna save her life! How many women fall in love with their doctors? How many prisoners fall in love with their captors? It's a wacky thing, but it happens all the time.

"Connally, being a cocky, successful lawyer, figures he'll get her off, no matter what. He's *obsessed* with this woman and not thinkin' straight. His ego is out of control. Even though Ann called him on the seventh, asking for an appointment to discuss divorce, Connally figures it'll never happen. He thinks that as long as Marty Cohen is alive, he doesn't stand a Chinaman's chance with this woman. So he just lets it happen.

"Being a clever bastard, he sets the frame up in such a way that there are a lot of unanswered questions. Like the clothes. Connally got Peters to wear woman's clothes, but not just any women's clothes. He had Peters dress a certain way, making sure he was dressed opposite to what the Cohen woman was wearing. If she'd been wearing a dress, he would have had Peters wear slacks. Connally probably had Ann under surveillance the whole night. He counted on somebody seeing the killer leave. That's why Peters took his time! It was planned that way! Peters is just a little guy. In the dark, who the hell would know?

"And the shells!" he went on. "Now that was really cute. Connally made sure the shells had no prints, even the ones in the gun. That way, he was sure to be able to throw a lot of flak at the jury. So you've got the clothes being a mystery, and the spent shells are confusing. Just enough to screw up a jury, but not enough to stop the charges from being laid in the first place."

Rex was almost beside himself. "And me! He was cute about that too. He picked me because I'd been out of touch for a while. Some other guy might have started checking things like— Jesus!"

"What?" asked Luther.

"Once, I asked him to let me talk to Bellesario. I wanted to confirm that Marty was a heavy gambler. He said *he'd* do it. Now I know why. He probably never talked to the man at all."

Luther nodded. "Yeah. Again, I'm only guessing, but I think this was strictly a private thing with Connally. Johnny Bellesario probably doesn't know squat about it."

Luther leaned forward, propped his head in his hands, and said, "Well, there you are. That's what I think happened. And the only problem we got is we can't prove any of it. Not a thing!"

"What about the prints on the car?" asked Rex.

Luther shook his head. "We did that on the quiet. Sure, we sealed the trunk lid, so we can always go back and redo the prints, but it's all still just circumstantial stuff. The phone calls are the same. We've really got nothing. Gibbons won't talk. Neither will Peters. So we're up shit creek."

Rex banged a fist on the table. "We can't just sit here and let it happen. I know this much. Ann is in love with this guy. At least that part of your theory checks out."

"Thank you."

"Jesus!" Rex continued. "It all fits. It really does. And the thing that really scares me is the fact that the jury may very well convict her, Connally notwithstanding. Even the best get beat sometimes."

"So what do we do?" Peter asked. "How do we find a way to get this on the record and get the investigation reopened?"

"It has to be done before the trial's over," Rex said. "If the jury convicts her, it could take years to get her out. Telfer doesn't like to admit mistakes. Even if we get solid evidence, they might try to bury it."

"I've been thinking about that," Luther said.

"So what do we do?" Peter repeated.

"Well," Luther said, "this is something only Rex can do. You and me, Peter, we're gonna have to stay out of this one."

It was almost an hour before Rex was able to get past Lionel Telfer's secretary, and even then the State Attorney had come to the telephone reluctantly. "What's all this about a press conference?" he snapped.

Rex took a deep breath and said, "Mr. Telfer, that's what's going to happen unless we have a chance to talk. I've got some new evidence on the Cohen case."

Telfer was incensed. "You're working for William Connally, are you not?"

"I was."

"What do you mean, you were?"

"That's what I have to talk to you about."

"Look," Telfer said, "if you have something, the proper procedure is for you to give it to Mr. Connally. If he deems it significant, he can bring it up during the trial. I don't understand why you're bothering me with this."

Rex took a breath, exhaled slowly, and said, "Mr. Telfer, I have reason to believe that William Connally is personally responsible for the deaths of Martin Cohen and Elizabeth Winters."

For a moment, there was silence. "Do you have any evidence to support such a preposterous statement?" Telfer snapped.

"Yes," Rex answered, "there's a lot of it, but it's all circumstantial."

Again, there was silence. Finally, Telfer said, "I want you in my office at four o'clock this afternoon."

"I'll be there," Rex said, as he hung up the phone.

LIONEL TELFER LISTENED CAREFULLY AS REX KELSEY laid it out. When the private investigator was finished, Telfer seemed unmoved.

"Here's what I'm going to do, Mr. Kelsey," he said tersely. "I'm going to send you down the hall where you will dictate your sworn statement to one of our investigators. This office will then begin an official investigation that will be conducted with deliberate speed and in total secrecy. You can appreciate the need for discretion. You can also appreciate the fact that should you decide to take your case to the media, you will not only expose yourself to the many and varied counteractions at the disposal of the eminent Mr. Connally but you will also scuttle the secret investigation. In that event, the investigation will have to be conducted openly. To be frank with you, I think that would be counter to the interests of the person you are trying to help. Agreed?"

"I guess so," Rex said.

"Now," Telfer continued, "should we find that your allegations are simply a concoction dreamed up by you and your supposedly former employer as a means of forcing a mistrial, I guarantee you that you—and he—will face the full fury of this office."

"Mr. Telfer, there's—"

Telfer held up a hand demanding silence. "If your allegations are a result of some dispute between you and Mr. Connally," he went on, "which has driven you to some vindictive insanity, you will face that fury alone. On the other hand, if there is some merit to your allegations, we will see it through."

Rex seemed unsure. "What if you don't get this done in time? What if the jury comes back and finds Mrs. Cohen guilty?"

Telfer frowned. "Mr. Kelsey, what you have presented to me is purely circumstantial evidence. I will do the best I can. In the event that Mrs. Cohen is convicted, the appeals process is automatic. While the appellate court cannot consider evidence not presented at the original trial, there are other remedies.

"You'll have to trust me, Mr. Kelsey. I have no desire to see an innocent person suffer. And that includes William Connally. As far as I'm concerned, he's innocent until we have solid evidence to the contrary. Can I count on your support?"

"I don't know."

Telfer stood up. "Who the hell do you think you're talking to, Kelsey? You think I'm some third-year law student? What you've presented is pure supposition! If I tried to stop the trial based on what you've given me, I'd be lucky to get a job as a bag boy at Publix.

"You leave this with me. Speak to the goddam press, and you'll wish you hadn't. Clear?"

Kelsey hesitated for a moment, then nodded.

CHAPTER
30

JEFF SMYLIE'S WITHERING CROSS-EXAMINATION OF Ann Cohen took almost six hours. For Ann, it was the most humiliating experience of her entire life. Drawing courage from a nearly empty reservoir, she managed to answer most of the prosecutor's questions with a forth-rightness she didn't feel—questions that examined, in microscopic detail, every facet of her relationship with Marty, her personality, her character, even her faith.

She felt her very soul had been autopsied, laid open for all to see in this public place, to be discussed and debated in the press and on television, like the weather. All remaining shreds of privacy had been stripped away. She was naked, every weakness exposed like a large unsightly wart on someone's nose. There was nowhere to hide, nothing left to be hidden.

When the cross-examination ended, she walked back to the defense table with her head held high, her shoulders back, and her eyes fixed on Bill. But inside she felt cold, and alone, and dead.

For the next five days, she sat immobile and impassive at the table as Bill presented witnesses on her behalf.

First came the character witnesses: Della, Gina, and Anita. Smylie cross-examined them all, and when he asked them if Marty had ever made a pass at them, Gina and Anita both answered yes. Connally had warned her that Marty's actions would be brought up, so it wasn't a surprise. On redirect, both insisted that they had never told Ann about the overtures, thereby confirming Ann's testimony. But Ann wondered if the jury believed them.

Bill called a doctor to the stand, the young intern who had examined her when she'd been taken to the hospital.

"You examined the defendant on the morning of July eighth. Is that correct?"

"Yes."

"And did you find any blood on her person?"

"No."

"Did you find any powder burns on her hands?"

"No."

"Exactly what did you find on the defendant when you examined her?"

The doctor hesitated, then said, "She was covered in her own vomit. She'd been ill."

"So they let the defendant lie in her own vomit?" Connally thundered.

"They had to," the doctor answered. "It's the law. She

could not be cleaned up until an examination had been performed."

On cross, Smylie had asked, "Doctor, if the defendant had managed to take a bath immediately prior to her admittance to the hospital, would you have known?"

"No."

"Thank you."

How clever Smylie was, Ann had thought. This vain, conceited yuppie was expertly twisting the facts to suit his purpose, oblivious to the truth, bent only on putting another notch in his gun. It was all just a game. The truth meant nothing to him.

Bill brought in an expert on forensics, a Dr. Louis Chalmers, who testified that in his forty years as a pathologist and forensics expert, he'd never experienced a case where a single set of prints were found on a murder weapon, with no prints at all having been found on the empty shell casings. On cross, Smylie had asked few questions.

"How much are you being paid to appear here today, doctor?"

"Two thousand dollars."

"As an expert, can you say, in all certainty, that the evidence presented by the State excludes the possibility of the defendant having used the gun to commit the crimes?"

Bill had objected to the question, to no avail. The doctor had answered that he could not say that, in all certainty.

Then there was a man named Jake Michell. He was a thin, wrinkled man in his eighties.

"Where do you live, Mr. Michell?" Connally asked.

"I live in the Sunlight Retirement Home, down in St. Pete."

"I see. You're retired?"

The little man laughed and said, "Yeah. I am now. Arthritis got so bad I couldn't work anymore."

"How old are you?"

"I'm eighty-three."

"What kind of work did you do?"

The little man grinned a toothless smile and said, "I'm a burglar. One of the best." Almost everyone smiled. He seemed so proud of it. "How long have you been a burglar, Mr. Michell?"

"Since I was fifteen. That would make it about—what, fifty years? No, more'n that, I guess."

Connally grinned. "Well, according to my figures, you've been a burglar for sixty-eight years."

"I guess so."

"Tell me, Mr. Michell, how do you do it? I mean, how do you break into a house?"

Michell shrugged. "It really ain't all that hard. First I pick a nice quiet neighborhood. Then I go door-to-door, looking for keys stuck under mats or above the doorsill or in flowerpots and things. I make notes of the houses that have keys stuck somewhere and then I plan the ones I'm gonna rob."

"Do you ever use lock-picking tools?"

"Not me."

"What about windows. You ever break them?"

"Nope. All I look for is houses where I can get in with a key. The rest I leave alone. I don't touch no houses with alarm systems either."

"I see. Now, tell the court and the jury this: Approximately how many homes do you have to check out before you find one with a hidden key?"

Michell thought about it for a moment, then said, "Oh, I'd say maybe twenty. Yeah. About one in twenty houses has a key hid somewheres."

"Thank you, Mr. Michell."

Then, suddenly, the testimony of the witnesses was at an end.

After Bill requested, for the second time, that the charges be dismissed, a motion that was promptly denied, he rested his case. It was time for closing arguments. Smylie was to go first. As he approached the lectern, Ann braced herself for what was sure to be another attack on her character. By now, she thought she'd be inured, but she wasn't.

In the back of the room, Peter Quill and Rex Kelsey looked at each other, then silently shook their heads.

There had not been a single word from Telfer since the meeting four days ago. Rex was beginning to wonder if the whole idea had been a mistake. Maybe, he thought, he *should* go to the media. Maybe Telfer was stroking him, hoping to keep him quiet until after the verdict. If Ann was convicted, Telfer could claim the investigation had proven nothing. Jesus! Once the case was in the hands of the jury, anything could happen. Despite Connally's histrionics, it didn't look all that great right now. Rex listened to Smylie with increasing anxiety.

"Ladies and gentlemen of the jury, I told you in my opening remarks that you would hear some basic facts and a lot of things that are designed to confuse you. I asked you to keep your minds completely open but to pay close attention to those facts, and I'm confident that you've done that. It's the facts that are important here, and the facts must speak for themselves.

"Ann Cohen had many motives to kill her husband and Elizabeth Winters. There was the infidelity, the insurance policy worth half a million dollars, and the marriage that was a marriage in name only. Aside from motive, Ann Cohen had the means and the opportunity. Three powerful factors.

"You have heard the testimony. You have heard the claim made by the defendant that she was framed. By whom? Who but Ann Cohen had anything to gain by these deaths? No one. Few murders are committed for no gain, ladies and gentlemen. There are criminals who kill in the course of committing other crimes, and there are criminals who kill because they are sick. But by and large, most murders are committed because of revenge, hate, jealousy, simple meanness, or escape from the law, or they are committed for gain.

"Ann Cohen killed for gain.

"If Ann Cohen had murdered her husband and his mistress at the moment she saw them in bed together, you might consider what she did an act of passion. But that isn't what happened. What happened was this. Ann Cohen went home, encouraged her friend to leave, then took her gun, went back to the Winters house, and brutally murdered her husband and Elizabeth Winters in cold blood, meticulously committing a crime she'd planned for years.

"This was no act of passion. This was an act of unbridled hatred. And that is why you must find Ann Cohen guilty of murder in the first degree."

He dropped his arms, smiled at each member of the jury, and said, "I thank you very much."

Rex Kelsey squirmed in his seat. Smylie had put on a convincing argument. It made Rex very uncomfortable. He stood up.

"Where are you going?" Peter Quill whispered.

"I've got to talk to Telfer," Rex said. "If he doesn't come through soon, I'm going to the press, no matter what the consequences."

"I'll go with you," Peter said.

The call to Lionel Telfer was put through immediately. Before Kelsey could say a word, the veteran prosecutor was one step ahead of him. "I know why you're calling, Kelsey. I can almost see the concern through the telephone line."

"So, what the hell is going on?"

"The thing we talked about is moving apace. It's taking time, yes, but that was to be expected. I can assure you that it has my full attention and things are happening."

"That's not good enough," Rex snapped.

"It has to be. We cannot do more than we are doing."

"I can't be sure of that."

"You don't trust me? You think going to the press will speed things up? Let me tell you, Mr. Kelsey, all that will do is create a massive problem. I explained all that to you. If you truly want to help your friend, trust me. There's still time. The jury is not yet out. Even if this is not settled in time, there is the appeals process, should she be unfortunate enough to be found guilty."

Rex was almost beside himself with frustration. "Big

deal," he said. "In the first place, Ann Cohen is not a friend of mine. In the second place, she's coming apart at the seams here. I can see it in her eyes. If she's found guilty and goes to prison, she'll never be able to put her life together again. It won't matter what the hell you do, it will all be too damn late."

There was a pause before Telfer said, "All the more reason for you to let me handle this, Mr. Kelsey. You asked me to do something, and I'm doing it. The longer we talk about it, the more time is wasted. If you don't trust me, go to the press. And when you see what a screw-up that creates, you can pat yourself on the back." Rex slammed the receiver home and headed back to the courtroom, with Peter right behind him.

"I'm sorry," the bailiff said, holding up his hand as they approached the door to the courtroom, "the room is full. You'll have to wait out here."

Rex glared at him for a moment, then leaned against the wall. "God," he said to Quill, "I really hate this, you know? I mean, I really hate it."

Peter slapped a hand on Kelsey's shoulder. "Hang in there, Rex," he said.

CHAPTER

31

WILLIAM CONNALLY STOOD AT THE LECTERN FACING the jury, slowly shaking his head, knowing that everyone in the room waited in tense anticipation. He was, after all, one of the country's top criminal lawyers, renowned, at the top of his form, on the threshold of winning yet another case.

The small spectator section was jammed, as it had been ever since the start of the trial. Today, in anticipation of his closing argument, the bailiffs had allowed a few favored defense lawyers to stand by the back wall and in the two corners, so they might watch the master in action. It was a small but welcome tribute. Just above them, two sets of television recording equipment silently transferred the scene from reality to precisely arranged molecules of iron oxide affixed to thin strips of Mylar.

For a brief instant, Connally turned and stared at the glass panes covering the two holes that had been cut into the wall to allow for the cameras. This was the penultimate moment of this trial, the time to nail it down tight. The final act would be up to the jury, but he was sure of the outcome—so sure, he had prepared one of the shortest summations of his career.

"Ladies and gentlemen," he began, "to suggest that Ann Cohen would enter the home of Elizabeth Winters, tie her up, then tie her husband Martin up, shoot both of them three times, getting blood all over the place, then pull and yank and finally place her husband's dead body on top of the body of Elizabeth Winters, leave the house, go home, change clothes, get rid of the bloody clothes but not the gun, and very carefully put the gun back in the bedside table—this is so outrageous, it's beyond belief!"

Connally started pacing slowly in front of the jury, his radio announcer's voice purring softly, his hands chopping the air. "The prosecution talked about facts. Well, here are some facts." He started ticking them off on his fingers.

"One. Ann Cohen was wearing a white blouse, black slacks, and black loafers when she was last seen by Cathy Pollard at one o'clock in the morning.

"Two. Three hours later, when the police arrived at her home, she was wearing the very same thing.

"Three. You heard a witness testify that the woman seen leaving the Winters house was wearing a skirt or a dress and high heels. He was very sure about that. You'll remember that we took the trouble to test that witness's eyesight. It was very good. He accurately described a man in the rear of the courtroom.

"The prosecution wants you to believe that a clever woman took three years to plan the murder of her husband and his girlfriend. She's so careful that she changes into a special outfit just for the purpose of committing murder. And she makes sure that she wears high heels. High heels? A woman is going to put on high heels for this?" He shook his head again. "After the murders have been committed, she makes sure she gets rid of the clothes she was wearing to ensure that the police don't get their hands on them. But this same woman takes the gun she used to commit the murders and puts it back in the bedside table." He threw his hands in the air again. "Does that make the slightest bit of sense to you?"

He stopped pacing and leaned forward, placing his hands on the wooden railing. "It's important that you understand something here. From the very outset, the police assumed that Ann Cohen was guilty. By doing so, they shut off a complete investigation of this crime, instead expending all of their energy in developing a case against the defendant. Had they looked elsewhere, who knows what they would have found?

"With my limited resources, I was able to discover that any number of people knew about the key in the flowerpot. Anyone could have entered the home of the defendant, used her gun to commit the crimes, and returned the gun to the bedside table. The defendant's fingerprints were found on the gun but not on the shells inside the gun. Why? The only answer that makes the slightest sense is that the real killer had to remove his fingerprints from the shells. That's why they were cleaned.

"Why in the world would the defendant take the trouble to clean the unused shells and leave them to be found in her house? What was the purpose? If she took the time to get rid of her bloody clothes, why did she not get rid of all damaging evidence?

"You've heard the testimony of witnesses, unrefuted by the prosecution, that Martin Cohen was a gambler and a cheat. There are scores of people who had a motive to kill Martin Cohen, and had the prosecution used their considerable resources to investigate these people, they might very well have found the killer."

Connally slammed a fist into the palm of his hand.

"The only reason Ann Cohen is on trial today is because the killer of her husband wanted all suspicion directed away from him. He knew that by framing Ann, the police, being busy people, would stop right there. It shouldn't have worked, but it did, and if you find Ann Cohen guilty, you will have helped him succeed.

"As you know, the burden of proof in any criminal case is on the prosecution. They must prove beyond a reasonable doubt that the defendant is guilty of the crime. Beyond reasonable doubt.

"If you find Ann Cohen guilty, you will be throwing that instruction out the window. There's more doubt here than reasonable doubt. There's a ton of doubt. In fact, I'm convinced that if the police had not found the murder weapon in Ann Cohen's house, we would not be here today. Because the gun is the single piece of evidence on which they've based their case—a gun that could have been easily and successfully hidden.

"Why wasn't it? Because the killer wanted it to be found. There can be no other explanation."

Crossing his arms in front of his chest, he said, "Almost every married couple has life insurance policies on each other. Almost every married couple has problems at one time or another. Some have very serious problems. And sad to say, I've read figures that indicate upwards of sixty percent of husbands cheat on their wives. But their wives don't go out and kill them. The fact that Ann Cohen had a motive to kill her husband is not enough. The fact that she had the opportunity is not enough. It's the gun that makes it look bad. The gun!

"So the real key to this entire trial, the root of the prosecutor's case, is the gun found in the home of Ann Cohen, complete with fingerprints. Only her fingerprints. The empty shell casings were completely clean but the gun wasn't. When you consider *all* of the facts surrounding that gun, you can see that something just doesn't fit. The empty shell casings, the unused cartridges, the clothes. It makes no sense.

"Ladies and gentlemen, you have more than reasonable doubt here. I know that after you've considered everything you've seen and heard during this trial, you will come to the realization that Ann Cohen could not possibly have committed these crimes. It's inconceivable. And I'm sure you will not allow the prosecutor to insult your intelligence by accepting as fact a story so crazy, so ludicrous, it defies all credibility.

"I'm sure you'll find Ann Cohen not guilty of the crimes with which she is charged. Because she's not a stupid woman, and you're not a stupid jury."

Then, like an actor taking a bow, Connally bent forward slightly and said, "Thank you very much."

As the defense attorney walked back to his table, Judge Clark started to give his lengthy instructions to the jury—which took over an hour—and then the jury was sent off to consider the case.

Ann watched them leave with the same mixed emotions she had felt a few days ago. What did it really matter?

"Ann?" Connally whispered.

She turned and looked at him vacantly. "Yes?"

He took her hands in his. His eyes were gleaming, and his face was wreathed in a big grin that deepened the lines around his eyes and mouth. "We're going to win, Ann! I just know it! I watched those people. They're with you all the way. There's no way they're going to bring in a guilty verdict. I told you I would save you, and I have! Don't you see? It's all but over. We've won!"

She looked at his brightly shining eyes. They seemed to be glowing, as if a micronuclear generating station had been placed within each one. She thought she saw them pulsing like a heartbeat, the glow gaining strength with each beat of his heart. She'd looked into his eyes many times, but never had she seen anything like this.

She turned away from what had now become a frightening vision. What's happening to me? she wondered. Am I losing my mind?

CHAPTER

32

LIONEL TELFER'S CHAUFFEUR-DRIVEN BUICK STOPPED at the closed wrought-iron gates that surrounded a house on Davis Islands, a short distance from downtown Tampa. Telfer pressed a small button, lowering the heavily tinted window. A large bald-headed man leaned forward and peered at the two men seated in the back of the Buick. "Mr. Telfer and Mr. Scott to see Mr. Bellesario," Telfer said. "He's expecting us."

Without a word, the bald-headed man turned, walked to the gate, and spoke into a telephone. Then he entered a series of numbers into a small electronic keyboard attached to one of the massive stone pillars that supported the gate. Immediately, the gate rolled to one side and the Buick proceeded up a long winding tree-lined road.

The road led to a large rambling California-style house that stood within a hundred feet of Tampa Bay. Johnny Bellesario, flanked on either side by men openly carrying semiautomatic weapons, stood waiting as the car neared the front of the house. As the car began to slow, Telfer turned to his companion and said, "The sonofabitch has seen too many movies. Does he think two state attorneys are about to make a hit?"

Warren Scott laughed. "I keep forgetting. You've never talked to Bellesario before, have you?"

"No, I haven't."

The black Buick came to a halt in front of the house. One of Bellesario's bodyguards grabbed the rear door and jerked it open. The other opened the door on Scott's side. Telfer and Scott climbed out of the Buick, put on sunglasses, and shook hands with a beaming Johnny Bellesario.

"Welcome, gentlemen," he said, gripping each man's hand tightly, first Scott's and then Telfer's. "Francesca has prepared some lemonade for us out back, by the bay. It's a little cool today, but I enjoy the fresh air, don't you?"

Telfer nodded, and the three men started walking along a wide flagstone path to the rear of the house, where a vast expanse of manicured Tifgreen sloped gently toward a concrete breakwater that included a large dock. They were followed by the two bodyguards, who maintained a discreet ten-pace distance. Both Telfer and Scott spotted the gleaming-white eighty-foot yacht tied up to the dock. It was impossible to miss. And it wasn't Bellesario's. The man hated going out on the water. He just loved being near it.

Johnny Bellesario, sixty-two years old, looking tan and fit, led his guests to an elaborate gazebo positioned almost exactly midway between the rear of the house and the bay. A large pitcher of lemonade and three crystal tumblers sat on a silver tray resting on a linen-covered table.

He was the king of central and northern Florida, this diminutive figure with the white hair and the ready smile, the boss of one small region in organized crime's network of illegal activities. Unlike most of his contemporaries, he hated publicity. That was not to say he lacked ego. Bellesario was known to be ruthlessly efficient.

He had old-world charm, this one-time common thief who'd worked his way up to the second-highest echelon in the mob hierarchy. He also had principles—of a sort. Telfer and Scott had noticed they'd not been allowed to enter his home. He'd agreed to meet with them, a rare condescension, but at no time would the State Attorney for Pinellas County and the State Attorney for Hillsborough County ever be allowed inside. Not without a warrant, they wouldn't. That would be against Bellesario's principles. They were his enemies. It was enough that he would speak to them.

Scott sipped his lemonade, surveyed the view for a moment, then got down to business. "Mr. Bellesario," he said, almost choking on the appellation. It did no good to insult Johnny Bellesario. To do so would be to bring an immediate halt to any conversation. "The matter at hand is really something that is of no concern to my office. However, it could become a matter of great interest. I asked for this meeting at the request of Mr. Telfer, who is, as you know, the State Attorney for Pinellas County. What he has to say is quite important. I just want you to know that we both appreciate the opportunity to discuss it with you. I'll let Mr. Telfer take it from here."

Bellesario leaned forward and said, "How may I be of service, Mr. Telfer?"

Lionel Telfer studied the smooth-skinned face of the man sitting across the table from him. Bastard, he thought. Holding court like some goddam potentate. A smiling lizard in expensive clothes, living off the weaknesses of others, enjoying the good life when he should be breaking rocks in some godforsaken prison. Trying to hide his contempt and cursing his need to talk to this man, Telfer forced a smile to his lips. "Mr. Bellesario, we find ourselves in a situation that could prove to be embarrassing to a number of people, not the least of whom would be yourself."

Bellesario said nothing.

"We're trying to find a man named Jimmy Gibbons," Telfer continued. "We have evidence that Gibbons and another man who works for you, Frank Peters, are involved in the murders of two people in my jurisdiction."

Bellesario never blinked an eye. He simply sat there, a Mona Lisa smile fixed on his face, and waited. Telfer rubbed his chin for a moment, then decided to drop the niceties. "Look, I'm not going to play games here. I'll get to the point. Gibbons works for you. Peters works for you. These two men killed two people at the request of your attorney, William Connally." Telfer waited for a reaction. There was none. The son of a bitch probably knew all about it.

"I know it and you know it," Telfer continued. "We can't prove it yet, but we will, sooner or later. Right now, a jury across the bay is considering the fate of a person who's been charged with both murders. We all know she didn't do it, but because we don't have the evidence we need, we aren't in a position to drop the charges against her. In time, we'll get it straightened out, and when that happens, there'll be one hell of a stink. I can guarantee you that when the shit hits the fan you'll be dragged into this thing."

"Why?" Bellesario asked quietly.

"Let's face it," Telfer said, the forced smile gone. "All three men work for you. Even both victims are tied to you in a small way. Martin Cohen was a gambler. From time to time, he owed you a lot of money. Maybe he owed a lot of money when he was killed. Who's to know? As for the woman, she was a hooker off and on. Maybe she never worked for you and maybe she did. Frankly, I doubt it. Nevertheless, when this whole pile of shit blows up, some of it is bound to stick to you.

"To be candid, I don't think you had anything to do with the murders. I think that Connally slipped a cog somewhere and hired your people to do a private job for him. You may not have known the first goddam thing about it, but that won't matter a damn to the media. You sure as hell didn't use your influence to stop it. When the media boys get their hands on this, your face will be plastered all over the tube for months. You'll look bad and so will I. It will appear as though an innocent woman was hounded by my office because we were incompetent assholes. But I'm not about to take the heat alone.

"The fact is, we went with what we had. Nobody could have dreamed that William Connally would have two people killed just so he could have the privilege of defending some woman he has the hots for. It's crazy. But that's what happened, sure as hell."

He paused while he sipped some of his lemonade.

"Why are you telling me this?" Bellesario asked.

"I'm telling you this because we want Gibbons in custody. We want to talk to him and make a deal. If he talks, and repeats his testimony in court, we'll give him immunity. We want him to testify against Peters and Connally. I want you to find him and convince him to cooperate."

Bellesario's eyebrows rose. "Me? Why would I do such a thing?"

Telfer gritted his teeth. "I just finished telling you why. This case is already a sensation all over the country. When the media people find out the truth, that Ann Cohen had nothing to do with it, it's going to be an even bigger sensation. All three men—Gibbons, Peters, and Connally—work for you. There's no way on God's green earth it won't look like you're involved as well. And I can assure you we'll make every effort to fuel that particular fire. The heat will be on, Johnny." Telfer noticed the frown. "Heat the likes of which you've never seen. I don't like being taken for a fool. And that's exactly how I'm gonna look. It won't be very hard for me to make it look like you're the mastermind behind this whole thing. Not too many people are going to buy the real story. Not unless we have some solid evidence. And the only way we can get that is by having Gibbons cooperate. He'll do it if you tell him to."

He took a deep breath. "I've talked to the feds, and they've agreed to place Gibbons in their witness protection program if he talks. He'll be moved and given a new identity."

Bellesario said, "You seem to have it all worked out."

"I think I have," Telfer said.

Bellesario just sat there, appraising Telfer for a moment. Then, after sipping some more lemonade, he said, "Your idea is that Gibbons, being a rather small fish in the ocean, will be given immunity to testify against Peters, who is in the eyes of the feds, a larger fish. Is that not so?"

"You could put it that way."

"I just did. Now, would you say that I'm a larger fish than Frank Peters?"

Telfer's face reddened. "I know what you're thinking, but this isn't a federal beef. It's a local beef. The feds have nothing to do with it, other than to give Gibbons a free ride somewhere. They won't lean on Peters. Neither will we."

Bellesario smiled. "So if Frank Peters offers to say things about me that are untrue there is no one who will listen to him, is that what you're saying?"

"Basically, yes."

"You say that Frank Peters works for me. Not so. But if we pretend for the moment that he did at one time, and if we further pretend that he faces a murder charge that could lead to his execution, you're sure he would not be allowed to make any sort of deal for himself? Is that what you're saying?"

"Yes."

Bellesario stroked his nose for a moment, then said, "There is also the problem of William Connally himself. If he learns that I have become involved in this . . . matter, he may well breach the confidentiality that now exists between us. I wouldn't like that."

Warren Scott stood up, patted Lionel Telfer on the shoulder, and said, "I think I'll let you two talk about this in private for a while. If you don't mind, I'll take a look at that magnificent boat you have, Mr. Bellesario."

Bellesario leaned back in his chair and nodded. "Yes. Well, unfortunately, it does not belong to me. I have guests. Right now, they would rather not be disturbed, so please confine your inspection to the exterior. If you don't mind."

Scott nodded. "I understand," he said. As he walked toward the water, he noticed two uniformed men peering at him from the upper bridge of the yacht. Neither man seemed to be overly concerned, but their Uzis were clearly in view.

Bellesario turned his attention back to Telfer. "Mr. Telfer," he said, lighting a cigar, "William Connally has represented my interests for a number of years. I find him to be professional and highly competent. I can't imagine what might cause you to think that he would have anyone murdered—for any reason."

Telfer's jaw tightened. "Look, I didn't come here to play games with you. I came here because I'm in deep shit. Sooner or later, you will be too. You help me out, d I help you out. What goes around comes around, hnny; you know all about that.

"Here's the deal," Telfer continued. "Connally can oot off his mouth till doomsday about you and we n't use any of it. Neither can the feds. You know at as well as I do. As for Peters, I'm sure he'll see the isdom of keeping his mouth shut about any business e might have had with you. Even if he doesn't, no one ill make a deal with him. It's Connally and Peters we ant, not you."

Bellesario blew a cloud of smoke in Telfer's direction. o you say, Mr. Telfer. But you're just one man. There e others who would like to see an end to my career d are not above making deals of their own. There nothing to prevent the feds from talking to Peters r Gibbons—or Connally, for that matter. Rules were ade to be broken, and the government breaks as any of them as anyone else when there are things be gained by doing so. I have no assurance from nyone except yourself that things will go as you say ey will. That is not enough, I'm afraid. No offense, ut experience has taught me that things never go as tended. Experience has also taught me that the FBI nd the DEA have no honor. None at all.

"I tell you this. Gibbons has done some work for me in he past, but he has worked for many others as well. As r Peters, I don't know the man. He's never worked for e. Ever. We don't kill people, Mr. Telfer. We leave that the punks in the projects. Mr. Connally has worked r me many times, as I have already stated. When you ssume that these three got together without my knowl- dge, you assume correctly. I had no knowledge of any

killings on your side of the bay. Nor do I now, oth-
than what I read in the papers and see on television

"I am a man of honor, Mr. Telfer. I don't impose n
personal interests on the lives of others. If you hav
a problem, you'll have to solve it on your own. If th
means dragging me into a situation that has nothin
whatsoever to do with me, you would be acting impr-
dently. I can assure you that I will take whatever step
necessary to protect my interests. There are other layers at my disposal. If you involve me in something th.
does not concern me, you may find yourself in more h-
water than you already are. I think it would be unwise
involve me, in any way whatsoever. Very unwise. Yo
understand?"

Telfer glared at Bellesario for a moment, then stoc
up. Without another word, he waved at Scott and starte
walking back to the front of the house. Once inside th
car, he turned to Scott and said, "The son of a bitc
wouldn't hear of it. He had the balls to threaten m
Can you imagine that?"

Scott sighed. "Well, you threatened him, after all. Th.
business about making it look like he's behind it, I don
think that was your cleverest move."

"I couldn't help it. I hate those bastards."

Scott leaned back in the seat. "I'm not surprised h
didn't agree to help you. He didn't get where he is b
helping law enforcement agencies."

Telfer decided to change the subject. "Did you get
make on the ocean liner?"

Scott grinned and said, "Sure did. It belongs to Vincer
Sabbatino himself. Every year at this time, they cruise t
Miami. I guess they stopped in to say hello to Johnn

n their way. They always like to spend Christmas in
iami."

Telfer snorted. "Why the hell would somebody want
) spend Christmas in Miami? And who was the asshole
ho said crime doesn't pay?"

Vincent Sabbatino walked slowly from the boat to the
azebo and pulled back the chair just vacated by Lionel
elfer. He wedged his considerable bulk into the chair.
Was it as you expected?"

Johnny Bellesario nodded. "Yeah. Just like I figured.
here's nothing to worry about, though. I got it covered.
his was a private thing with Connally. It's got nothin'
o do with me. Telfer's just suckin' wind because he's
onna look like a real asshole. He's gotta be crazy,
oming here like this. Even crazier if he thinks he can
on me into helping him out."

Sabbatino smiled, then asked, "I was reading the pa-
ers. They say this woman—this Cohen woman—is an
ccountant, and that her father is a retired lawyer from
hicago."

"That's right."

"The papers say she uses her maiden name, Martino,
or her company."

"Yeah."

For a moment, the big man said nothing. "I want you
o check on something for me."

"Be happy to. What?"

"This woman. Find out if her father's name is Luigi.
Find out he was a lawyer in Chicago in 1946."

Bellesario looked confused. "He's been at the trial
every day. What the hell do you care?"

Sabbatino didn't answer. "Will you find out for me?

Bellesario noticed the look in his boss's eye. "C course," he said quickly. "I'll have the answer in mi utes."

He was sixteen years old then. Just a punk. Whe he'd been arrested, a reform-minded judge had ordere that he be tried as an adult. The judge had arrange for him to be defended by an attorney with n previous criminal experience, a rookie wet behin the ears. It was a goddam setup. But the lawyer, Lui Martino, had busted his ass for two weeks to kee Vincent out of jail. And he'd succeeded.

Six months later, Vincent's family had moved t New York, where young Vincent had picked up wher he'd left off in Chicago. The next time he'd bee arrested, there'd been no Luigi Martino, and he' gone to jail for three long years.

He'd met people in jail. People who'd taught hir things and introduced him to other people. Upon h release, he was an older, wiser man. His career ha been meteoric. Now, he was at the top. Boss of bosses

Still, he remembered that first brush with the lau Especially the lawyer who'd fought like a tiger t help him.

That first time.

CHAPTER

33

THE JURY HAD BEEN OUT A DAY AND A HALF. DURING that time, Rex Kelsey had become increasingly agitated. He'd made three more calls to Telfer, who'd been as terse as before. "Look," Telfer had said during their last conversation, less than three hours ago, "we're doing everything we can. I told you that before. As soon as I have something, you'll be the first to know." There was never an explanation of just what was going on, only the vague promise that it was a top priority.

Rex was unconvinced. If Telfer was so sure Ann Cohen was getting a raw deal, why didn't he just have this thing stopped? He had enough evidence to tell the judge that the State didn't think she was guilty. That was all. Why the stall?

Because Telfer wasn't convinced, Rex thought. There

could be no other explanation. Telfer was simply trying to keep Rex away from the media so the trial could
proceed without a hassle. If Ann was found innocent,
he could wash his hands of the entire affair, saying the
jury had screwed up. Only if she was found guilty would
he have a problem.

Rex was tired of it. Tired of playing Russian roulette
with Ann Cohen's life. Anyone could see she was falling apart. Now, as he sat on a windowsill in a hallway
just outside the courtroom at two o'clock on the afternoon of December twenty-second, Rex came to a decision. It was time to put an end to this. It was time to
go to the media. It might not help Ann Cohen for the
moment, but it would certainly bring everything out in
the open.

He turned and faced Peter Quill, his constant companion for the last two weeks. "I've had it," Rex said.
"I'm going to the press. They're crawling all over the
building. It shouldn't take much to get them together."

Peter, exhausted from working a full night shift and
watching the trial every day, looked at him with bloodshot eyes. "Are you sure?"

"Damn sure," Rex said. "That bastard is conning us.
He probably hasn't done a goddam thing. He's worried
he's gonna look bad, is all. He doesn't give a shit about
what's happening to that poor woman. It's just another
goddam case to him."

Peter shook his head. "I dunno. I've always heard that
Telfer was a real straight arrow. Maybe we should hang
on, like he says."

Rex shook his head. "No. Not anymore. I've waited
too long already. The damn jury could come back at

any—" He was interrupted by Peter, tugging at his arm and pointing down the hall.

It was Telfer himself, walking briskly down the hall, two men with briefcases at his side, while behind him a flurry of reporters struggled for position. Telfer stopped at the entrance to the hallway leading to the judges' chambers, noticed Rex, gave him a thumbs-up signal, and disappeared down the hallway. A reporter who'd noticed the contact between the two rushed over to ask, "What was that all about?"

Rex leaned back against the wall, utterly exhausted, lit a prohibited cigarette, and said, "I'm damned if I know."

Judge Sam Clark, sans official robes, his forehead deeply furrowed, his eyebrows seemingly suspended in space, his ear lobes a light pink, sat stiffly in his chair and eyed Lionel Telfer. "You're telling me you want to withdraw the charges?"

"Yes, Your Honor."

The pink was spreading. "I warn you, Mr. Telfer, you had better have a very good reason for this most unusual behavior. If this is something that should have been presented during the course of this trial, you're in serious trouble."

Telfer shifted his feet. He looked nervous. "Your Honor, this is probably the screwiest deal I've ever run into. This is the only way I can think of to handle it."

"What do you mean?"

Telfer motioned to one of his aides, who removed two documents from a briefcase and gave them to the judge. "These," Telfer said, waving the papers in the air, "are warrants for the arrest of William Connally and Frank Peters. Conspiracy and murder, two counts."

Judge Clark stood straight up so quickly it looked as though he'd been ejected from his chair. "What?"

Telfer took a deep breath, then said, "For the past few days, we've been accumulating a significant amount of circumstantial evidence which points to Connally as the man behind these killings. There wasn't much I could do without something solid, but now I have it. An hour ago, an ex-con named Jimmy Gibbons walked into my office and gave me a complete statement.

"Frank Peters killed Marty Cohen and Elizabeth Winters, with Gibbons's help. Both men were paid by William Connally, who conceived the plan. Gibbons received fifteen thousand dollars and Peters thirty thousand."

"My God!" Judge Clark said, as he sank slowly into his chair, leaning back, one hand on top of his head as if trying to press this astounding information into his brain. Then he leaned forward. "Go on."

"The method of killing and the arrangement of the bodies was Connally's idea," Telfer said. "Connally wanted it to look like Ann Cohen killed them both in a fit of rage. Gibbons has confessed to removing the gun from Mrs. Cohen's house before the murders, then putting it back in the nightstand afterward. The thing with the clean shell casings and the clothes was part of the plan. Peters dressed up as a woman."

"Plan?"

"Connally knew that once Ann Cohen was arrested, she'd come to him to defend her. That was the whole idea. It appears Connally has been obsessed with her for some time. It's pretty sick."

"Gibbons told you all this?" the judge asked.

"Yes," Telfer said. "Before you bring it up, let me assure you that I've considered the possibility that this is some sort of ploy. I've also considered the possibility that Ann Cohen and William Connally are in this together. I think the chances of either scenario being valid is remote. However, as you know, if I withdraw the charges against Ann Cohen now, there's a slim chance I can bring them back later if it turns out I'm wrong. But if the jury comes back with an acquittal, I can never prosecute her again. I don't want to take that chance.

"My office is continuing with a very thorough investigation. We'll find out what's what. Meanwhile, I want the charges against Ann Cohen withdrawn and Connally arrested."

Judge Clark shook his head. "You had five months to investigate this case, Mr. Telfer. You presented evidence to the grand jury and they returned an indictment. Now, at this late date, everything is thrown into a cocked hat. This has become a circus. I don't appreciate it."

"Your Honor, with all due respect, the evidence we presented was placed in our hands by a very clever man. Anyone in my position would have done exactly the same thing. I had no choice in the matter. The fact that my office refuses to allow a possible miscarriage of justice does not merit criticism."

For a moment, the judge glared at Telfer. Then, almost imperceptibly, he nodded. Pointing a finger at senior bailiff George West, he asked, "Where is Mr. Connally now?"

"Last I saw, he was with his client in one of the witness rooms on the second floor."

"Where's Mr. Smylie?"

"In his office."

Judge Clark grunted. "Okay. George, you arrange for some bailiffs to accompany Mr. Telfer, then notify Smylie I want to see him."

"Yes, Your Honor."

"Don't leave just yet."

The bailiff nodded and stood by the door. "Mr. Telfer," the judge said, "I want to meet with Mr. Smylie. He can make the motion. Once we have an escort ready, you and your people can exercise the warrant for Connally, but I want all of you out of this building before the press gets wind of this. I won't have a media feeding frenzy in this courthouse. Take him out of the building via the freight elevator. Understand?"

"Yes, Your Honor."

Clark pointed a finger at one of Telfer's assistants. "What's your name?"

"Homer Jenson, Your Honor."

"You an attorney?"

"Yes, Your Honor."

Telfer interjected. "Mr. Jenson has recently joined my office, replacing Kemphill."

Judge Clark nodded. "Is there any reason why he can't officially represent the defendant when the motion is heard?"

"No, sir."

"All right." The judge faced Jenson. "Mr. Jenson, you stay with Mrs. Cohen. You explain to her what's going on. I'm appointing you her counsel for the purpose of hearing the motion." Clark shook his head. "What a mess." He stood up and put on his black robe. "Everyone clear on this?"

There was a chorus of assent.

"All right. Once I know Connally's out of here and Mrs. Cohen is ready to go, I'll call back the jury to hear the motion. George, you can call Smylie now."

Ann Cohen and William Connally looked up as Telfer, another man, and two bailiffs entered the small witness room. Ann had never seen any of the men before, but she felt Bill stiffen beside her.

Telfer nodded at Ann. "Mrs. Cohen, I'm Lionel Telfer, State Attorney." He waved a hand at the other man and said, "This is my assistant, Homer Jenson." None of the men were smiling. The one named Telfer looked especially tough.

"What's the big occasion, Lionel?" Bill asked. "You here to see me win another one?"

"Not exactly," Telfer answered. "I'm here to arrest you for the murder of Elizabeth Winters and Martin Cohen."

"You're what?"

For the first time, Telfer smiled. "You have the right to remain silent. You have the right to an attorney—"

Connally was on his feet. "Are you insane?"

Telfer didn't answer. He just kept on with the Miranda warning. When he was finished, he said, "Do you understand these rights as I have explained them to you?"

Connally's face was livid with rage. "You're crazy, Telfer."

Ann was now standing, trying to comprehend the insanity of the moment. "You think we were in this together? Is that what you think?"

Telfer, some of the hardness gone from his face, said, "Mrs. Cohen, I'll tell you what I think. I think the man standing beside you paid two men to kill your husband and make it look like you did it. I think he did it so he could have you for himself. I think he figured he could win this case and have you feel forever grateful to him. I think he's one of the cruelest, most selfish-human beings on the face of the earth. And I'm going to prove it in court."

"You know nothing!" Connally shouted.

Telfer turned his attention back to Connally. "Gibbons talked," he said coldly. "He told us how he and Frank Peters worked hand in glove. He told us about the money you paid them. He told us about the gun and the clothes and the shells. All of it."

The blood drained from Connally's face. "That's impossible," he croaked.

Telfer smiled. "You underestimated me, Connally. The other day, I leaned pretty hard on Johnny Bellesario. Put the fear of God in him, in fact. He persuaded Gibbons to cooperate. That surprise you?"

"Bellesario is an ex-con," Connally retorted. "So is Gibbons. You think their testimony will stand up in court? I'll tear them both apart."

"I don't think so," Telfer said, motioning to the bailiffs.

Connally's hands formed into fists as the two bailiffs moved slowly toward him. "Face the wall," one of them said.

Ann watched in stunned silence as handcuffs were placed on William Connally's wrists. Then, without thinking, she tried to pull one of the bailiffs away. "Stop this," she cried. "You're making a terrible mistake."

Homer Jenson restrained her. "I'm sorry, Mrs. Cohen, but there's no mistake."

Ann ignored him. "Bill," she cried. "Tell them! Tell them to stop."

Connally looked at her for a moment, then let his gaze fall to the floor.

Suddenly, as if struck by lightning, Ann remembered something Bill had said months ago, something that had shocked and saddened her. It was a cruel, heartless remark.

Whoever killed your husband did you a favor.

At the time, he was angry, and she'd assumed the comment was born of rage. Could she have been wrong? Could the outburst have been an inadvertent manifestation of his true feelings?

She felt her throat constricting and a tightness in her chest. For months, she'd tried desperately to think of someone with a motive to kill Marty and frame her. She'd always assumed that the killer was someone who'd hated them both. Even when Bill had told her no one could possibly hate her that much, that the killer was just trying to deflect suspicion, she'd clung to the belief that it had to be someone consumed by hate. She'd never considered someone consumed by another emotion.

This was madness.

"Bill, tell them," she repeated, her voice less sure this time.

His eyes remained downcast.

"You couldn't have," she cried, her hand to her mouth.

"I love you," he said softly, not looking at her.

"You love me? Bill, tell me you had nothing to do with this. Tell me this is a mistake."

"Of course it's a mistake," he thundered. "Gibbons is lying. Bellesario is lying. They're all lying. I don't know why, but I'll find out, and when I do, God help them all!"

His face was almost purple with rage, but in his eyes she could see that same cold look of arrogance she'd seen in Marty's eyes so many times.

He was lying.

She felt her body quivering.

Jenson gently pulled her away and held her while Telfer and the two bailiffs escorted Bill out of the room and down the hall.

"Mrs. Cohen," Jenson said softly, "I know this has been one hell of a shock, but I must talk to you. The judge is calling the jury back. The charges against you are being withdrawn. If you can pull yourself together, this will all be over in minutes."

She looked into his face. "Over?" She turned away and sat down, holding her head in her hands.

Quietly, patiently, Jenson explained it to her. As he explained, Ann wept. When he was finished, she removed a linen handkerchief from her handbag, wiped her eyes, and blew her nose. She let out a sigh, then shook her head. "He told me he loved me," she said softly. Then, looking at Jenson with misty eyes, she said, "That's not love at all. He was sicker than Marty."

EPILOGUE

PETER QUILL ROLLED OVER AND OPENED HIS EYES. IT was almost six o'clock in the evening. For the first time in weeks, he'd slept solidly for eight straight hours. Still, every muscle in his body ached from the tension that had gripped him during that time. He reached over and switched on the small television set by the bed. Some commercials were running, but in a minute the news would be on. He waited.

"Good evening. I'm Bill Conners."

"And I'm Brittany Gold."

Peter snorted at the mention of the woman's name, as he did every time he heard it.

"Our top story tonight still concerns the incredible events that unfolded in front of our cameras yesterday in Pinellas County District Court. Ron Fields has the latest update."

The scene switched to a young man holding a microphone and standing in front of the courthouse. "Thank you, Brittany. In dramatic fashion, State Prosecutor Lionel Telfer announced today that the body found lying beside I-Seventy-five early this morning has positively been identified as that of Frank Peters, suspected of being the person responsible for the actual killing of Martin Cohen and Elizabeth Winters last July eighth.

"At a press conference held an hour ago, Telfer said that Peters had been shot three times in the head, probably while in an automobile, and his body dumped out on the highway. The State Attorney said there is no evidence to link the death of Peters to Johnny Bellesario, though Peters and James Gibbons, the man whose confession broke this case, are both rumored to be employees of the reputed Tampa mobster.

"While Telfer refused to discuss further details regarding the Gibbons confession, informed sources have told this reporter that Gibbons will be granted immunity in return for his testimony against attorney William Connally, one of the bay area's best-known criminal attorneys, the man who was defending Ann Cohen until yesterday.

"Connally made his first appearance in district court today. Bond was denied, and Connally remains in jail. The lawyer was represented by Hugh Smith, a member of Connally's law firm, but word has it that Connally is looking for someone else to take his case. We've heard many names being mentioned, but as of this moment we have nothing solid on that. The expected trial promises to be a major one.

"Earlier this morning, this bizarre case took another turn, when it was revealed that the jury hearing the case against Ann Cohen had taken a vote just before the charges against her were withdrawn. The vote was eleven to one to convict. Juror Mrs. Thelma French was asked why the jury was so close to coming in with a guilty verdict. This is what she had to say."

The face of an obviously confused, bespectacled woman appeared on the screen. "It was the evidence," she said. "We just couldn't imagine why someone else would go to such trouble to make it look like she did it. Now, of course, we know, but at the time all we had was the evidence. I'm sorry, but we really thought she was guilty."

"What about the defense offered by William Connally?" the reporter asked. "The clothes and the fact that no fingerprints were found on the empty shell casings?"

Mrs. French grimaced. "We just thought—well, most of us anyway—that she had done that herself just to confuse things. We thought the only reason she put the gun back was because she simply forgot to throw it away."

The door to the bedroom flew open, and Connie Quill rushed into the bedroom. "Oh, you're awake!" she exclaimed. "Then you heard?"

Peter grinned. "Yeah, I heard. Frank Peters murdered. How about them apples?"

"Who do you think did it?"

"Bellesario, probably," Peter said.

"Why would he do that?"

"Because of what happened with Gibbons."

"I don't understand," she said, nuzzling his chest.

Peter brought an arm up, put it around her neck, and drew her close to him. "Where are the kids?"

"Over at Jane's. Tell me about Peters."

"Okay," he said. "Gibbons turned himself in, right?"

"Right."

"He simply walked into Telfer's office and said he wanted to make a deal, and he got it. There's only one possible way that could have happened. Bellesario told him to."

"But that's what I don't understand. Why would Belle-sario do that?"

"I haven't a clue," Peter said. "Maybe he was afraid the investigation would cause him trouble. Who knows?"

"Why kill Peters?"

"To keep him quiet. Once Gibbons shot his mouth off, Peters had to know it was Bellesario's doing. Since Gib-bons had made a deal, Peters's only alternative was to go to the feds and try to make a deal for himself by giving them some stuff on Bellesario. Bellesario couldn't let that happen, so he had Peters killed. He probably had it done before Gibbons turned himself in. Gibbons was probably shown the body, as a further incentive to do what he was told."

Connie shook her head. "God! Wheels within wheels. These people are something else."

"Indeed they are."

"But I still don't understand why Bellesario would do this. What was in it for him?"

"I don't think we'll ever know the answer to that one,"

Peter said. "Maybe Bellesario had a beef with Connally and wanted to handle it this way. Whatever the reason, t finally worked out for Ann."

She snuggled closer. "I'm sorry I doubted you, Pete."

"It's okay."

"Forgive me?"

"Of course."

"Prove it."

"Be happy to. What if the kids come back?"

"They won't. I asked Jane to keep them until eight."

They were interrupted by the sound of the telephone ringing. "Let it ring," Connie said huskily.

Ann Cohen sat at the kitchen table, cradled a cup of coffee in her hands, and stared at the squirrels as they cavorted just outside the window. Across from her, a worried look on his face, Luigi Martino rubbed his arthritic wrist. "You mustn't blame yourself," he said softly.

Ann sighed. "Oh, Daddy," she said, "I'm not blaming myself. I was just thinking."

"What?" he asked.

She turned and looked into his eyes. "I was thinking how fortunate I really am. All my friends stood by me the whole time. They never for one minute thought I could do such a thing. Then there's you. How many children are blessed with such loving, caring parents?"

He blushed.

"Look at that dear man Clive Bennett," she continued. "He knew me only from my work, but he made it possible for Cathy and me to start our own business. Such courage. It would have been so easy to just let it be, but he made it a point to put his money where his mouth was."

"They say there are some who have the ability to see within a person's soul," he said. "Perhaps he's one of them."

She laughed. "I wish I had that."

"You have other attributes," he said.

"I must. Why else would a rookie cop risk his job for a woman he didn't know? Another act of courage. I'm going to stop by and see him tomorrow to thank him. Kelsey, too. If it wasn't for them, where would I be?"

"We won't think about that."

She stood up, went behind him, and gave him a big hug. "I'm a very lucky woman, when you add it all up."

"I agree," he said.

As Ann refilled her coffee cup, Luigi put on his glasses, picked up the newspaper, and started reading again.

"You've read that same story at least ten times," Ann said.

"I know," he said. "I just can't figure it out."

"Figure what out?"

"This thing with the thugs. Connally I understand. He was obsessed. It's not that uncommon. The country is full of crazy people, but this Gibbons is something else. Why would he confess? They say Johnny Bellesario was behind it all. Maybe so, but why would he do such a thing?" He shook his head. "I just don't understand it."

"They said Mr. Telfer talked him into it."

"Nonsense," Luigi replied. "These people aren't intimidated by the law."

She sat down and looked out the window again, lost in thought. Luigi turned his attention back to the newspaper. One name in the story stood out as if set in thirty-point type: Vincent Sabbatino. The same Vincent Sabbatino Luigi had defended when he was a young lawyer in Chicago.

The newspaper reported that Vincent Sabbatino had been in Tampa, visiting one of his lieutenants, Bellesario. The reporter had speculated on Sabbatino's possible involvement in the decision by Gibbons to confess. For what purpose? The reporter couldn't guess.

Each time Luigi had read the report, he'd considered the possible connection and discarded it as impossible fantasy. Sabbatino had been a kid. He probably didn't even know Luigi Martino still existed. And even if he did know, what difference would it make? Why would a powerful man like Sabbatino care what happened to Luigi Martino or his daughter? They meant nothing to him.

Once again, Luigi brushed away the thoughts as those of an old man clinging to some outdated old-world code. Silliness.

The doorbell rang. "I'll get it," Luigi said.

He glanced through the window and saw a young woman with a massive bouquet of flowers in her arms, at least three dozen red roses. He opened the door, accepted the bouquet, tipped the woman, and brought the flowers inside.

As he searched the cupboards looking for an appropriate vase, Ann glanced at the small envelope accompanying the roses. Her eyebrows arched as she said, "They're for you."

"Me?"

"Yes. The envelope says Luigi Martino." She handed

it to her father, who opened the envelope and looked at the card.

Suddenly, he looked stricken. He walked unsteadily toward the table and sat down heavily.

"Daddy? What's wrong?"

Ann took the card from his quaking hand and read it. "It's unsigned," she said. "Who could it be?"

"Probably a client . . . from the old days," he mumbled. "He must have read about this in the papers."

"What does he mean, *A good turn repaid*?"

"I have no idea."

"But you're upset," she insisted.

He shook his head. "No. I'm fine. I'm just not used to receiving flowers. The last time was when I was in the hospital, years ago. Your mother sent them to me. It just made me think of her, that's all."

"You're okay?"

"I'm fine," he assured her. He picked up the flowers and brought them to his nose. Breathing deeply, his face broke into a broad smile.

Now he knew.

HARRISON ARNSTON'S success as founder, chairman, and CEO of an automotive accessory manufacturing company enabled him to retire in 1984 to pursue his dream of a writing career. He has had five novels published. He also enjoys playing jazz piano, reading, and traveling in the United States. He currently lives in Florida with his attorney wife, Theresa.